THE NIGHT
STALKER

About the author

Born in Brazil of Italian origin, Chris Carter studied psychology and criminal behaviour at the University of Michigan. As a member of the Michigan State District Attorney's Criminal Psychology team, he interviewed and studied many criminals, including serial and multiple homicide offenders with life imprisonment convictions.

Having departed for Los Angeles in the early 1990s, Chris spent ten years as a guitarist for numerous rock bands before leaving the music business to write full-time. He now lives in London and is the *Sunday Times* bestselling author of *The Executioner* and *The Crucifix Killer*.

Visit www.chriscarterbooks.com

Also by Chris Carter

The Crucifix Killer
The Executioner

CHRIS
CARTER
THE NIGHT
STALKER

**SIMON &
SCHUSTER**

London · New York · Sydney · Toronto · New Delhi

A CBS COMPANY

First published in Great Britain by Simon & Schuster UK Ltd, 2011
A CBS Company
First published in paperback in 2012

3 5 7 9 10 8 6 4

Simon & Schuster UK Ltd
1st Floor
222 Gray's Inn Road
London WC1X 8HB

www.simonandschuster.co.uk

Simon & Schuster Australia
Sydney

Simon & Schuster India
New Delhi

A CIP catalogue record for this book
is available from the British Library

Paperback B ISBN 978-1-47114-308-3
Paperback A ISBN 978-0-85720-298-7

Typeset by Hewer Text UK Ltd, Edinburgh
Printed and bound by CPI Group (UK) Ltd, Croydon, CR0 4YY

This novel is dedicated to my family and to
Coral Chambers, for being there for me
when I most needed someone.

Acknowledgements

I am tremendously grateful to several people without whom this novel would never have been possible.

My agent, Darley Anderson, who is not only the best agent an author could ever hope for, but also a true friend. Camilla Wray, my literary guardian angel, whose comments, suggestions, knowledge and friendship I could never do without. Everyone at the Darley Anderson Literary Agency for striving tirelessly to promote my work anywhere and everywhere possible.

Maxine Hitchcock, my fantastic editor at Simon & Schuster, for being so amazing at what she does. My publishers, Ian Chapman and Suzanne Baboneau, for their tremendous support and belief. Everyone at Simon & Schuster for working their socks off on every aspect of the publishing process.

Samantha Johnson for lending a sympathetic ear to so many of my terrible ideas.

My love and most sincere thanks go to Coral Chambers, for keeping me from breaking.

One

Doctor Jonathan Winston pulled the surgical mask over his mouth and nose and checked the clock on the wall of autopsy room number four on the underground floor of the Los Angeles County Department of Coroner. 6:12 p.m.

The body on the stainless steel table a few feet in front of him was of an unidentified white female in her late twenties, early thirties. Her shoulder-length black hair was wet, its tips plastered to the metal table. Under the brightness of the surgical light, her pale skin looked rubbery, almost unhuman. It hadn't been possible to identify the presumed cause of death at the location where the body was found. There was no blood, no bullet or knife wounds, no lumps or abrasions to her head or torso and no hematomas around her neck to indicate she'd been strangled. Her body was clear of traumas, except for the fact that her mouth and vagina had been stitched shut by whoever had killed her. The thread used was bulky and heavy – the stitches untidy and careless.

'Are we ready?' Doctor Winston said to Sean Hannay, the young forensic assistant in the room.

Hannay's eyes were glued to the woman's face and her sealed lips. For some reason he felt more nervous than usual.

'Sean, are we OK?'

'Umm, yes, Doctor, sorry.' His eyes finally met Doctor Winston's and he nodded. 'We're all set here.' He positioned himself to the right of the table while the doctor activated the digital recording device on the counter closest to him.

Doctor Winston stated the date and time, the names of those present, and the autopsy file number. The body had already been measured and weighed, so he proceeded to dictate the victim's physical characteristics. Before making any incisions, Doctor Winston meticulously studied the body, looking for any marks that could help identify the victim. As his eyes rested on the stitches applied to the victim's lower body, he paused and squinted.

'Wait a second,' he whispered, stepping closer and carefully moving the victim's legs apart. 'Please pass me the flashlight, Sean.' He extended his hand towards the forensic assistant without taking his eyes off the victim. Concern crept into his gaze.

'Something wrong?' Hannay asked, handing Doctor Winston a small metal flashlight.

'Maybe.' He directed its beam towards something that had caught his eye.

Hannay shifted his weight from foot to foot.

'The stitches aren't medical suture,' Doctor Winston said for the benefit of the audio record. 'They're amateurish and imprecise. Like a teenager sewing a patch onto an old pair of ripped jeans.' He moved closer still. 'The stitches are also too spread apart, the gaps between them are too wide, and . . .' he paused, cocking his head, '. . . no way.'

Hannay felt his whole body shiver. 'What?' He stepped forward.

Doctor Winston drew a deep breath and slowly looked up at Hannay. 'I think the killer left something inside her.'

'What?'

Doctor Winston concentrated on the flashlight beam for a few more seconds until he was sure. 'The light is being reflected off something inside her.'

Hannay bent down, following the doctor's gaze. It took him only a second to see it. 'Shit, the light *is* reflecting off something. What is it?'

'I don't know, but whatever it is it's large enough to show through the stitches.'

The doctor straightened up and grabbed a metal pointer from the instrument tray.

'Sean, hold the light for me; like this.' He handed the flashlight to the young assistant and showed him exactly where he wanted him to focus the beam.

The doctor bent over and inserted the tip of the metal pointer between two of the stitches, guiding it towards the object inside the victim.

Hannay kept the flashlight steady.

'It's something metallic,' Winston announced, using the pointer as a probe, 'but I still can't say for certain what it could be. Pass me the stitch-cutting scissors and the forceps, will you?'

It didn't take him long to slice through the stitches. As he cut through each one, Doctor Winston used the forceps to pinch and pull the thick black thread from the victim's skin, placing it into a small plastic evidence collection container.

'Was she raped?' Hannay asked.

'There are cuts and bruises around her groin that are consistent with forced penetration,' Doctor Winston confirmed, 'but they could've been caused by the object that's been inserted into her. I'll take some swabs and send them up to the lab together with the thread samples.' He placed the scissors and the forceps on the used instrument tray. 'Let's find out what the killer has left us, shall we?'

Hannay tensed as Doctor Winston inserted his right hand into the victim. 'Well, I was right, it's not a small object.'

A few silent, uneasy seconds went by.

'And it's oddly shaped too,' the doctor announced. 'Sort of squared with something strange attached to its top.' He finally managed to grab hold of it. As he pulled it out, an attachment at the top clicked.

Hannay stepped forward to gain a better look.

'Metal, relatively heavy, looks handmade . . .' Doctor Winston said, staring at the object in his hand. 'But I'm still not sure what . . .' He paused and felt his heart hammer inside his chest as his eyes widened in realization. 'Oh my God . . .'

TWO

It took Detective Robert Hunter of the Los Angeles Robbery Homicide Division (RHD) over an hour to drive from the Hollywood Courthouse to the disused butcher's shop in East LA. He was paged over four hours ago, but the trial in which he was testifying had run a lot later than he'd expected.

Hunter was part of an exclusive elite; an elite that most LAPD detectives would give their right arm *not* to become part of. The Homicide Special Section (HSS) of the RHD was created to deal solely with serial, high-profile and homicide cases requiring extensive investigative time and expertize. Inside the HSS, Hunter had an even more specialized task. Due to his criminal behavior psychology background, he was assigned to cases where overwhelming brutality had been used by the perpetrator. The department tagged such cases as UV, *ultra-violent*.

The butcher's shop was the last in a parade of closed-down businesses. The whole neighborhood seemed to have been neglected. Hunter parked his old Buick next to a white forensic crime lab van. As he stepped out of the car, he allowed his eyes to study the outside of the buildings for a while. All the windows had been covered by solid metal shutters. There was so much graffiti on the outside walls Hunter couldn't tell what color the buildings had originally been.

He approached the officer guarding the entrance, flashed his badge and stooped under the yellow crime-scene tape. The officer nodded but remained silent, his stare distant.

Hunter pushed the door open and stepped inside.

The foul smell that hit him knocked him back and made him gag – a combination of putrid meat, stale sweat, vomit and urine that burned his nostrils and stung at his eyes. He paused for a moment before pulling the collar of his shirt up and over his nose and mouth as an improvised mask.

'These work better,' Carlos Garcia said, coming out of the back room and handing Hunter a surgical nose mask. He was wearing one himself.

Garcia was tall and slim with longish dark hair and light blue eyes. His boyish good looks were spoiled only by a slight lump on his nose, where it had been broken. Unlike all the other RHD detectives, Garcia had worked very hard to be assigned to the HSS. He'd been Hunter's partner for almost three years now.

'The smell gets worse once you enter the back room.' Garcia nodded towards the door he'd just come out of. 'How was the trial?'

'Late,' Hunter replied as he fitted the mask over his face. 'What have we got?'

Garcia tilted his head to one side. 'Some messed up stuff. White female victim, somewhere in her late twenties, early thirties. She was found on the stainless steel butcher's work-top in there.' He pointed to the room behind him.

'Cause of death?'

Garcia shook his head. 'We'll have to wait for the autopsy. Nothing apparent. But here comes the kick. Her lips and her vagina were *stitched* shut.'

'What?'

Garcia nodded. 'That's right. A very sick job. I've never seen anything like it.'

Hunter's eyes darted towards the door behind his partner.

'The body's gone,' Garcia offered before Hunter's next question. 'Doctor Winston was the Forensics lead here tonight. He wanted you to see the body and the scene in the exact way in which it was found, but he couldn't wait any longer. The heat in there was accelerating things.'

'When was the body taken away?' Hunter mechanically checked his watch.

'About two hours ago. Knowing the doc, he's probably halfway through the autopsy already. He knows you hate sitting in on those, so there'd be no point in waiting. By the time we finish looking around this place, I'm sure he'll have some answers for us.'

Hunter's cell phone rang in his pocket. He grabbed it and pulled his surgical mask down, letting it hang loosely around his neck. 'Detective Hunter.'

He listened for a few seconds. 'What?' His eyes shot towards Garcia, who saw Hunter's entire demeanor change in an instant.

Three

Garcia made the trip from East LA to the Los Angeles County Department of Coroner in North Mission Road in record time.

Their confusion doubled as they approached the entrance to the coroners' parking lot. It was blocked off by four police vehicles and two fire engines. More police cars were inside the lot. Several uniformed officers were moving around chaotically, shouting orders at each other and over the radio.

The media had descended upon the scene like ravenous wolves. Local TV and newspaper vans were everywhere. Reporters, cameramen and photographers were doing their best to get as close as they could. But a tight perimeter had already been established around the main building, and it was being strictly enforced by the LAPD.

'What the hell is going on here?' Hunter whispered under his breath as Garcia pulled up by the entrance.

'You'll have to move along, sir,' a young policeman said, coming up to Garcia's window and frantically gesturing for him to drive on. 'You can't—'

He stopped as soon as he saw Garcia's badge. 'I'm sorry, Detective; I'll clear a path right away.' He turned to face the other two officers who were standing next to their vehicles. 'C'mon guys, make way.'

Less than thirty seconds later, Garcia was parking his Honda Civic just in front of the stairway that led up to the main building.

Hunter stepped out of the car and looked around. A small group of people, most of them in white coats, were huddled together at the far end of the parking lot. Hunter recognized them as lab technicians and coroner staff.

'What happened here?' he asked a fireman who had just come off the radio.

'You'll have to ask the chief in charge for more details. All I can tell you is that there was a fire somewhere inside.' He pointed to the old hospital-turned-morgue.

Hunter frowned. 'Fire?'

Certain arson cases were also investigated by the HSS, but they were rarely considered UV. Hunter had never been assigned as the lead detective in any of them.

'Robert, over here.'

Hunter turned and saw Doctor Carolyn Hove coming down the steps to greet them. She'd always looked a great deal younger than her forty-six years. But not today. Her usually perfectly styled chestnut hair was disheveled, her expression solemn and defeated. If the Los Angeles County Coroner had ranks, Doctor Hove would be second in command, just under Doctor Winston.

'What in the world is going on, Doc?' Hunter asked.

'Absolute hell . . .'

Four

Hunter, Garcia and Doctor Hove climbed up the steps together and entered the main building via its large double doors. Several more police officers and firemen were lingering around in the entry foyer. Doctor Hove guided both detectives past the reception counter, down another set of stairs and onto the underground floor. Even though they could all hear the extraction fans working at full power, a sickening smell of chemicals and burned flesh hung in the air. Both detectives cringed and reflexively cupped their hands over their noses.

Garcia felt his stomach churn.

Right at the end of the corridor, a section of the floor directly in front of autopsy room four was drenched in water. Its door was open but it seemed to have been dislodged off its hinges.

The fire chief in charge was giving instructions to one of his men when he saw the group approaching.

'Chief,' Doctor Hove said, 'these are Detectives Robert Hunter and Carlos Garcia of the RHD.'

No handshakes, only polite nods.

'What happened here?' Hunter asked, craning his neck to try to see inside the room. 'And where's Doctor Winston?'

Doctor Hove didn't reply.

The chief took off his helmet and wiped his forehead with a gloved hand. 'Some sort of explosion.'

Hunter frowned. 'Explosion?'

'That's right. The room has been checked and there are no hidden fires. In fact, the fire itself looked to have been minimal. The sprinklers put it out even before we got here. At the moment we don't know what caused the blast, we'll have to wait for the fire investigator's report.' He looked at Doctor Hove. 'I was told that this is the largest of all the autopsy suites, and it doubles as a lab, is that right?'

'Yes, that's correct,' she confirmed.

'Are any volatile chemicals – maybe gas canisters – stored in there?'

Doctor Hove closed her eyes for a moment and let out a heavy breath. 'Sometimes.'

The chief nodded. 'Maybe there was a leak, but as I said, we'll have to wait for the investigator's report. It's a sturdy building with solid foundations. As it's a basement room, the walls down here are much thicker than the ones through-out the rest of the building, and that helped contain the blow. Though it was a powerful enough blast to cause a lot of internal damage, it wasn't powerful enough to compro-mise the structure. For now, there isn't much more I can tell you.' The chief took off his gloves and rubbed his eyes. 'It's very messy in there, Doctor, in a *very* bad way.' He paused as if unsure of what else to say. 'I'm really sorry.' His words were coated with grief. He nodded solemnly at the rest of the group and made his way back upstairs.

They all stood in silence at the entrance to what used to be autopsy room four, their eyes taking in the destruction. At the far end of the room tables, trays, cabinets and trol-leys were bent out of shape and turned over everywhere, showered in debris and bits of skin and flesh. Part of the ceiling and the back wall were damaged and covered in blood.

'When did this happen?' Garcia asked.

'An hour, maybe an hour and fifteen minutes ago. I was in a meeting in the second building. There was a muffled bang and the fire alarms went berserk.'

What was bothering Hunter was the amount of washed-up blood and the number of black impermeable covers he could see scattered around the room, covering bodies or body parts. The cooler body storage facility was located on the wall opposite where the blast occurred. None of the fridges looked damaged.

'How many bodies were out of the coolers in here, Doc?' Hunter asked tentatively.

Doctor Hove knew Hunter had already caught on. She lifted her right hand, showing only the index finger.

Hunter let out a laden breath. 'An autopsy was taking place.' It was a statement rather than a question and he felt a shiver grab hold of his spine. 'Doctor Winston's autopsy?'

'Shit!' Garcia ran a hand over his face. 'No way.'

Doctor Hove looked away, but not fast enough to hide the tears that were forming in her eyes.

Hunter's gaze stayed on her for a couple of seconds before returning to what was left of the room. His throat went dry, and a choking sadness surrounded his heart. He'd known Doctor Jonathan Winston for over fifteen years. He'd been the Los Angeles Chief Medical Examiner for as long as Hunter could remember. He was a workaholic and brilliant at his job. He always tried his best to conduct most of the autopsies on murder victims whose death circumstances had been deemed out of the ordinary. But most of all, to Hunter, Doctor Winston was like family.

The best of friends. Someone on whom he'd counted on numerous times. Someone who he respected and admired like few others. Someone he'd sincerely miss.

'Two people were present.' Doctor Hove's voice faltered for an instant. 'Doctor Winston and Sean Hannay, a 21-year-old forensic assistant.'

Hunter closed his eyes. There was nothing he could say.

'I called as soon as I found out,' Doctor Hove said.

Garcia's expression was one of pure shock. He'd seen many dead bodies in his career, several of them grotesquely disfigured by a sadistic killer. But he'd never personally known any of the victims. And despite meeting Doctor Winston for the first time only three years ago, they'd quickly become friends.

'How about the kid?' Hunter finally asked. And for the first time, Garcia heard Hunter's voice quiver.

Doctor Hove shook her head. 'I'm sorry. Sean Hannay was finishing his third year of pathology at UCLA. His ambition was to become a forensic scientist. I was the one who approved his internship only six months ago.' Her eyes glistened. 'He wasn't even supposed to be in this room. He was just helping out.' The doctor paused and considered her next words carefully. 'I asked him to do so. It was supposed to be me assisting Jonathan.'

Hunter noticed that the doctor's hands were shaking.

'It was a special circumstances death,' she continued. 'Jonathan always asks me to assist on those. And I would've, but I got held up in my meeting and asked Sean to take over for me as a favor.' Her eyes filled with horror. 'He wasn't the one who was supposed to have died here today – I was.'

Five

Hunter understood what was going through Doctor Hove's mind. In the immediate aftermath of the blast, her self-preservation instinct had kicked in and she had felt relief. She'd had a lucky escape. But now reason and guilt were settling in and her mind was punishing her in the worst possible way. *If my meeting hadn't run late, Sean Hannay would still be alive.*

'None of this is your fault, Doc,' Hunter tried to reassure her, but he knew that words would have little effect. Before accepting anything, they all needed to understand what had happened in that room.

Hunter took a step up to the autopsy room door as his mind tried to process the scene in front of him. Right now, nothing was making sense. Suddenly, something caught his eye and he squinted for a second before turning to face Doctor Hove.

'Are autopsies ever videotaped?' he asked, pointing to something on the floor that resembled a camera tripod leg.

Doctor Hove shook her head. 'Very rarely, and the request has to be approved either by me or . . .' her eyes moved from Hunter to the inside of the room, '. . . the chief medical examiner.'

'Doctor Winston himself.'

A single, hesitant nod from Doctor Hove.

'Do you think he might've chosen to record this autopsy?'

Doctor Hove considered it for a moment and her face flared with hope. 'There's a chance. If he considered the case intriguing enough.'

'Well, even if he did,' Garcia cut in, 'how would that help us? The camera was certainly blown to shit like most of the room. Just look at it.'

'Not necessarily,' the doctor said slowly.

All eyes went back to her.

'Do you know something we don't?' Hunter asked.

'Autopsy room four is sometimes used as a lecture room,' the doctor explained. 'It's the only examination suite we have equipped with a video camera connection hub. It links directly to our mainframe computer. That means that the images are simultaneously stored into our mainframe hard drive. To videotape a lecture or an examination, all a doctor has to do is set up a digital camera, hook it to the hub and they're good to go.'

'Can we find out if Doctor Winston did that?'

'Follow me.'

Doctor Hove moved purposefully back to the same stairway they'd come down and went up to the ground floor. They passed the reception area before continuing through a set of metal double doors and into a long and empty hallway. Three-quarters of the way down, they turned right. A single wooden door with a small frosted glass window stood at the end of the corridor. Doctor Hove's office. She unlocked it, pushed the door open, and led them inside.

Doctor Hove went straight to her desk and logged onto her computer. Both detectives gathered behind her.

'Only mine and Doctor Winston's login has administrator's

rights access to the video directory on the mainframe computer. Let's see if we got anything.'

It took Doctor Hove only a few clicks to get to the video directory where all recordings were stored. Inside the main folder there were three subdirectories – New, Lectures and Autopsies. The doctor expanded the directory named *new* to find only one .mpg file. The timestamp on it indicated that it had been created an hour ago.

'Bingo. Jonathan did record the autopsy.' Doctor Hove paused and anxiously looked at Hunter. He noticed that she had fractionally pulled her hand away from the mouse.

'It's OK, Doc; you don't have to watch this. We can take it from here.'

Doctor Hove hesitated for a second. 'Yes I do.' She double-clicked the file. The screen flickered and the computer launched its default video player application. Hunter and Garcia moved closer.

The pictures weren't of great quality, but clearly showed a white female body on an autopsy table. The image had been filmed from above and at an angle, and was partially zoomed in so that the table occupied most of the screen. On the right, two other people in white lab coats could be seen from mid-torso down.

'Can you zoom out?' Garcia asked.

'The image was recorded this way,' Hunter replied, shaking his head. 'We're not controlling a camera here. This is just playback.'

On the screen, one of the two people to the right of the table moved towards the body's head and bent down to examine it. Doctor Winston's face suddenly appeared in the shot.

'There's no sound?' Garcia asked as he watched Doctor Winston's lips move in silence. 'How come there's no sound?'

'The microphones on the cameras we use to video examinations aren't of great quality,' the doctor explained. 'We usually don't even turn them on.'

'I thought pathologists had a habit of dictating every step of their examinations.'

'And we do,' she confirmed. 'Onto our own personal recording devices. We take them into the examination rooms with us. Whatever Jonathan was using, is now mangled up with everything else in that room.'

'Great.'

'*Eyes – hazel, skin is well cared for, earlobes look like they've never been pierced . . .*' Hunter said before the video showed Doctor Winston turning away from the camera. 'Damn! I can't see his mouth any more.'

'You can lip-read?' The question came from Doctor Hove, but her surprised look was mirrored on Garcia's face.

Hunter didn't reply. He kept his attention on the screen.

'Where in the world did you learn to do that?' Garcia asked.

'Books,' Hunter lied. Right now, the last thing he wanted to do was talk about his past.

They watched in silence for the next few seconds.

'Jonathan is performing a regular external examination of the body,' Doctor Hove confirmed. 'All the victim's physical characteristics are listed, including first impressions of their wounds, if any. He'd also be looking for any physical marks that could help identify the victim – she was brought in as a Jane Doe.'

On the screen, Doctor Winston paused and an intrigued look passed across his face. They all watched as his assistant handed him a small flashlight. Bending over, he focused the light directly on the stitches applied to the victim's lower body, moving the light up and down and from side to side. He seemed baffled by something.

'What is he doing?' Garcia instinctively tipped his head to one side, trying to get a better view.

The video played on and they all watched as Doctor Winston used a metallic pointer to probe through the stitches and into the victim's body. The doctor's lips moved and they all looked at Hunter.

'*It's something metallic,*' Hunter translated, '*but I still can't say for certain what it could be. Pass me the stitch-cutting scissors and the forceps, will you?*'

'There was something inside her?' Doctor Hove frowned.

On the screen, Doctor Winston turned away from the camera again and proceeded to use a pair of scissors to slice through the stitches. Hunter noticed there were five in total. The doctor inserted his right hand into the victim.

Moments later, Doctor Winston managed to retrieve an object. When he turned, only its edge flashed past the camera.

'What was that?' Garcia asked. 'What was left inside the victim? Did anyone see?'

'Not sure,' Hunter replied. 'Let's wait, he might turn and face the camera again.'

But he never did.

Within seconds there was a blast and the whole image was substituted by static. The words – *Room 4. Signal fail* – flashed across the center of the screen.

Six

Absolute silence filled the room for several seconds. Doctor Hove was the first to speak.

'A bomb? Someone put a bomb inside a murder victim? What the hell . . . ?'

There was no reply. Hunter took over at the computer and was already clicking away, rewinding the images. He pressed play again, and the video resumed from just a couple of moments before Doctor Winston pulled his hand from inside the victim's body, gripping the unidentified metallic object. All eyes reverted back to the screen.

'I can't make it out exactly,' Garcia said. 'It moves past the camera too fast. Can you slow it down?'

'It doesn't matter what it looks like,' Doctor Hove said almost catatonically. 'It was a bomb. Who the hell puts a bomb inside a victim, and why?' She took a step back and massaged her temples. 'Terrorist?'

Hunter shook his head. 'The location of the attack alone defeats the very essence of terrorism. Terrorists want to cause as much damage as possible with as much loss of life as possible. I hate to state the obvious, Doc, but this is a morgue, not a shopping mall. And the blast wasn't even powerful enough to destroy a whole medium-sized room.'

'Besides,' Garcia said, with no sarcasm in his voice, 'most bodies in here are already dead.'

'So why would someone place a bomb inside a dead body? It doesn't make any sense.'

Hunter held the doctor's gaze. 'I can't tell you the answer to that question right now.' He paused for a moment. 'We need to stay focused here. I'm assuming that no one else has seen this footage?'

Doctor Hove nodded.

'We need to keep it this way for now,' Hunter said. 'If news gets out that a killer has placed a bomb inside a victim, the press will turn this into a carnival. We'll spend more time giving pointless interviews and answering stupid questions than investigating anything. And we can't afford to lose any more time. Despite our emotions on this, what we have here is someone who is crazy enough to kill a young woman, place an explosive device inside her body and stitch it shut. Consequently, he also took the life of two other innocent people.'

New tears started to form in Doctor Hove's eyes. But she had worked with Hunter in many cases over the years and there was no one in law enforcement she trusted more than him. She nodded slowly and for the first time Hunter saw anger in her face.

'Just promise me you'll catch this sonofabitch.'

Before leaving the coroners building, Hunter and Garcia stopped by the Forensics lab and picked up all the available information the team had collected so far. Most of the lab test results would take at least a couple of days. Since Hunter had never got a chance to see the body as it was found at the crime scene, the reports, notes and photographs were all he had to go on at the moment.

He already knew that the body had been found eight hours ago in the back room of the disused butcher's shop in East LA. An anonymous phone call had tipped off the police. Hunter would get a copy of the recording later.

On their way back to East LA, Hunter slowly flipped through all the information in the forensic file. The crime-scene pictures showed that the victim had been left naked, lying on her back on a dirty metal counter. Her legs were together and stretched out but not tied. One of her arms was hanging off the side of the counter, the other rested on her chest. Her eyes were left open, and Hunter had seen the expression in them many times before – pure fear.

One of the pictures showed a close-up of her mouth. Her lips had been stitched shut with thick black, thorn-like thread. Blood had seeped through the needle punctures and ran down her chin and neck, indicating that she was still alive when it was done. Another close-up showed that the same thing had been done to her lower body. Her groin and inner thighs were also smeared with blood that had seeped through the puncture wounds. There was some swelling around the stitches – another indication that she had died hours after being violated by needle and thread. By the time she died, the wounds had already started to go septic. But that wouldn't have caused her death.

Hunter checked the location photographs. The butcher's shop was a dirty mess. Its floor was covered in crack pipes, old syringes, used condoms, and rat droppings. The walls were plastered with graffiti. Forensics had found so many different fingerprints it looked like a party had taken place in that back room. The truth was: right now only an autopsy examination could shed light onto the case.

Seven

Everyone had already left by the time Garcia dropped Hunter back to his car. Crime-scene tape still marked the perimeter around the butcher's shop. A sole uniformed cop guarded the entrance.

Garcia knew Hunter would take his time, looking at every possible detail inside the shop.

'I'm gonna head back and see what I can do with the crime-scene photos and the Missing Persons database. As you said, our priority is in identifying who she was.'

Hunter nodded and stepped out of the car.

The foul smell seemed to have intensified threefold as Hunter flashed his badge at the officer and entered the shop for the second time that evening.

As the door shut behind him, Hunter was left in pitch-black darkness. He clicked his flashlight on and felt a surge of adrenalin rush through his body. Every step was accompanied by the crunching of glass or the squelching sound of something moist under his feet. He moved on past the old meat display counter and approached the door at the back. As he got closer, Hunter heard the buzzing of flies.

This new room was spacious and linked the front of the store to the small freezer-room at the back. Hunter paused by the door, struggling with the putrid stench. His stomach was begging him to leave, threatening to erupt at any moment and causing him to gag and cough violently a few times. His surgical mask was having little effect.

He slowly allowed the beam of his flashlight to move around the room. Two oversized metal sinks sat against the far wall. To their right was an empty floor-to-ceiling storage module. Rats moved freely on its shelves.

Hunter screwed up his face.

'There had to be rats,' he cursed under his breath. He hated rats.

In an instant his mind took him back to when he was eight years old.

On his way back from school, two older kids stopped him and took his Batman lunchbox from him. The lunchbox had been a birthday present from his mother a year earlier, just months before cancer robbed him of her. It was his most prized possession.

After taunting Hunter for a while by throwing the lunchbox back and forth to each other, the two bullies kicked it down an open manhole.

'Go get it, deaf boy.'

Hunter's mother's death was devastating for him and his father, and coping with its aftermath proved particularly difficult. For several weeks, as her disease progressed, Hunter sat alone in his room, listening to her desperate cries, feeling her pain as if it was his own. When she finally passed away, Hunter started experiencing severe loss of hearing. It was his body's psychosomatic way of shutting off the grief. His temporary deafness made Hunter an even easier target to the bullies. To escape being cast aside even more, he'd learned to lip-read by himself. Within two years, with the same ease that it had gone away, his hearing came back.

'You better go get it, deaf boy,' the bigger of the two bullies repeated.

Hunter didn't even hesitate, hurrying down the metal ladder as if his life depended on it. That was exactly what the bullies wanted him to do. They pushed the lid back over the manhole and walked away, laughing.

Hunter found the lunchbox down at the bottom and made his way back up the ladder, but no matter how hard he tried, he just didn't have the physical strength to push the lid aside. Instead of panicking, he went back down to the sewage passageways. If he couldn't get out the same way he went in, he'd simply have to find another way out.

In semi-darkness, clenching his lunchbox tight to his chest, he started down the tunnel. He'd traveled only about fifty yards through filthy, stinking sewage water when he felt something drop from the ceiling onto his back and tug at his shirt. Reflexively, he reached for it, grabbed it and threw it as far away from him as he could. As it hit the water behind him, it squeaked, and Hunter finally saw what it was.

A rat as big as his lunchbox.

Hunter held his breath and slowly turned to face the wall to his right. It was alive with rats of every shape and size.

He started shivering.

Very carefully, he turned around and faced the wall to his left. Even more rats. And he could swear all their eyes were locked on him.

Hunter didn't think, he simply ran as fast as he could, splashing water high in the air with every step. A hundred and fifty yards ahead he came to a metal ladder that led him to another manhole. Again, the lid would not budge. He returned to the passageway and carried on running. Another two hundred yards, another manhole, and Hunter finally hit a little luck. At the top, the lid was half on, half off. With his skinny body, he had no problem squeezing through the gap.

Hunter still had the Batman lunchbox his mother had given him. And ever since then, rats had made him very uneasy.

Now, Hunter pushed the memory away, bringing his attention back to the butcher's shop back room. The only other piece of furniture in it was the stainless steel counter where the victim's naked body had been laid out. It was positioned about six feet from the open freezer-room door on the back wall. Hunter studied the counter from a distance for a long while. There was something odd about it. It was way too high off the ground. When he checked the floor, he found that bricks had been placed under each of its four legs, elevating the counter another foot to foot and a half.

Just like the crime-scene photos showed, the floor was littered with dirty rags, used condoms and discarded syringes. Hunter moved inside, taking short steps, carefully checking the floor before each one. The temperature in the room seemed to be at least five degrees higher than outside, and he felt sweat trickling down the small of his back. As he approached the stainless steel counter, the buzzing noise coming from the flies got louder.

Despite the flies, the nauseating smell and the melting heat, Hunter took his time. He knew the Forensics team had done the best job they could, but crime scenes could offer a lot more than simple physical evidence. And Hunter had a gift when it came to understanding them.

He carefully circled the metal counter for the fifth time. The main question swimming around in his mind was whether the victim had died in that room, or whether the butcher's shop had been nothing more than a simple dumping ground.

Hunter decided to take the victim's place.

He hopped onto the metal counter before lying down in the exact position the victim had been found and switching off his flashlight. He kept absolutely still, allowing the sounds, the smell, the heat, and the darkness of the room to envelop him. His shirt was clinging to his body, wet with sweat. From the photographs, he remembered the look in her eyes, the horror expression frozen on her face.

He switched on his flashlight but remained in the same position, his eyes taking in the graffiti that adorned the entire ceiling.

A moment later, something caught his eye. He squinted and sat up. His gaze locked onto the ceiling directly above the metal counter. The realization came in three seconds flat and his eyes widened.

'Oh Jesus!'

Eight

Katia Kudrov stepped out of her bathtub and wrapped a fluffy white towel around her shoulder-length black hair. Scented candles illuminated her luxurious bathroom in the penthouse of an exclusive apartment block in West Hollywood. The candles helped her relax. And tonight she wanted nothing more than to unwind.

Katia had just finished her first American tour as the principal violinist concertmistress with the Los Angeles Philharmonic. Sixty-five concerts in as many cities in seventy days. The tour had been a tremendous success, but the grueling schedule had left her exhausted. She was looking forward to a well-deserved break.

Music found its way into Katia's life at a very early age, when she was only four. She remembered vividly sitting on her grandfather's lap while he tried to rock her to sleep to the sound of Tchaikovsky's *Violin Concerto in D Major*. Instead of falling asleep, she fell in love with the sounds she heard. The next day, her grandfather gave Katia her first violin. But Katia wasn't a natural, far from it. For years her parents endured the agonizing and ear-piercing noises of her long practice sessions. But she was dedicated, determined and hard-working, and eventually she began playing music that could make the angels smile. After a long spell in

Europe, she had come back to LA thirteen months ago after being offered the concertmistress seat with the Los Angeles Philharmonic.

Katia stepped out of the bathroom, paused in front of the full-length mirror in her bedroom, and studied her reflection. Her features were nearly perfect – large brown eyes, a small nose, high cheekbones and full lips that framed a faultless smile. At thirty, she still had the body of a high-school cheerleader. She checked her profile, sucking her stomach in for several seconds before deciding that she'd gained a small potbelly. Probably from all the junk food she ate at the many cocktail parties she'd had to attend during the tour. Katia shook her head in disapproval.

'Back on the diet and in the gym from tomorrow,' she whispered to herself, reaching for her pink bathrobe.

The cordless phone on her bedside table rang and she looked at it dubiously. Not many people had her home number.

'Hello,' she finally answered after the fifth ring, and could swear she heard a second click on the line, as if someone had picked up the extension in her study, living room or kitchen.

'How's my favorite superstar?'

Katia smiled. 'Hi Dad.'

'Hi there, baby. So how was the tour?'

'Fantastic, but extremely exhausting.'

'I bet. I read the reviews. Everyone loves you.'

Katia smiled. 'I'm so looking forward to two weeks of no rehearsals, no concerts, and certainly no parties.' She made her way out of her bedroom and onto the mezzanine that overlooked her spacious living room.

'But you have some time for your old man, right?'

'I always have time for you when I'm not touring, Dad. You're the one who's always so busy, remember?' she challenged.

He chuckled. 'OK, OK, don't rub it in. I'll tell you what. I can tell you're tired by your voice, how about you have an early night and we catch up over lunch tomorrow?'

Katia hesitated. 'What are we talking about here, Dad? One of your quick "I gotta go, let's grab a sandwich" deals, or a proper sit-down, three-course, no-cells-allowed lunch?'

Leonid Kudrov was one of the most famous film producers in the USA. His lunch engagements usually never lasted more than thirty minutes, which Katia knew well.

There was a small pause and this time Katia was sure she heard a click on the line. 'Dad, are you still there?'

'I'm here, baby. And I'll take option number two, please.'

'I mean it, Dad. If we're having a proper lunch, there'll be no phone calls, and you're not rushing away after half an hour.'

'No cells, I promise. I'll clear my afternoon schedule. And you can pick the restaurant.'

Katia's smile was more animated this time. 'OK. How about we meet at Mastro's Steak House in Beverly Hills at one o'clock?'

'Great choice,' her father agreed. 'I'll make the reservation.'

'And you won't be late, will you, Dad?'

'Of course not, honey. You're my superstar, remember? Look, I gotta go. An important call just came in.'

Katia shook her head. 'What a surprise.'

'Have a good sleep, darling. I'll see you tomorrow.'

'See you tomorrow, Dad.' She rang off and placed the receiver in her bathrobe pocket.

Taking the stairs down to the living room, Katia made

her way into the kitchen. She felt like having a glass of wine, something to relax her even more. She selected a bottle of Sancerre from the fridge. As she fumbled inside one of the worktop drawers for the corkscrew, the phone in her pocket rang again.

'Hello?'

'How's my favorite superstar?'

Katia frowned.

Nine

'Oh please, tell me you're not cancelling on me already, Dad?' Katia wasn't impressed.

'Dad?'

Katia suddenly realized that the voice at the other end of the line wasn't her father's. 'Who is this?'

'Not your daddy.'

'Phillip, is that you?'

Phillip Stein was the new conductor for the Los Angeles Philharmonic, and Katia's latest affair. They'd been seeing each other for four months, but three days before the end of the tour they'd gotten into a heated argument. Phillip had fallen head over heels for Katia, and wanted her to move in with him. Katia liked Phillip and she had enjoyed their affair, but certainly not with the same intensity as he did. She wasn't ready for that type of commitment, not now. She had hinted at the idea that maybe they should take a few days off from seeing each other – just to see how things panned out. Phillip hadn't taken the suggestion well, throwing a tantrum and conducting the worst concerto of his career that night. They hadn't spoken since.

'Phillip? Who's Phillip? Is that your boyfriend?' the voice asked.

Katia shivered.

'Who is this?' she asked again, firmer this time.

Silence.

An uncomfortable sensation made the hairs on the back of Katia's neck stand on end. 'Look, I think you dialed the wrong number.'

'I don't think so.' The man chuckled. 'I've been dialing this number every day for the past two months.'

Katia breathed out, relieved. 'See, now I'm sure you've got the wrong number. I've been away for a little while. I actually just got back.'

There was a pause.

'It's no big deal, it happens,' Katia said kindly. 'Look, I'm gonna put the phone down so you can redial.'

'Don't put the phone down,' the man said calmly. 'I haven't dialed the wrong number. Have you checked your answering machine yet, Katia?'

The only phone in Katia's apartment with an answering machine was the one at the far end of the worktop in the kitchen. She covered the mouthpiece with her hand and quickly made her way towards it. She hadn't noticed the blinking red light until then. Sixty messages.

Katia gasped. 'Who are you? How did you get this number?'

Another chuckle. 'I'm . . .' there was a click on the line again, '. . . a fan, I guess.'

'A fan?'

'A fan with resources. The kind of resources that make information very easy to come by.'

'Information?'

'I know you are a fantastic musician. You love your Lorenzo Guadagnini violin more than anything in this world. You live in a penthouse apartment in West Hollywood. You're allergic to peanuts. Your favorite composer is Tchaikovsky and you love driving that torch red, convertible Mustang of yours.' He paused. 'And you're having lunch with your father tomorrow at one o'clock at Mastro's Steak House in Beverly Hills. Your favorite color is pink, just like the bathrobe you're wearing now, and you were just about to open a bottle of white wine.'

Katia froze.

'So how dedicated a fan am I, Katia?'

Instinctively, Katia's eyes shot towards her kitchen window, but she knew she was too high up for anyone in one of the neighboring buildings to be able to spy on her.

'Oh, I'm not peeping on you through the window,' the man said with a sneer.

The light in the kitchen went out and the next voice Katia heard didn't come from her phone.

'I'm standing right behind you.'

Ten

On any given night Hunter's insomnia would rob him of at least four hours of sleep. Last night, it had kept him awake for almost six.

It was after cancer took his mother from him when he was just seven years old that his sleeping problems started. Alone in his room, missing her, he would lie awake at night, too sad to fall asleep, too scared to close his eyes, too proud to cry. Hunter grew up as an only child in an underprivileged neighborhood of South Los Angeles. His father made the decision never to remarry, and even with two jobs, he struggled to cope with the demands of raising a child on his own.

To banish the bad dreams, Hunter kept his mind occupied in a different way – he read ferociously, devouring books as if they empowered him.

Hunter had always been different. Even as a child, his brain seemed to work through problems faster than anyone else's. At the age of twelve, after a battery of exams and tests suggested by the principal of his school in Compton, he was accepted into the Mirman School for the Gifted on Mulholland Drive as an eighth-grader.

But even a special school's curriculum wasn't enough to slow his progress down.

By the age of fifteen, Hunter had glided through Mirman,

condensing four years of high school into two, and amazing all of his teachers. With recommendations from everyone, he was accepted as a 'special circumstances' student at Stanford on its Psychology School Program.

In college, his advancement was just as impressive, and Hunter received his PhD in Criminal Behavior Analysis and Biopsychology at the age of twenty-three. And that was when his world was shattered for a second time. His father, who at the time was working as a security guard for a branch of the Bank of America in downtown Los Angeles, was shot dead during a robbery gone wrong. Hunter's nightmares and insomnia came back then – even more forcefully, and they hadn't left him since.

Hunter stood by the window in his living room, staring at a distant nothing. His eyes felt gritty and the headache that had started at the rear of his skull was quickly spreading. No matter how hard he tried, he simply couldn't shake the images of the woman's face from his mind. Her eyes open in horror, her lips swollen and sealed together. Did she wake up alone in that butcher's shop and try to scream? Was that why the thread had dug so deep into the flesh around her lips? Did she claw at her mouth in desperate panic? Was she awake when the killer placed a bomb inside her before sewing her shut? The questions were coming at him like tidal waves.

Hunter blinked and the woman's face was substituted by Doctor Winston's and the video images they'd retrieved from the morgue – his eyes wide in shock as he finally understood what he was holding in his hand, as he finally realized that death had caught up with him, and there was nothing he could do. Hunter closed his eyes. His friend was gone, and he had no clue why.

A distant police siren brought Hunter out of his daze and he shivered with anger. What he saw on the ceiling of the butcher's shop last night changed everything. The bomb was meant for no one else but the woman who was left there. Doctor Winston, his friend, someone he considered family, had died for no reason – a tragic mistake.

Hunter felt a pain start in his right forearm. Only then did he realize he'd been clutching his fist so tight blood couldn't find its way to his arm. He swore to himself that whatever happened, he'd make this killer pay for what he'd done.

Eleven

Due to the sensitivity of Hunter's investigation, the entire operation was moved from the third to the fifth floor of Parker Center, LAPD's Robbery Homicide Division HQ in North Los Angeles Street. The new room was spacious enough for two detectives, but with only a small window on the south wall it felt claustrophobic. When Hunter arrived, Garcia was studying the crime-scene photographs that had been placed on a large magnetic board to the right of Hunter's desk.

'We're a little stuck when it comes to identifying her,' Garcia said as Hunter fired up his computer. 'The crime-scene team got several close-up shots of the stitches to her lips, but only one shot that shows her entire face.' He pointed to the top photograph on the board. 'And as you can see, it isn't a great one.'

The photo had been taken at an angle and the left side of the victim's face was partially obscured. 'Apart from the video, we've got no pictures from the autopsy room,' Garcia continued. 'This is all we have to work with. If she was local to where she was found, we can't really go around asking people and showing them a photograph of someone with her lips stitched shut. It'll creep the hell out of everybody. And someone would no doubt talk to the media.' He stepped back from the board.

'Missing Persons?' Hunter asked.

'I got in touch with them last night, but because this is the only photo we have, and the stitches and swelling to her lips are so prominent, the face-recognition software they use won't work. If they run this picture against their database and she happens to be in there, they'll never get a match. We needed a better picture.'

'Sketch artists?'

Garcia nodded, checking his watch. 'They aren't in yet, neither are the computer guys. But you know they can perform miracles with airbrushing and retouching, so there's hope. The problem is, it can take a while.'

'We don't have a while,' Hunter replied.

Garcia scratched his chin. 'I know, Robert, but without an autopsy report, a DNA profile, or the knowledge of any specific physical marks that could help us identify her, we're stuck.'

'We've gotta start somewhere, and right now the only place we can start is with the Missing Persons files and those pictures,' Hunter said, clicking away on his computer. 'The two of us will have to go through them manually until we get something from the composite drawing team.'

'The two of us? Manually? Are you serious? Do you know how many people get reported missing in LA every week?'

Hunter nodded. 'On average eight hundred, but we can narrow the search down using what we already know – Caucasian woman, brunette, hazel eyes, age between twenty-seven and thirty-three. Judging by the length of the counter and the position the body was left, I'd say she was somewhere between five five and five eight. Let's start the search with women who have been missing for anywhere up to two weeks. If we get nothing, we'll go back further.'

'I'll get right on it.'

'How about her fingerprints?'

Garcia quickly shook his head. 'I've checked with Forensics. They've been running them against the National Automated Fingerprint ID System since last night. So far no matches. She doesn't seem to be in the system.'

Hunter had a feeling she wouldn't be.

Garcia poured himself some coffee from the machine on the counter. 'Any clues from the butcher's shop?'

Hunter had emailed himself the photo of the ceiling he'd taken with his cell phone last night. When the file downloaded, he hit the print button.

'Yes, this.' He showed Garcia the printout.

'Graffiti?' Garcia asked after studying the photograph for a moment.

Hunter nodded. 'I took this picture while lying on the counter in the same position the victim was found.'

Garcia raised an eyebrow. 'You lay on that?' He pointed to the photograph of the dirty metal counter on the pictures board, but didn't wait for a reply. 'What exactly am I looking at here?'

'Blended with the graffiti colors, Carlos. Look for the different lettering.'

A moment later Garcia saw it and his whole body tensed. 'Well, I'll be dipped in shit.'

Hidden amongst the colors and shapes, a line of small spray-painted black letters seemed out of place. It read: IT'S INSIDE YOU.

Twelve

Before Garcia could ask anything further, Captain Blake entered the room without knocking.

Barbara Blake had taken over the Los Angeles Robbery Homicide Division's leadership after the retirement of its long-standing captain, William Bolter, two years earlier. Her name had been put forward for captaincy by Bolter himself, upsetting a long list of candidates. She was an intriguing woman – elegant, attractive, with long black hair and mysterious dark eyes that never gave anything away. Despite reservations by some at the division, she had quickly gained a reputation for being a no-nonsense, iron-fist captain. She wasn't easily intimidated, took shit from no one, and she didn't mind upsetting high-powered politicians or government officials if it meant sticking to what she believed was right. In just a few months she had earned the trust and respect of every detective under her command.

Captain Blake and Doctor Winston's friendship went back a long way – over twenty years. The news of his death had hit her like a sucker punch to the gut, and she wanted answers.

As she stepped into the room, she instantly picked up on the tension coming from Garcia. Her eyebrows rose. 'What happened? Have we got something already?'

Garcia handed her the printout. 'From the butcher's shop.'

Just like Garcia, she didn't see it at first. 'What the hell am I looking at?'

Garcia pointed at the letters.

The captain's eyes shot in Hunter's direction. 'This was on the wall in the shop?'

'On the ceiling. Directly above where the victim was left.'

'But the ceiling is covered in graffiti. Why do you think these words have anything to do with our victim?'

'Two reasons. One, that's not graffiti like the rest of the ceiling, that's a handwritten message. Two, the paint was more vivid than the rest of the graffiti, too fresh.'

The captain's eyes returned to the printout.

Hunter paused and all of a sudden started searching his desk.

'What are you looking for?' the captain asked.

'The DVD with the video file we got from the morgue yesterday. I want to check something.' He found it and popped it into his computer's disk drive.

Garcia and Captain Blake joined Hunter by his desk.

As the video started playing, Hunter fast-forwarded it to the scene where Doctor Winston retrieved the bomb from inside the stitched victim. The player application in Hunter's computer didn't have a frame-by-frame function. He had to keep on clicking the play/pause button to slowly advance it to the exact spot he wanted. He watched a small segment a couple of times before turning to face Garcia and the captain.

'His back is towards the camera, so we have to guess the correct moment,' Hunter said, 'but look at Doctor Winston's arm movement right here.'

All eyes were glued to the screen.

Hunter rewound and played the sequence twice over.

'There's a small jerk.' Garcia nodded. 'As if his hand came unstuck.'

'Exactly,' Hunter agreed. 'Do you have a stopwatch?'

Garcia pulled his sleeve up to reveal his wristwatch. 'Sure.'

'Time it. Ready? Go.' Hunter clicked the play button. Exactly ten seconds later, the screen was filled with static.

'A ten-second delay trigger mechanism?' the captain said, looking at Hunter. 'Like a grenade?'

'Something like that.'

'Most grenades' trigger mechanisms have to be manually activated,' Garcia said. 'Who activated that one?'

Hunter rubbed his face. 'That's the question that's been knocking around in my head. Whoever placed the bomb inside the victim couldn't be sure of the exact moment of extraction. That means that the bomb couldn't have been on a timer or have been remotely activated.'

Garcia nodded.

'So what if in this case the trigger was held in place not by a pin like most grenades, but by the confined space where the bomb was placed?' Hunter suggested. 'A spring trigger of some sort, held tight by the victim's own body.'

Garcia and Captain Blake exchanged glances as they considered it for a moment.

'So extracting the bomb from the victim would've released the trigger,' Garcia said, scratching his forehead. 'It's possible – and very creative.'

'Fantastic,' the captain said, pinching the bridge of her nose. 'To the killer this is all just a game.' She showed Hunter the printout again. 'He even told us it was inside her.'

Hunter shook his head. 'The killer wasn't informing us, Captain.'

'Sorry?'

'The killer was informing the *victim*.'

Thirteen

Captain Blake leaned against the edge of Garcia's desk and folded her arms. 'You've lost me, Robert.'

'Have a look at that printout again, Captain,' Hunter said. 'The killer wrote "It's inside *you*" not "It's inside *her*". He wasn't communicating with us.'

'Why would the killer try to communicate with a dead body?'

'Because she wasn't dead when he left her.'

The captain ran a finger over her right eyebrow and pulled a face. 'You lost me even more now.'

Hunter walked up to the pictures board. 'There were several things that were bothering me about the crime-scene photos. That's why I wanted to have a look at the butcher's shop again myself.' He pointed to one of the pictures. 'Look at the position the body was found in, the arms in particular. One is hanging down from the side of the counter and the other is resting awkwardly on her chest. The fingers on her right hand are spread apart and half bent, as if she was trying to dig at something. I don't think the killer left her in this particular position.'

'The body might've been interfered with, Robert,' the captain countered. 'It was an anonymous phone call that gave us the body's location, remember?'

Hunter nodded. 'Yes, and I listened to the 911 recording. It's a girl's voice. Not older than sixteen or seventeen, and she sounded hysterical. The reason why she didn't wanna give us her name is probably because she was going into that room to shoot up.'

'OK, so the girl didn't touch the body,' the captain said, accepting his theory. 'But maybe you're reading too much into this message. Maybe the killer didn't put a great deal of thought into it. So he wrote *you* instead of *her*, no big deal.'

It was Garcia's turn to disagree. 'That would suggest that the writing on the ceiling was a spur-of-the-moment thing, Captain.' He rubbed the lump on his nose. 'We're talking about someone who put together his own explosive device and probably engineered the trigger mechanism himself. He then placed it all inside the victim in some way that it wouldn't be triggered until found and extracted. All of that while she was still alive.' He shook his head and faced the pictures board. 'Whatever this killer did, Captain, nothing was on the spur of the moment. He thought it all through. And that's what makes him so dangerous.'

Fourteen

Captain Blake let out a frustrated breath and started pacing the room. Her high heels clicked against the wooden floor.

'It doesn't make any sense. If the victim was still alive when she was left in that butcher's shop, and the message on the ceiling was meant for her, how come she was dead when we found her? Who killed her, the rats?' She pulled a photograph from the board and studied it for a moment. 'Independently of whatever happened to the victim, the fact still remains that someone placed a bomb inside her and stitched her shut. The only way of getting that bomb out was to cut through the stitches and pull it out.' She paused and allowed her eyes to move from one detective to the other. 'Don't tell me you think the killer expected the victim to do that by herself?'

No one replied.

Hunter massaged the back of his neck, and for a moment allowed his fingers to rub the rough scar on his nape.

The captain turned towards him. 'I know you, Robert. If you think the message was left for the victim instead of us, you must have a theory on this. I'm all ears.'

'I don't have a proper theory yet, Captain, just too many ifs.'

'You've gotta have something brewing in that brain of

yours,' the captain pushed. 'Indulge me, because right now I hate what I'm hearing.'

Hunter took a deep breath. 'Maybe the bomb's how the killer wanted her to die.'

Captain Blake's eyes narrowed. 'You think the bomb was supposed to blow up inside her, while she was still alive?'

Hunter tilted his head to one side, musing over the possibility.

Captain Blake sat down in Hunter's chair. 'You're going to have to develop on that, Robert. If this killer thought everything through so thoroughly as Garcia has suggested, and if the bomb was supposed to blow up inside the victim as you're suggesting, why didn't it? What happened? Did the killer make a mistake? How would the trigger mechanism be activated while the bomb was *inside* her? And if he didn't kill her, how the hell did she die?'

'As I said, too many ifs, Captain,' Hunter replied calmly. 'And at the moment I don't have the answers. With everything that's happened, we don't have much to go on. I don't know if the killer made a mistake or not. I don't know why the bomb didn't blow up inside her, or how it was supposed to be activated in the first place. Without the autopsy report we'll probably never know the real cause of death. What we do know is that it's nothing apparent. She wasn't shot, stabbed, or strangled. I also don't believe she was poisoned.' He paused. 'But there's a possibility she suffocated.'

Captain Blake threw Hunter a perplexed look. 'How's that?'

Hunter pointed to an enlarged picture of the victim's face. 'Suffocation causes the blood vessels around the eyes and behind the delicate skin on the cheeks to burst. See here.' He indicated on the photo. 'This sort of old-person's-skin look is a consequence of burst blood vessels. There's a good chance she suffocated. I confirmed it with Doctor Hove. But again, without an autopsy we'll never be certain.'

'So you're saying that you think she might've suffocated by herself, after the killer left her there?'

Hunter nodded.

'On what? The foul smell of the place?'

Hunter shrugged. 'Her own vomit ... her tongue ... Who knows? Maybe the victim had a bad heart. But just imagine if she was still alive when she was left in that butcher's shop – unconscious, but still alive. She wakes up, naked, frightened, in pain, and with parts of her body stitched shut. That'd certainly be enough to trigger a severe panic attack in most people.'

Captain Blake massaged her closed eyelids, considering Hunter's suggestion. She knew that a panic attack could easily cause someone to vomit, gag or hyperventilate. With the victim's mouth sewn tightly shut, she'd have no way of drawing in breath and increasing the flow of oxygen to her lungs. That would've made the victim's panic turn into mindless desperation. If she'd puked, the vomit had nowhere to go. Choking and asphyxiating would've been just a breath away. And then ... certain death.

Fifteen

The results of the chemical tests done on the spray paint used on the ceiling of the butcher's shop came in by 2:00 p.m. and threw up nothing special. The paint came from a can of Montana Tarblack – probably the most popular brand of spray paint in the USA. Every graffiti artist in the country used it. The handwriting analyses confirmed what Hunter already suspected – the killer had used his non-writing hand to spray the words onto the ceiling. Simple, but effective. Hunter had requested that the whole room be dusted again, and this time they should include the ceiling. Every print found was to be run through the National Automated Fingerprint ID System.

Hunter leaned back in his chair, closed his eyes and gently ran the tip of his finger up and down the bridge of his nose. His brain kept trying to make sense of such a senseless act.

If there had been no bomb, if the victim had been found simply stitched shut, Hunter would have a steadier psychological path to follow. The stitches to the mouth on their own would have suggested the possibility of a retaliation kill – a lesson being taught. The victim might have said something she shouldn't have – about the wrong person, to the wrong person, or both. The act could have been performed as a way to symbolize shutting her up.

The stitches to her mouth and lower body together would have upped the stakes to a possible sexual or love betrayal and revenge. *If you can't keep your mouth and legs shut, I'll shut them for you.* That would've clearly placed a deceived husband, boyfriend or lover right at the top of their list of persons of interest. And that possibility was still pretty much alive in Hunter's mind. But he still had the bomb to deal with. Why place a *bomb* inside the victim? Experience also told him that the overwhelming majority of what were considered crimes of passion were spur-of-the-moment acts, generated by irrational anger and an almost total loss of control. Very rarely did it come in the form of a planned, calculated and brutal vengeance act.

One possibility that kept nagging Hunter was that there could have been more than one perpetrator, more specifically, a gang. Crimes like this one weren't beyond the scope of certain gangs in Los Angeles. Some were notorious for their violence and their bad-ass, don't-fuck-with-us attitude. Sending a warning to other gangs in the form of brutal beatings and murders happened more often than the mayor of Los Angeles would care to admit. These gangs also had a direct link to gun trafficking. Getting hold of a ready-made bomb, a grenade, or materials to make their own wouldn't have been a problem. The victim could've belonged to some gang leader. Some of them liked to think of their women as possessions. If she'd betrayed him, especially if she did it with a rival gang member, this could have been their way of blowing her off.

And then there was the possibility that the stitches carried no symbolism whatsoever. As Captain Blake had suggested, they could simply be dealing with an extremely sadistic killer, someone who enjoyed hurting people for the sheer pleasure of it. And Hunter knew that if that were the case, more victims would follow.

'The Missing Persons files we requested should be with us in the next forty-five minutes or so,' Garcia said, coming off the phone and dragging Hunter away from his thoughts.

'Great. You can start going over them if I'm not here.' Hunter reached for his jacket. There was only one person he knew in LA who'd have knowledge of guns, explosives, trigger mechanisms and gangs. It was time to call in some favors.

Sixteen

D-King was probably the best-known dealer in Hollywood and Northwest Los Angeles. Though he was known as a dealer, no one was ever able to prove it, least of all the District Attorney's office. They'd been trying to nail him to anything substantial without success for the past eight years.

D-King was young, intelligent, a fierce businessman, and very dangerous to anyone who was stupid enough to ever cross him. Allegedly, he dealt not only in drugs, but prostitution, stolen goods, weapons . . . the list went on and on. He also had a string of legitimate businesses – nightclubs, bars, restaurants, even a gym. The IRS couldn't touch him either.

Hunter and D-King's paths had crossed for the first time three years ago, during the notorious Crucifix Killer investigation. An unprecedented chain of events forced them into a standoff, and into reaching a decision that despite them being on different sides of the law, made them respect each other.

Hunter pulled D-King's address from the police computer. Where else but Malibu Beach, where the super-famous and the super-rich called home.

As he brought his car to a stop by the enormous double iron gates fitted with security cameras, Hunter had to admit he was impressed. The two-story building was majestic: an ivy-covered, double bow-front brick construction with square granite piers every twenty feet.

Before Hunter had a chance to reach for the intercom button, a strong male voice called out.

'May I help you?'

'Yes, I'm here to see your boss.'

'And you are?'

'Tell D-King it's Robert Hunter.'

The intercom clicked off and a minute later the iron gates parted.

The driveway was flanked by millimeter-perfect trimmed hedges. Hunter parked his rusted Buick Lesabre next to a pearly white Lamborghini Gallardo, just in front of a six-car garage. He climbed up the steps to the main house, and as he reached the top, the door was opened by a six-foot-three, two-hundred-and-seventy-pound muscle-bound black man. The man frowned at Hunter's car.

'It's an American classic,' Hunter retorted.

Not even a ghost of a smile from the muscleman.

'Please, follow me.'

The interior of the house was just as impressive as the outside. Twelve-feet-high ceilings, designer furniture and walls covered with oil paintings – some of them Dutch, a few of them French, all of them valuable.

As Hunter crossed the Italian-marbled floor in the living area, he noticed a jaw-droppingly beautiful black woman in a bright yellow bikini sitting among overstuffed cushions. She lifted her eyes from the glossy magazine in her hands and gave Hunter a warm smile. He politely nodded back and smiled internally. *Even rock stars and sports superstars don't have it this good.*

The muscleman guided Hunter through a pair of sliding

glass doors and out to the backyard and pool area. Four young and attractive topless women were by the edge of the pool, giggling and splashing water at each other. Three other musclemen in suits were strategically positioned around the yard. D-King was sitting at one of four artfully weathered teak tables at the poolside, under a white umbrella. His blue silk shirt was unbuttoned, revealing a muscular torso adorned with chains and diamonds. The blonde woman sitting with him was also topless. A single white gold loop ring pierced her left nipple.

'Detective Robert Hunter?' D-King said with a smile but without getting up. 'Yo, wuz up, dawg? Now that's a moth-erfucking surprise. How long has it been, three years?' He indicated the chair opposite his.

Hunter took it. 'Something like that.' He nodded at the blonde woman, who replied with a wink.

'Can I offer you something, Detective?' D-King said, tilt-ing his head towards his blonde friend. 'Lisa here can mix you the most amazing cocktail.'

Hunter's eyes stole a peek at Lisa, who smiled naughtily. 'Anything you like.'

Hunter shook his head. 'I'm fine for now, thanks.'

'OK,' D-King cut in, 'so now that I know you're not here for the company or the drinks, what can I do for you, Detective?'

Hunter's eyes subtly moved to Lisa and then back to D-King. He got the hint.

'Lisa, why don't you go play with the other girls?' He didn't phrase it as a request. She undid the sarong around her waist and stood up. Only then Hunter realized that she was fully naked. Not a hint of embarrassment crossed her face as she paused in front of him for a long moment. Her body was as close to perfection as Hunter had ever seen. Lisa slowly turned and walked away, her hips swinging as if she were on a catwalk. The tattoo on her lower back read – *I know you're looking.*

'That's right, baby, dance it up,' D-King called out before turning to Hunter. 'Admit it, Detective,' he teased, 'I know how to live, don't I? Hugh Heffner and Larry Flynt have got shit on me. *Playboy* and *Hustler* can kiss my black ass all the way to Mississippi. My girls are hotter.'

'What do you know about homemade explosive devices?'

The smile vanished from D-King's lips. 'I know they go bang.'

Hunter kept a poker face.

'Officially, notta thing.'

'And unofficially?'

D-King scratched the small scar above his left eyebrow with his pinky while scrutinizing Hunter. 'If you're here unofficially, why don't you have a drink?'

'I'm not thirsty.'

They regarded each other for a few more seconds.

'First time we met you bullshitted for a while before coming clean. I hope we're past that crap. What's this really about, Detective?'

Hunter leaned forward and placed a close-up photograph of the victim's face on the table in front of him, rotating it around to face D-King.

'Oh, hell no, dawg.' He cringed and moved back. 'Last time you showed me a picture of a dead woman, all fucking hell broke loose.'

'Do you know who she is?'

'And that's exactly the question that started it all.' His eyes moved back to the picture, and involuntarily D-King rubbed his lips with the tips of his fingers. 'Oh damn. That's some nasty shiiit. Some motherfucker stitched her mouth shut?'

'Do you know who she is?' Hunter asked again.

'She ain't none of my girls if that's what you're asking,' he replied after a brief pause.

'Could she have been on the game?'

'Not looking like that.' Instantly D-King's hands came up in surrender. 'Sorry, bad joke. Anybody could be on the game these days. She looks to have been attractive enough. I don't think I've ever seen her before though.' He tried to read Hunter's expressionless face and failed. 'The problem is that nowadays a lot of girls are trying to go it alone, creating websites and all, doing their own thang, you know what I'm saying? It's hard to be sure. But if she was a top working girl in the Hollywood area, I'd know.'

The other four women who were playing by the edge of the pool decided to join Lisa, who was now sitting on a floating chair sipping a colorful drink.

D-King's eyes moved down to the picture again. 'This is too fucking nasty, man. And knowing the kind of shit you get involved with, I'm sure whoever did this did it while she was still alive, right?'

'Could this have been done by a gang?' Hunter asked. 'Or a pimp?'

D-King's face clouded over. Helping the police was never part of his agenda. 'I wouldn't know,' he replied coldly.

'C'mon, D-King, look at her.' Hunter tapped the photograph on the table, but kept a steady voice. He was aware all three musclemen around the yard had their eyes on him. 'Her mouth wasn't the only part of her body that was stitched shut. Whoever did this did a real nasty job on her. And you were right. It was done while she was still alive.'

D-King shifted in his seat. Violence against women had a way of lighting a fuse inside him. His mother had been beaten to death by his own drunken father while he was locked in the closet. He was ten. D-King never forgot her screams and pleas for mercy. He had never forgotten the sound of her bones breaking as his father repeatedly hit her, over and over again. He heard those sounds almost every night in his dreams.

D-King sat back and looked at his fingernails, flicking the end of each one with his thumb. 'You mean could this be some sort of trademark retaliation?' He shrugged. 'Who knows? Possibly. If she belonged to a homeboy and she either stole from him or decided to fuck around, I wouldn't be surprised. Some people don't look kindly at being fucked with. Examples have to be made, do you feel me? This could even be considered mild by some standards.' He paused and looked at the picture again. 'But if this is payback for her being somebody's woman and getting dirty somewhere else, you can expect to get another body – the motherfucker she was doing it with. This kind of revenge comes in twos, Detective.' He pushed the photo back towards Hunter. 'What does this have to do with homemade explosive devices?'

'More than it looks.'

D-King chuckled. 'You never give anything away, do you?' He had a sip of the dark green colored drink in front of him. 'Actually, if last time we saw each other is anything to go by, I don't really fucking wanna know what this is all about.' He regarded Hunter like a poker player about to bet his whole stash before tapping the picture with his index finger. 'But this is fucking offensive, man, and I owe you one anyway. Let me look into it and I'll get back to you.'

Seventeen

Garcia turned on the fan and stood in front of it for a minute before going back to his desk. He couldn't even imagine how hot that room would be during summer.

He'd been going over the crime-scene pictures in his computer, enhancing and scrutinizing them, looking for anything they could use to point them in the right direction as to the victim's identity. So far, nothing. No tattoos or surgery scars. The moles and freckles he could see on her arms, stomach, neck and cleavage were too common and not prominent enough to really be classed as identifying marks. As far as he could tell, she was a natural brunette and her breasts were her own.

Her arms showed no signs of needle marks and her frame wasn't skinny and wasted. If she was a junkie, she certainly didn't look like one. Despite the small patches on her cheeks that carried that old-person's-skin look Hunter had mentioned, the victim couldn't have been any older than thirty-three, at a stretch. If the old saying that the eyes are the windows to the soul was true, then her soul was scared beyond belief when she died.

Garcia leaned forward, placed his elbows on his desk and rubbed his eyes with the heels of his hands. He reached for his coffee cup, but it had long gone cold. Before he could pour himself a new one, a clicking sound announcing the arrival of a new email came from his computer. The Missing Persons files he'd requested. They'd promised to send them over in forty-five minutes. That had been two hours ago.

Garcia read the email and let out a high-pitched whistle. Fifty-two brunette Caucasian women with hazel eyes, aged between twenty-seven and thirty-three, and somewhere between five five and five eight in height had been reported missing in the past two weeks. He unzipped the attachment containing all the files and started printing them out, first the photographs, then their personal information sheets.

He poured himself a new cup of coffee and gathered all the printouts into one pile. The photos would have been brought into the Missing Persons Unit by the person who reported them as missing. Even though Missing Persons would have asked for a recent picture, Garcia knew that some of those photographs could be over a year old, sometimes more. He'd have to allow for subtle changes in appearance such as hair length and style, and fullness of the face due to weight loss or gain.

The main problem Garcia faced was that he had only the close-up photo of the victim, the one from the crime scene, to compare them to. The swelling on the victim's lips together with the thick black threaded stitches forcing them tightly together deformed the bottom half of her face. Matching any of the photographs sent from Missing Persons to that one would be a long and laborious task.

An hour later Garcia had reduced the possible matches from fifty-two to twelve, but his eyes were getting tired, and the more he looked at the pictures, the fewer distinguishing features he saw.

He spread the twelve printouts out on his desk, creating

three lines of four with their respective information sheets next to them. The photos were all of reasonable quality. There were six face portraits, passport-style; three where the subject had been cropped from a group picture; one showed a wet-haired brunette sitting on a jet ski; another smiling brunette was by the pool; and the last picture showed a woman at a dinner table holding a glass of champagne.

Garcia was about to start the whole process again when Hunter walked through the door and saw him hunched over his desk, staring intensely at the group of neatly arranged photographs.

'Are those from Missing Persons?' Hunter asked.

Garcia nodded.

'Anything?'

'Well, I started with fifty-two possibilities and have been comparing them to our crime-scene photos for over an hour now. The swelling on our victim's face makes things a lot harder. I'm now down to these,' he nodded at the twelve photos on his desk, 'but my eyes are starting to play tricks on me. I'm not sure what I'm supposed to look for any more.'

Hunter stood in front of Garcia's desk and allowed his eyes to jump from photo to photo, spending several seconds on each one. A moment later his gaze settled on the facial close-up of the unidentified victim. He moved them all nearer together, making a new photo group before reaching for a blank sheet of paper.

'Every face can be looked at in several ways,' Hunter said, placing the sheet of paper over the first photo at the top of the group, covering two-thirds of it. 'That's how composite sketches are created. Individual characteristics added together one by one.'

Garcia moved closer.

'The shape of the head and ears, the shape of the eyebrows, eyes and nose, the mouth, the jaw line, the chin . . .' As he mentioned each facial feature, Hunter used the paper sheet to cover all the other ones. 'We can very crudely use the same principle here.'

A few minutes later they had discarded another eight photographs.

'I'd say our victim could be any of these four,' Hunter said finally. 'They share all the same physical features – oval face, small nose, almond-shaped eyes, arched eyebrows, prominent cheekbones . . . the same as our victim.'

Garcia agreed with a nod.

Hunter checked the personal fact sheets Garcia had stapled to the back of each picture. They'd all been reported missing over a week ago. Their home and work addresses were scattered all over town. At first glance there seemed to be no other similarities between the four women other than their looks.

Hunter glanced at his watch. 'We've gotta check them all out today.'

Garcia reached for his jacket. 'I'm ready.'

Hunter handed him two of the photographs. 'You take those and I'll take these two.'

Garcia nodded.

'Call me if you get lucky.'

Eighteen

Whitney Myers drove through the tall iron gates of the sumptuous mansion in Beverly Hills just forty-five minutes after she had received the call. She parked her yellow Corvette C6 at the far end of the wide cobblestone court-yard, took off her dark glasses, and placed them on her head like an arc to hold her shiny, long black hair back. She grabbed her briefcase from the passenger's seat, checked her watch and smiled to herself. Considering LA's afternoon traffic and the fact that she had been in Long Beach when she got the call, forty-five minutes was lightning fast.

She was greeted at the steps that led up to the mansion's main entrance by Andy McKee, a short, overweight, brilliant attorney-at-law.

'Whitney,' he said, using a white handkerchief to wipe the sweat from his forehead. 'Thank you for coming so quickly.'

'Not a problem,' she smiled as she shook his hand. 'Whose house is this? It's gorgeous.'

'You'll meet him inside.' He looked at her appraisingly and the sweat returned to his forehead.

Whitney Myers was thirty-six years old with dark eyes, a small nose, high cheekbones, full lips and a strong jaw. Her smile could be considered a weapon with the power of turning steady legs into gelatinous goo. Many strong and eloquent men had babbled incoherently and giggled like kids after she hit them with it. She looked like a model on a day off, even more beautiful because she wasn't trying.

Myers started her career as a police officer at the age of twenty-one. She worked harder than anyone in her bureau to move through the ranks and make detective as quickly as she could. Her intelligence, quick thinking and strong character also helped push her forward, and by the age of twenty-seven she finally received her detective's shield.

Her captain was quick to recognize that Myers had a gift when it came to persuasion. She was calm, articulate, attentive and extremely convincing when putting her point across. She was also good with people. After six months on an intensive and specialized course with the FBI, Myers became one of the chief negotiators for the West and Valley bureaus of the LAPD and the Missing Persons Unit.

But her career as a detective with Los Angeles' finest came to an abrupt end three years ago, after her efforts to negotiate a suicidal jumper off the roof of an eighteen-story-high skyscraper in Culver City went terribly wrong.

The aftermath of what happened that day put Myers' entire life under severe scrutiny. An investigation was launched into her conduct, and Internal Affairs came down on her like a heavy downpour. After several weeks, the IA investigation was inconclusive and no charges were brought against her, but her days with the LAPD were over. She'd been running her own missing persons investigation agency since then.

Myers followed McKee through the house, past a double staircase and down a hallway lined with pictures of famous movie stars. The hallway ended in the living room. The room was so imposing it took Myers a few seconds to notice a six-foot-two, broad-shouldered man standing at an arched window. In his right hand he held an almost empty glass of Scotch. Despite being in his mid-fifties, Myers could see he had a boyish charm about him.

'Whitney, let me introduce you to Leonid Kudrov,' McKee said.

Leonid put his glass down and shook Myers' hand. His grip was tense and the expression on his face was the same she'd seen in every face that had ever hired her – desperation.

Nineteen

Myers declined the offer of a drink and listened attentively to Kudrov's account of events, taking notes every other sentence.

'Have you called the police?' she asked while Leonid refilled his glass.

'Yes, they took my details but they barely listened to what I was saying. Gave me some bullshit about elapsed time, independent adult, or something like that, and kept putting me on hold. That's when I called Andy and he called you.'

Myers nodded. 'Because your daughter is thirty years old and you couldn't substantiate your reason for believing she's gone missing, it's normal practice to wait at least twenty-four hours before she can be officially considered a missing person.' Her voice was naturally confident, the kind that inspired trust.

'Twenty-four hours? She could be dead in twenty-four hours. That's bullshit.'

'Sometimes it's even more, depending on the evidence given.'

'I tried telling him that,' McKee added, wiping his forehead again.

'She's an adult, Mr. Kudrov,' Myers explained. 'An adult who has simply failed to turn up for a lunch appointment.'

Kudrov glared at Myers and then at McKee. 'Has she heard a fucking word I said?'

'Yes,' Myers replied, crossing her legs and flipping through her notes. 'She was thirty minutes late for your lunch. You called her several times. She never answered and never returned any of your messages. You panicked and went to her apartment. Once there you found a towel on the kitchen floor, but nothing else seemed out of place except for a bottle of white wine that should've been in the fridge. Her car keys were on a tray upstairs. You found her priceless violin in her practice room, but you said that it should've been in the safe. From what you could tell there was no sign of any sort of struggle or a break-in, and the place didn't seem to have been burgled. The building's concierge said that no one had visited her that night.' She calmly closed her notebook.

'Isn't that enough?'

'Let me explain how the police would think, how they are trained to think. There are way more Missing Persons cases than there are detectives working them. The number one rule is to prioritize, only allocate resources when there's no doubt the person in question has really gone missing. If she were a minor, an amber alert would've been issued all across the country. But as an independent adult who's only been unreachable for less than twenty-four hours, protocol dictates the police go through a checklist first.'

'A checklist? You're shitting me.'

A quick headshake. 'I shit you not.'

'Such as?'

Myers leaned forward. 'Is this an adult who: one – may be in need of assistance? Two – may be the victim of a crime or foul play? Three – may be in need of medical attention? Four

– has no pattern of running away or disappearing? Five – may be the victim of parental abduction? And six – is mentally or physically impaired?' Myers placed her sunglasses on the coffee table next to her. 'From that list, only having no pattern of running away or disappearing checked out. The police's initial thoughts would be – because Miss Kudrov is a sane, independent, financially sufficient and unattached adult woman, she could've simply decided she needed a break from everything. There's no one she really needs to give account of her actions to. She doesn't have a nine-to-five job, and she isn't married. You said she just got back from a long tour with the Los Angeles Philharmonic.'

Kudrov nodded.

'It must be very stressful. She could've jumped on a plane and gone to the Bahamas. She could've met someone in a bar last night and decided to spend a few undisturbed days with that person somewhere else.'

Leonid ran a hand though his cropped hair. 'Well, she didn't. I know Katia. If she had to cancel an appointment with me or anyone else, she would've called. It's just the way she is. She doesn't let people down, least of all me. We have a great relationship. If she had decided that she needed a break, she would've at least let me know where she was going.'

'How about her mother? Am I right in assuming you and she aren't together any more?'

'Her mother passed away several years ago.'

Myers kept her eyes on Leonid. 'I'm sorry to hear that.'

'Katia didn't just decide to take a trip somewhere. I'm telling you, something is wrong.'

He started pacing the room. Emotions were starting to fly high.

'Mr. Kudrov, please—'

'Stop calling me Mr. Kudrov,' he cut her short. 'I'm not your teacher. Call me Leo.'

'OK, Leo. I'm not doubting you. I'm just explaining why the police acted the way they did. If Katia hasn't showed up in twenty-four hours, they'll be all over this case like ugly on a moose. They'll use every resource available to find her. But you better be prepared, because with your celebrity status, the circus will come next.'

Leonid squinted at McKee before moving his stare back to Myers. 'Circus?'

'When I said that the LAPD will use every resource available, I meant that. Including you and your status. They'll want you to make your own appeal to the public, to personalize the case. Maybe even hold a conference here at your house. They'll broadcast Katia's photo on TV and in the newspapers, and they'll prefer a family picture instead of a lone shot – it's more . . . *touching*. The picture will be copied and plastered all over LA, maybe even the whole of California. Search parties will form. They'll ask for clothes for the dog search teams. They'll want hairs and other samples for DNA tests. The media will camp outside your gates.' Myers paused for breath. 'As I said, it will turn into a circus, but the LAPD Missing Persons Unit is very good at what they do.' She hesitated for effect. 'Leo, given your status and social class, we have to consider the possibility that your daughter was kidnapped for ransom. No one has attempted to contact you?'

Leonid shook his head. 'I've been in the house all day and have left specific instructions at my office to divert any unidentified caller to my home line. No calls.'

Myers nodded.

'Something is wrong. I can feel it.' Leonid pinned Myers down with a desperate stare. 'I don't want this splattered all over the news unless it's really necessary. Andy told me you are the best at what you do. Better than the LAPD Missing Persons. Can *you* find her?' He made it sound less of a question and more like a plea.

Myers gave McKee a look that said, *I'm flattered.*

He returned a shy smile.

'I will do my best.' Myers nodded, her voice confident.

'So do it.'

'Do you have a recent picture of your daughter?'

Kudrov was already prepared and handed Myers a colored eight-by-twelve-inch photograph of Katia.

Myers' eyes grazed the picture. 'I'll also need the keys to her apartment, the names and phone numbers of everyone you can think of who she could've contacted. And I need it all by yesterday.'

Twenty

Hunter called both contacts on the two Missing Persons personal fact sheets he had with him. Mr. Giles Carlsen, a hair salon manager from Brentwood, had contacted the police ten days ago to report Cathy Greene, his roommate, as missing. On the phone, Carlsen told Hunter that Miss Greene had finally turned up the morning before. She'd been away with a new male friend she'd met in her dance class.

The second contact, Mr. Roy Mitchell, had contacted the police twelve days ago. His 29-year-old daughter, Laura, had simply disappeared. Mr. Mitchell asked Hunter to meet him at his home in Fremont Place in an hour.

Hancock Park is one of the most affluent and desirable areas in all of Southern California. In sharp contrast to most Los Angeles neighborhoods, houses in Hancock Park are set well back from the street, most power and telephone lines are buried, and fences are strongly discouraged. As Hunter turned into Fremont Place, it became obvious that invasion of privacy wasn't one of the area's main concerns.

The house's half-moon-shaped driveway was paved in cobble block and merged into a parking area large enough for two buses. At the center of it stood a massive stone fountain. The sun was just reaching the horizon, and the sky behind the terracotta brick two-story house was being painted in 'photo moment' fiery red streaks. Hunter parked his car and climbed out.

The front door was answered by a woman in her mid-fifties. She was a picture of elegance, with longish hair neatly tied in a ponytail, a magnetic smile, and skin most women half her age would kill for. She introduced herself as Denise Mitchell and showed Hunter into a study rich with art, antiques, and leather-bound books. Standing before a tall mahogany sideboard crowded with photographs was a stocky man, a donut shy of being fat. He was at least half a foot shorter than Hunter with a full head of disheveled gray hair and a matching moustache.

'You must be the detective I spoke to on the phone,' he said offering his hand. 'I'm Roy Mitchell.'

His handshake was as practiced as his smile, strong enough to show strength of character but soft enough not to intimidate. Hunter showed him his credentials and Roy Mitchell tensed.

'Oh God.'

His whisper wasn't quiet enough to escape his wife's ears. 'What's wrong?' she asked, moving closer, her eyes pleading for information.

'Can you give us a moment, honey,' Roy replied, trying in vain to conceal his concern.

'No, I'm not giving you a moment,' Denise said, her stare now fixed on Hunter. 'I want to know what happened. What information do you have on my daughter?'

'Denise, please.'

'I'm not going anywhere, Roy.' Her eyes never left Hunter. 'Did you find my daughter? Is she OK?'

Roy Mitchell looked away.

'What's going on, Roy? What got you so spooked?'

No reply.

'Somebody talk to me.' Her voice faltered.

'I'm not with the Missing Persons Unit, Mrs. Mitchell,' Hunter finally offered, showing her his credentials once again. This time she looked at them a lot more attentively than she had at the door.

'Oh my God, you're from Homicide?' She cupped her hands over her nose and mouth as tears filled her eyes.

'There's a chance that I'm in the wrong house,' Hunter said in a steady but comforting voice.

'What?' Denise's hands started shaking.

'Maybe we should all have a seat.' Hunter indicated the leather Chesterfield sofa by a six-foot-tall Victorian lampshade.

The Mitchells took the sofa and Hunter one of the two armchairs facing it.

'At the moment we're trying to identify someone who shares several physical characteristics with your daughter,' Hunter explained. 'Laura's name is one of four which have come up as a possible match.'

'As a possible match to a homicide victim?' Roy asked, placing a hand on his wife's knee.

'Unfortunately, yes.'

Denise started crying.

Roy took a deep breath. 'I gave the other detective a very recent picture of Laura, do you have it?'

Hunter nodded.

'And still you can't be sure if this victim of yours is Laura?' Denise asked, her mascara starting to run down her face. 'How come?'

Roy clamped his eyes shut for an instant and a single tear rolled to the tip of his nose. Hunter could see he'd already picked up on the possibility of the victim being unrecognizable. 'So you're here to ask us for a blood sample for a DNA test?' he said.

It was obvious that Roy Mitchell was a lot more clued up on police procedures than most people. Since the introduction of DNA testing, in a situation such as the one Hunter was facing, it was a lot more practical for the police to collect samples and match them to the victim first. That way they could later approach only the identified family, instead of putting several innocent ones through the panic and the traumatic experience of looking at a photograph of a gruesomely disfigured victim.

Hunter shook his head. 'Sadly, a DNA test won't help us.'

For a moment it was as if there wasn't enough air in the room for all three of them. 'Do you have a picture of the victim?' Roy finally asked.

Hunter nodded and flipped through several sheets of paper inside the folder he'd brought with him. 'Mrs. Mitchell,' he said, catching Denise's eyes, 'this woman might not be your daughter. There's no reason for you to look at this picture right now.'

Denise stared at Hunter with glassy eyes. 'I'm not going anywhere.'

'Honey, please.' Roy tried again.

She didn't even look at him.

Hunter waited, but the determination in her eyes was almost palpable. He placed the close-up of the victim on the coffee table in front of them.

It took Denise Mitchell just a fraction of a second to recognize her. 'Oh my God!' Her shivering hands shot to her mouth. 'What have they done to my baby?'

All of a sudden the room they were in looked different

– darker, smaller, the air denser. Hunter sat in silence for several minutes while Roy Mitchell tried to console his wife. Her tears weren't hysterical; they were simply full of pain – and rage. In different circumstances Hunter would have left, giving the Mitchells some time to grieve before coming back the next morning with a list of questions, but this wasn't like any other case, this killer wasn't like any other killer. Right now Hunter didn't have a choice. Laura's parents were his best, and at the moment, only source of information on Laura. And he needed information like he needed air.

Denise Mitchell grabbed a tissue from the box on the side table and wiped her tears away before finally standing up. She approached a small desk next to the window where several photo frames were arranged, most of them containing pictures of Laura at different stages of her life.

Roy didn't follow, instead slumping himself deeper into the sofa, as if he could somehow escape the moment. He made no attempt to wipe away his tears.

Denise turned to face Hunter, and she looked like a complete different woman from the one who'd greeted him at the door minutes earlier. Her eyes were horribly sad.

'How much did my daughter suffer, Detective?' Her voice was low and hoarse, her words coated in pain.

Their eyes locked for a long moment and Hunter saw a mixture of grief and anger burning deep inside her.

'The truth is that we don't know,' he finally replied.

With a trembling hand Denise brushed a strand of loose hair behind her right ear. 'Do you know why, Detective? Why would someone do something like that to anyone? Why would someone do it to my Laura? She was the sweetest girl you could ever meet.'

Hunter held her gaze firmly. 'I'm not gonna pretend I understand what sort of pain both of you are going through, Mrs. Mitchell. I'm also not gonna pretend this is easy. We're after the answers to those same questions and at the moment I can't tell you much because we don't have much. I'm here because I need your help to catch who did this. You knew Laura better than anyone.'

Denise's eyes never left Hunter's face, and he knew what her next question would be even before the words left her lips.

'Was she . . .' her voice croaked as she fought the tears catching in her throat yet again, '. . . raped?'

Roy Mitchell finally looked up. His stare went from his wife to Hunter.

There were very few things in life Hunter hated more than having to hide the truth from grieving parents, but without an autopsy on Laura's body, the best he could do was tell Denise and Roy that again he didn't know. As a psychologist, he knew that the uncertainty of never knowing the answer to such a question would torture them for the rest of their lives, putting their marriage, even their sanity, in jeopardy.

'No, Laura wasn't raped,' Hunter said with unflinching eyes and without an ounce of hesitation. Certain lies were worth telling.

Twenty-One

The uncomfortable moment stretched until Denise broke eye contact with Hunter, returning her stare to the photographs on the desk. She picked up a small silver frame.

'Laura was always talented, you know? Always very artistic.' She walked over and handed Hunter the frame. The photograph showed a little girl of about eight surrounded by crayons and tiny pots of watercolor paint. She looked so happy and her smile was so contagious, Hunter couldn't help but smile back, for a second forgetting that that little girl was gone and in the most horrifying manner possible.

'In school, every year without fail, she was awarded an honors certificate in arts,' Denise said proudly.

Hunter listened.

A sad grin threatened to part Denise's lips but she held it back. 'She only started painting professionally late on, but she'd always loved it. It was her refuge from all things bad. Every time she got hurt, she went back to the brushes. It was what cured her when she was a child.'

'Cured her?' Hunter's expression tightened and his gaze bounced between Denise and Roy.

'One day when Laura was eight, for no apparent reason, she had some sort of seizure,' Denise explained. 'She couldn't move or breathe properly, her eyes disappeared into her head and she almost choked to death. It petrified us.'

Roy nodded and then took over. 'We took her to four different doctors. Experts, they said.' He shook his head as if irritated. 'But none of them could diagnose what had happened. In fact, they didn't have a clue.'

'Did it happen again?'

'Yes, a few more times.' Denise again. 'She went through every possible examination, including CAT scans. They found nothing. No one knew what was wrong. No one could tell us what was triggering her seizures. About a week after her last episode, Laura picked up a brush for the first time. And that was it. The seizures never came back.' Denise touched the edge of her right eye with the tip of her fingers, trying to stop the new tear that had just formed from rolling down her cheek. 'No matter what anyone says, I know her painting is what made them stop. It's what made her well again.'

'You said her seizures made her choke?'

Denise nodded. 'It terrified us every time. She couldn't breathe. Her skin changed color.' She paused and looked away. 'She could've died so many times.'

'And the seizures simply stopped all together?'

'Yes,' Roy continued. 'Right after she started painting.'

Hunter got up and handed the frame back to Denise. 'Was Laura in a relationship?'

Denise let out a deep sigh. 'Laura didn't really get deeply involved with anyone. Another of her self-defense mechanisms.' She walked over to the bar by the large bookcase. 'If you read any of the articles about her and how she got her career started, you'll read about her pain of being cheated on by her fiancé. She found him in bed with another woman.

It destroyed her inside.' Denise poured herself a double dose of whiskey from a decanter and dropped two ice cubes in it. 'Would you like one?' She raised her glass.

Hunter's biggest passion was single malt Scotch whiskey, but unlike most, he knew how to appreciate its flavor and quality instead of simply getting drunk on it.

'No, thank you.'

'Roy?' She faced her husband.

He shook his head.

Denise shrugged, took a small sip and closed her eyes as the liquid traveled down her throat.

'To drown her pain, Laura went straight back to painting. Something that she hadn't done for several years. By chance, a gallery curator saw one of her canvases, and that was how her new career started. But not before she suffered a great deal.'

'From a broken heart?' Hunter said.

Denise nodded and looked away. 'Patrick was the one who insisted they moved in together after only four months,' she continued. 'He told Laura he couldn't stand being away from her, that he loved her more than anything. He was one of those who had a way with words. A charmer who usually got what he wanted. I'm sure you know the type. And Laura believed him. She fell desperately in love with him and his seductive charm.'

'You said his name is Patrick?'

Denise nodded. 'Patrick Barlett.'

Hunter wrote the name down in his notebook.

'Laura used to work in a bank. Patrick was a big investor. That's how they met. She found out about his affair because that day she felt unwell just after lunch,' Denise recalled. 'Something she'd eaten. Her boss told her to take the rest of the day off and she went home. Patrick was in their bed with his slut secretary or PA or something.' She shook her head. 'For someone who was supposed to be intelligent, you'd thought that he would've at least gone to a motel.' She chuckled nervously. 'So much for loving Laura more than anything, huh? That was only three months after they'd moved in together. Since then, relationships became a thing of the past for Laura. She had flings, affairs, but nothing serious.'

'Any recent ones?'

'No one Laura thought was worth mentioning.'

'So after Laura split from Patrick, was that it between them?'

'For her, yes.'

'And for him?'

'Ha!' Denise said with contempt. 'He never let go. He tried apologizing with flowers and gifts and phone calls and whatever else he could think of, but Laura didn't wanna know any more.'

'How long did he carry on all that for?'

'He never stopped.'

Hunter's eyebrows arched in surprise.

'He visited her exhibition last month and begged her to have him back yet again. She obviously told him where to go.'

'So he's been after her, asking for forgiveness and trying to get her back for . . . ?'

'Four years,' Roy confirmed. 'Patrick is not the sort of man who takes no for an answer. He's the sort of man who gets what he wants, no matter the price.'

Twenty-Two

The word *obsession* flashed at the back of Hunter's mind. Four years was more than enough time for most people to take the hint and move on. Denise told him how possessive and jealous Patrick used to be of Laura, and though during the time they were together he'd never been violent towards her, he did have a problem with his temper.

'Do you know if anyone other than you had an extra set of keys to Laura's apartment?'

Denise had another sip of her drink and thought about it for a minute before looking at Roy.

'Not that we know of,' he said.

'Laura never mentioned if she'd given the keys to anyone else?'

A firm shake of the head from Denise. 'Laura never allowed anyone to go into her apartment or her studio. Her work was very private to her. Even though she was successful, she never did it for the money. She painted for herself. It was a way of expressing what was going on inside her. She didn't even like exhibiting that much, and that's what most artists live for. As far as I know, she never took any dates back to her apartment. And she never, never got emotionally involved.'

'How about any close friends?'

'I was her closest friend.' A slight quiver came into her voice.

'Anyone other than family?'

'Painters are very lonely people, Detective. They spend most of their time by themselves, working on a piece. She had acquaintances, but no one she could really call a close friend.'

'She didn't keep in touch with any of her old school, university or work friends?'

Denise shrugged. 'Maybe, by phone or the odd drink, but I couldn't tell you who.' She paused. 'The only other person I can think of is Calvin Lange, the curator of the Daniel Rossdale Art Gallery. The person who kick-started her career. He was very fond of her, and she of him. They talked on the phone and met quite frequently.'

Roy nodded his agreement.

Hunter noted Calvin Lange's name down and his eyes returned to the photo frames on the wooden desk. 'Being a successful artist consequently means having fans, I suppose.'

Denise nodded proudly. 'Her work was admired and loved by many.'

'Did Laura ever mention any . . .' he searched for the right words, ' . . . *insistent* fans?'

'You mean . . . like a stalker?' Her voice faltered for an instant.

Hunter nodded.

Denise finished the rest of her whiskey in one gulp. 'I never thought of it, but she did mention something a few months ago.'

Hunter put down the picture frame he was holding and took a step in Denise's direction. 'What exactly did she tell you?'

Denise's gaze moved to a neutral point on the white Nepalese rug in the center of the room as her memory struggled to remember. 'Just that she'd started receiving some emails from someone who said he was in love with her work.'

'Did she ever show you any of these emails?'

'No.'

Hunter looked at Roy questioningly, who shook his head.

'Did she tell you what they said?'

Denise shook her head. 'Laura played it down, saying that it was just a fan being flattering of her work. But I did get the feeling that something about it had spooked her.'

Hunter wrote again in his notebook.

Denise moved closer, stopping at an arm's reach from Hunter. She looked into his eyes. 'How good are you and your team, Detective?'

Hunter frowned as if he hadn't understood the question.

'I wanna know if you can catch the sonofabitch who hurt my daughter and took her from me.' The grief in her voice was gone, substituted by undeniable anger. 'Don't tell me you're gonna do the best you can. The police are always doing the best they can, and their best is rarely good enough. I know you're gonna do your best, Detective. What I want you to do is look me in the eyes and tell me your best *will* be good enough. Tell me you'll catch this sonofabitch. And tell me you *will* make this sack of shit pay.'

Twenty-Three

Whitney Myers used the little gadget Leonid Kudrov had given her to activate the gates to the underground garage in Katia's apartment block. As she drove in, she immediately spotted Katia's torch red V6 convertible Mustang parked in one of the two spaces reserved for her penthouse apartment. Myers took the empty spot next to it, got out and placed her right palm on the Mustang's hood. Stone cold. Through the window, she checked its interior. All seemed fine. The car alarm light was blinking on the dashboard, indicating that it was active. Myers paused and allowed her eyes to roam the whole of the garage. The place was well lit, but there were many dark spots and corners where someone could hide. She noticed only one security camera, on the ceiling, facing the garage's entrance door.

Myers retrieved a pair of latex gloves from the box in the back seat of her car and rode the elevator up to the penthouse. There, she used the keys Leonid Kudrov had given her to gain access to Katia's apartment. No alarm. No signs of forced entry.

She softly closed the door behind her and paused for an instant. The living room was immense and decorated with a lot of style. Myers took her time looking around. Nothing seemed out of place. No signs of a fight or struggle.

She made her way to the spiral stairwell in the corner and moved up to the top floor. On the mezzanine landing, she found Katia's car keys in a tray on a tall chest of drawers crowded with family photographs.

Myers moved on down the corridor and entered Katia's bedroom. The walls were painted in pink and white, and there were enough stuffed toys on the perfectly made king-size bed to keep a crèche occupied for weeks. Myers checked the pillows on it. No smell. No one had slept in that bed last night.

Katia's two suitcases lay on the end of the bed seat. They were both open, but it looked like she hadn't had time to unpack them. The bedroom's balcony door was locked from the inside. Again, no signs of forced entry.

Myers moved on to the walk-in closet. Katia's collection of dresses, shoes and purses took her breath away.

'Wow.' She ran her hand down the front of a Giambattista Valli dress. 'A dream wardrobe,' she whispered. 'Katia had taste.'

In the en-suite bathroom, she noticed a hair towel was missing from the rail.

Myers moved out of the bedroom and into the next room along – Katia's practice den. The room was spacious but simple. A stereo system on a wooden sideboard, a couple of music stands, a mini fridge on the corner and a comfortable armchair pushed up against a wall. Katia's violin case was on a small coffee table by the door. Her priceless Lorenzo Guadagnini was lying inside it.

Leonid had told her that Katia was obsessed with her Guadagnini violin. If it weren't by her side, it'd be in her safe behind the large painting of Tchaikovsky on the wall, no exceptions.

Myers found the painting and checked the safe. Locked. Despite her previous confidence that Katia had just skipped town for a few days, she was getting a very bad feeling about this.

Myers returned downstairs and walked into the kitchen. It was as big as most studio apartments in Los Angeles. Black marble worktops and floors, polished steel appliances and enough pots and pans hanging from a center island that could give any small restaurant a run for their money.

The first thing Myers noticed was the missing hair towel from the en-suite bathroom upstairs. It was lying on the floor a few steps away from the fridge. She picked it up and brought it to her nose – a sweet, fruity smell that matched the bottle of designer hair conditioner in Katia's bathroom.

Myers looked around. There was a bottle of white wine on the breakfast table. No glasses were out. No corkscrew either. But what really caught her attention was the blinking red light on the answerphone at the far end of the worktop. She walked over and looked at the screen.

Sixty messages.

'I guess Katia is a popular woman.'

Myers pressed play.

'You have sixty new messages,' announced the prerecorded woman's voice. 'Message one.'

Absolute silence.

Myers frowned.

At the end of it there was a beep, and the machine moved on to the next message.

Silence.

And the next.

Silence.

And the next.

Silence.

'What the hell?' Myers took a seat on the barstool next to her. Her eyes settled on the large clock hanging from the wall above the door.

The messages kept on playing, not a whisper in any of them. After maybe the fifteenth or twentieth message, Myers picked up on something that made her skin crawl.

'No fucking way.' She pressed the stop button and then rewound the messages back to the very first one. She started from the beginning again. Her eyes returned to the clock above the door, and this time she let them play all the way to the fifty-ninth message. Silence in every single one of them, but the pattern she found told her that that silence had its own chilling meaning.

'I'll be goddamned.'

The last message started playing, and suddenly the silence was substituted by a long stretch of static, catching Myers by surprise and making her jump.

'Jesus . . .' She brought a hand up to her thumping heart. 'What the hell was that?' She rewound it, leaned closer to the machine, and played the message again.

Static noise blasted through the tiny answerphone speaker.

Myers moved even closer.

And what she heard, half-hidden by the static sound, sent a cold shiver down her entire body.

Twenty-Four

From the car, even before leaving the Mitchells' driveway, Hunter called the Office of Operations and asked them to gather all the information they could on Patrick Barlett, Laura's ex-fiancé. He'd just become a priority person of interest in the investigation.

Hunter disconnected and speed-dialed Garcia's number. He gave him the lowdown on everything he'd found out from the Mitchells and they met half an hour later at the entrance to an old warehouse turned apartment block in Lakewood, minutes away from Long Beach.

Hunter looked subdued but Garcia didn't have to ask. He knew that breaking the news to parents that their daughter had been the victim of a monstrous killer was already hard enough. But to have to tell them that they couldn't even give her a proper burial because the body had been blown to pieces was really the stuff of nightmares.

They rode the elevator up to the top floor in silence.

Laura Mitchell's apartment was an astonishing two thousand square feet loft conversion. The living area was simple but stylish with black leather furniture and sumptuous rugs. The kitchen was to the right of the entrance door and the sleeping area to the left – both modern, spacious and decorated with taste. But the bulk of the apartment was taken by her art studio.

Set at the far end and surrounded by large windows, including two skylights, it was filled with canvases of all sizes. The largest one was at least twelve foot by six.

'Wow, I always loved loft conversions,' Garcia said looking around. 'I could fit four of my apartment in here.' He paused and checked the door. 'No forced entry. You said that her parents told you that they last heard from her two and a half weeks ago?'

Hunter nodded. 'Laura and her mother were close. They called or met each other almost every other day. The last time they talked was on the 2nd of this month. A Wednesday. That was just a couple of days after the last night of Laura's latest exhibition in a gallery in West Hollywood. Her mother tried to contact her again on the 5th, and that's when alarm bells started ringing.'

'In between the 2nd and the 5th?' Garcia said, his eyes narrowing. 'That's around two weeks ago.'

Hunter drew a deep breath and his expression hardened. 'And if she was taken by the killer ...' He didn't complete his thought, allowing the gravity of his suggestion to simply hang in the air.

'Shit!' Garcia said in realization. 'She was killed yesterday. If the same person who killed her also kidnapped her, it means he kept her hostage for two weeks.'

Hunter walked towards the sleeping area.

'Have Missing Persons been through here?'

'Yes, Detective Alex Peterson, from the West Bureau was in charge of the investigation,' Hunter confirmed, opening the drawer on the bedside table – a sleeping eye mask, two cherry-flavored Chapsticks, a small pen flashlight and a packet of Tic

Tacs. 'I've already got in touch with him and explained that the case has now escalated to a homicide investigation. He said he didn't have much, but he'll send us everything he's got. He found her laptop on the sofa in the living area. They've processed it but got only her fingerprints.'

'How about the files in the hard drive?'

Hunter tilted his head to one side. 'It's password protected. The computer is with the Information Technology Division, but there was no urgent request until I talked to them a few minutes ago, so nothing yet.'

They checked her wardrobe – several dresses, a few of them designer, jeans, T-shirts, blouses, jackets and a substantial collection of shoes and handbags. In the kitchen Hunter checked the fridge, the cupboards, and the trash can. Nothing out of the ordinary. They moved to the living area and Hunter spent a few minutes looking through the photos and the book titles on the shelf unit next to the sofa before making his way into the studio.

Laura Mitchell was a lyrical abstractionist painter, and her work consisted mostly of collections of colors and shapes loosely applied to canvases. The studio floor was littered by a rainbow of paint splashes – almost a work of modern art in itself. Tens of finished paintings were organized against the west wall. Spread around the main working space were three canvas stands, two of them covered by once-white sheets. The third one, occupying a center position, held a thirty-six-by-twenty-four-inch semi-completed painting. Hunter studied it for a few moments before lifting the sheets from the other two stands. Both paintings also appeared unfinished.

Garcia took his time looking through some of the completed canvases resting against the wall.

'I never understood modern art, you know.'

'What do you mean?' Hunter asked.

'Look at this painting.' He stepped out of the way so Hunter could take a look. It was another thirty-six-by-twenty-four-inch canvas displaying pastel green and orange colors surrounded by vibrant red and a touch of blue and yellow. To Garcia the colors seemed to have no co-ordination.

'What about it?'

'Well, this is named "Lost men in a forest of giant trees".'

Hunter raised an eyebrow.

'Exactly. I see no men, there is no forest and nothing on it resembles a tree.' He shook his head. 'Go figure.'

Hunter smiled and walked over to the large window on the left of the studio. Locked from the inside. He looked around the studio again before frowning and returning to the bedroom where he rechecked Laura's wardrobe.

'Did you find something?' Garcia asked while he watched Hunter move purposefully into the bathroom.

'Not yet.' He searched through the dirty laundry basket.

'What are you looking for?'

'Her painting clothes.'

'What?'

'In her living room you'll find three photos of Laura taken while she was working. In all three she's wearing the same old greenish shirt and track pants, both covered in paint splashes.' He checked behind the door. 'And an old pair of tennis shoes. Have you seen them anywhere?'

Instinctively Garcia looked around. 'No.' Confusion started to settle in. 'Why do you need her clothes?'

'I don't, I'm just trying to establish that they are missing.' Hunter returned to the studio and motioned towards the easel holding the uncovered and unfinished painting. 'It looks like Laura was last working on this canvas. Now check this out.' He indicated a paint palette thick with crusts of different dried colors. It was casually lying on a wooden unit next to the stand. To its right was a jar containing four different-sized brushes. The water in the jar was muddy with oil paint residue. Resting on the palette, and now sticking to it as if glued, was another brush. Its tip was dry, hard and caked in bright yellow paint. 'Now look around her studio,' Hunter continued. 'She seemed to have been pretty organized. But even if she wasn't, painters don't just simply leave the brush they're working with laying around thick with paint to dry out. It would be just as easy for her to drop it into the cleaning jar.'

Garcia thought for a moment. 'Something caught her attention while she was working, maybe a sound, a knock on the door . . .' he said, following Hunter's line of thought. 'She put the brush down to go check it out.'

'And the probable reason why we can't find her working clothes and shoes is because she was wearing them when she was abducted.'

Hunter paused next to several finished canvases arranged against the back wall. Something about the long one on the far right called his attention. It displayed an astonishing gradient variation moving from yellow at one end to red at the other. He took a few steps back and tilted his head sideways. The canvas was leaning tall against the wall at a sixty-five-degree angle, but it was supposed to be looked at horizontally, not vertically. From a distance, the color combination became almost hypnotic. Laura certainly had talent and an astounding understanding of colors, but that wasn't what had caught Hunter's eye.

He approached the painting, crouched down next to it, and studied the floor around the canvas for a moment before looking behind it.

'Now *this* is interesting.'

Twenty-Five

Whitney Myers got to her office in Long Beach to find Frank Cohen, her assistant and expert researcher, flipping through computer printouts. He looked up when Myers closed the door behind her.

'Hey there,' he said, pushing his glasses up his long and pointy nose. 'Any luck?' He knew Myers had spent most of the day going over Katia's penthouse apartment in West Hollywood.

'A few clues.' She dumped her bag on the chair behind her glass-top desk and reached for the jug of freshly brewed coffee that perfumed the entire office. 'Whoever abducted Katia . . .' she poured herself a cup and stirred in a teaspoon of brown sugar, '. . . did it from inside her apartment.'

Cohen leaned forward.

'Just as her father said, I found the towel in the kitchen. The smell on it was very faint, but it matched the hair conditioner in her bathroom upstairs. Both of her suitcases were at the end of her bed.'

'Suitcases?' Cohen frowned.

Myers walked to the large window that overlooked West Ocean Boulevard. 'Katia Kudrov had just returned from her tour with the Los Angeles Philharmonic. She had been away for two months,' she explained. 'She didn't even have time to unpack.'

'Did you find her purse, cell phone?'

Myers shook her head. 'Only her car keys, as her father had said.'

'Any signs of forced entry?'

'None. All locks intact. Doors, windows, balcony.'

'Struggle?'

'None, unless you count a towel on the kitchen floor and a bottle of white wine sitting out of the fridge as one.'

Cohen twisted his lips from side to side. 'Was she in a relationship?'

'Not with anyone who'd be waiting for her in her apartment if that's what you're thinking. Katia had started seeing the Philharmonic's new conductor, a guy called Phillip Stein. Apparently he was just a fling, though, nothing serious.'

'Did he feel the same?'

'Oh, he fell for her. Her father said it's always just a fling with her. Katia doesn't do heavy relationships. Music is her real love.'

Cohen pulled a face. 'Deep.'

'Katia and this Phillip guy were on the same tour together, and before you ask, there were no signs that he'd been home with her that night. She broke everything off a few days ago, just before their last concert.'

'I bet he didn't like that at all.'

'Not one bit.'

'So where is he now? Better yet, where was he on the night they got back to LA?'

'In Munich.'

'Munich, Germany?'

A quick nod. 'He was *that* upset. Never came back with the Philharmonic after their last concert. Flew directly to Germany. That's where his family is from. He couldn't have done it. No matter how much motive he had.'

Cohen paused and tapped the top of his pen against his teeth. 'Aren't those flashy apartment blocks in West Hollywood packed with security – CCTV cameras and all? If someone took this Katia woman from her apartment, it must've been picked up somewhere.'

'You would've thought so, wouldn't you? You're right, there's a camera inside the elevator, two at reception, one on the penthouse landing and one in the underground car park. Conveniently, there was a power surge that blew the fuse box on the night Katia returned from her tour. All the cameras were down for a few hours. We've got no footage.'

'Nothing at all?'

'Nothing. Her father never thought to ask the building's concierge about cameras. That's why he never mentioned anything when we met.'

Cohen pulled a face.

'I know. This thing screams professional kidnapping, doesn't it?'

'Has anyone got in touch with the family yet? Ransom request?'

Myers shook her head and returned to her desk. 'Nothing, and that's what gets me. Everything so far points to a professional job. Professionals are always after money. Katia and her family are rich enough for the ransom to be in the millions. She's been gone for over forty-eight hours and nothing, no communication of any sort.'

Cohen tapped the pen against his teeth again. He'd been working with Myers for long enough to know that in a professional kidnapping, communications between the kidnappers and the ransom party were usually established quickly, if possible, before the party had a chance to involve the authorities. If the abductor wasn't after money, then

Cohen knew they weren't dealing with a kidnapper, they were dealing with a predator.

'But this gets worse,' Myers said, sitting back in her chair. 'Our kidnapper likes to play.'

Cohen stopped with the pen tapping. 'What do you mean?'

'There was an answerphone in her kitchen.'

'Yes, and . . . ?'

Myers allowed the suspense to stretch. 'The machine was full to capacity. There were sixty new messages.'

Cohen's left eye twitched. 'Sixty?'

Myers nodded. 'I listened to every single one of them.' She paused and took a sip of her coffee. 'Not a word, zip, absolute silence, not even heavy breathing.'

'They were *all* blank?'

'It sounded that way. I thought there was something wrong with the phone or the machine, until I got to the last message.'

'And . . . ?' Cohen's eager eyes widened.

'Have a listen yourself.' Myers searched her handbag for her digital voice recorder and tossed it over to Cohen.

He quickly placed it in front of him on his desk, readjusted his glasses on his nose and pressed play. Several silent seconds went by. Then a low-pitched white noise oozed out of the tiny speaker. It lasted a few seconds.

'Static?'

'That's what it sounds like at first, doesn't it?' Myers replied. 'But listen again – like you mean it this time.'

Cohen reached for the voice recorder, rewound it, brought it close to his right ear, and listened carefully to it one more time – very attentively this time.

His blood ran cold.

'What the fuck?'

Covered up by the static-like sound there was something else, something that sounded like a whisper. Cohen listened to it a couple more times. There was no denying it; the undecipherable murmur was definitely there.

'Is somebody saying something or just trying to catch his breath?'

'Not a clue.' Myers shrugged. 'I did exactly what you just did. Listened to it over and over again. I'm still none the wiser. But I'll tell you something. If the intention of whoever left that message was to scare Katia, that would've done it. It sounds like a poltergeist ready to come through the phone. It freaked the hell out of me.'

'You think this could be the abductor's voice?'

'Either that or someone with a very sick sense of humor.'

'I'll get this to Gus at the studio.' Cohen jiggled the voice recorder in his hand. 'If we transfer this into his voice analyzing program, we could clean it up and slow it down. I'm sure we'll decipher whatever it is that he's saying. If he *is* saying something, that is.'

'Great, do it.'

'Does her father know about this?' Cohen knew that Myers was in constant contact with Leonid Kudrov, but with nothing of significance to report back, it was fast getting frustrating.

'Not yet. I'll wait and see if Gus can make something out of it before giving Mr. Kudrov another call.' Myers ran her hand through her hair. 'Now are you ready for the next twist?'

Cohen's eyes shot in Myers direction. 'There's more?'

'When I was listening to the messages, for no specific reason, I kept looking at the clock in Katia's kitchen.'

'OK.'

'Suddenly, I realized that there was a common factor that linked all of those messages.'

'What factor?'

'A time signature.'

'A what?'

'I know it sounds crazy, but I went over every message twice. It took me a while.' She moved to the front of her desk and leaned back against its edge. 'They're all twelve seconds long.'

Cohen's eyes narrowed. 'Twelve seconds? All sixty of them?'

'Precisely. Not a second more, not a second less. Even the last message with the noise and the creepy murmur – twelve seconds exactly.'

'And that's not a fault with the machine?'

'Nope.'

'Did anyone set the message recording time to only twelve seconds?'

Myers looked at Cohen inquisitively. 'I didn't even know you could do that.'

'I'm not sure you can, but I'm just trying to cover all angles.'

'Even if that's possible, who'd set a message recording time to only twelve seconds?'

Cohen had to agree. 'OK,' he said as his stare returned to the voice recorder. 'Now that's officially messed up, and I'm officially intrigued. There's gotta be a meaning to it. No fucking way the twelve seconds thing is a coincidence.'

'No fucking way,' Myers agreed. 'Now we're just going to have to find out what it means.'

Twenty-Six

'What?' Garcia asked, facing Hunter and moving towards the canvas. 'What have you found?'

'We need to get the Forensics guys in here, now.' He paused and looked up at his partner. 'Someone was hiding behind this canvas.'

Garcia crouched down next to Hunter.

'Look at this.' Hunter pointed to the floor just behind the canvas base. 'Can you see the dust marks?'

Garcia squinted as he moved his face so close to the floor it looked like he was about to kiss it. Moments later he saw it.

Since it had been placed there, regular house dust had settled on the floor around the canvas edge. Garcia saw a long, dragging dust mark.

'The canvas was moved forward,' he finally admitted.

'Enough for a person to get behind it,' Hunter noted.

Garcia bit his bottom lip. 'Laura could've moved it forward herself.'

'She could've, but check this out.' Hunter pointed to a spot further behind the canvas, closer to the wall.

Garcia squinted again. 'What am I supposed to be looking at?'

Hunter reached for his pen flashlight. 'Look again.' He handed it to Garcia.

Garcia directed the light beam to the spot Hunter had indicated. This time it didn't take him long to see it.

'I'll be damned.'

Just a few inches from the wall, he identified the faint outline of foot imprints left in the dust. Clear indications that someone had been standing there.

'Look at it one more time,' Hunter said. 'See anything that strikes you as odd?'

Garcia returned his attention to the imprints. 'Nope, but you obviously have, Robert. What am I missing?'

'The amount of variation on the imprints.'

Garcia looked for a third time. 'There's barely any.'

'Exactly. Isn't that strange?'

It finally clicked. When standing in a confined space for even a small amount of time, it was natural for anyone to fidget and shift his or her weight from foot to foot, to try to move into a more comfortable position every time the old one becomes uncomfortable. That shifting should, in theory, leave behind several different onionskin imprints. There were none. And that could only mean two things – either the killer didn't wait long, or – and the thing that really bothered Hunter – the killer was preternaturally patient and disciplined.

Hunter's cell phone rang in his pocket.

'Detective Hunter.'

'Detective, it's Pam from Operations,' said the voice at the end of the line. 'I've emailed you all the information we managed to get on Patrick Barlett. At the moment he's out of town.'

'Out of town?'

'He's been away at a conference in Dallas since Tuesday evening. He's flying back tomorrow – mid-afternoon. Everything checked out.'

'OK, thanks, Pam.'

Hunter disconnected and returned his attention to the space behind the large canvas and the faint foot imprints. A strong and fast perpetrator could have covered the distance between there and where Laura would have been standing in a flash, too fast for her to react. But Hunter didn't believe her attacker had surprised her in that way. If he had, there would have been some sort of a struggle, and there were no such signs anywhere. If someone had crept up behind her and sedated her in some way, Laura would have no doubt dropped her paint palette and brush, not placed it on the unit next to the stand. The surrounding floor area where Laura would have stood while working on her canvas was covered in small speckles and splashes of paint, not blotches and smudges caused by a palette hitting the ground.

'Pass me the flashlight, Carlos.'

Garcia handed it to him and Hunter moved its beam to a point on the brick directly behind the large canvas.

'Something else?' Garcia asked.

'Not sure yet, but brick walls are notorious for pulling fibers out of fabrics if you lean against them.' Hunter kept inching the beam up. When he got to a point about six feet from the floor, he paused and moved forward, stopping just millimeters from the wall, careful not to disrupt the dust. 'I think we might have something.'

He reached for his phone and dialed the number for the Forensics team.

Twenty-Seven

West Hollywood is famous for its nightlife, celebrity culture and diverse atmosphere. Themed bars, chic restaurants, futuristic and exotic nightclubs, art galleries, designer boutiques, sports centers, and the most varied selection of live music venues will keep you entertained from sunset to sunset. Informally referred to as 'WeHo' by most Angelinos, the word is that if you can't get your kicks in West Hollywood, then you're probably already dead.

It was just past 6:00 p.m. when Hunter and Garcia got to the Daniel Rossdale Art Gallery in Wilshire Boulevard. The building was small, but stylish. Smoked glass together with concrete-and-metal frames were used to create a pyramid-style structure that could be considered a sculpture on its own.

Calvin Lange, the gallery's curator and Laura Mitchell's closest friend, had agreed to a meeting. Laura's last exhibition had been at his gallery.

Hunter and Garcia were shown to Calvin Lange's office by an attractive and elegantly dressed assistant.

Lange was sitting behind his desk, but stood up as both detectives entered the room. He was a wiry, sandy-haired, smiling man in his early-thirties.

'Gentlemen,' he said as he firmly shook their hands.

'You said over the phone that this was about Laura Mitchell?' He indicated the two leather chairs in front of his desk and waited for both detectives to have a seat. 'Have there been any problems with any of her paintings purchased from this gallery?' He paused and quickly studied both detectives' expressions. Then he remembered Laura's mother's phone call to him two weeks ago. 'Is she OK?'

Hunter filled him in.

Calvin Lange's eyes flicked from Hunter to Garcia and then back to Hunter. His lips parted but no words came out. For an instant he looked like a little kid who'd just been told Santa Claus was a con. Still in shocked silence, he approached the minibar built into the tall wooden unit on the north wall, and with a trembling hand reached for a glass. 'Can I offer you a drink?' His voice quivered.

'We're fine,' Hunter said, taking in all his movements.

Lange poured himself a large glass of Cognac and quickly took a mouthful. That seemed to bring some of the color back to his face.

'I was told by Mrs. Mitchell that you were probably Laura's closest friend outside the family,' Hunter said.

'Maybe . . .' Lange shook his head as if disoriented. 'I'm not sure. Laura was a very private person, but we got on well. She was . . . fantastic: funny, talented, intelligent, beautiful . . .'

'She exhibited in this gallery not so long ago, is that right?' Garcia asked.

Lange told them that Laura's exhibition had run from the 1st to the 28th February and it'd been a tremendous success – very well attended, and all of the twenty-three pieces she'd exhibited had been sold. Laura had only been present for about two hours on the opening and closing nights, and Lange said she hadn't seemed at all upset, worried or anxious at either of them.

'Was that the last time you saw her?' Hunter asked.

'Yes.'

'And did you use to keep in contact regularly? Phone calls, texts, that sort of thing?'

Lange moved his head from side to side. 'Not that regularly. We usually chatted on the phone two maybe three times a month. It really depended on how busy we both were. Sometimes we did lunch, dinner or drinks together, but again, nothing regular.'

'Mrs. Mitchell also told me that her ex-fiancé was here on her closing night,' Hunter said.

Lange's eyes shot in Hunter's direction.

'Do you remember seeing him talking to Laura at all?'

Lange took another sip of his Cognac and Hunter noticed his hands had started shaking again.

'Yes, I'd forgotten all about that. He'd had a little too much to drink. He really upset her that night,' Lange recalled. 'They were by the staircase at the back of the gallery, away from the main floor and the crowd. I was looking for her because I wanted to introduce her to an important buyer from Switzerland. When I finally found her, I went over and that's when I noticed she looked unhappy. As I joined them, he walked away angrily.'

'Did she tell you what happened?'

'No, she didn't want to talk about it. She went straight into the ladies' room and came out again about ten minutes later, but before doing so, she asked me to get him out of here, before he made a scene with the guests.'

'A scene?' Hunter questioned. 'Did she tell you why?'

Lange shook his head. 'But I sensed it was because he was jealous.'

Garcia craned his neck. 'Jealous of whom? Did Laura have a date with her that night?'

'No, but I saw her talking to someone earlier that night. And I know they swapped phone numbers because she told me.'

'Could you describe him?' Garcia asked.

Lange bit his lower lip and looked at a distant nothing as if considering something. 'I can do better than that. I think I might have a picture of him.'

Twenty-Eight

Calvin Lange lifted his right index finger at both detectives, asking them for a minute, and reached for the phone on his desk.

'Nat, we still have the photos from Laura Mitchell's exhibition, right? . . . Great, can you bring your laptop into my office, please . . . Yeah, now is good.' Lange put the phone down and explained that they always photographed and sometimes videoed their exhibitions, especially the artists' nights. The photos were used for brochures, advertisement campaigns and their own website.

'How about your CCTV footage?' Hunter asked. He'd noticed six cameras in total on their way up to Lange's office.

Lange gave him an embarrassed headshake. 'We recycle hard drive space every two weeks.'

There was a soft knock on the door and the same assistant who had guided Hunter and Garcia into Lange's office earlier stepped into the room carrying a white laptop.

'You've met Nat,' Lange said, motioning her to his desk.

'Not properly,' she replied with the same smile she'd given them earlier. Her eyes stayed on Hunter.

'Natalie Foster is my assistant,' Lange explained, 'but she's a great photographer and very good with computers. She's also our webmaster.'

Natalie shook both detectives' hands. 'Please, call me Nat.'

'These are detectives from the Homicide Division,' Lange told her.

Natalie's smile quickly slipped from her face. 'Homicide?'

Hunter explained the reason for their visit and Natalie's entire body tensed. Her eyes searched for Lange's and Hunter could tell her mind had flooded with questions.

'We need to take a look at the photographs from Laura's exhibition, Nat,' Lange said.

It took a few seconds for his words to register. 'Umm . . . yes, of course.' She placed the laptop on Lange's desk and fired it up. As the computer booted, an anxious silence hovered over the room. Natalie typed in a password and scrolled a trembling finger across the laptop's mouse pad as she searched for the pictures directory.

Hunter grabbed a small bottle of water from the drinks cabinet. 'Here, have some of this, it'll help.' He poured some into a glass with ice and brought it over to her.

'Thank you.' She forced a smile before taking two large sips and returning her attention to the computer.

A few more mouse clicks later and Natalie set the picture display to full screen.

'OK, here they are.'

The first picture was a wide shot of the main gallery floor on the opening night of Laura Mitchell's exhibition. It looked full to capacity.

'How many people were here that night?' Hunter asked.

'About a hundred and fifty.' Lange looked at Natalie for confirmation. She nodded. 'And there were a few more outside waiting to get in.'

'Entry wasn't by invitation only?' Garcia asked.

'Not always, it depends on the artist,' Lange replied. 'Most, especially the more famous and egocentric ones, like to make their launch nights invitation- and RSVP-only.'

'But not Laura.'

'Not Laura,' Lange confirmed. 'She wasn't like most artists who think they're God's gift. She insisted her exhibitions were open to everyone and anyone. Even on artists' nights.'

Most of the photographs were of Laura smiling and chatting to people. She was usually surrounded by a group of four or five. A few of the photographs showed her posing in front of a canvas or with a fan. She certainly was a very attractive woman. Hunter could hardly make the connection with the crime-scene photos he'd seen.

'Wait,' Lange said, stepping closer. His eyes squinted as he studied the photograph that had just appeared on the screen. 'I think that's him – the guy who swapped numbers with Laura.' He pointed to someone standing at the back of the frame. He was tall with short dark hair and was dressed in a dark suit, but his face was partially obscured by a waiter carrying a tray of drinks. Natalie used the zoom feature at the bottom of the screen to enlarge it, but it didn't make the man's face any clearer. He looked to be around the same age as Laura Mitchell.

'Have any of you seen him before?' Hunter asked.

Lange shook his head, but Natalie looked uncertain. 'I think I have, at one of our previous exhibitions.'

'Are you sure? Can you remember which one?'

She took a moment. 'I can't remember which exhibition it was, but he looks familiar.'

'Are you sure you saw him here in the gallery? Not in a coffee shop, restaurant, nightclub . . . ?'

Natalie searched her memory again. 'No, I think it was here at the gallery.'

'OK, if you see him again, or you remember which exhibition, you call me, all right? If he comes in, don't try to talk to him, just call me.'

Natalie nodded and moved on with the pictures.

'Stop,' Lange said again a few pictures later. This time he indicated another tall, well-built man standing just a couple of paces behind Laura. He was looking at her as if she was the only person in the room. 'That's her ex-fiancé. I think his name is . . .'

'Patrick Barlett,' Hunter confirmed, once again enlarging the picture. 'We'll need a copy of all these files.'

'Sure,' Natalie said. 'I can burn them onto a CD for you before you leave.'

Just a few pictures from the end of the archive, Lange told Natalie to stop again. There he was. The tall, mysterious, phone-swapping stranger. He was standing right next to Laura. But this time he was looking straight at the camera.

Twenty-Nine

Small but very well equipped, Gustavo Suarez's studio was set in the basement of a single-story house in Jefferson Park, South Los Angeles.

Gus had been an audio engineer for twenty-seven years, and with a perfect-pitch ear it took a single note from any instrument for him to immediately place it on a music scale. But his understanding of sounds went much beyond musical notes. He was fascinated by their vibrations and modulations, what created them and how they could be altered by location and the environment. Because of his knowledge, gifted ear and experience, Gus had been called upon by the LAPD on several occasions where some sort of sound, noise or audio recording played a critical part in an ongoing investigation.

Whitney Myers had met Gus for the first time through the FBI, while training to be a negotiator. Their paths crossed again soon after, when she became a detective for the LAPD. As a private investigator, Myers had required Gus' expertize on only two other occasions.

Gus was forty-seven years old, with a shaved head and more tattoos than a Hell's Angel. But despite the intimidating look, he was as docile as a puppy. He opened the door to Frank Cohen and was instantly disappointed.

'Where's Whitney?' he asked, looking past Cohen's shoulders.

'Sorry, Gus, it's only me. She's tied up.'

'Damn, man. I got my best shirt on.' He ran his hands down the front of his freshly ironed dark blue shirt. 'Even splashed on some cologne and all.'

'Splashed?' Cohen took a step back and covered his nose. 'You smell like you bathed in the stuff. What the hell is it, Old Spice?'

Gus frowned. 'I *like* Old Spice.'

'Yeah, no shit. More than most by the smell of it.'

Gus disregarded his comment and guided him down to the basement and into his studio.

'So how can I help you guys this time? Whitney didn't tell me much over the phone.' He took a seat in his engineer's chair and wheeled himself closer to his sound desk.

Cohen handed him Myers' digital recorder. 'We got this from an answering machine.'

Gus brought the device closer to his right ear and pressed play. As the strange sound came through, he reached for the bowl of Skittles next to the recording console. Gus had a thing for Skittles, they helped him relax and concentrate.

'We think there's a voice, or a whisper, or something hidden in the middle of all that static,' Cohen offered.

Gus swirled a bunch of Skittles from his right cheek to his left one. 'It's not hidden, it's just there,' he announced, playing the recording from the beginning again. 'Definitely someone's voice.' He got up, walked over to a cabinet and retrieved a thin cable that looked like iPod headphones. 'Let me hook this thing up so we can have a better listen.'

Through the studio speakers, the sound was louder, the out-of-breath whisper more evident, but not clearer.

'Is he using a device to conceal his voice?' Cohen asked, stepping closer.

Gus shook his head. 'It doesn't sound like it. This is pure static. Interference caused by another radio wave electronic device or a bad signal. Whoever made the call was probably standing next to something, or on a spot affected by a signal dip. I'd say the static noise was unintentional.'

'Can you clean it up?'

'Of course.' Gus smiled smugly and turned on the computer monitor to his left. As the recording played again, audio lines vibrated animatedly on the screen. Gus had another handful of Skittles while watching them attentively.

'OK, let's tweak this baby a little.' He clicked a few buttons and slid some faders on the digital equalizer inside the application on his screen. The static noise was reduced by at least 90 per cent. The out-of-breath whisper now came through much clearer. Gus reached for a pair of professional headphones and listened to the whole thing again. 'OK, now *this* was deliberate.'

'What was?' Cohen craned his neck in Gus' direction.

'The forced whisper. Whoever's voice this is, it isn't naturally hoarse and whispering soft. And *that* is clever.'

'In what way?'

'Every human voice travels along certain frequencies that are part of one's personal identity, as identifiable as fingerprints or the retina. They have certain high, low and medium tones that don't vary, even if you try to disguise your voice by naturally altering it in any way, like a falsetto or baritone or whatever. With the right equipment, we can still identify those tones and match them to someone's voice.'

'You have that equipment, right?'

Gus looked offended. 'Of course I've got that equipment.

Look around. I've got whatever you need for voice identification.'

'So what's the problem?'

Gus leaned back in his chair and let out a long sigh. 'I'll show you. Place the tips of your fingers just below your Adam's apple.'

'What?'

'Like this.' Gus placed the tips of two of his fingers on his throat.

Cohen pulled a face.

'Just do it.'

Reluctantly Cohen copied Gus' movement.

'Now, say something, anything, but try to disguise it in some way ... high, low, gravel, child's voice, it doesn't matter. When you do, you'll feel your vocal cords vibrate. Trust me.'

Cohen looked at Gus with a you've-gotta-be-kidding-me face.

'Go on.'

He finally conceded and, putting on an extremely high-pitched voice, recited the opening three lines of *Othello*.

'Wow, profound. I never took you for a Shakespeare fan,' Gus said, suppressing a smile. 'Did you feel them vibrate?'

Cohen nodded.

'When we have any sort of vocal cord vibration, then we have those distinct frequencies I told you about. Now, do the same thing but go for a *very* soft whisper instead.'

Cohen repeated the same three lines in the most delicate whisper he could muster. His eyes narrowed as he looked back at Gus. 'No vibration.'

'Exactly,' Gus confirmed. 'That's because the sounds aren't being formed by your vocal cords, but by a combination of the air being exhaled from your lungs, and your mouth and tongue movements.'

'Like whistling?'

'Like whistling. No vibration, no identifiable frequencies.'

'Smart motherfucker.'

'That's what I said.'

'So this is the best we can do? We still don't know what he's saying.'

Gus smiled cynically. 'You don't pay me the big bucks just to give you back a tape with undecipherable whispering, do you? What I mean is that because he forced his own voice into a slow, dragging whisper, we won't be able to clean it or alter it back to its original pitch. So even if you have a suspect, it will be very hard to get a voice match from this. And I'm pretty sure he knew that.'

'But you'll be able to alter it enough so we can understand what he's saying, right?'

A confident smile came back from Gus. 'Watch my magic.' He went back to the digital equalizer, twisted a few more buttons and slid some more faders before loading a pitch shifter onto a separate screen. He placed a small section of the audio recording into a constant loop and worked on it for a few minutes. 'Oh, hello,' he said, frowning.

'What? What?'

Gus automatically reached for the Skittles. 'We've got something else. Some sort of faint hissing noise right in the background.'

'Hissing?'

'Yeah, something like a frying pan or maybe rain against a distant window.' He listened to it again. His eyes went back to one of his monitors and he pulled a face. 'Its frequency is very similar to the static noise. And that messes things up a little.'

'Can't you do something with all this?' Cohen nodded at all the equipment in the studio.

'Is today stupid-question day? Of course I can, but to properly identify it I'll have to run it against my library of sounds.' Gus started clicking away on his computer. 'All that can take a while.'

Cohen checked his watch and let out a deflated breath.

'Relax, that won't affect me cleaning up the whispering voice. That'll take me no time at all.' Gus went back to his buttons and faders. A minute later he seemed satisfied. 'I think I got it.' He pressed play and rolled his chair away from the mixing desk.

The same whispering voice Cohen and Myers had tried so hard to decipher poured out of the loudspeakers, as clear as daylight.

Cohen's jaw dropped as he looked at Gus.

'Motherfucker.'

Thirty

The first thing Hunter did when he and Garcia got back to Parker Center was get a copy of all the photographs taken at Laura Mitchell's exhibition to Brian Doyle, the IT Unit supervisor at ITD. Hunter knew that potentially every single person in those pictures was a suspect, but his immediate interest was in identifying the stranger who'd swapped phone numbers with Laura. The photograph Hunter had flagged showed a clear enough image of the stranger's face to allow Doyle to blow it up and run it against the unified police database.

'That laptop you called about earlier,' Doyle said as he transferred all of the pictures to his hard drive, 'the one that was sent to us by Missing Persons about two weeks ago, belonging to . . .' He started searching his messy desk.

'Laura Mitchell,' Hunter confirmed. 'That's her in those pictures.'

'Oh, OK. Anyway, we bypassed her password.'

'What? Already?'

'We're fantastic, what can I say?' Doyle smiled and Hunter pulled a face. 'We ran a simple algorithm application against it. Her password was just a combination of the first few letters of her family name and her date of birth. Now, you said you needed to have a look at her emails?'

'That's right. Her mother said she'd received a few fan emails that'd scared her.'

'Well, that won't be easy, I'm afraid. The email application on her computer was never used,' Doyle explained, 'which means she didn't download emails, she simply read them online. We checked the computer registry, and at least there she was smart. She never said "yes" when the operating system asked her if she wanted the computer to remember her password every time she logged onto her email online. Her Internet history was also automatically deleted every ten days.'

'Her email password ain't the same as her computer's?'

A quick headshake.

'How about this algorithm application you ran on her PC?'

'It won't work online. Internet security against email account attacks has gotten a lot tougher over the years. All the major email service providers lock you out for several hours, sometimes indefinitely if you try a certain number of incorrect passwords.' Doyle shook his head again. 'Also, if she didn't keep these emails in her account, I mean, if she deleted them after she read them, which is probable since you said they scared her, then the chances of retrieving the full message is basically zero. Unless you find the email provider where the message originated from, the best you gonna get are fragments. And you'll have to go straight to her provider – Autonet. We can't do shit from here. You know what that means, right? Warrants and court orders and what have you. Plus, you can be searching for days, weeks . . . who knows . . . and still get zip.'

Hunter ran a hand over his face.

'I have people going over the rest of the files on her hard drive now. I'll let you know if we come across anything.'

Thirty-One

Whitney Myers stood still, staring at the computer screen and the audio lines as they vibrated like electrified worms. Cohen had just loaded the digital recording Gus had given him onto his computer. The once jumbled whisper she'd retrieved from Katia Kudrov's answering machine was now as clear as daylight.

'YOU TAKE MY BREATH AWAY . . .' Pause. 'WELCOME HOME, KATIA. I'VE BEEN WAITING FOR YOU. I GUESS IT'S FINALLY TIME WE MET.'

The recording was on an endless loop, playing through Cohen's loudspeakers. After the fifth time, Myers finally tore her eyes away from the screen and hit the Esc key.

'Gus said this is actually his voice, there's no electronic device disguising it?'

Cohen nodded. 'But he was clever. He used his own whisper to alter it. If he's ever caught, we'll never get a voice match. At least not with this recording.'

Myers stepped back from Cohen's desk, lightly running two fingertips against her top lip. She always did that when she was thinking. She knew she had to play the recording to Leonid Kudrov when she met him at his house in two hours' time. She had no doubt it would drive terror into an already petrified heart.

'Do you still have my Dictaphone with all the sixty messages?' she asked, returning to her desk and flipping through her notebook.

'Yep, right here.'

'OK, play the last message again.' She paused. 'Actually, just *after* the last message. What I'm interested in is the electronic answering machine voice announcing the time the message was left.'

'Eight forty-two in the evening,' Cohen replied automatically.

Myers' eyebrows rose.

'I listened to it so many times it's etched on my brain,' he explained.

'You're sure?'

'Positive.'

Myers' eyes returned to her notebook. 'According to Katia's father, he called his daughter from his cell phone at eight fifty-three that night. The call lasted four minutes and twelve seconds.'

'She answered that call, didn't she?'

Myers nodded.

'But eleven minutes earlier the answering machine picked it up. Was she out?'

Myers flipped a page. 'Nope, the building's concierge said that she arrived at around eight o'clock. He took her suitcases up to the penthouse for her.' Myers' fingers returned to her upper lip for an instant. 'Of course. The towel on the kitchen floor. Katia must've been in the shower.' She quickly checked her notes again. 'Shit! Remember I told you we have no CCTV footage from the cameras in her building because there was a power surge that blew the fuse box.'

'Yep.'

'Well, the cameras went down just before eight.'

Cohen cleared his throat as he leaned forward. 'And we already know there's no fucking way that was a coincidence.'

'That means the kidnapper knew *exactly* the time she'd be arriving home.' Myers paused and fought back an uneasy feeling. 'He was already waiting for her inside her apartment when she got there. That's why he says welcome home. He *knew* she was home.'

Cohen's whole expression changed. 'So he made that last call from *inside* her apartment?'

'It looks that way.'

'Why? Why make the call if he was already there?'

'I'm not sure. Fear factor? Sadism? It doesn't matter.'

Cohen felt every hair on his body stand on end. 'Oh my God.'

'What?'

'The background hissing noise that Gus picked up in the recording. At the studio he told me that it sounded like rain hitting a window far away, or maybe even a strong shower somewhere.' Cohen's eyes moved to Myers'. 'The kidnapper was inside her bedroom when he made that call. He was watching her shower.'

Thirty-Two

The next morning Captain Blake was already waiting for Hunter in his office by the time he walked in at 7:51 a.m.

'Carlos told me you identified the victim.'

Hunter nodded. 'Her name is Laura Mitchell.' He handed the captain a two-sheet report.

She scanned it and paused. 'The killer stalked her from inside her own apartment?' Her stare quickly bounced between both detectives.

'That's what it looks like, Captain,' Hunter confirmed.

'How did he get in? Any signs of forced entry?'

He quickly shook his head.

'She could've let the killer inside herself,' Garcia offered.

The captain nodded. 'Which means that the killer could've used a false identity to sneak into the building and ring her doorbell, or maybe he was known to her, or he posed as a collector or buyer and made an appointment or something. But still, why hide behind a painting? It makes no sense.'

'Exactly,' Hunter agreed. 'And that's why I don't think Laura opened the door to the killer and invited him in, but the possibility that he was known to her is real.'

Captain Blake thought for a moment. 'The perpetrator could've had his own set of keys.'

Hunter nodded. 'Either that or he's a master locksmith.'

'Did she have a boyfriend, a lover?'

'We're talking to her ex-fiancé later today. His flight from Dallas lands at 2:45 p.m.'

'How long has he been away?'

Hunter rubbed his forehead. 'Since Tuesday evening.'

'Well, that takes him off the suspects list, doesn't it?'

'I wouldn't say that just now, Captain.'

Captain Blake faced Hunter. 'Well, let's see, he's been out of LA since Tuesday evening. Our victim's body was found two days ago – Wednesday afternoon, remember? No exact time of death, but the crime-scene forensic report said that it wouldn't have been more than three to six hours prior to the discovery of the body. That means that he wasn't in Los Angeles when she died, Robert.'

'Yes,' Hunter agreed, 'but we also have no proof that our killer *actually killed her*, remember, Captain? He could've dumped her in that butcher's shop – alive – hours before she died. Even the night before, giving the ex-fiancé an almost perfect alibi. We need more information before we start discarding suspects at this point.'

'OK, I can go with that,' the captain agreed. 'How about this other guy Carlos told me about? The one who tried to pick Laura up on the last night of her exhibition?'

Hunter searched his desk for a copy of the picture of the stranger she was referring to and handed it to her. The captain stared at it for a few seconds.

'We've been running this picture against the unified police database since yesterday. No matches yet. We've also got a team of uniformed officers going around every art gallery, exhibition hall, museum, art school, cafe, anywhere and everywhere where exhibitions take place. The chaperone at the Daniel Rossdale Art Gallery said she was certain she'd seen him before at a previous exhibition. Which means this guy is probably genuinely into art. Hopefully someone, somewhere will recognize him.'

'The door to door of Laura's apartment building gave us nothing,' Garcia said. 'Two to three weeks is a hell of a long time for any of the neighbors to remember hearing anything out of the ordinary, or seeing anyone suspicious.'

'Have Forensics found anything else in her apartment?'

Hunter poured himself a glass of water. 'They recovered several black fibers from a brick wall. No results yet, but a possible clue.'

'Which is?'

'A few of the fibers came from a point about six foot from the floor.'

'Any hairs?' Captain Blake asked.

'None.'

'So whoever was there was wearing a hat or a ski mask or something,' she concluded.

'The assumption is that while hiding, the attacker flattened his back against the brick wall,' Hunter said. 'If we're right and the fibers came from some sort of head garment, he should be between six foot and six four.'

'And if they haven't?'

'Then the fibers could've come from a sweater and we're looking for a seven-foot giant.'

'At least he'll be easy to spot,' Garcia joked.

'No sign of a struggle?' the captain asked without a hint of a smile.

'None.'

She turned and stared at the crime-scene photographs pinned to the pictures board. No matter how often she looked at them, they made her wince every time. Violence in this city seemed to get worse with each passing year.

'Talk to me, Robert, 'cause I'm really starting to dislike this whole thing. It's been two days since we found Laura's body. Two days since this scumbag blew a bomb inside a morgue and killed two other people, one of them being one of my best friends, and we've got shit so far. Why was she kept hostage for so long before being murdered? Has the Mitchell family received any sort of ransom requests or demands?'

Hunter shook his head. 'No. And if we're right, whoever this killer is, he's not after a ransom. Murder/kidnappings are rarely about money.'

Captain Blake felt a chill start at the base of her neck. 'You think he kept her for sexual pleasure?'

'It's possible. But with no autopsy report we'll never know if Laura Mitchell was raped or not.'

Captain Blake let out a heartfelt sigh.

'There's always a reason why a kidnapper would keep a hostage without demanding money for the victim's return,' Hunter offered. 'The two most common are revenge or an obsession with the victim, where the aggressor just can't let go. Nine times out of ten it starts out as some sort of platonic love ... to the power of a thousand.' Hunter paused and allowed his eyes to rest on the portrait photograph of Laura Mitchell. 'And almost undoubtedly that obsession is, or becomes, sexual.'

The captain shifted her weight from one foot to another.

'But something here isn't matching,' Hunter continued.

'What do you mean?'

'One thing we do know for sure from the crime-scene pictures is that the killer didn't torture Laura.'

The captain's brow furrowed.

'Torture, degradation and sadistic sexual abuse are a big part of most murder/kidnappings,' Hunter explained. 'When the reason behind the kidnapping isn't money, if and when the victim is found, there are usually clear indications of physical torture and abuse.' He walked up to the pictures board. 'Before identifying her, Garcia and I went through these pictures with a fine-toothed comb and a magnifying glass trying to identify any physical marks that could point us in the right direction.' He shook his head. 'Not a scratch. Laura had no bruises other than the ones caused by the stitches and her own nails.'

'If whoever kidnapped her was after revenge,' Garcia said, 'he would've tortured her, Captain. If he were obsessed with her, there's a good chance he would've raped her. In both cases, her body should've shown bruises.'

'Once the aggressor starts using violence to get what he wants . . .' Hunter continued, '. . . then we're into a very fast downward spiral. His dominance over her, the false sense of power it gives him, will hook him like a drug. The violence will escalate, the rapes will become more aggressive until . . .' He let the sentence hang in the air.

'But that's not what we have here.' Garcia took over. 'We've got the kidnapping, the keeping of the victim and the murder, but not the violence.'

Captain Blake almost choked on Garcia's words. '*Not* the violence?' She glanced at the pictures board and then back at both detectives. 'He placed a bomb inside her and stitched her shut – while she was still alive. What the hell do *you* consider violent?'

'That's precisely the problem, Captain,' Hunter cut in. 'The violence only came at the end, with the murder. And we all agree it was gruesomely sadistic. But the lack of any bruising on Laura's body indicates that the killer wasn't violent towards her while she was held captive. There was no escalation. It went from zero violence to monstrous in one quick step.'

'And that tells us what?'

Hunter held her stare. 'That we're dealing with an extremely unstable, explosive individual. When he loses his temper, someone loses their life.'

Thirty-Three

Patrick Barlett was one of the top financial advisors in the whole of California. He ran his own company from the fortieth floor of the famous 777 Tower.

Barlett's company reception office was decorated to impress. Hunter thought he no doubt subscribed to the theory that money attracts money.

There were two receptionists standing behind a semicircular steel and green-glass reception counter. Their synchronized smiles greeted Hunter and Garcia as they approached the counter. Hunter flashed his credentials, but was careful to keep his thumb over the word *homicide*. The receptionists' smiles lost some of their sparkle. Two minutes later, Hunter and Garcia were shown into Patrick Barlett's office.

If his company's reception was impressive, Barlett's office was majestic. The entire west wall was one huge floor-to-ceiling window, offering the sort of panoramic views of Los Angeles few had ever seen. The floors were pristine bare oak boards. The walls were painted white with just a hint of blue. The entire office was full of sharp edges and gleaming surfaces.

Barlett greeted both detectives with an overpowering handshake.

'Please, come in,' he said in a smooth, deep voice. 'I'm

sorry for the mess, I just got in. I came straight from the airport.'

Barlett was thirty-one years old, as tall as Garcia but with a strong, quarterback frame, tanned skin and a full head of brown hair. His eyes were dark, nearly black. His facial bone structure was as attractive as any Hollywood superstar.

As Hunter explained the reason for their visit, he saw something change inside Barlett's eyes, as if something precious had been smashed to pieces.

Barlett sat behind his imposing desk unable to speak for a minute. His stare stayed on Hunter for several seconds before switching to a small picture frame on his desk. The photo showed three couples at what looked like a gala dinner. Patrick and Laura were sitting side by side. They looked happy. They looked in love.

'There's got to be some sort of mistake.' The smoothness in his voice had given way to an anguished quiver.

Hunter shook his head. 'Unfortunately, no.'

'There must've been. Who identified the body?'

'Mr. Barlett,' Hunter's voice sounded firmer this time, 'there's no mistake.'

Patrick's eyes returned to the photo frame for an instant before breaking away and finding refuge in the panoramic view. His hands moved from his desk to his lap, like a kid trying to hide the fact that they were shaking.

'When did you last see Miss Mitchell, Mr. Barlett?' Garcia asked.

Silence.

'Mr. Barlett?'

His gaze moved back to both detectives. 'Huh? Please call me Patrick.'

'When did you last see Miss Mitchell, Patrick?' Garcia repeated, a fraction slower this time.

'Weeks ago, on the last night of her exhibition at . . .' he searched the air for the name but didn't find it, '. . . in West Hollywood somewhere.'

'The Daniel Rossdale Gallery?' Hunter helped him.

'Yes, that's the one.'

'Were you invited?' Garcia again.

'It wasn't an invitational exhibition.'

'I mean, did Miss Mitchell know you were going? Did she ask you to go?'

Barlett's entire demeanor changed into something a lot harder.

'Am I being accused here?' He didn't wait for a reply. 'This is absolutely ridiculous. If you think I'd ever be capable of hurting Laura, then you guys are probably the worst detectives this town has ever seen. Either that, or you didn't bother doing a background check on us. We have history together. I love Laura. I'd take my own life before I hurt her.'

Hunter noticed that Barlett didn't even mention the fact that he wasn't in town when Laura's body was found.

'Did you try contacting her again after the exhibition? Apparently you didn't part on very good terms that night.'

'What?' Patrick glared at Garcia. 'That's bullshit. You need to get your facts right, Detective. I drank a little too much that night and I acted like a jerk, I admit it. But that was all. Nothing more. And yes, I tried calling her the next day to apologize, but all I got was her answering service.'

'Did you leave a message?'

'Yes.'

'Did she call you back?'

Barlett gave Garcia a nervous chuckle. 'No, she never does. I'm used to it.'

'Why do you say you acted like a jerk?' Garcia again. 'What happened?'

Barlett paused, trying to decide if he should say any more. 'Since it's obvious you have me as a suspect, I think we should adjourn this conversation until I have my lawyer present.'

'We're not accusing you of anything, Patrick,' Garcia countered. 'We're just clearing up a few points.'

'Well, it looks and sounds like an interrogation to me. So, if it's all the same to you, I really think I should have my lawyer present.' He reached for the phone on his desk.

Garcia leaned back in his chair and ran a hand over his stubbled chin.

'That's your prerogative, Patrick,' Hunter took over, 'but that won't help anyone. It will certainly waste time, though. Time we could spend hunting Laura's killer.'

Patrick paused mid-dial and stared at Hunter.

'I understand this line of enquiry might seem upsetting to you, but at the moment everyone is a suspect and we wouldn't be doing our job if we didn't come knocking at your door. Laura's final exhibition night seems to be the last time anyone saw Miss Mitchell alive. You were seen arguing with her that night.' Hunter leaned forward. 'You're an intelligent man, so think about it. Given your well-documented outbursts, your history with Laura Mitchell, and the fact that you've been trying to get her back for the past four years without success, does it come as a surprise to you that we're here? What would you do if you were us?'

'I would never hurt Laura,' Barlett repeated.

'Fine, but this ain't the way to prove it. No matter what

you do, lawyer or no lawyer, you'll still have to answer our questions. We'll just get a warrant and drag this thing out for a lot longer.' Hunter emphatically allowed his eyes to focus on the photo on the desk. Barlett followed his stare. 'Whoever killed Laura, the woman you loved so much, is still out there. Do you really think that fighting us and wasting time is such a good call?'

Barlett's eyes didn't leave the photograph.

Hunter and Garcia waited.

'I was jealous, I admit it,' he finally said as his eyes became glassy. 'That guy was shadowing Laura everywhere she went like a hungry dog. Staring at her all the time as if she were naked or something. Then I saw them talking. Laura was a very private person, not the flirty type, so of course I was jealous. But there was something different about that guy.'

'Different how?' Hunter asked.

'I don't know. The look in his eyes when he stared at her. As I said, he was shadowing her. Just a few steps away from wherever she was, but he wasn't there for her art.'

'How do you know that?'

'Because not once did he look at any of the paintings. While everyone else was walking around, admiring the exhibition, his eyes were on her . . . *only* on her. As if Laura *was* the exhibition.'

'Don't you think that your opinion of this man could've been distorted by the fact that you were jealous of him?' Garcia suggested.

Barlett shook his head. 'I was jealous of him, all right, especially after I saw him chatting to Laura and the way she was smiling at him, but that's not the reason he caught my attention. I spotted the way he was staring at her way before they talked. I'm telling you, he wasn't there for the exhibition. He was there for her.'

'And you told Laura that?' Garcia asked.

'Yes, but she wouldn't listen. She got angry. She thought I was jealous. But I was just trying to protect her.'

Hunter retrieved a snapshot from a folder he'd brought with him. It was one of the photos they'd got from the Daniel Rossdale Gallery. The one showing the tall, dark-haired stranger who had swapped phone numbers with Laura. He was standing next to her, staring at the camera. Hunter placed the photo on the desk in front of Patrick. 'Is this the person you're referring to?'

Patrick moved closer. His eyebrows contracted. 'Yes, that's him.'

'And you'd never seen him before?'

'Not before that night, no.'

Hunter's phone rang in his pocket.

'Detective Hunter,' he answered and listened for a long moment. His eyes lit up as he faced Garcia.

'You're kidding me.'

Thirty-Four

'So, where exactly are we going?' Garcia asked, easing his car out of the parking spot.

'Norwalk,' Hunter said, punching the address he was given over the phone into the GPS system.

One of the officers they had visiting art galleries with a snapshot of the man who'd swapped phone numbers with Laura Mitchell on the final night of her exhibition had hit gold. The owner of an exclusive gallery in Manhattan Beach had recognized the person in the photo. Nine months ago he'd purchased a canvas by Laura Mitchell from the gallery during one of their exhibitions.

Most art galleries will ask their clients to allow the purchased piece to remain on display until that particular show is over. The Manhattan Beach Gallery always insisted on taking down a name and contact number for its clients.

The man's name was James Smith.

Norwalk is a mostly middle-class neighborhood located seventeen miles southeast of downtown Los Angeles. It took Hunter and Garcia fifty-five minutes to get from South Figueroa Street to the address they were given on the poorer side of Norwalk.

The address led them to an old, gray concrete monstrosity. A six-story-high public housing unit with dirty windows which was in desperate need of a coat of paint. Garcia parked his car across the road from the building's entrance. A group of five guys who were bouncing a basketball around just a few yards away stopped all activity. Ten eyes were glued to Hunter and Garcia.

'*¿Que passa* five-o?' the tallest and fittest one of the group called as both detectives crossed the street. He had no shirt on and his muscles glistened with sweat. Most of his torso, arms and neck were covered in tattoos. Hunter recognized some of them as prison branding. '*¿Qué quieres aquí, puercos?*' He let go of the ball and folded his arms defiantly. The other four grouped up behind him like a defensive line-up.

'*No somos policías*,' Hunter said, flashing his gym membership card. He knew the group was way too far away to be able to see it properly. 'I'm from the City of Los Angeles Housing Authority.' He flicked his head towards Garcia. 'He's from Pensions and Welfare.'

The whole group's hard-ass demeanor evaporated in an instant.

'Oh man, I gotta go,' the one with glasses said, checking his watch. 'I've got a job interview in an hour.'

'Yeah, me too,' the skinny, shaven-headed one said.

They all nodded and mumbled in Spanish as the group broke away, all five of them reaching for their cell phones.

Garcia couldn't hide his smile.

The entrance lobby was in as much need of attention as the rest of the building. Dirty walls, water stains on the ceilings, and the stale smell of cigarettes greeted Hunter and Garcia as they came through its metal and wired-glass doors.

'Which floor?' Garcia asked.

'Fourth.'

Garcia reached for the elevator call button.

'You gotta be kidding, right?' Hunter chuckled. 'Have you noticed the state of this place? That's a risk too far.' He gestured towards the stairs. 'Safer to use those.' They took the steps two at a time.

The fourth floor corridor was long, narrow, badly lit and it smelled of old fried onions and piss. They passed a semi-open door where a baby was crying somewhere inside. The TV in the living room was on, showing some sort of court-room program.

'Not really the sort of place you'd expect an art lover to live,' Garcia commented.

Apartment 418 was two doors from the end of the corridor. Hunter knocked and waited fifteen seconds.

No reply.

He knocked again and moved his ear to the door. Ten seconds later he heard someone approaching from inside. The door unlocked with a loud clang and then was pulled back a fraction, just the length of the security chain. The lights inside the apartment were off. All he could see was a pair of eyes looking out from about a foot away from the door. The sweet smell of jasmine seeped through from inside.

'Mr. Smith?' Hunter asked. 'James Smith?'

Silence.

Hunter subtly placed the tip of his boot against the bottom of the door and lifted his badge. 'We were wondering if we could ask you a few questions?'

Two more seconds of silence. Suddenly, in a desperate reaction, the door was pushed forward with a jerk, but Hunter's foot stopped it from slamming shut.

'James . . . ? What the hell?' Hunter called.

The tension on the door relaxed as Smith let go of it.

They heard the hustle of foot scuffing inside the apartment, moving deeper within, and away from them. Hunter looked at Garcia quizzically for a split second. They both realized it at the same time.

'Fire escape . . .'

Thirty-Five

Hunter pointed to the far end of the hall. 'Back alley . . . go . . . now.'

Garcia spun around on the balls of his feet and took off down the corridor like a locomotive. Hunter pushed the apartment's door open but it halted at the security chain. He slammed his left shoulder hard against it. Once was all it took. The chain came undone from the doorframe, wooden splinters flying through the air. Hunter saw and heard the door at the end of the apartment's hallway slam shut. He dashed towards it but didn't get there in time. A step away from it he heard the lock turn. Mechanically he tried the handle. Nothing.

'Smith, c'mon . . .' He shoved his shoulder against the door. It didn't budge. He tried again, harder this time. Solid as stone. He took two steps back and sent his boot straight onto the door handle. Once, twice, three times. The door rattled a little but that was all. He knew it was pointless carrying on. The door probably had surface-mounted deadbolt locks on the other side. Hunter could shoot the hinges off, but that would be overkill, and way too hard to justify in a report.

'Smith, c'mon, open up.'

Chances were he was already halfway down the fire ladder.

'Fuck!'

Hunter backtracked down the corridor to the next room along on the right, which was on the same side as the room James had locked himself in. The door was shut but not locked. He pushed it open and stepped inside. The room was in almost complete darkness. Hunter didn't look for a light switch – no time – and dashed towards the window on the far wall, almost tripping over something on the floor. Just like the room James had gone into, the window faced the building's back alley. There were no curtains, but the glass had been sprayed with black paint. It was an old-style window. Two panels. The bottom one had slots for fingers at the bottom. No locks, just a single rotating latch. Hunter undid it and pushed the bottom panel up. Stuck.

'Shit.'

With his fingers in the slots he shook the window so vigorously the entire frame rattled. He tried again. The panel slid up a couple of inches, enough for him to get his hands under the frame. Much better grip. With one big push, the panel creaked and slid all the way up. Hunter craned forward and looked out. James was rushing down the last rungs of the metal fire escape ladder.

'Goddamnit.'

Smith didn't look back. He jumped from the ladder and hit the ground running. He was fast and agile.

Hunter searched the alley for Garcia. He saw Smith zigzag between a few large trash cans and then dive through an open door about twenty yards ahead.

Garcia finally appeared, coming from the alley's entrance on the right, sprinting like an Olympic champion.

'The Chinese restaurant's back door,' Hunter called from

the window. 'Past those trash cans on the right. He got in through the kitchen.'

Garcia hesitated for a beat, considering if he should run back the way he came in and try to cut James off at the front of the shops. Going back and around would take too long. By the time he got there James would be gone. He carried on forward, sidestepping the trash cans and disappearing through the same door James had done seconds earlier.

Hunter turned around and hurried back out of the room. If he was fast and lucky enough, he could cut Smith off at the top of the street. He'd taken only two steps away from the window when his eyes caught a glimpse of something on the walls.

The light that now poured in through the open window had erased the darkness.

What he saw made him stop dead.

Thirty-Six

Garcia rushed through the back door of the Chinese restaurant and found himself inside a crowded kitchen. Lunchtime was in full swing. Three chefs were standing by a large ten-burner cooker where several woks were sizzling away. One of the woks seemed to have caught on fire and flames were shooting up from its bowl at least a foot and a half high. Two sous chefs were by a long metal workstation covered with freshly cut vegetables along with three waitresses. One of them had her back flat against the wall next to the double swinging doors that led to the restaurant's dining room, as if she'd just been pushed out of the way. On the floor directly in front of her was an overturned metal tray. Several bowls of noodles and soup were scattered on the ground. All eight of them were yelling loudly in Mandarin. Garcia didn't have to understand them to know that they weren't yelling at each other, or about the spilled food. It was a nervous reaction.

Garcia figured from their reaction that he was about ten to fifteen seconds behind Smith.

All eyes were on Garcia as he came through the alley door. Everyone took a step back. A fraction of a second later they were all yelling and gesticulating at him. Garcia didn't even miss a step. As he skipped over the dishes on the floor and burst through the swinging doors, he could understand only one word – *asshole*.

The shocked expression from the kitchen staff was mirrored on the faces of every customer in the main dining room. Some had turned to look at this new crazy man who'd blasted out of the kitchen, and some were still staring at the restaurant's front door, where the previous one had just exited.

Garcia ran through the restaurant, expertly avoiding the manager and a waitress on the way.

Outside, the street was full of people coming and going in both directions. Garcia looked left, then right. No one was running. No one looked surprised. There was no commotion. Garcia took two steps forward, lifted himself onto the tips of his toes and looked both ways again. He cursed under his breath as he realized that he didn't even know what Smith was wearing. Only his eyes had been visible when he opened the door to his apartment. From the exhibition picture, he knew what Smith looked like, but not from the back. Any tall male walking away from him could be Smith.

Garcia searched the street for Hunter. He was certain that while he followed Smith in through the restaurant, Hunter would be trying to cut him off at the top end of the street, but he was nowhere in sight.

'Shit, Robert, where are you?'

He approached a group of three guys standing just a few yards away. 'Did any of you see a tall guy come running out of that restaurant just a few seconds ago?'

They all looked at him, then at the restaurant's door, then back at him.

'Sure,' the short stocky one said, and they all nodded at each other at the same time. 'He went . . . that way.' One of them pointed left, the other one right, and the stocky guy pointed at his crotch. All three burst out laughing. 'Get the fuck outta here, cop. We ain't seen shiiit.'

Garcia didn't have time to argue. He took a step back and checked up and down the street once again.

No Hunter.

No Smith.

Garcia had to hand it to him. Smith was smart. He knew no one had gotten a good look at him. He could be wearing a suit or a hooded jacket. As soon as he hit the street in front of the restaurant, instead of carrying on running and sticking out like a sore thumb, he slowed down to a walking pace. Just another guy strolling along a street full of shops. He'd look as suspicious as everyone else.

Garcia took his cell out of his pocket and called Hunter. 'Where are you? Did you get him?' His eyes were still roaming up and down the street.

'No, I'm still at the apartment.'

'What? Why? I thought you'd try to cut him off.'

'I take it you don't have him either.'

'No. He was clever. He mixed in with the crowd. And I don't have a clue what sort of clothes he was wearing.'

'I'll call and put an APB out on him right now.'

'Why are you still at his apartment?'

A short pause.

'Robert?'

'You've gotta come see this room.'

Thirty-Seven

Garcia stood motionless by the door to the small square room. The window was now fully open, allowing daylight in. The weak light bulb at the center of the ceiling was also on. A musty smell of old paper and dust lingered in the air, the kind of smell you'd get inside a basement storage room of a bookshop, or a newspaper archive. Hunter was standing next to a large wooden table piled high with magazines, journals, printouts and newspapers. Piles and piles of them were stacked all around the floor, overcrowding the room – Smith was either some sort of collector, or one of those people who was scared of throwing anything away.

Garcia's eyes crawled around the room, trying to take everything in. Every inch of every wall was taken by some sort of drawing, article, clipping, sketch or photograph. They came from newspapers, magazines, websites, journals, and many of them had been drawn, written or taken by Smith himself. There were literally hundreds of images and articles. Garcia stepped inside and his eyes moved to the ceiling. The bizarre collage continued there as well. Every available space was covered.

'Jesus . . .' Something tightened low in Garcia's gut. He recognized the woman in all the pictures and sketches straight away. There was no mistake. Laura Mitchell. A love heart had been drawn around several of the photographs with a thick red marker pen. Like kids do with pictures of their idols.

'What the fuck is this place?' Garcia whispered.

Hunter turned and looked around the room again as if he was seeing it for the first time.

'A sanctuary of some sort? His own private archive? Maybe a research room? Who knows?' A shrug. 'This guy seems to have collected everything that was ever published about Laura. Judging by the discoloration of some of the pictures and newspaper articles, some of these are quite old.' His gaze flickered to the piles of paper everywhere.

Garcia turned his attention to the magazines and newspaper stacks. 'Is she in every one of these?'

'I haven't checked them all. But if I had to have a guess, I'd say yes.' Hunter pulled a newspaper from the bottom of one of the stacks. It was a copy of the *San Diego Union-Tribune*.

Garcia's left eyebrow lifted a fraction. 'San Diego?' He noticed the date. 'That paper is three years old.'

Hunter started flipping through the newspaper. 'The problem is: none of the newspapers, magazines or journals are folded or opened onto a particular page or article. I've checked a few already. I assume he kept them because of something on the entertainment section.' He folded the paper and showed it to Garcia. 'But as you can see, there are no marks. Nothing is circled, underlined or highlighted.'

'Anything about Laura?'

Hunter scanned the page.

Most of the articles were music-related – gig and album reviews. He flipped the paper over and carried on. At the bottom corner of the page he saw a review for an art exhibition and nodded. 'She was exhibiting in San Diego back then.'

Garcia craned his neck. There were no pictures. He randomly pulled another newspaper from the bottom of another pile. He came up with a copy of the *Sacramento Bee*. 'This one is from a year and a half ago.' He quickly found the entertainment section and scanned through another exhibition review. 'He's been stalking her for years,' he said, looking around the room one more time. 'He knew everything there was to know about her. Collected everything there was to collect. Talk about being patient. He waited years for the right moment to make his move. Laura never had a chance.'

Thirty-Eight

Hunter and Captain Blake had to pull all the stops to get an overworked and understaffed Forensics division to send two evidence technicians to a non-crime scene so fast. First impressions showed no indications that anyone else other than James had been inside that apartment. There was no hidden cell or prison room. If Smith was their killer, he'd kept Laura Mitchell captive in a secret location somewhere else. And that secret location was probably where he was heading to right now. The difference this time was that he now knew the police were onto him, and that would certainly influence his actions. He'd be edgy, maybe even in a panic. And a killer in a panic was catastrophic. Hunter knew that only too well from harsh experience.

They needed to catch him fast. Before he left Norwalk. Before he disappeared.

They didn't.

Hunter had immediately arranged for James Smith's snapshot to be emailed from Parker Center to Norwalk's LA Sheriff's Department Station. Available black-and-white units were dispatched to search the streets almost immediately. Officers on foot patrol and inside Norwalk's Metrolink

Station were also sent Smith's picture via SMS text. Airports, train and bus stations were put on high alert. But six hours after Hunter and Garcia had knocked on Smith's door, he still hadn't been sighted.

Both evidence techs had been going over the apartment for the past three and a half hours. They'd need confirmation from the lab, but their best guess, based on what they'd seen, was that all the fingerprints they'd found so far seemed to have come from only one person – James Smith.

Key points inside Smith's bedroom and both bathrooms were sprayed with Luminol but no blood was detected. They also ran a UV light test on all the bed linen and on the fabric sofa and rug in the living room. No evidence of semen stains either.

Hunter and Garcia kept out of the way, staying in the collage room. There was enough in there to keep a platoon occupied for a week. Initially, Hunter wasn't worried about sieving through everything. All the information on those pages seemed to pertain to Laura Mitchell, not James Smith. What he was looking for was some sort of personal diary, or journal, or notebook. Anything that could give them a clue to where Smith might have gone or who he was.

They found nothing. No documents, no passport, no driver's license. Not even any utility bills.

'Anything that could give us any sort of lead, guys?' Hunter asked one of the techs some time later.

'Yeah, my guess is you're looking for a cleaning freak,' he said, bending down and sliding his index finger across the top of the skirting board before showing the result to Hunter. 'Nothing, no dust. My wife is pretty tight on her housecleaning, but even she doesn't dust the skirting boards every time she cleans. The only place with any dust is that freaky room you guys have been in. There's a cupboard in the kitchen packed solid with cleaning materials. Enough bleach to fill a Jacuzzi. This guy is either obsessed with cleaning, or he was expecting us.'

The door to door of the building also produced no information of interest. Most residents said they'd never even seen the person who lived in apartment 418. The ones who did never talked to him. The next-door neighbor, a small, fragile man in his sixties with glasses as thick as bulletproof glass, said Smith always said hi to him whenever they bumped into each other on the corridor. He said Smith was always very polite. That sometimes Smith went out dressed in a suit. No one else in that building ever wore a suit. The old man also said that the walls in the building weren't very thick. He could often hear Smith cleaning, vacuuming, scrubbing and moving around. He did that a lot.

The Forensics agents took shoes and underwear from Smith's wardrobe, and a razor blade, a comb, a toothbrush and a deodorant spray can from his bathroom. They didn't want to take any chances where a DNA signature was concerned.

Night had darkened the sky when Hunter received a call from Operations.

'Detective Hunter? It's Pam from Operations.'

'What have you got for me, Pam?'

'Well, next time you decide to go after someone, please can you pick a person with a more unique name. James is the most common first name in the United States. Smith is the most common last name in the United States. Put them together and we have approximately three and a half million males in the USA called James Smith.'

'Great.'

'In the LA area alone there are about five hundred of them. But the interesting thing is: none are registered to the Norwalk address you gave me.'

Thirty-Nine

Her eyelids flickered in rapid succession but she failed to open them. Her consciousness was returning to her like waves breaking over a beach. But each time her mind hinted at clearing, an undertow of blackness would pull her back into nothing.

The only thing she seemed to be certain of at that moment was the smell. Something like mothballs and strong disinfectant all rolled up into one. It felt as if the vile odor had traveled in through her nose, down her throat and into her stomach, burning everything in its way. Her guts felt like writhing snakes trying to climb out of her body.

Her eyes flickered again, this time for a little longer, and with great effort she managed to force them open. The light around her was dim and weak, but it still burned at her retinas like lightning bolts. Gradually, she began taking in her surroundings. She was lying on her back on some hard and uncomfortable surface, inside a hot and humid place. Old and rusty metal pipes ran across the ceiling in all directions, disappearing as they reached the mold-infested cinder block walls.

She tried lifting her head, but the movement sent waves of nausea rippling through her stomach.

Slowly, the numbness that controlled her body started to subside, and as it did, it was substituted by agonizing pain.

Her lips felt as if they were being ripped from her face by several pairs of pliers at the same time. Her jaw hurt as if it had been broken. She tried opening her mouth, but the pain that rose from the effort almost sent her back into unconsciousness. Tears started streaming down her face as she urged her brain to work and tell her what to do. She tried moving her arms – surprisingly, no pain. More surprisingly, they weren't restrained.

Shivering, she brought her hands to her face and touched her lips with the tips of her fingers. The shivering turned into uncontrollable convulsions of fear as she realized why she couldn't move them.

Her mouth had been stitched shut.

Desperation took over.

Robotically and without any sense of reality, her trembling fingers tapped the stitches on her lips like a mad pianist. Her wailing and frantic muffled screams echoed throughout the room, but there was no one there to hear them. The thread used on her mouth dug deeper into her skin as she tried to move her lips again. She tasted blood.

Suddenly, as if a switch had been flicked on inside her head, she became aware of a much more intense and terrifying pain. It was coming from between her legs. It shot through her body with such ferocity it felt like evil had just climbed inside her.

Instinctively, her hands moved towards the source of the pain, and as they touched her body and the other stitches, she felt her strength leaving her.

Panic erupted inside her, and her body's defense mechanism inundated her bloodstream with adrenalin, numbing the pain just enough for her to be able to move. Guided now by pure survival instinct, she forced herself to sit up.

Sound disappeared, time slowed, and the world turned black and white in front of her eyes. Only then did she realize she was naked and had been lying on some sort of stainless steel table. Strangely, the tabletop seemed higher off the ground than one would expect. At least another foot or so.

She looked down at her bare feet, and all of a sudden it dawned on her. Her legs were also unrestrained. Frantically her terrified eyes searched the room – large, square with a concrete floor and a metal door directly in front of her. The door didn't seem to be locked. The walls were lined with empty wooden shelves.

Without wasting any more time or caring if this was a cruel trap or not, she jumped to the floor. The impact as her feet hit the ground sent a shudder up her spine. A millisecond later, the most unimaginable pain exploded inside her. Her legs lost all their strength and she fell to her knees, shivering. She looked down and all she saw was blood.

Forty

It was now three full days after Laura Mitchell's body had been found and not much had materialized. James Smith, or whoever he really was, had simply vanished. The Forensics agents were right: all the fingerprints found in the apartment did come from a single person. They'd been running them against the National Automated Fingerprints ID System for several hours. So far no matches. It didn't look like James Smith had ever been in the system.

The DNA result would still be at least another day or so. Whoever James Smith was, he was smart.

Choosing the most common American male name automatically hid him under layers upon layers of other people. Even if Hunter asked Operations to narrow the LA's James Smith list down by filtering on age and approximate height, it'd still be too long. Besides, it was obvious that James Smith wasn't his real name.

The apartment in Norwalk had been rented and paid in cash, a year in advance. Hunter talked to the landlord, a Mr. Richards. He was a retired shop owner and lived in Palmdale. He told Hunter that he'd only seen James Smith twice – first when he initially rented the property two years ago, and then again twelve months later when he renewed his lease agreement and paid the next full year in advance, plus extras – more than enough to cover all utility bills. So that was the reason they found no bills in the apartment.

Mr. Richards told Hunter that in the two years Mr. Smith had been renting his apartment, he'd been a great tenant, the best he'd ever had.

'He never causes any trouble,' Mr. Richards told Hunter. 'He's also never requested anything else, unlike most of my previous tenants. They were always calling and asking me for a new fridge, or stove, or mattress, or electric shower, or whatever. They were always complaining that there was something wrong with the apartment, but not James. He never complained.'

'Did you check any documentation when Mr. Smith rented your apartment?' Hunter asked. 'You know, background checks, references or anything like that?'

Mr. Richards shook his head. 'There was no need. He paid cash and the full year in advance, which means he could never default on a payment.'

Hunter was more than aware that Los Angeles was definitely the city for if you've got the cash, you get the goods, no questions asked.

'Did Mr. Smith ever tell you what he did for a living?'

Another shake of the head from Richards.

The snapshot Hunter had of James Smith was quickly released to the press. The picture was by no means perfect. His face was at least 30 per cent obscured, but it was the best they had. With a little luck, someone out there would know who he was. A dedicated phone line was created to receive calls. So far they'd got a mountain of dead ends and people claiming to be James Smith himself, challenging the police to come and get them.

They'd also found the painting Smith had purchased nine months ago along with several DVDs in his apartment. All of them homemade. All of them of Laura Mitchell. Apparently, all of them shot by Smith himself. Hours and hours of footage of Laura at exhibitions, dinner parties, arriving at and leaving her art studio, walking into her gym, browsing in shopping malls, and so on. There were no time-stamps on any of the footage, but judging by her different hairstyles and slight differences in weight, they had been shot over a period of years. They could be seen as surveillance in preparation for an abduction, or plain obsessive stalking. Hunter didn't want to jump to any conclusions until he had more evidence.

'OK,' Captain Blake said, putting the ten-page report she was reading down on her desk. 'What's confusing me is . . . if this James Smith is our killer, and he's obviously been collecting intel on Laura Mitchell for a few years, how come he only decided to strike now?'

'That's not unusual, Captain,' Hunter said, walking over to the window in the captain's office. 'Very few people have the mental strength to become a killer overnight. The vast majority of serial killers, or people who have shown tendency to becoming one, have fantasized about their actions for months, years, sometimes decades. For most, the fantasy alone is enough to satisfy them. Some will go as far as doing all the preparation, the research, the stalking, the surveillance, collecting intel, maybe even capturing the victim, but bottle out right at the last minute. Maybe it took James all these years to gather the courage to finally act out his fantasy.'

'And we know our killer doesn't mind waiting,' Garcia said.

The phone on Captain Blake's desk rang. She answered it on the third bell.

'What?' she barked.

As she listened her eyes darted towards Hunter.

'Shit! Seal the entire place and keep everyone else away from that building, do you hear me? And I mean *everyone*. We're on our way.'

Forty-One

The abandoned preschool was located in Glassell Park, Northeast Los Angeles. Cracked walls, broken windows, subsiding floors, cobwebs, and crumbling wooden door-frames was all that was left of the once bustling single-story building. Instead of cartoon characters, gang graffiti now decorated the walls both outside and inside. Several police vehicles and a forensic crime-scene van took over the park-ing lot to the right of the school. The press had parked all over the place. Reporters and photographers, together with an ever growing crowd of onlookers were being held back at the twenty-five-yard perimeter line created by yellow crime-scene tape and numerous officers.

Hunter, Garcia and Captain Blake got out of the car, sidestepped the crowd and quickly stooped under the tape, approaching the two police officers standing by the main building's entrance. They were both silent.

'Sorry, sir, but I got orders from high up not to let anyone in there for now,' the most senior of the two officers said, acknowledging both detectives' badges.

'I gave that order,' Captain Blake replied firmly, display-ing her credentials.

Both officers immediately stood to attention.

'Captain,' a short, overweight male reporter with thick

glasses and a terribly disguised bald patch called from the pack. 'What's going on? Who is the victim? Why are you here? Care to give the people of Los Angeles some information?' His questions ignited an onslaught of frantic shouts from everyone.

All Los Angeles crime beat reporters knew that LAPD captains didn't usually attend crime scenes, no matter what division or bureau they were from. When they did, there was always a reason. And it was never good news. When the captain of the LAPD Robbery Homicide Division turned up at a crime scene, something was definitely wrong.

Captain Blake ignored the questions and returned her attention to the officer. 'Were you first response?'

He nodded but avoided her eyes.

'C'mon, Captain, give us something. Why are you here? What's going on in there?' The bald reporter insisted.

Captain Blake still paid no attention. 'Who else other than Forensics has seen the body?'

'Only me and my partner, ma'am, Officer Gutierrez.' He tilted his head in the direction of the building behind him. 'He's inside, guarding the entrance to the basement.'

'No one else?' she pressed.

'No one else, ma'am. We got a call from dispatch earlier to come down here and investigate a 911 call – someone claiming to have found a body. We radioed Homicide and Forensics as soon as we walked into that room. We got our orders back almost immediately – not to let anyone else in. Forensics are the only ones we've allowed through.'

'The body is in the basement?' Hunter asked.

'Yes, at the end of the corridor turn left and you'll be in the old kitchen. At the back of it you'll see a few steps that'll take you down to a storage room. The body is in there.' His next words came out no louder than a whisper. 'What in God's earth . . . ?'

Minutes later, Hunter, Garcia and Captain Blake found Officer Gutierrez at the back of the old kitchen, guarding the steps to the storage room just like his partner had said. His youthful face couldn't hide the shock of what he'd seen down in that room.

The cement staircase going down to the basement was worn out, narrow and steep, illuminated by a single light bulb that hung from the water-infiltrated ceiling above the landing at the top. With each step they took, the smell of disinfectant grew stronger. Brilliant forensic light seeped through the rusty metal door at the bottom. As they approached it, Hunter felt his blood rush and warm his skin as if he'd just stepped out into the baking sun. He opened the door, and all he saw was blood.

Forty-Two

Doctor Hove was standing by the far wall talking to her lead Forensics agent, Mike Brindle. They were both wearing white Tyvek coveralls. A stainless steel table occupied the center of the large room. The concrete floor was covered in sticky, coagulated blood. Not splashes and sprinkles, but thick, vampiric pools of it. A few small and delicate bloody handprints traced a short trajectory from the table to the ghostly pale, naked body of a brunette woman lying on her back just a few steps from the door. Her arms had been carefully placed by her side, her legs stretched out.

'Jesus Christ,' Captain Blake murmured, bringing a hand to her mouth as she felt her stomach churn.

The woman's lips had been stitched shut, and though her torso and legs were caked in blood, the black, thorn-like stitches to her lower body were clearly visible.

Doctor Hove approached them in silence and Hunter shot her a questioning look.

The doctor nodded in confirmation. 'Judging by what we have in this room, I'd say it's the same killer,' she said in a hushed voice.

Hunter and Garcia did their best to avoid stepping into the pools of blood and approached the body on the floor. Captain Blake stayed by the door. Hunter crouched down and examined what he could of the woman without touching her. Garcia did the same but his eyes kept returning to her once attractive face, as if something was bothering him. A few seconds later he frowned at Hunter. 'Jesus, she's a carbon copy of Laura Mitchell. They could've been sisters.'

Hunter nodded. He'd noticed the uncanny resemblance from the door.

Captain Blake pinched the bridge of her nose, closed her eyes and took a deep breath. She knew exactly what that meant.

Hunter turned to Doctor Hove. 'Is this how you found the body?'

'No,' Mike Brindle replied, stepping closer. 'We photographed everything and then turned her over. Her body was facing down; right cheek against the floor, facing left towards the wall. Her left arm was extended as if she was reaching for something. Her position gave us the impression that she was probably crawling towards the door, but lacked the strength to get there.'

Hunter's eyes wandered the room again, taking in more of the scene. 'The handprints?'

'They're hers,' Brindle confirmed. 'The few bloody sneaker shoeprints you saw on the floor outside and on the steps going up haven't been confirmed yet. But judging by the runaway smear pattern in some of them, I'd say they belong to the scared teenager who dialed 911 – anonymously, he left no name and no address.' He paused and his stare returned to the woman on the floor. 'Rigor mortis started not long ago, but the heat and humidity in this room could have delayed it for up to five hours, maybe a little more.'

'So she definitely died today?' the captain asked.

Brindle nodded.

Garcia's attention went from the body to the large distribution of blood on the floor. 'She's got no wounds I can see other than her stitches. Where did all this blood come from?'

Doctor Hove and Mike Brindle exchanged an uneasy glance. 'I'll have proper confirmation with the autopsy,' the doctor replied, 'but right now, all this indicates some sort of internal hemorrhage.'

Captain Blake's eyes widened.

'All this blood . . .' the doctor shook her head as if she was struggling to find the right words, ' . . . dripped out of her through the stitches.'

'Holy shit.' Garcia rubbed his face with his right hand.

'She's also got tiny abrasions on both of her hands and knees,' Doctor Hove continued. 'We think she came off that table and collapsed to the ground. Maybe because she was dizzy or in tremendous pain, but she was still alive. The abrasions were probably caused by the fall and her crawling towards the door. Her prints are on that table, so we concluded that she was left there by the killer, but there isn't a speck of blood on it. She didn't start bleeding until she was on the ground.'

'And then there's this,' Brindle said, walking over to where Captain Blake was standing. 'Excuse me, Captain.'

She frowned and took a step to her right.

Brindle pointed to the wall directly behind where the captain was standing. Only then did they see the set of small spray-painted black letters – IT'S INSIDE YOU.

Forty-Three

Captain Blake's lips parted in disbelief. They were exactly the same words Hunter had found spray-painted on the ceiling in the butcher's shop where Laura Mitchell's body had been found. Her stare refocused onto the body on the floor for a moment before moving back to Doctor Hove.

'OK, I thought what we had here was just suspicion and conjecture. I was obviously wrong. But if you knew this was the same killer, given that he placed a bomb inside his first victim that took the lives of two other people inside one of your autopsy rooms . . .' she pointed to the letters on the wall, ' . . . and again he's telling us he did the same here, what the hell are we doing in this room? Where's the bomb squad? And why did you risk turning the body over?'

'Because whatever it was the killer placed inside her this time,' Hunter replied, gently rubbing between his eyebrows, 'it's already gone off inside her.'

'Judging by where she bled from,' the doctor added, 'that's exactly what we think. As we said, it all points to an internal hemorrhage, but not one we've ever seen before.'

'What do you mean?' Captain Blake asked.

'Internal hemorrhages usually occur from traumatic injuries, blood vessel rupture or certain specific diseases, carcinoma being one of them. But the blood accumulates inside the body, hence the term *internal*. And the amount is just a fraction of what you see here. This woman bled as if she had been mutilated. Whatever it was that caused it, it was inside her.'

No one said anything for a moment.

'There was nothing else in this room other than what you can see,' Brindle took over. 'The body, those old shelves on the walls and that stainless steel table.' He gestured towards it. 'There are no chains, no ropes or any sort of restraints anywhere. A closer look at the victim's wrists and ankles shows no abrasions or marks. She wasn't tied down. She also couldn't have been locked in here because there's no lock on that door.' He shook his head as he considered it. 'The truth is: we can't find anything that suggests why she wasn't allowed to just walk out of here. So far there are no indications that anyone else was in here with her when she died. It looks like the killer simply dumped her on that table and left. And as we said, she wasn't bleeding then. But the killer somehow knew she would never get out of this room alive.'

Hunter had already noticed that the table in the room had been raised higher off the ground than normal. 'Does this look strange to anyone?' He pointed to the wooden blocks under each of the four table legs.

Everyone frowned.

'The first victim, Laura Mitchell,' he continued, 'was left on a stainless steel counter inside a butcher's shop in East LA. That counter had also been raised higher off the ground by bricks. First I thought that maybe the old butcher there had been some sort of a giant, but no, I checked. He was five foot eight.'

'So you think the killer did this deliberately?' the captain asked. 'Why?'

'I'm not sure yet.'

They all paused as they heard heavy footsteps coming down the stairs. A couple of seconds later a crime lab agent also dressed in white Tyvek coveralls pulled the door open. He brought with him a large, black plastic flight case.

'It's OK, Tom,' Brindle said, reaching for the case. 'I know how to set it up.'

The agent left the case with Brindle and exited the room.

'This is why we had to turn her body over,' Doctor Hove explained as Brindle undid the locks to the case and started unpacking its contents. 'That's a portable tactical X-ray unit. It's mainly used for the investigation of small- to medium-sized objects like parcels, boxes and luggage. The picture it produces is not of the same quality as you'd get from a proper hospital X-ray machine, but it'll serve our purposes here. We're pretty confident that whatever was placed inside her has, as Robert said, gone off, and that's what killed her. But we all know what this killer is capable of.' She looked at Captain Blake. 'I don't wanna move her before I have an idea of what we're dealing with.'

They all watched as Brindle set up the equipment. 'Since we don't have a tripod,' he said, 'can somebody hold the camera over her?'

'I'll do it,' Garcia said, returning to the body and once again carefully avoiding the pools of blood. He took the small digital camera from Brindle.

'Just keep it directed at her stomach. Two to three feet away will do,' Brindle explained before approaching the laptop he'd set up on top of the black plastic flight case. 'That's all there is to it. The camera connects wirelessly to the computer and produces an X-ray image. You can press the on button now, Carlos.'

He did, and all eyes reverted to the laptop screen as the image materialized.

Brindle and Doctor Hove's eyes widened in amazement and confusion, and they both craned their necks a little closer.

Hunter squinted, trying to understand what he was looking at.

Captain Blake's jaw dropped and her mouth went instantly dry, but she was the only one who managed to ask the question in everyone's mind.

'In the name of God, what . . . the *hell* . . . is that . . . inside her . . . ?'

Forty-Four

Hunter knew that with everything his brain was trying to process, sleep just wouldn't come. And he'd have to wait until morning for any sort of answer. Forensics were still processing the basement room in the old preschool, though he didn't hold out any great hopes about what they'd find. Doctor Hove would expedite the body's autopsy, but that'd only be at first light.

He collected some files from his office before making his way back to his place and then onto Jay's Rock Bar, a joint just two blocks away from his apartment. It was one of his favorite drinking spots. Great Scotch, fantastic rock music and friendly staff. He ordered a double dose of Glenturett 1997 with a single cube of ice and sat at a small table towards the back.

Hunter sipped his drink slowly for a minute, allowing its strong flavor to take over his palate. In front of him, spread out on the table, were all the photographs they'd received from Missing Persons. He scanned through them carefully, and despite the disfigurement to the new victim's face caused by the rough stitches, he knew she wasn't among them.

He needed to search the MPU database again, go back four, maybe five weeks, but as before, with the stitches and swelling, the face recognition software wouldn't work.

Doing it manually again would take too long. Hunter would have to wait until the end of the autopsy and use the new face close-ups once the stitches have been removed from the victim's mouth.

He finished his drink and debated if he should have another one. His eyes rested on the wall closest to him and all its paintings and decorations. He observed them for a moment. That's when a new thought entered his mind.

'It can't be . . .' he whispered as he shook his head.

Hunter gathered all his files together and rushed back to his apartment.

Sitting at the table in his living room, he fired up his computer and accessed the MPU database. He knew the criteria he used for the new search would reduce the output result considerably. He wasn't expecting any more than three, maybe five matches.

He was wrong.

Seconds later the screen flickered and the displayed table showed that his search had produced a single match. Hunter double-clicked it and waited for the file to upload.

As the new photograph materialized on his screen, Hunter let out a heavy breath.

Forty-Five

Special autopsy room one was located down a different corridor, separate from all the other chambers. It was usually used for postmortem examinations of bodies that could still pose some sort of contamination threat – highly contagious viral diseases, exposure to radioactive materials and so on. The room, with its own cold storage facility and separate database system, was sometimes used during high-profile serial killer cases, like the Crucifix Killer investigation a few years ago – a security precaution to better contain sensitive information.

The image they got from the portable tactical X-ray unit in the basement of the disused preschool in Glassell Park didn't reveal much, but whatever it was that the killer had placed inside his second victim, it sure as hell wasn't a bomb, Doctor Hove had no doubt of that. The picture showed a solid, triangular shape with a rounded base. Something that resembled a large but very thin slice of pizza. She'd never seen anything like it, and the only way she could find out any more about it was by extracting it from the body.

Doctor Hove had had almost no sleep, and turned up at the LACDC even before the crack of dawn. She just wanted to get on with things. At that time in the morning she had to perform the autopsy of the new victim on her own, no assistant. It would take longer than usual.

It was just past 7:00 a.m. when Doctor Hove called Hunter's cell.

During the short trip from Hunter's apartment to the morgue, he heard a report of shots fired in Boyle Heights and another of an armed robbery in progress in Silver Lake through the police radio. He drove past three light-flashing, siren-wailing police cars and two ambulances. The day had barely started. How could such an incredible city be so saturated with insanity?

The main coroners building at the LACDC was an intriguing piece of architecture with hints of Renaissance styling. Terracotta bricks and light gray lintels gave it an Oxford college look. Its business hours were the same as any city office – Monday to Friday, 8:00 a.m. to 5:00 p.m. Except under special request, no autopsies were ever carried out in the evenings or weekends. This was certainly one of those.

Hunter had called Garcia from the car and he wasn't surprised to find him already waiting in the empty parking lot.

'You got here quick,' Hunter said, stepping out of his old Buick.

'I got no sleep. I was waiting for this call.'

Hunter looked at him suspiciously. 'How about Anna?'

Garcia bobbed his head to one side. 'She got no sleep either. She insisted on staying up with me. She said that at least we could spend a few hours together since we haven't had much time for each other lately. But you know how perceptive she is. She's already picked up that the case we're working on isn't just a regular one. She never says anything, but you can see the worry in her face.'

Hunter nodded understandingly. He was very fond of

Anna. She was the unseen strength behind his partner. Most cops' wives would never understand or stick by their husbands like Anna did. Divorce numbers amongst the police in Los Angeles were around 70 per cent. But Hunter could never see that happening to Anna and Garcia. They were made for each other.

On the other hand, Hunter himself had never been married. The few relationships he'd had over the years had never really worked out. They'd always start well. But the pressures and commitments imposed by his job had a way of taking their toll on most love stories.

Hunter paused and turned as he heard the sound of another car entering the lot.

Captain Blake parked her silver metallic Dodge Challenger next to Garcia's Honda Civic.

'I wanna see this for myself,' she explained as she closed the door and pressed a button on her key. The car's headlights flicked twice followed by a muffled click. 'I want to get a better idea of who the hell we're dealing with here. What kind of freak has claimed the lives of four people in my city so far.'

A silent and haggard-looking Doctor Hove let them into the building. With most of its lights turned off, and without the hustle and bustle of people, orderlies, and pathologists moving around, the place looked and felt like a horror movie mausoleum. The cold, antiseptic odor that was all too familiar to them seemed stronger this early in the morning. The underlying smell of death and decomposition followed their every step, scratching the inside of their nostrils. Garcia fought the shiver that threatened to run up his spine as they walked past the empty reception area and turned into a desolate hallway. No matter how many times he and Hunter had walked those corridors, he'd never get used to the empty feeling that took over him every time.

'There's no point in explaining it until you see it for yourselves,' Doctor Hove said, punching the code into the metal keypad by the door to the special autopsy room. 'And if you thought the bomb left inside the first victim was crazy, wait until you see this.'

Forty-Six

The room was large and bright, lit by two rows of florescent lights that ran the length of the ceiling. Two steel tables dominated the main floor space, one fixed, one wheeled.

They stepped through the door and were immediately hit by a blast of cold air and an immense feeling of sadness that seemed to chill their bones. The brunette woman's body was lying uncovered on the fixed table. The stitches to her mouth and body had been removed, now substituted by new ones that outlined the Y incision. In a strange way she looked peaceful. The immeasurable suffering that was etched on her face just a few hours ago seemed to have vanished, as if she was grateful to someone for removing those terrible stitches from her body.

They all put on latex gloves and approached the table in silence. Doctor Hove buttoned up her white lab coat and moved around to the other side of the body.

Hunter stared at the woman's face for a long time. There was little doubt in his mind.

'I think her name is Kelly Jensen,' he said quietly, retrieving a black-and-white printout from the folder he'd brought with him and handing it to the doctor.

Captain Blake and Garcia craned their necks across the table. Doctor Hove had a good look at it before holding it close to the woman's face. Without the stitches to her lips, and washed of all that blood, the resemblance was undeniable.

The doctor nodded in agreement. 'On looks alone I'd say you're right, Robert.'

'Her file says that when she was a teenager she tripped and fell through a glass window in school,' Hunter continued, reading from a file sheet. 'Two large shards pierced the back of her left shoulder leaving a V-shaped scar. Her right elbow was also cut and she should have a semicircular scar just below the joint.'

Doctor Hove lifted her right arm and they all bent over to take a look at her elbow. An old and faint semicircular scar marked the skin a couple of centimeters below the joint. Very quickly they all repositioned themselves around the head of the table. The doctor didn't have to lift her upper body far, just a few inches was all that was needed. On the back of her left shoulder, scar tissue marked by the evidence of old stitches formed a sideways V-shape.

'I don't think there's much doubt now, is everyone agreed?' Doctor Hove lowered the victim body back down.

'Who is she?' the captain asked.

'The information I have at the moment isn't much, just what was passed to Missing Persons. Thirty years old from Great Falls in Montana. She was reported missing twenty-one days ago.' Hunter paused to clear his throat. 'Now here comes the punch. The person who reported her as missing was her agent.'

'Agent?' Garcia asked.

Hunter nodded. 'Kelly Jensen was a painter.'

Forty-Seven

Everyone held their breaths. Captain Blake was the first to slash the silence.

'How old was the first victim?'

'Laura Mitchell was thirty,' Garcia replied.

'And when did she go missing?'

Garcia looked at Hunter.

'She was reported missing fifteen days ago,' he replied.

Captain Blake closed her eyes for an instant. 'Fantastic,' she said, 'so we're dealing with some psycho killer who's after pretty, brunette, 30-year-old painters, and has a hard-on for stitching their bodies shut?'

Hunter didn't reply.

'Are there any more brunette 30-year-old painters who are missing?'

'I searched all the way back to ten weeks, Captain, Laura Mitchell and Kelly Jensen were the only two.'

The captain's gaze returned to the body on the table. 'Well, that's something I guess.' She turned to face Hunter and Garcia. 'We'll talk about this back at PC. What do we have here, Doc?' she asked Doctor Hove.

The doctor stepped a little closer to the autopsy table.

'Well, just like the first victim, the stitches the killer applied to his second one were amateurish, to say the least.'

The doctor pointed to Kelly Jensen's mouth. 'Actually, they were more like knots than anything else. Ten in total, five to each body part.'

'Same as the first one,' Hunter confirmed.

Doctor Hove nodded.

'So you're saying we shouldn't be looking for anyone with medical knowledge?' the captain asked.

'If he has any, he didn't show it here. The thread used is also very thick. What in medical suture we call a number six or seven. Thread sizes are identified by the United States Pharmacopeia,' she explained. 'Seven is the thickest. In comparison, a size four thread is roughly the diameter of a tennis racquet string. The thread used here will be going to the lab for proper analysis today, but there's no doubt he used some sort of nylon.' Doctor Hove turned and retrieved a folder from behind her. 'Her organs were healthy, but dehydrated. They also showed symptoms of mild malnutrition.'

The captain shifted on her feet. 'The killer starved her?'

'Possibly, but not for long. The symptoms are consistent with one, maybe two days of starvation at the most. She was deprived of food and water either on the day or the day before she died.' She lifted her right hand in a wait gesture. 'Before any of you raise this point, the stitches to her mouth were brand new, probably inflicted just hours before she died. That wasn't the reason why she'd had no food or water.'

'Any guesses?' Captain Blake asked as her eyebrows arched.

Doctor Hove tucked her dark hair behind her ears. 'There could be any number of reasons. Some sort of ritual on the killer's part, the victim herself refusing to eat as an act of

defiance or because she felt sick, or angry, or anything . . .'
She shrugged almost imperceptibly.

'Did you find any sort of marks at all on her body, Doc?'
Hunter took over.

The doctor's face morphed as if Hunter had asked the
million-dollar question.

'Now here is where it starts to get interesting.' She took
a step to her right and allowed her eyes to refocus on Kelly
Jensen's ghostly white face. 'I couldn't find a single scratch
on her.'

Captain Blake looked puzzled. 'Nothing?'

'Nothing,' Doctor Hove confirmed. 'As we said earlier,
her wrists and ankles are totally free from marks and abrasions. We know she wasn't restrained to that table in the
kitchen basement of the preschool. But I can't find anything
that suggests she was restrained *at all* during the time she
was held captive either.' The doctor paused. 'My examination of the inside of her mouth and the skin around it also
showed no evidence that she was gagged.'

'Which means the killer wasn't concerned with the victim
making any sort of noise,' Garcia noted.

Doctor Hove nodded. 'She was either drugged up to her
eyeballs, or locked inside a very secure and soundproofed
room, or both. Toxicology results will take a few days.'

'Needle marks?' Hunter asked.

'Not even a little nick. Except for the tiny scrapes to her
palms and knees, which I'm pretty sure she got when she
fell to the floor, she doesn't have a scratch on her. Take away
the stitches, and there's not a shred of evidence the killer
ever touched her.'

Everyone went silent for a moment.

Hunter thought back to how long he'd spent going over

every inch of the crime-scene pictures of Laura Mitchell. Just like Kelly Jensen, she didn't have a scrape on her.

Hunter's attention shifted to Kelly's hands and his brow furrowed. Every one of her nails had been filed, witch-style. As pointy and as sharp as possible.

'Did you find anything under her nails, Doc? Why are they so . . . claw-like?'

'Good spot, Robert,' the doctor agreed. 'And the answer is – I'm not sure why. But I did find something under them, yes – some sort of dark copper-colored dust. It could be clay or brick dust, maybe even dry dirt. Again, we'll need to wait for the lab results to be sure.'

Hunter bent down and examined Jensen's hands more closely.

'I'll put an urgent tag with anything related to this case that gets sent to the lab,' the doctor reassured them. 'Hopefully we'll start getting results in a day or two. But unfortunately, due to the severity of her internal injuries and the amount of blood that was discharged, we won't be able to establish with any certainty if she was raped or not. If there was any trace of it, it's been washed away by her own blood.'

The entire room seemed to tense with those words.

Doctor Hove walked over to the metal counter and retrieved something from a plastic tray. 'Now this is the cause of it all, and it's as grotesque as it's ingenious,' she said, returning to the autopsy table. The strange metallic object she was holding was about eight inches long, a quarter-inch wide and two inches deep. At first glance it looked like several long and narrow slices of metal stacked up on top of each other like a deck of cards.

There were curious looks all round.

'This is what the killer placed inside her,' the doctor said, her voice a touch sadder than before.

The curious looks turned into confused frowns.

'What?' Captain Blake spoke first. 'I don't know what that is, Doc, but it sure as hell isn't what we saw through that X-ray machine of yours.'

'Not in this state, no,' the doctor agreed.

'And what in God's creation does that mean?'

Doctor Hove moved back to the other side of the autopsy table, putting some distance between herself and the other three.

'What this is, is a weapon like I've never seen before. Here we have a stack of twelve quarter-inch-wide razor blades held together by a very strong and potent spring mechanism. These blades are laser sharp. And when I say laser sharp, I mean a Samurai sword cuts like a baseball bat when compared to these.'

Hunter rubbed his eyes and shifted uncomfortably.

'I don't get it,' Garcia said, shaking his head. 'As the captain said, that isn't what we saw. So what did you mean when you said not in this state, Doc?'

'You obviously remember what we saw inside her body when we used the X-ray machine, right?' Doctor Hove clarified. 'Big, triangular shape with a rounded base? Something like a large protractor?' She didn't wait for a reply. 'OK, how do you suppose the killer managed to get that inside her? You'll have to agree that its rounded base was way too wide for it to be simply inserted into her body.'

Hunter let out a deep, heavy breath, his eyes back on the object in the doctor's hands. 'Some sort of spreading knife.'

Captain Blake's attention swung to Hunter. 'Some sort of what?'

'That's exactly it,' the doctor confirmed, showing everyone the long and thin metal object again. 'In this closed format, the killer would've had no problems inserting this thing into her before sewing her shut.'

The shiver Garcia had fought off as he entered the building returned, and this time he was powerless against it.

'Once inside,' the doctor continued, 'this happened.' She held the object by one of its tips using only her thumb and index finger. With her other hand's forefinger she clicked an almost invisible button at the top of it.

WHACK.

Forty-Eight

Caught completely by surprise, everyone jumped back.

'Shit!' Captain Blake let out in a high-pitched voice, bringing a hand to her mouth.

'Holy crap, what the fuck?' Garcia's hands shot up towards his face in a protective reflex.

In a fraction of a second, with a loud metallic thwack, the blades on the object in Doctor Hove's hands had snapped open exactly like a Chinese hand fan. Every shocked eye in the room was on it, and though their mouths were half-open, not a word was uttered. Doctor Hove carefully placed the object down on Kelly's stomach, its narrower tip just touching her pubic bone.

'This is about the position this thing was found inside her,' she finally said, her voice quieter, her tone darker than before. 'As you can see, the area it covers is almost the entire width of her abdomen.'

Captain Blake let go of the breath she had been holding for the past minute.

'As I said,' the doctor moved on, 'these blades are laser sharp on both edges. The springs that were used to smack them open are small but very powerful. Able to generate several pounds of pressure. Probably the equivalent to someone hatching down with a meat cleaver. This thing sliced through everything in its path.'

She indicated a large female body organ diagram on the wall behind her.

'Her urethra, bladder, cervix, uterus, ovary, vaginal cavity, everything in her reproductive system was mutilated instantly. The blades also managed to rip through muscle, her appendix and part of her large intestine. Her pelvic bone was chipped. There was no way she could've survived this. The internal hemorrhage she suffered was . . . unthinkable, but death wouldn't have been instantaneous. The pain she went through is something that even Satan would've had trouble imagining.'

Hunter ran a hand over his mouth. 'How long?'

'How long did she suffer for?' The doctor shrugged. 'Depends on how strong she was. A matter of minutes, probably. But to her I'm sure it felt like days.'

All eyes returned to the object the doctor had placed on Kelly's stomach.

'So how does this thing work again?' Captain Blake asked.

'Simple,' the doctor said, picking it up. 'The blades are way too sharp for anyone to touch them, so moving them back to their starting position could pose a problem, but there's a retracting mechanism built into it.' She indicated a round screw just a couple of centimeters from the object's base – the side that held one of the ends of the blades together. Using a screwdriver she retrieved from a glass-fronted cabinet, Doctor Hove began to turn it slowly. As she did, the blades started retracting behind each other, closing the fan-like knife. Less than a minute later they were all stacked up like a deck of cards just like before.

'The trigger is this button,' the doctor indicated it with her finger, 'very similar to the ones you see in click pens.'

They all moved closer to have a better look.

'So if this thing went off inside her, who clicked it on?' the captain asked.

'Well, I said the trigger is very similar to a clicking pen mechanism, but not identical. The difference is that this one is much more sensitive. I also said this was an ingenious piece of work. Check this out.' She stepped back, holding the strange knife just as she had moments earlier. This time, instead of clicking the trigger with her finger, she simply jerked it down about four inches, as if shaking a cocktail shaker, but only once.

WHACK. The knife fanned out with a metallic thud once again.

'It activates itself,' the doctor said. 'All it needs is a little bump.'

Hunter's mind went into overdrive. 'Fuck! The table . . . and the counter . . . that's why . . . the impact.'

Captain Blake gave him a slight headshake, still not with him.

'Do you think a clicking trigger mechanism just like that one could've been used to activate the bomb that was placed inside Laura Mitchell?' Hunter faced the doctor.

She thought about it for a second and her face transformed as realization dawned. 'It could've been easily adapted, yes. It's such a sensitive mechanism that Doctor Winston could've activated it by mistake as he pulled the bomb out of the victim without even noticing it.'

'How tall was she?' Hunter asked, nodding at Kelly Jensen's body.

'Five six,' the doctor replied.

Hunter turned to Captain Blake. 'The table inside the old preschool, and the butcher's counter in East LA had both been raised off the ground about a foot by wooden blocks or bricks. Neither of the victims was very tall. Laura Mitchell was five seven. The killer was making sure that his victims wouldn't just climb down from where they were once they woke up. They had to *jump* down. Like a kid out of a bunk bed.'

'Oh God!' Doctor Hove's eyes returned to the knife. 'The impact as their feet hit the ground would've jerked the object inside them.'

'Enough to activate the trigger mechanism?' Captain Blake asked.

'Easily,' Doctor Hove replied. A moment later she brought a hand to her mouth as she realized what it all meant. 'Jesus! The killer wanted to make them kill themselves without them knowing it.'

Forty-Nine

'OK,' Captain Blake said closing the door to Hunter and Garcia's office just minutes after getting back to Parker Center. 'What the hell is going on? I can almost get my head around a psycho being obsessed with painters. Both of them brunettes. Both of them somewhere in their thirties. Both of them attractive. In this city, that kind of obsession is *normal crazy*. But this thing about placing something inside the victims . . . something as absurd as a bomb, or as . . .' she shook her head as words escaped her ' . . . fucked up as a fan-out knife, and then stitching their bodies shut, that's completely dancing-around-the-room-naked-smothered-in-peanut-butter crazy.' She looked at Hunter. 'But this isn't what we're dealing with here, is it? This guy isn't insane. He's not hearing the devil's voice in his head or drinking his own piss, is he?'

Hunter shook his head slowly. 'I don't think so.'

'An obsessed stalker going after his idols, then?'

Hunter tilted his head from side to side. 'First impressions . . . maybe, but if you look closely at the evidence, it goes against the possibility of an obsessed fan being behind these murders.'

'How so? What evidence are you talking about?'

'The lack of bruising.'

Captain Blake's brow furrowed so hard, her eyebrows almost met.

'Two victims,' Hunter indicated with his fingers. 'Both kidnapped and held hostage for around two weeks. You remember what Doctor Hove said, right? That if we take away the savagery of the stitches and the way in which they died, they were both untouched. Not a scratch. The killer didn't lay a finger on them while they were in captivity.'

'OK,' the captain agreed. 'And how does that relate to the obsessed fan theory?'

'Obsessed fans spend a lot of time creating fantasies in their heads about their idols, Captain,' Hunter explained. 'That's why they become obsessed in the first place. Most of these fantasies are sexual, some are violent, but none is about kidnapping their idols so they could chat for weeks over hot milk and donuts. If this guy were a fan obsessed enough to kidnap, chances are he wouldn't be able to resist acting out at least one of his fantasies. Especially if he was prepared to kill them anyway. And if he did that, there would've been some sort of bruising somewhere on their bodies.'

Captain Blake looked pensive. They'd never be able to obtain confirmation that either of the victims had been raped. But Hunter was right; the lack of bruising on both of their bodies suggested that wasn't what this killer was after. An obsessed fan was starting to sound improbable.

'So who the hell could be capable of something like this?' she asked. 'A split personality job?'

'Again, possible, but with what we have so far it's hard to say.'

'Why?' she challenged. 'You said so yourself, the killer went from passive to absurdly violent in one quick step.

Isn't that an indication of extreme mood swings? A drastic change in personality?'

Hunter nodded. 'Yes, but the way he carries out his violence contradicts the theory.'

'How's that?'

'The time and preparation behind both murders was too extensive.'

'Slow down, big brain, I ain't following you,' she countered.

Hunter continued. 'Mood swings and extreme personality changes have to be triggered, usually by a very strong emotion – like rage, or love, or jealousy. They don't simply occur out of the blue. The new mood, or personality, takes over and stays for a while, but as soon as that rage, or whatever emotion it was that triggered it is gone, so is the personality. The person goes straight back to his or her normal self.' He snapped his fingers. 'Like waking up from a trance. How long do you think this trance can last, Captain?'

She started to catch on. 'Not long enough.'

'Not long enough,' Hunter agreed. 'The killer crafted a bomb and that knife from hell himself, not to mention the unique self-activating trigger mechanism. He also took time preparing the location where the victims were left, and then calmly sewed their body parts shut. All that takes a lot of time. Both preparing and executing it.'

'And that would mean that the killer would've had to have been in an altered state of mind for days, maybe weeks,' Garcia added. 'Highly unlikely.'

Hunter nodded. 'And then there's also the current accepted opinion of modern psychology that Multiple Personality Syndrome doesn't really exist. It's a therapist-induced disorder perpetuated by a never-ending barrage of TV talk shows, novels and ill-conceived Hollywood movies.'

'What?'

'Basically, modern psychology believes that Multiple Personality Syndrome is complete bullshit.'

Captain Blake leaned against Hunter's desk and undid both buttons on her suit jacket. 'So we're dealing with someone who knows exactly what he's doing?'

'I'd say so, yes.'

'His creativity is proof of that,' Garcia added.

Hunter nodded. 'He's also patient and self-disciplined, a rare virtue nowadays, even in the calmest of individuals. Add that to the level of craftsmanship he's showed so far, and it wouldn't surprise me if he were a watchmaker or even an artist himself. Maybe some sort of sculptor or something.'

The captain's eyes widened. 'Like a *failed* sculptor? Someone who was never as successful as his victims? You think this could be payback?'

Hunter shifted his weight to his left foot. 'No. I don't think this is born out of revenge.'

'How can you be sure? Envy is a powerful emotion.'

'If the killer is a failed artist after revenge because he never made it big, he wouldn't target other artists. It'd make no sense. They wouldn't be the reason he never made it.'

Garcia bit his bottom lip and bobbed his head in agreement. 'The revenge would've been against agents, or gallery curators, or art critics and journalists, or all of the above. People who can make or break an artist's career, not fellow artists.'

Hunter nodded. 'Also Laura Mitchell and Kelly Jensen's resemblance to each other isn't just a coincidence, Captain.

His victims mean more to him than just a vehicle for revenge.'

'The killer also used the same MO, but inserted a different killing device into each of his victims,' Garcia added. 'I don't think that was random. I think there's a meaning behind it.'

'What?' Captain Blake asked. A speck of irritation crept into her tone as she crossed to the window. 'What kind of relation could a bomb and a knife that didn't even exist on this earth until a few days ago have with two painters?'

No one replied. The silence that followed held a different meaning for each of them.

'So this new victim fucks up our lead on the James Smith guy, right?' the captain blurted. 'Everything we found in his apartment was about Laura Mitchell, not Kelly Jensen.'

'Maybe not,' Garcia argued. He started fidgeting with a paper clip.

'And how's that?'

'Maybe he's got another room somewhere else. Another apartment maybe,' Garcia offered.

'What?' Captain Blake glared at him.

'Maybe he's that smart, Captain. He knows that with two victims, if he gets caught and only one of the rooms is found, he has a good chance of walking.' He placed the paper clip, now bent out of shape, down on his desk. 'As we already know, he adopted the name James Smith because he knew if anything happened, his name alone would hide him under a mist of people.' He showed the captain his right index finger. 'He pays his rent up front.' Now the middle finger. 'He pays his bills up front. If he *is* our guy, we know for sure he's got at least one more place somewhere else: the place where he keeps his victims, 'cause we know he didn't keep them in that apartment. If that's the case, he could easily have another rented apartment somewhere else. Maybe under a complete different name. That's why we can't find him.'

Captain Blake leaned against the windowsill. 'It's an unlikely possibility.'

Garcia cracked his knuckles. 'It's also unlikely that anyone would create his own bomb, his own crazy knife, his own trigger mechanism and place it inside a victim before stitching her body shut.' He paused for effect. 'C'mon, Captain, the evidence says this guy is everything but predictable. He's smart, very slick and very patient. Would it really surprise you if he *did* have another collage room somewhere else? It gives him deniability.'

'Garcia is right, Captain,' Hunter said, sitting at the edge of his desk. 'We can't discard James Smith simply because the room we found didn't have anything about Kelly Jensen.'

'And has he been sighted anywhere yet? Have the phone lines produced any useful tips?'

'Not yet.'

'That's just great, isn't it?' She pointed to the street outside. 'Over four million people in this city and no one seems to know who this James Smith really is. The guy has simply vanished.' She crossed to the door and opened it. 'We're chasing a fucking ghost.'

Fifty

When Hunter got back to his office, he found an email from Mike Brindle in Forensics – the lab results from the fibers found on the wall behind the large canvas in Laura Mitchell's apartment were in. They had been right in their assumption. The fibers had come from a common wool skullcap. That meant that whoever had hid behind that canvas was somewhere between six foot and six four.

The results for the faint footprints were also in, but because they were set on house dust, and therefore smudged, they weren't 100 per cent accurate. The conclusion was that they'd probably come from size eleven or twelve shoes, which was consistent with the height theory. The interesting fact was that they had found no sole marks. No trademark imprints, or grooves, or anything. A completely flat sole. Mike Brindle's take on it was that whoever had waited in Laura's apartment had used some sort of shoe cover. Probably handmade. Probably soft rubber or even synthetic foam. That would have no doubt also muffled the perpetrator's footsteps.

After analyzing the entire studio floor for any more size eleven or twelve foot imprints, Brindle arrived at the same conclusion as Hunter and Garcia had. After hiding behind the large canvas resting against the back wall, Laura

Mitchell's attacker had somehow diverted her attention and very quickly gotten to her with a strong sedative, probably an intravenous one.

'I've got the personal info on Kelly Jensen from research,' Garcia said as he walked through the door, carrying a green plastic folder.

'What do we have?' Hunter asked looking up from his computer.

Garcia took a seat behind his desk and flipped open the folder. 'OK, Kelly Jensen, born in Great Falls, Montana, thirty years ago. Her parents haven't been notified yet.'

Hunter nodded.

Garcia continued. 'She started painting in high school . . . At the age of twenty, against her parents' wishes, she relocated here to Los Angeles . . . She spent several years struggling and being rejected by every agent and art gallery in the business . . . blah, blah, blah, your typical LA story, except she was a painter, not an actress.'

'How did she get noticed?' Hunter asked.

'She used to sell her work on the oceanfront – a street stall. Got noticed by none other than Julie Glenn, New York's top art critic. A week later, Kelly got an art agent, a guy called Lucas Laurent. He was the one who reported her as missing.' He paused and stretched his arms high above his head. 'Kelly's career took off quickly after that. Julie Glenn wrote a piece about her in the *New York Times*, and within a month, the canvases Kelly couldn't give away at the beach were selling for thousands.'

Hunter checked his watch before grabbing his jacket. 'OK, let's go.'

'Where?'

'To see the person who reported her missing.'

Fifty-One

The traffic was like a religious procession and it took Garcia almost two hours to cover the twenty-three miles between Parker Center and Long Beach.

Lucas Laurent, Kelly Jensen's agent, had his office on the fifth floor of number 246 East Broadway Street.

Laurent was in his thirties, with olive skin, dark brown eyes and neatly cut hair that was starting to gray. The wrinkles that already surrounded his lips came from heavy smoking, Hunter guessed. His navy blue suit was well fitting, but his tie was a masterpiece of bad taste. A Picasso-style monstrosity of chunky color pieces that only someone with enormous amounts of confidence could wear. And confidence Laurent certainly had – the quiet kind that came with wealth and success.

He stood up from behind his twin pedestal desk and greeted Hunter and Garcia by the door. His handshake was as firm as a businessman's ready to close a large deal.

'Joan told me you're detectives with the LAPD?' he said as he eyed Hunter. 'I hope you're not actually artists and this was just a trick to get you into my office without an appointment.' He smiled and deep crinkles appeared at the edges of his eyes. 'But if it was, it certainly shows you've both got creativity and ambition.'

'Unfortunately, we're the real thing,' Hunter said, showing Laurent his credentials. The agent's smile faded fast. Only then did he remember he'd reported Kelly as missing a couple of weeks ago.

Hunter told him only what he needed to know and watched as the color vanished from his face. Laurent slumped back in his chair, his eyes catatonically looking through Hunter.

'But that's just ludicrous ... murdered? By whom? And why? Kelly was an artist, not a drug dealer.'

'That's what we're trying to find out.'

'But she had an exhibition scheduled in Paris in less than two months' time ... it could have made us close to a million.'

Hunter and Garcia exchanged a quick, concerned glance. *Strange time to be thinking about money.*

Laurent ruffled inside his desk's top drawer for a pack of cigarettes. 'I don't usually smoke in my office,' he explained, 'but I really need this. Do you mind?'

Both detectives shrugged.

Laurent brought a cigarette to his lips, lit it up with a shaking hand and took a drag as if his life depended on it.

Hunter and Garcia sat in the two salmon-colored armchairs in front of Laurent's desk and began asking him about his relationship with Kelly and his knowledge of her personal life. From Laurent's answers, just like from his comment about making millions a moment ago, they quickly gathered that Laurent's relationship with Kelly had been 99 per cent business.

'Did you have a set of keys to her apartment?' Garcia asked.

'God, no.' Laurent had one last drag of his cigarette,

walked over to the window and stubbed it out on the ledge before flicking the butt onto the street below. 'Kelly didn't like having people in her apartment or her studio. She wouldn't even allow me to see any of her pieces until they were completely finished, and even then I almost had to beg her to show them to me. Artists are very self-centered and eccentric people.'

'Her apartment is in Santa Monica and her art studio in Culver City, is that right?' Garcia asked.

Laurent nodded nervously.

'Am I right in thinking you and Miss Jensen attended some social engagements together? Dinners ... receptions ... exhibitions ... awards, things like that?'

'Yes, quite a few over the three years I've been representing her.'

'Have you ever met anyone she was seeing? Has she ever taken a date to any of these engagements?'

'Kelly?' He laughed tensely. 'I couldn't think of anything that'd be farther from her thoughts than a relationship. She was stunning. She had men throwing themselves at her, but she just didn't wanna know.'

'Really?' Hunter said. 'Is there a reason why?'

Laurent shrugged. 'I never asked, but I know she was really hurt by someone she was in love with a few years ago. The kind of hurt that never goes away. The kind of hurt that makes you wary of every relationship you have from that day on. You know what I mean?'

'Do you know if she had casual relationships?' Garcia asked.

Another shrug. 'Probably, as I said, she was stunning; but I never met anyone she was dating. She never mentioned anyone either.'

'Did she ever mention anything about emails? Something that'd scared or upset her lately?' Hunter took over.

Laurent frowned, taking a few seconds to remember. 'Nothing in particular. I'm not sure about any of them being scary or upsetting, but I'm sure she got a few strange ones from infatuated fans. It happens more than you think. I just tell all my artists to disregard them.'

'Disregard them?'

'Fans come with fame, Detective; it's a package deal that you can't opt out of. And unfortunately some of them are just plain weird, but they usually mean no harm. All the artists I represent get them every now and then.' His eyes moved back to the pack of cigarettes on his desk and he quickly debated if he should have another one. He started fidgeting with a black-and-gold Mont Blanc pen instead. 'I've been Kelly's agent for three years, and in that time I've never seen her unhappy, or worried. She always had a smile on her face, as if it were tattooed to her lips. I really can't remember ever seeing Kelly unhappy.'

'When did you last speak to Miss Jensen?' Garcia asked.

'We were supposed to meet up for lunch on the . . .' he flipped open a leather-bound diary on his desk and quickly leafed through it, ' . . . the 25th February, to discuss Kelly's upcoming exhibition in Paris. Kelly had been very excited about that particular trip for months, but she never turned up for the meeting, and she never called to cancel either. When I tried getting hold of her, all I got was her answering service. Two days later I gave up trying and contacted the police.'

'Was she involved with drugs, gambling, anything of the bad sort you know of?' Garcia asked this time.

Laurent's eyes widened for an instant. 'God, no. At least

not that I know of. She barely drank. Kelly was your typical good girl.'

'Financial difficulties?'

'Not with the kinda money she was making. Every one of her paintings sells for thousands. Probably more now.'

Hunter wondered if he threw a hundred bucks out the window, would Laurent jump after it?

Before leaving, Hunter paused by the door to the office and turned to face Laurent again. 'Do you know if Miss Jensen was friends with another LA painter – Laura Mitchell?'

Laurent looked at him curiously before shaking his head. 'Laura Mitchell? I'm not sure. Their styles are very different.'

Hunter turned to look back at him curiously.

'Believe it or not,' Laurent clarified, 'many painters are funny in that way. Some won't mix with different style artists.' He pouted reflexively. 'Some won't mix with other artists at all. Why do you ask?'

'Just wondering.' Hunter handed Laurent a card. 'If you think of anything else, please don't—'

'Wait!' Laurent cut him short. 'Laura Mitchell and Kelly *did* meet. It was a few years ago. I'd forgotten all about that. Right at the start of Kelly's career. I had just started representing her. She was interviewed for a cable TV documentary. Something about the new wave of American artists from the West Coast, or something along those lines. Several artists took part in it. I think it was all filmed at the . . .' his eyes moved to a blank spot on the wall ' . . . Getty Museum or maybe at the Moca, I can't be sure. But I'm in no doubt Laura Mitchell was one of the artists who was there that day.'

Fifty-Two

Night had already darkened the sky by the time Hunter and Garcia got back to Parker Center. They both felt exhausted.

'Go home, Carlos,' Hunter said rubbing his eyes. 'Spend the night with Anna. Take her out for dinner or a movie or something. There ain't much we can do now but review information, and our brains are both too fried to process anything at this time.'

Garcia knew Hunter was right. And Anna would really appreciate having her husband for an entire night. He reached for his jacket.

'Aren't you coming?' he asked as Hunter turned his computer on.

'Five minutes,' Hunter replied with a nod. 'Just gonna check something on the net.'

It took Hunter a lot longer than he expected to find any references to the documentary Kelly Jensen's agent had mentioned. It was a low budget production by the Arts and Entertainment cable TV Channel called *Canvas Beauty, The Upcoming Talents from the West Coast*. It had only aired once, three years ago. He called the A & E TV network office in LA, but at that time of night, there was no one there who could assist him. He'd have to contact them again in the morning.

Hunter didn't go straight home after he left his office. His mind was too full of thoughts for him to try to brave the solitude of his apartment.

If the killer was really forcing his victims to kill themselves by impact-activating a trigger mechanism, then they were right about Laura Mitchell, the first victim. She wasn't supposed to have died on that butcher's counter. She was supposed to have jumped down from it. The bomb was supposed to have gone off inside her. But the trigger was never activated. She died from suffocation. Her mother had told Hunter about the choking seizures Laura used to suffer when young. Possibly some psychological condition that had ceased to manifest itself after she started painting. Hunter knew that such conditions could easily be shocked back to life by a traumatic experience, like severe panic. The kind of panic she would have experienced in that dark back room, alone, with her mouth and body stitched shut.

Hunter drove around aimlessly for a while before ending up at the oceanfront on Santa Monica Beach.

He liked watching the sea at night. The sound of waves breaking against the sand together with the quietness calmed him. It reminded him of his parents and of when he was a little kid.

His father used to work seventy-hour weeks, jumping between two awfully paid jobs. His mother would take any work that came her way – cleaning, ironing, washing, anything. Hunter couldn't remember a weekend when his father wasn't working, and even then they struggled to pay all their bills. But Hunter's parents never complained. They simply played the cards they were dealt. And no matter how bad a hand they got, they always did it with a smile on their faces.

Every Sunday, after Hunter's father got home from work, they used to go down to the beach. Most times they got there as everyone else was packing up and getting ready to leave. Sometimes the sun had already set. But Hunter didn't mind. In fact, he preferred it. It was like the whole beach belonged to him and his parents. After Hunter's mother passed away, his father never stopped taking him to the beach on Sundays. Sometimes, Hunter would catch his father wiping away tears as he watched the waves break.

There were tourists everywhere, especially down Third Street Promenade and in the many beach bars that lined the oceanfront. A boy sped past him in rollerblades, quickly followed by a younger girl, clearly struggling with her technique.

'Slow down, Tim,' she called after the boy pleadingly. He didn't even look back.

Hunter sat on the sand for a while, watching the waves and breathing in the sea breeze. He spotted a group of night surfers in the distance. Five in total, two of them female. They seemed to be having a great time. A boy was practicing his soccer juggling skills close to the water. He was good, Hunter had to admit. A couple holding hands walked past in silence and both nodded a cordial hello at Hunter, who returned the gesture. He watched them walk away, and for a moment he lost himself in a memory. Something few people ever knew about him – he'd been in love once, long ago.

Unconsciously his lips spread into a melancholic smile. As the memory developed, the smile faded and an empty pit took hold of his stomach. A lonely tear threatened to form at the corner of his eye. But the memory was interrupted by his cell phone ringing in his pocket. The display window read – unknown number.

'Detective Hunter.'

'*Wassup, dawg?*' D-King said in his chilled-out lilt. Loud hip-hop music was playing in the background.

'Not much,' Hunter replied.

D-King wasn't one for beating around the bush. 'Sorry, dawg, there's no word on the street, you know what I'm saying. The Chicanos, the Jamaicans, the Russians, the Chinese, the Italians, whoever ... no one knows anything about no girl getting a stitch job. She wasn't a gang hit, at least not a known gang.'

'Yeah, I figured that out since we last talked.'

'Did you find out who she was?'

'Yeah.'

D-King waited, but Hunter didn't follow up.

'Let me guess, she wasn't a working girl.'

'That's right.'

'I told you, dawg. I would've known if she was.' There was a hesitant pause. 'Listen, I gotta go, but I'll keep asking around. If I hear anything, I'll give you a holler.'

He disconnected, brushed his hands against each other, clearing off the sand before grabbing his jacket and walking back to his car. The throng of people around the bars was starting to die down, and for a moment Hunter considered going inside. He could do with a shot of single malt ... or five. Maybe *that* would completely clear his mind.

A woman sitting at one of the many outside tables laughed loudly, catching Hunter's attention. She was attractive with short brunette hair and a magnificent smile. Their eyes met for a brief instant and he remembered that Kelly Jensen's apartment was in Santa Monica. Her art studio wasn't far either. Culver City was practically the next neighborhood.

The file Hunter had got from Missing Persons said that the investigating officer had visited both locations without any major breakthroughs. The suspicion was that Kelly had been abducted from her home address as she parked her car and made her way into her apartment building. There were no witnesses and no CCTV camera footage.

Hunter checked his watch. He and Garcia had planned on checking out both places tomorrow, but what the hell. He was already there, and there was no way he'd be getting any sleep anytime soon.

Fifty-Three

Kelly Jensen's apartment was on the second floor of a luxurious building on the exclusive San Vicente Boulevard, a stone's throw away from the west end of Santa Monica Beach.

Hunter parked his car just outside her apartment block and observed the traffic for a while. Cars came and went every ten to fifteen seconds. As he got out and closed the door behind him, he recognized Kelly's car as described in the information sheet he'd received from Missing Persons – a candy white 1989 anniversary Pontiac Trans-Am T-top in pristine condition. It was parked just a few spaces from where he had pulled up. Hunter put on a pair of latex gloves before mechanically looking up at the surrounding buildings. There were several lights on. He approached Kelly's car and cupped his hands over the driver's window. Its interior looked to be spotlessly clean.

Hunter already had the keys to Kelly's apartment. They had been sent to Parker Center together with the MPU case files, and those were in the back seat of his car. He let himself into the building and made his way up to the second floor. After fumbling for the right key, he unlocked the door to Kelly's apartment, stepped inside and paused by the entrance for a moment before trying the light switch. Nothing.

'Great.' He flicked on his flashlight.

Her living room was spacious and nicely decorated. Hunter took his time looking around. The tidiness was almost compulsive, except for the dust that had accumulated since Kelly had gone missing. Every object seemed to have its place.

There were a few photo frames on a long glass sideboard against one of the walls – most of the photos were of her and her parents.

The kitchen was open plan, on the west side of the living room. No lights worked there either. Hunter opened the fridge and was immediately slapped across the face by a gust of warm, putrid air.

'Damn!' He jumped back, slamming the door shut. The power must've been off for a few days now. He exited the kitchen and moved further into the apartment.

The bedroom was enormous, probably bigger than Hunter's entire one-bedroom flat. In the en-suite bathroom he found a large collection of make-up items and several bottles of face, hand and body creams. Her bed was perfectly made. On her dresser Hunter found another portrait of her parents, some necklaces and bracelets, and a collection of fragrances. The drawers were overflowing with lingerie and summer clothes.

Hunter returned his attention to Kelly's parents' portrait. She looked a lot more like her mother than her father. Hunter couldn't help but think about the pain they were about to go through when the sheriff in Great Falls knocked on their door. It was the worst news any parent could ever receive. He'd been the bearer of such news more times than he cared to remember.

As he placed the frame back on the dresser, his flashlight beam reflected on the silver frame and his body tensed. The frame worked like a mirror, and he caught a glimpse of a dark figure standing right behind him.

Fifty-Four

Click.

Hunter heard the muffled sound of a semi-automatic pistol being cocked inches away from the back of his head. But before the person standing there had a chance to say or do anything, he spun on the balls of his feet and swung his arm around with purpose. The flashlight caught the intruder's pistol-holding arm with a loud thud.

Gun and flashlight flew across the room, smashing against the wardrobe door and falling to the floor. The flashlight ended up under the bed, facing the wall, its deflected beam now just strong enough to keep the room from slipping into total darkness.

Hunter's left hand was already at his shoulder holster. He'd managed to wrap his fingers around the handle of his gun when the intruder delivered a well-placed kick to his abdomen, catching Hunter right at the pit of his stomach. Air left him like a ripped balloon and he stumbled backwards, gasping for oxygen. Hunter knew another kick would quickly follow. This time it came in the form of a side sweep to the right side of his body, around the same height as the first one, but Hunter was ready for it. He blocked it with the outside of his forearm and unleashed a devastating blow with his left fist, catching the intruder square in the chest. Hunter used his momentum to step forward and sent in a follow-up punch to the face. It was blocked with martial-art precision. Hunter didn't miss a step, another left punch to the side of the torso – blocked. Right punch to the chest – blocked. Left elbow to the face – blocked.

What the fuck? Hunter thought. Can this guy see in the dark or what?

A new, higher and more powerful jump kick came from the intruder. Hunter saw it late, but even so, his rapid reaction allowed him to swerve most of his head out of the way. The tip of the intruder's boot grazed Hunter's right eyebrow, nicking it. Hunter used his swerving motion to gain speed and pirouetted his body around three hundred and sixty degrees. The movement took only a split second, and at the end of it Hunter delivered a new punch with his left fist straight to the intruder's ribcage. But some last-minute intuition told him to take some of the power off the strike. Even so, this time there was no blocking. The intruder doubled over and stumbled back. In a blink of an eye Hunter reversed his movement, spinning his body in the opposite direction. As he faced his attacker again, he was holding his gun with his right arm fully extended. The barrel of his weapon just inches away from his attacker's face.

'Move and you'll be having dinner with Elvis.'

'Fuck, that was a fast draw.'

Hunter frowned. It was a woman's voice.

'Who the fuck are you?' she asked.

'Me?' Hunter cocked his gun. 'Who the fuck are you?'

'I asked first.'

'Well, I have a gun.'

'Yeah? So did I.'

'Well, guess what? I still have mine, and it's pointing right at your face.'

A split-second pause.

'OK, point taken.' She lifted her hands but didn't say a word.

'I'll ask again, in case you forgot – who the hell are you?'

'My name is Whitney Myers.' Her voice was calm.

Hunter waited but Myers offered nothing else. 'And . . . ? Is your name supposed to mean anything to me . . . ?'

'I'm a private missing persons investigator. If you allow me to move I can show you my credentials.'

'Your hands are going nowhere for now, buttercup.'

He looked at her suspiciously. Even through the weak light coming from under the bed, Hunter could tell Myers was wearing dark trousers and shirt, flat-soled shoes, a small pouch belt around her waist and a black skullcap.

'You dress more like a burglar than a PI.'

'Well, you don't dress like a cop either,' she stabbed back.

'How do you know I'm a cop?'

She tilted her head in the direction of the wardrobe. 'Standard issue LAPD flashlight.' A short pause. 'Unlike your gun. Nothing standard about that. HK USP tactical pistol. A Navy Seals favorite. You're obviously part of some special section, or a pretty big gun fanatic. I'm guessing both.'

Hunter's gun was still aimed dead at her eyes. 'If you knew I was a cop, why the hell did you attack me like that?'

'You never gave me a chance to say a word. I was about to politely ask you to turn around slowly when suddenly you turned into Captain America on crack. I was just defending myself.'

Hunter considered it. 'If you're a PI, who hired you?'

'You know I can't tell you that. It's privileged information.'

Hunter's gaze moved to his gun and then back to Myers. 'Under the circumstances, I don't think you've got much of a choice.'

'You and I both know you're not gonna shoot me.'

Hunter chuckled. 'I wouldn't be so confident if I were you. All I need is a reason.'

Myers didn't reply.

'Plus I can arrest you for breaking and entering. You know how it goes. You'll have to drag a lawyer down to the station, then you'll be properly interrogated . . . yada, yada, yada . . . and we'll find out anyway. So you'd better tell me something, or this is about to become a *very* long night for you.' Hunter could feel thin lines of blood running down the right side of his face from the cut just above his eyebrow. He stood perfectly still.

Myers fixed Hunter down with a solid stare. She could see the resolve in his eyes. He wasn't about to let her go easy. But Myers also wasn't about to tell Hunter the truth about Katia and Leonid Kudrov. She wasn't prepared to tell him her secrets, or that – out of habit and as a way of keeping her updated with who her potential clients could be – Myers was sent a daily list of names, including photographs, of new additions to the Missing Persons Unit database. The list was compiled and filtered by her LAPD informer, Carl O'Connor.

O'Connor wasn't a detective with the MPU. Pure and simple, he was a computer geek, an old friend, and the database administrator for the Valley Bureau of the LAPD. His unlimited access to essential information where missing persons were concerned had given Myers the advantage she needed in many cases. When she received Kelly

Jensen's photograph, Myers immediately saw the resemblance to Katia Kudrov, and that was why she was at Kelly Jensen's apartment in that specific moment. She was looking for clues.

There was no way she was telling Hunter all that. But Myers knew she had to tell him something. She improvised as fast as she could.

'OK. The person I'm working for is an ex-boyfriend,' she lied with the steadiest of faces.

Hunter frowned. 'Name?'

Myers smiled. 'You know I can't give you his name. Not without his consent or a court order. You have neither.'

'And he went to you instead of the Missing Persons Unit?'

'What can I say? Some people just don't trust the LAPD.' Myers relaxed her right arm.

'Hey, hey, hey,' Hunter called with a lilt in his voice. 'Easy there, pumpkin. What are you doing?'

She brought her hand to the side of her body, rubbing it while taking a deep breath. 'I think you've broken a couple of my ribs.'

Hunter didn't move. 'No I haven't. And at least you're not bleeding.'

Myers glanced at the cut above Hunter's eyebrow. 'I've never seen anyone move that fast. I had you right in my sights. You were supposed to be knocked out cold.'

'Lucky for me I got out of the way, then,' Hunter said, gently stretching his neck. 'How did you get in here? There were no signs of forced entry.'

Myers gave Hunter a charming smile. This was getting complicated. She stood her ground.

'I'm doing all the talking here, and you still haven't told me your name or shown me any police ID yet. Hell, I'm not even sure for a fact that you *are* LAPD. I know you're not MPU. So who are you?'

'How do you know I'm not with the Missing Persons Unit?'

Her face went dead serious. ''Cause I used to be part of them.'

Fifty-Five

Hunter kept his gaze on Myers for several seconds. She held his stare with identical determination.

'OK,' Hunter finally said, 'let's see that PI license you were talking about. But very slowly.'

'Let's see that police badge you were talking about,' Myers challenged.

Hunter pulled open the left side of his leather jacket. His badge was clipped onto his belt.

Myers acknowledged it with a nod, unzipped her pouch belt and handed Hunter a black leather wallet.

He scrutinized her identity card before returning his attention to Myers. Dark eyes, small nose, high cheekbones, full lips, perfect skin, and an athlete's body.

Hunter finally holstered his weapon before picking up his flashlight together with Myers' gun – a Sig Sauer P226 X-5 semi-auto pistol.

'Being a PI must pay well,' he said, releasing the magazine and checking for a chambered round before handing the empty pistol back to Myers. 'This is a two and a half grand gun.' He slipped the magazine into his pocket.

'Why? Are you looking for a new job? I could certainly use a guy like you. Good benefits and health insurance.'

Hunter took a paper tissue from a dispenser on the

dresser and cleared some of the blood from his face. 'Yeah? Well, I couldn't use a boss like you.'

Myers smiled. 'Oh, you're quick with the comebacks too? I guess the chicks dig that.'

Hunter ignored her comment.

'Are you gonna tell me who you are now, or shall I just call you Mr. Detective?' she asked, folding her arms.

'My name is Robert Hunter.' He handed her wallet back to her. 'I'm a detective with the LAPD.'

'Which section?' She nodded at his badge. 'As I said, I know you're not Missing Persons.'

Hunter placed the flashlight on the dresser. 'Homicide Special.'

Myers eyes widened. She knew exactly what that meant. For a beat she seemed lost for words. 'When?' she asked.

'When what?'

'Don't play dumb. You don't look the type, and I'm through fucking around. Do you know when Jensen died?'

Hunter studied Myers' face and saw a hint of desperation there. He mechanically checked his watch before conceding. 'Yesterday.'

'Was her body found yesterday or did she die yesterday?'

'Both. She'd been dead for only a few hours when we found her.'

'Whoever took her kept her for almost three weeks before killing her?'

Hunter didn't reply. He didn't need to. Myers knew exactly the implications of such an act by a kidnapper/murderer.

'How was she murdered?' she asked.

Silence.

'Oh c'mon, I'm not asking for any major investigation secrets. I know the protocol and I know what you can and cannot disclose. If not from you, how long do you think it'll take me to find that information out? A couple of phone calls, maybe. I've still got contacts and connections in the force.'

Hunter still said nothing.

'Fine. I'll find out my way then.'

'The killer used a knife.'

Myers ran the tips of her fingers against her upper lip.

'How many victims?'

Hunter looked back at her curiously.

She continued. 'How many victims have you got so far? If you're Homicide Special it means this guy has either killed before or Kelly Jensen was killed in a particularly horrific way . . . or both. And if I had to take a guess I'd say both.'

Hunter remained silent.

'You're looking for a serial killer, aren't you?'

'For someone who used to be a cop, you sure jump to conclusions very quickly.'

Myers' eyes moved away from Hunter.

'OK, it's your turn to share,' he said. 'Who's this ex-boyfriend you're working for?'

Myers didn't want to embroil herself further in her lie. 'You want information from me now?' Her eyebrows arched.

'Are we back playing games again, sweetheart?' Hunter challenged. 'I thought you said you were through fucking around.'

Myers glared at him again.

'Kelly Jensen is dead. Murdered in a way your nightmares

couldn't produce. Your Missing Persons case is over. That's all you need to know.'

'Client/investigator confidentiality privileges don't end once the case is over. You know that.'

'The ex-boyfriend could be a suspect.'

A second of hesitation.

'He isn't,' Myers said confidently. 'Or do you think I didn't have him thoroughly checked out before taking the case. And you said that Kelly was killed yesterday. He's been out of the country for five days.'

'If you're so sure of his innocence, why not give me his name and let me check him out too.'

A long, uncomfortable moment played out between them before Myers put out her right arm, the palm of her hand facing up. Her eyes staring straight into Hunter's. 'Can I have my ammunitions clip back?'

Hunter knew she was asking for a trust gesture. A give in order to receive kind of thing. He slowly retrieved the magazine from his pocket and placed it in her hand. Myers didn't load it into her gun. Instead, she just stared at it for a long moment. Her lie was snowballing into something she knew she wouldn't be able to control. She needed to get out of there before she made a mistake.

'You know I can't give you his name. If I do I'll never get another client again. But I can hand you everything I have on the case. Maybe you can find something there.'

Hunter saw her right eye twitch ever so slightly.

Myers looked down and checked her watch. 'Give me a few hours to gather everything together and you can have whatever I have.'

Hunter continued to observe her.

'I know where to find you.'

Hunter watched Myers leave the room before reaching into his pocket. He looked down at the Private Investigator's ID he'd slipped out of her leather wallet.

'And I know where to find you,' he whispered to himself.

Fifty-Six

Kelly Jensen's art studio was a refurbished mechanic's garage behind a row of shops in Culver City. The street was narrow and hidden away from the main roads, at the top of a small hill. To the right of her studio was a small parking lot, where all the shop owners kept their vehicles during the day. At that time at night it was completely empty. The only light came from a lamppost on the corner, its bulb old and yellowing. Hunter looked around for security cameras. Nothing.

The studio was spacious and well organized. There were shelves and drawers for every different paint color, type of brush, palette, and canvas sizes. All finished paintings were placed on a large wooden rack that occupied the entirety of the north wall. There was only one canvas stand, positioned just a few feet from the large window that faced west. Kelly liked watching the sunset while working, Hunter guessed. A paint-splattered cloth covered the painting on the stand. Unlike Laura Mitchell, Kelly seemed to only work on one canvas at a time.

Hunter lifted the stained cloth and checked the painting underneath it. Dark, shadowy skies against a placid lake that surrounded the ruins of an old building on top of a steep sloping hill. Hunter stepped back to get a better view.

Kelly was a realist painter, and the effect she achieved

with that particular canvas was so vivid it was like standing at the shore, looking out into the horizon. But she'd done something Hunter had never seen before. It was as though the whole scenery was seen through a smoky glass. Everything had a sad, gray tint to it, as if the weather was about to close in on you with a vengeance. The painting looked so real it made Hunter feel cold. He pulled the collar of his jacket tighter against his neck.

Kelly's ample working space was uncluttered. The only furniture around the place were the shelves and drawer units against the walls, the storing rack, and an old, beat-up armchair several feet away from the window, facing the canvas stand. There were no six-foot canvases, partitions, or anything else for that matter. No place for anyone to hide behind. There was an improvised kitchen area in one corner, and a small bathroom in the opposite one. Hunter checked everywhere. There was no way the killer could've waited and then sneaked up on Kelly in there without her noticing it.

Hunter walked back up to the window and stared out into the night. Because her studio was at the top of a hill, the view was unobstructed and quite astonishing. No wonder Kelly used to paint facing that view. He checked the locks. All quite new and very secure. The small parking lot was to the far left, but only part of it was visible from the window.

Suddenly, just a couple of feet from where he was, something moved outside the window with incredible agility.

'Shit!' Hunter jumped back, his hand going for his gun.

The black cat ran the length of the window ledge in just a split second. Hunter stood motionless, both arms extended, his grip tight around his pistol handle, his pulse racing.

'Goddamn it! Not twice in one night,' he finally breathed out. How could he not have noticed the cat? He moved closer and looked again. The lack of any light outside made the window work almost as a two-way mirror. At night, a person dressed all in black could have observed Kelly without being noticed. Hunter unlocked the window, pushed it open and welcomed the cool breeze that kissed his face. He leaned forward and looked out, first right then left, in the direction of the parking lot. That's when he noticed something at the far wall blink at him.

Fifty-Seven

The shrieking scream that came from her TV made Jessica Black wake with a start. She'd fallen asleep on the sofa and hadn't even noticed the old, black-and-white B-movie horror film that had started.

She rubbed her gritty eyes, pulled herself up into a sitting position, and looked around her living room for Mark, her boyfriend. He was nowhere to be seen.

The woman on the screen screamed again and Jessica groggily reached for the remote control that had fallen between her legs, and switched the set off. The scented candle she'd lit earlier had burned halfway through, and the entire room now carried the sweet smell of apples and cinnamon. Jessica watched the flame burn for a minute. Her Wechter acoustic guitar was resting by the side of the sofa next to her. Still watching the flame, she ran her hand across the strings and allowed her memories to catch up with her.

Jessica had got her first acoustic guitar on her tenth birthday. Her father had bought it for her as a present in a garage sale. It was an old and scratched plank of wood with rusty strings that sounded more like a dying dog than a musical instrument. But even at that age, Jessica understood her father had spent money he couldn't afford just to make her happy. And happy she was.

Her fascination with the instrument had started two years earlier. Just like every afternoon before she had gotten sick, her mother had taken Jessica to the park close to where they lived. That day there was an old black man playing guitar just yards away from the bench her mother liked to sit on. That day, instead of running around with the other kids, Jessica sat on the grass in front of the old man and watched him play all afternoon, mesmerized by the sounds he could get out of only six strings.

The old man never returned to the park, but Jessica never forgot him. A week later her mother fell ill with something no one could diagnose. Her disease advanced quickly, eating away at her from the inside and transforming her from a smiling, vital woman into an unrecognizable bag of skin and bones. Jessica's father faded along with his wife. As the disease progressed, so did his depression. His pay as a supermarket clerk was barely enough to keep them going, and when he lost his job two months after his wife had gotten ill, their financial situation collapsed.

Jessica's mother died the day after doctors finally found out she had developed a rare carcinoid tumor.

Jessica's last happy memory of her mother was that day in the park, both of them listening to the old guitar man.

Jessica took to the guitar as if that memory lived in every note she plucked. She had no money for lessons, magazines or music books, but she spent every possible second with her beloved instrument. Soon she'd developed her own unique style of tapping and fingerpicking the strings, exploring every sound the instrument could give her. She could play the guitar like no one had ever heard. At the age of nineteen she was offered a record deal by a small independent record company based in South Los Angeles. Through them she'd released six albums and done countless tours over the years. Jessica became well known and well respected in the jazz music scene, but her music wasn't mainstream enough to be played by the most popular radio stations.

Three years ago, the manager of her record company decided to go back to basics and record a few videos of Jessica playing by herself before uploading them onto YouTube. He was betting on her beauty as well as her talent.

Jessica was stunning in a simple way. Five foot six with a dancer's lithe body, straight shoulder-length black hair, magnetic dark brown eyes, full lips and flawless skin. She attracted looks anywhere she went.

The gamble paid off, but even he hadn't expected it to take off as it did. Through word of mouth and social networking, Jessica's YouTube videos went stratospheric. Over one million worldwide hits in the first month alone, placing her name on YouTube's front page as the most watched clip. Today, as many of Jessica's albums were sold and downloaded as those of mainstream, world-famous pop bands.

Jessica's attention returned to her living room. A single, empty dinner plate and a half-drunk bottle of red wine sat on the small glass table in front of her. Seeing that made her remember that she'd eaten alone, and reality finally caught up with her. Mark wasn't in. And he wouldn't be coming back anytime soon.

Jessica and Mark had met at the Catalina Jazz Club on Sunset Boulevard two years ago, after one of her gigs. That night she had been sitting at the bar, surrounded by fans and a few music reporters when she'd noticed someone hanging out by the stage. He was tall, with broad shoulders and a strong physique. His long midnight-black hair was tied back Viking-style. But his good looks weren't what caught Jessica's attention. It was the intriguing way he was studying her guitar.

She'd excused herself from the crowd and approached him, wondering what was so interesting about her instrument. They'd chatted for a while and she found out that Mark was also a guitarist. He'd been classically trained, but instead of following that route he'd formed his own hard rock band. They were called Dust, and they'd just signed their first record deal a few days before.

The chat turned into dinner somewhere along Sunset Strip. Mark was funny, intelligent and charming. Several more dates followed and eight months later they'd rented a large warehouse loft conversion in Burbank together.

With the help of the Internet and the music video channels, Dust's first album became a worldwide sensation. Their second had just been mixed down and it was scheduled for release in a month's time. Their grueling touring schedule was about to begin again. As a pre-tour warm-up they were doing a series of eight secret gigs in smaller venues all around California. The first one was tonight in Fortuna. Mark and the band had left that morning.

Jessica crossed her legs under her and checked her watch – 1:18 a.m. She'd fallen asleep in an awkward position and the left side of her neck had gone stiff. She sat there for a while longer, nursing the pain and dreading the loneliness of her bed. But spending the night in the living room would probably make her miss him even more. She had one last sip of her wine and blew out the scented candle before heading to bed.

Jessica wasn't the best of sleepers, and sometimes she would toss and turn for a long while before finally falling into a light sleep. Tonight though, with the help of the wine, she started dozing almost immediately.

Click, click.

She blinked a few times before opening her eyes. Had she really heard something or was that her mind playing tricks on her? The bedroom curtains weren't drawn, and the full moon just outside her window was enough to keep total darkness out. Jessica allowed her eyes to roam the room slowly – nothing. She lay still, listening attentively but the sound didn't repeat itself. A minute later she started drifting back into sleep.

Click, click.

Her eyes shot open this time. There was no doubt in her mind. She'd heard something. And it was coming from inside her apartment. Jessica sat up in bed and brushed her fingers against the touch lamp on her bedside table. Her eyes narrowed slightly. Had she left a tap on somewhere? But if that was it, why wasn't the sound constant?

Click, click.

She held her breath and her pulse surged in her neck. There it was again. It was coming from just outside her bedroom door. It sounded like a shoe heel lightly clicking against the corridor's wooden floor.

'Mark?' she called and instantly felt silly for doing so. He wouldn't be back for several weeks.

Jessica hesitated for an instant, debating what to do. But what else could she do? Stay in bed worrying for the whole night? It was probably nothing but she had to go check it out. Slowly, she slid out of bed. She was wearing nothing but a tiny pair of shorts and the thinnest of sleeveless shirts.

She stepped outside her room and switched on the hallway lights. Nothing. She waited a moment. No sound. She grabbed Mark's old baseball bat from the storage closet before proceeding cautiously down the corridor. An uncomfortable shiver ran through her as her bare feet touched the cold tiles of the bathroom floor. All the faucets were securely off. There were no drips. She walked back and checked the living room, the kitchen, Mark's games room and her practice den. The entire apartment was absolutely still, except for the tick-tock that came from the clock in the kitchen. She rechecked the windows – all closed – doors – all locked.

Jessica shook her head and chuckled as her eyes focused on the baseball bat in her hands.

'Yeah, I'm a real home-run hitter, me.' She paused. 'But just in case, I'm keeping you by the bed.'

Back in her room, Jessica looked around one more time before resting the baseball bat against her bedside table and getting back into bed. She switched off the lamp and snuggled under the covers once again. As her eyes closed, every hair on her body stood on end. Some hidden instinct inside her exploded into life. Some sort of danger sensor. And the only thing she could sense was that she wasn't alone in that room. Someone else was there with her. That's when she heard it. Not a clicking sound coming from outside, but a hoarse whispering voice coming from the only place she didn't check.

'You forgot to look under your bed.'

Fifty-Eight

Hunter had spent the rest of the night on the computer discovering who Whitney Myers really was.

In the morning, after a strong cup of black coffee, he made his way back to Culver City and Kelly Jensen's studio. The blinking red light he'd seen last night from her window was a wireless CCTV camera, hidden away in an alcove in the wall. The camera was pointing straight at the small parking lot. There were no computers in Kelly's studio, so the camera couldn't have belonged to her.

At 6:00 a.m. only one of the shops that shared the car parking lot with Kelly's studio was open – Mr. Wang's convenience store. Hunter's luck was in; the wireless camera belonged to the elderly bird-like Chinese man.

Mr. Wang's wrinkled face and observant eyes only hinted at how much he'd lived, what he'd seen and the tremendous knowledge he'd accumulated over so many years.

He told Hunter that he'd asked his son, Fang Li, to install the camera at the back after his old Ford pickup truck was broken into one too many times.

Hunter asked him how far back he kept the recordings.

'Year,' Mr. Wang replied with a wide smile that seemed to never fade.

Hunter's face lit up in surprise. 'You have recordings going back a year?'

'Yes. Every minute.' His voice was like a whisper, but the words came out quickly, as if he was about to run out of time for what he wanted to say. His pronunciation was perfect, indicating that he'd been in America for many years, but the sentences were staccato. 'Fang Li too smart. Good with computers. He make program that box files. Twelve months – files delete automatic. Don't need do nothing.'

Hunter bobbed his head. 'Clever. Can I have a look at them?'

Mr. Wang's eyes narrowed to such a thin line, Hunter thought he'd closed them. 'You wanna see in store's computer?'

A quick nod. 'Yes. I'd like to see the footage from a few weeks ago.'

Mr. Wang bowed and his smile spread even wider. 'OK, no problem, but me no good. Need talk to Fang Li. He not here. I call.' Mr. Wang reached for the phone behind the counter. He spoke Mandarin. The conversation didn't last longer than a few seconds. 'Fang Li coming,' he said, putting the phone down. 'Be here very fast. Not live far.' He consulted his watch. 'Not go to work yet. Too early.'

Hunter asked Mr. Wang about Kelly Jensen. He said that she came into the shop almost every day when she was around, but sometimes she'd disappear for weeks. He liked Kelly very much. He said she was very polite, always happy and very beautiful.

'In my country, whole village be asking her to marry.'

Hunter smiled and looked around the shop while he waited. He bought a cup of microwavable coffee and a packet of teriyaki-flavored beef jerky. A few minutes later Fang Li arrived. He was in his late twenties, with longish black hair that shined like in a shampoo commercial. His features were striking, a replica of what his father must have looked like when he was younger, but much taller and well built. He quickly spoke to his father before turning and offering his hand to Hunter.

'I'm Fang Li, but everybody calls me Li.'

Hunter introduced himself and told him the purpose of his visit.

'OK, come with me and I'll show you.' Li guided Hunter through a back door that led into a large, well-organized storage room. The entire place carried a sweet and pleasant smell, a combination of exotic spices, condiments, soaps, fruit and unburned incense. At the far end of it, up a set of wooden stairs was the shop's office. Hundreds of Chinese calendars hung from the walls – Hunter had never seen so many. It was like they used them as wallpaper. Apart from the calendars there were several old, metal filing cabinets, a wooden shelf rack, a water cooler and a large desk with a computer monitor on it. Chinese characters danced across the screen.

Li chuckled as he read them.

'What does that mean?' Hunter asked.

'Be yourself. There's no one better suited for the job.'

Hunter smiled. 'Very true.'

'My father likes this kinda thing. Proverbs and all, you know. But he prefers to create his own, so I programed a little screen saver for him. It reads from a list of his own wise sayings.'

'So is that what you do? Computer programing?'

'Pretty much.'

'Your father said that you could store as much as a whole year's worth of footage.'

'That's right. My father's pretty much obsessed with organization.' He pointed out the window at the storage room. 'Nothing's ever out of place with him.'

Hunter nodded.

'He's also big on security. We've got five cameras filming twenty-four hours a day. One picking up the front door, one facing the parking lot out back, and three inside the shop. There's no way we could archive that much data without having a ridiculous amount of hard drive space or compressing the hell out of the footage. So I created a small program that automatically compresses the files that are over three days old and then archives them into external high-capacity hard drives.' Li rolled his chair back and pointed at four small black boxes under the desk. 'At the end of twelve months, those files auto-delete to create more space.' He paused and faced Hunter. 'So what do you need, Detective?'

Hunter wrote something down on a piece of paper and placed it on the desk in front of Li. 'I need a copy of all the footage you have between those dates.'

Li looked at the paper. 'An entire week's worth? From all five cameras?'

'Maybe, but let's start with the footage from the one in the parking lot.'

Li coughed. 'That's one hundred and sixty-eight hours of footage. Even compressed that'll take . . .' his eyes narrowed and his lips moved without a sound for a second, '. . . around thirty DVDs. Maybe a few more. When do you need them for?'

'Yesterday.'

Li's face paled. He checked his watch. 'Even if I had a

professional multi-DVD copier, which I don't, it'd still take most of the day.'

Hunter thought about it for a beat. 'Wait a second. You said that older files are stored in those external hard drives, right?' He pointed at the black boxes. 'Will the files from those dates be in one of them?'

Li quickly picked up on what Hunter was suggesting and his lips spread into a smile. 'They will be, yes. Very good idea. You could take the whole hard drive. There's nothing in them but archived CCTV footage. Nothing that my father would need, anyway. You can link the drive to any computer, easy. It will save you tons of time, but you'll still have to uncompress the files on your side.'

'We can do that.'

Li nodded. 'Let me show you how to find them.'

Fifty-Nine

Hunter made it back to Parker Center in less than half an hour and went straight into the Information Technology Division. Brian Doyle was at his desk, speed-reading through a pile of papers. He was wearing the same clothes as yesterday. His eyes were bloodshot and his face unshaven. An empty pizza box was by the edge of the desk and the coffee percolator in the corner was practically empty.

'Have you been here all night?' Hunter asked.

Doyle looked up but said nothing. His stare went straight through Hunter.

'Are you OK?'

Doyle's eyes finally focused. 'Umm? Yeah, sorry, I'm fine.' He placed the sheet he was reading on the desk. 'Just under-staffed and overworked. Everyone always needs everything ASAP. I've got cases piling up everywhere. And this after-noon there's this huge sting operation going on.' He leaned back in his chair and studied Hunter for a second. 'What the hell happened to your face?' He pointed at the cut above his eyebrow.

Hunter shook his head. 'Walked into a door.'

'Of course you did. Just hope the door isn't gonna sue the department.'

'She won't.'

'*She*? A *woman* did that to you?'

'Long story.'

'I bet.' He cleared a space at the edge of his desk and leaned against it. 'OK, Robert, for you to be here, it's gotta be something urgent.'

Hunter nodded. 'But I only need about three minutes of your time, Jack. Then I'm out of here.'

'Is this about the psycho who killed Doctor Winston with that bomb?'

An almost imperceptible nod. Hunter felt his chest tighten around his heart as he remembered he'd never see his old friend again.

'He was a good man. I met him a couple of times.' Doyle checked his watch. 'What do you need?'

Hunter handed him the high-capacity hard drive and waited while Doyle hooked it up to his PC. Unsurprisingly, all the directories in the hard drive were perfectly organized – first by camera location and then by date.

'Can these files be uncompressed in bulk?' Hunter asked.

'Not simultaneously. They're massive. It'd be too processor intensive and it'd crash any machine, but . . .' Doyle lifted his index finger, 'you could line them up inside an application. As soon as one file finishes uncompressing, it'll automatically move to the next one in the list. That way you don't even have to be there. Just leave it working and come back when it's all done.'

'That'll work for me.'

Doyle smiled. 'Please tell me you don't need all of these files. There're hundreds of them. This will take days.'

'No.' Hunter shook his head. 'Just a handful of them – to start with.'

'OK, in that case I'll tell you the easiest thing to do.

Because this is an external drive, I can link it up to an empty laptop instead of clogging up the machine in your office. That way you can work on your machine if you need to and just leave the laptop on the side, as it does its thing. Give me five minutes and I'll have it all set up for you.'

Sixty

The phone on Hunter's desk rang almost the second he entered his office. It was Doctor Hove.

'Robert, I'm about to send you some lab results on Jensen. I got my team to fast-track whatever they could.'

'Thanks, Doc. What do we have?' He gestured for Garcia, who'd just come in, to grab his phone and listen in.

'OK, as we expected, the victim was sedated. We found traces of a drug called Estazolam in her blood. It's a sleeping agent.'

'Usually prescribed for short-term treatment of insomnia, right?' Hunter confirmed.

Doctor Hove had forgotten that Hunter knew more about insomnia than most doctors.

'That's right. Now, given its relatively high concentration, we figured that's what the killer used to sedate her on the day she died. Before dumping her in that basement. He didn't overdo it, though. He used just enough to knock her out for a couple of hours or so.'

Hunter leaned back in his chair.

'But the interesting thing is: we also found faint traces of another drug. Something called Mexitil. It's an anti-arrhythmic drug.'

'Anti- what?' Garcia blurted.

'A common drug used to treat a heart condition called ventricular arrhythmia.'

Hunter started leafing through sheets of paper on his desk.

'If you're looking for her medical records, Robert, don't bother,' the doctor said, recognizing the sound of pages turning. 'Her heart was as strong as a racing horse's. She didn't have the condition.'

Hunter stopped and thought for a split second. 'What are the side effects of this Mexitil, Doc?'

'Very good, Robert. Mexitil is pharmacologically similar to Lidocaine, which as you know is a local anesthetic. Its major side effect is light drowsiness and confusion. But if taken by someone who doesn't suffer from ventricular arrhythmia, that light drowsiness can become moderate to severe. And you don't even need high doses of the drug to cause it. But that's about all it does. It won't knock you out. It won't even make you doze off.'

Hunter considered it. It made sense. That was probably why neither of the victims had any restraint marks. If the killer kept them in a constant state of confusion and drowsiness, he didn't need to immobilize them.

'Would there be any other reason why the killer chose to use Mexitil?' Hunter asked. 'If he just wanted them high, he could've used a number of drugs.'

'It's an easy drug to obtain on the Internet.'

'So are most drugs nowadays, Doc,' Garcia countered.

'True.' There was a short pause. 'There's always the chance that he's familiar with the drug. He might suffer from the condition himself.'

Hunter was already clicking away on his computer, searching the Internet for more information about the drug.

'Could you check your database, Doc? Go back five . . . no, ten years. Look for any case where Mexitil was found in a murder victim's blood?'

'No problem.' This time the sound of pages turning came from Doctor Hove's side. 'I've also got a result on the dark copper-colored dust retrieved from under the victim's fingernails. It's brick dust.'

Hunter's eyebrows arched.

'We might be able to identify exactly what kind of brick it is. I'll let you know if we can.' The doctor coughed to clear her throat. 'At first I thought that maybe she tried to claw her way out of wherever she was kept. Somewhere with a brick wall. But as you well know, if that had been the case, she'd certainly have cracked and broken nails . . . maybe even missing ones. None were even chipped. They were filed down into claws, remember? Maybe the killer has a bizarre fetish for pointy fingernails.'

Hunter's eyes quickly moved from his computer to the pictures board. 'Nothing else was found under her nails?'

'Yes, bits of her own skin,' the doctor confirmed. 'She scraped at her mouth, her groin and the stitches before dying.'

'Only *her* skin?'

'That's right.'

Hunter nodded to himself. 'OK, Doc. Call me if anything else comes up.' He put the phone down and stared at his own fingernails for a moment. 'A weapon,' he whispered.

'A what?' Garcia asked, rolling his chair away from his desk.

'A weapon. That's why her fingernails were so claw-like.' Hunter stood up and approached the pictures board. 'Look at the crime-scene pictures of our first victim.' He pointed to the ones of Laura Mitchell's hands. There was nothing strange about her fingernails.

'No filing,' Garcia agreed.

'Having pointy fingernails didn't come from the killer, as the doctor suggested. Kelly used a brick wall to sharpen them herself. I think she wanted to attack her captor. In an empty cell, it was the only weapon she could think of.'

Garcia pinched his bottom lip. 'But nothing else was found under her nails except brick dust and her own skin. So she never got the chance to use them.'

'That's right.' Hunter had returned to his desk and was flipping through his notebook. 'The doctor said that Kelly's organs showed mild symptoms of dehydration and malnutrition, right? I think she starved herself.'

Garcia frowned.

'Mexitil. Kelly had no needle marks on her, remember?'

'He was feeding it to her through her food.'

Hunter leaned against his desk. 'Most probably, and she figured out the food was drugged.'

'So she stopped eating to get rid of the dizziness.' Garcia picked up Hunter's train of thought. 'But wouldn't that make her too weak to fight back?'

'It would if she'd gone without food for a few days, but that wasn't the case.'

'One day only. That's what Doctor Hove said, right?'

Hunter nodded. 'Mexitil isn't a proper sedative. Kelly would've only needed to be off it for a few hours.'

'Enough to get rid of the dizziness, but not enough to take all of her strength away. But how would she know that?'

'She didn't. She gambled.'

'So she filed her nails into the only weapon she could think of.' Garcia ran a hand through his hair while exhaling. 'She wanted out of there. She was trying to do something herself because she knew she was running out of time, and she'd run out of hope. She got tired of waiting for us to save her.'

Hunter's cell phone started ringing.

'Detective Hunter,' he said, bringing the clamshell phone to his ear.

'Detective, this is Tracy from the Special Operations switchboard. I'm managing the information line on the suspect you're looking for, James Smith.'

'Yes?'

'I've got someone on the line who claims to be him.'

Hunter pulled a face. 'Yeah, well, we've had about fifty of those so far. Just take his—'

'Detective,' Tracy interrupted, 'I think you should take this call.'

Sixty-One

Hunter snapped his fingers at his partner to get his attention. He didn't have to; Garcia had already noticed the change in Hunter's expression.

'Start a trace?' Hunter said to Tracy.

'We're all set here, Detective.'

Hunter nodded to himself. 'OK, put him through.'

There was a click on the line followed by a second of static.

Hunter waited.

So did the person on the other end of the line.

'This is Detective Robert Hunter.' Hunter eventually broke the silence. He was in no mood for games.

'Why are you after me?' The sentence was delivered in a calm, unrushed tone. The voice was like a muffled whisper, as if his phone's mouthpiece had been wrapped in several layers of cloth.

'James Smith?'

There was a short pause. 'Why are you after me?' he repeated in the same cool tone.

'You know why we're after you.' Hunter's calm voice matched Smith's. 'That's why you ran, isn't it?'

'The newspapers all across town have my picture in them. They say the police want to speak to me in relation to an ongoing investigation, but no other details are given. So I want you to tell me: why are you after me? How am I related to any ongoing investigation?'

'Why don't you come in, James? We can sit down and talk. I'll tell you anything you wanna know.'

A bitter chuckle. 'I'm afraid I can't do that just now, Detective.'

'Right now that's your best option. What else can you do? You can't run or hide forever. As you said, your photograph is all over the papers. And it's going to stay there. Sooner or later someone will recognize you – on the streets, in a shop, driving around. You know you're not invisible. Come in and let's talk.'

'The picture in the papers is crap and you know it – grainy, out of focus and partially obscured. It's a desperate attempt. I had trouble recognizing myself. The newspapers won't carry on publishing that picture forever, 'specially if you get no results from it. In a week's time I could dance naked on Sunset Strip and no one would recognize me.'

Hunter didn't reply. He knew it was only too true.

'So I'm gonna ask you one more time, Detective. Why are you after me? And how am I related to a major ongoing investigation?'

'If you don't know why we're after you, how do you know we're running a *major* investigation? None of the papers mentions it.'

'I'm not that stupid, Detective. If the LAPD got the papers to publish a snapshot of every person they'd like to talk to, there wouldn't be enough paper in California for all the pictures. The few that do get published are always related to a major investigation. Something big is going on, and somehow you think I'm involved.'

Smith was right, Hunter thought, he wasn't stupid.

'So you're telling me that you figured all that out by yourself, but you have no idea why we came to your door?'

'That's exactly what I'm telling you.'

Something in Smith's tone intrigued Hunter. 'So why don't you come in, and we can clear everything up?'

'Goodbye, Detective.'

'Wait.' Hunter stopped Smith before he was able to disconnect. 'Do you know which section of the LAPD I'm with?'

Garcia looked at his partner and frowned.

Smith hesitated for a second.

'Fraud?'

Garcia's brow creased even further.

The pause that followed stretched for several seconds.

'No, I'm not with the fraud squad.'

Silence.

'James? You still there?'

'Which section?'

Hunter noticed a different tension in Smith's voice.

'Homicide.'

'*Homicide*? Look, I don't like going through switch-boards. Give me a number where I can contact you directly.' The tension in his voice had morphed into anxiety.

'Why don't you give me your number?'

'If you wanna play games, suit yourself. Goodbye, Detective.'

'OK.' Hunter stopped him again. 'We'll play it your way.' He gave Smith his number and the line went dead. Hunter quickly pressed a button on his cell phone and got the Special Operations switchboard again. 'Tracy, are you there?'

'I'm here, Detective.'

'Tell me you've got something.'

'Sorry, Detective, whoever this guy is, he really ain't stupid. He's using a pre-paid cell phone. Either a very cheap one with no GPS chip, or he knows how to deactivate them.'

Hunter knew the logic of how GPS chip phones worked. They emitted a locator beacon every fifteen or so seconds, similar to the ones used by airplanes. GPS satellites could then very quickly pin the phone location down to the nearest fifteen to twenty feet. It was obvious James Smith knew that too.

'How about triangulation?' Hunter asked.

'As I said before, this guy ain't dumb, Detective. He was on the move during the call. And I mean he was moving fast. The phone was immediately switched off once he disconnected.'

'Shit!' Hunter ran a hand through his hair. He knew that triangulation is the most accurate method of locating a cell phone that doesn't send out a position signal. A live cell phone is in continual relay with surrounding cell phone towers to ensure they get the best signal available. Triangulation works by identifying the three towers receiving the strongest signal from the phone and drawing their coverage radius. At the point where the three orbits intersect, that's where the phone is located. Its accuracy depends on how close together the three signal receiving towers are. In a city like Los Angeles, where there are simply hundreds and hundreds of cell phone towers, the accuracy can be almost as precise as with a GPS chip. And that's where the being on the move problem comes from. In Los Angeles, cell phone towers are relatively close together. The process of triangulating can take as long as ten to fifteen minutes. If during that process the cell phone in question moves out of range of one of the three triangulating towers and into the range of a new one, the whole process fails and it has to start again from the beginning. If James Smith was calling from a moving car or even a bus, his signal would be constantly jumping from tower to tower in the space of minutes. Triangulation would be virtually impossible. Tracy was right. James Smith was no first-timer.

'OK, Tracy, here's what I want you to do . . .'

Sixty-Two

It was one of those Los Angeles spring mornings that made people happy to be alive. Crisp blue skies, gentle winds, and temperatures not higher than twenty-two degrees Celsius. People just couldn't help but smile. It was on days like these that every detective in the force wished the LAPD issued unmarked convertibles. In the absence of those, Garcia's Honda Civic would do. At least it had air conditioning, something that Hunter's ancient Buick didn't.

On their way to Century City and the A & E TV network studios, Garcia came level with a scarlet red convertible BMW with its top down. A short-haired brunette with her eyebrows plucked to the thinnest of lines had her head resting on the driver's shoulder. He was a brawny man with a bullet head polished to shine, wearing a gym vest that looked two sizes too small for his frame. Hunter observed them for a minute. The woman seemed completely loved up. She brushed her fingers through her hair casually, and for an instant she reminded him of Anna, Garcia's wife.

'Would you ever hurt Anna?' Hunter asked, suddenly turning to face Garcia.

The question was so surprising and out of character that Garcia had to do a double take and almost swerved. '*What*?'

'Would you ever physically hurt Anna?'

'That's what I thought I heard you say. What the hell, Robert? Is that question for real?'

A few seconds went by. If Hunter was joking, he wasn't giving anything away.

'I guess that means *no*, then,' Hunter said.

'It means *hell no*. Why would I ever hurt Anna? Physically or any other way?'

Garcia had met Anna Preston in high school. She was a sweet girl with an unusual beauty. Garcia fell in love almost immediately. It took him ten months to gather the courage to ask her out though. They started dating during their sophomore year and Garcia proposed straight after their graduation. Hunter didn't know of a couple whose love for and dedication to each other matched theirs.

'No matter what happened, no matter what she did,' Hunter pressed, 'you wouldn't hurt her, in any way?'

The confusion stamped across Garcia's face intensified. 'Have you lost your mind? Listen to me. No matter what she does, no matter what she says, no matter what anything – I would *never* hurt Anna. She's everything to me. Without her, I don't exist. Now what in the world are you trying to say, Robert?'

'Why?' Hunter's voice sounded even. '*Why* wouldn't you ever hurt her? No matter what she did . . . or said . . . or anything . . .'

Garcia had been Hunter's partner for almost four years, since he had joined the RHD. He knew Hunter wasn't a conventional detective. He could figure things out faster than anyone Garcia had ever met. Most of the time, no one even understood how he did it until he explained, and then it all seemed so simple. Hunter listened a lot more than he spoke. When he did speak, not everything he said made sense at first, but in the end, everything always slotted into place like a jigsaw puzzle. But sometimes Garcia had to admit Hunter seemed to inhabit a different dimension to everyone on this planet. This was one of those times.

'Because I love her.' Unconsciously, Garcia's words came out coated in tenderness. 'More than anyone or anything in this world.'

'Exactly.' A smile stretched across Hunter's lips. 'And, I think, so does our killer.'

Sixty-Three

The traffic began to unclog, but Garcia was still anesthetized by Hunter's words. Anxious drivers started sounding their horns behind them. The more impatient ones were already shouting abuse out of their windows. Garcia disregarded them and edged forward slowly in his own time. His attention was still on Hunter.

'Please tell me there's sense behind the madness. What are you saying, Robert? That the killer is in love with my wife?'

'No, not with Anna,' Hunter replied. 'But what if the killer thinks he's in love with all his victims.'

Garcia's eyes narrowed as he thought about it. 'What, *both* of them?'

'Yes.'

'At the same time?'

'Yes.'

'And we're not talking obsessed fan love?'

'No.'

His eyes narrowed further. 'If he's really in love with them, why would he kill them in such a brutal way?'

'I didn't say he *was* in love with them,' Hunter clarified. 'I said he *thinks* he's in love with them. But what he's really in love with is their image. Who they represent, not who they are.'

Silence.

Realization came seconds later.

'Sonofabitch! Both of the victims remind him of someone else,' Garcia finally caught on. 'Someone he loved. That's why they look so alike.'

Hunter nodded. 'It's not them he wants. It's who they remind him of.' He watched the convertible BMW pull away. 'The lack of bruising prior to the stitching on both victims has been bothering me from the start. I kept thinking: since he doesn't kidnap them for ransom, there's gotta be a reason why he keeps them instead of killing them straight away, but more importantly, there's gotta be a reason why he never touches them until the last minute. It didn't make any sense. No matter which path I followed, I couldn't see how there'd be no bruising. If the killer was keeping these women to satisfy his sexual needs, there'd be bruising . . . For revenge, there'd be bruising . . . Generalized hate against women, or even brunette painters induced by some past trauma, there'd be bruising . . . If he were an obsessed fan, there'd be bruising . . . Sadistic paranoia, there'd be bruising . . . Pure homicidal mania, there'd be bruising . . . Nothing fitted.'

Garcia raised his eyebrows.

'I heard it first a few days ago, when we were interviewing Patrick Barlett, but I guess it just got filed away in my subconscious.'

'Patrick Barlett?' Garcia frowned. 'Laura Mitchell's ex-fiancé?'

Hunter nodded as he watched the traffic flow. A black woman driving a white Peugeot to their right was shaking her head and gesticulating while apparently singing along to something. She noticed Hunter looking at her and smiled, embarrassed. He smiled back before continuing.

'Patrick said that he'd never hurt Laura, no matter what. He loved her too much.'

'Yeah, I remember that.'

'Unfortunately, that day I was more worried about observing Patrick's reactions than anything else. It just escaped me. But it happens more often than you think. It's a spin-off of the combination of two conditions known as *transference* and *projection*.'

Garcia frowned.

'Some husbands look for prostitutes that remind them of their own wives,' Hunter explained. 'Some people look for girlfriends or boyfriends that look like an old high-school sweetheart or a teacher, or even their own mothers or fathers.'

Garcia thought back to a childhood school friend who, in fourth grade, had fallen in love with his history teacher. When he was old enough to date, every girlfriend he had was the spitting image of that teacher, including the one he'd gone on to marry years later.

'Anyway,' Hunter moved on, 'it wasn't until a moment ago that the idea of resembling someone paired up with transference and projection came into my head.'

'Shit!' Garcia let out a slow breath through clenched teeth, the confusion finally starting to clear in his mind. 'When he looks at the women he's abducted, his mind sees someone else, because he *wants* them to be someone else. Someone he was *truly* in love with. Someone he would never hurt, no matter what. That's why there's no bruising.'

A quick nod from Hunter. 'That's the projection side.'

'But wait a second.' Garcia shook his head. 'He still kills them . . . very brutally. Doesn't that go against this theory?'

'No, it strengthens it. The stronger the transference and projection, the easier it is for the killer to be disappointed.

They might have the same looks as the person he wants them to be, but they won't act, or talk, or do anything else in the same way. No matter how much he wants it, they'll never be who he wished they were.'

Garcia thought about it for a beat. 'And as soon as he realizes that, why keep them, right?'

'That's right. But he still can't bring himself to kill them directly. That's why they're still alive when he leaves them. That's why he's not even there when they are supposed to die. He can't bear to see them go. And that's why he created the self-activating trigger mechanism.'

'So he doesn't have to be there.'

'Exactly,' Hunter agreed.

Garcia remained thoughtful. 'So this true love of his, is she dead?'

'Most probably,' Hunter admitted. 'And that might be why he cracked. His mind just can't let go of her.'

Garcia puffed his cheeks out before letting them deflate slowly. 'Do you think she died in the same way his victims died, stitched up? Do you think he killed her as well?'

Hunter stared out the window at a cloudless, baby blue sky, and wished his thoughts were just as clear. 'There's only one way we can find out.'

He reached for his phone.

Sixty-Four

The Los Angeles branch of the A & E TV network was located in Century City. It occupied fifteen offices on the ninth floor of building two of the famous Twin Century Plaza Towers. It was no coincidence that the buildings resembled the twin towers that were destroyed in 2001 during the terrorist attack in Manhattan's World Trade Center. They'd been designed by the same architect.

The red-haired woman behind the reception counter at the A & E TV network entry lobby was what you'd call striking rather than pretty.

She smiled politely as Hunter and Garcia approached the counter before lifting her index finger to signal that she'd only be a moment.

Seconds later she touched her earpiece and a blinking blue light went off.

'How can I help you, gentlemen?' Her gaze bounced between both detectives and settled on Hunter. Her smile gained an extra twinkle. He explained that they needed to talk to someone about an old documentary their studio had produced. The receptionist glanced at their badges and her demeanor changed. A quick internal call and two minutes later they were being shown into an office at the end of a long corridor. The placard on the door read Bryan Coleman – Director of Production.

The man sitting behind the desk smiled as Hunter and Garcia appeared at his door. He too had a hands-free earpiece on. The blue light was blinking. He motioned both detectives inside, stood up and moved to the front of his desk. He was at least two inches taller than Hunter, with close-cropped dark hair and piercing brown eyes set closely together behind horn-rimmed glasses.

Hunter closed the door behind him and waited. The two chairs in front of Coleman's desk were occupied by boxes. Both detectives stood.

'We need to get that redelivered today . . .' Coleman said into the hands-free while nodding at Hunter and Garcia. He listened for only half a second before cutting off whomever he was speaking to. 'Listen, if we don't get it redelivered today, we're gonna get our account transferred to a different company, do you get me?' Another pause. 'Yeah, this afternoon is fine, before three o'clock even better . . . I'll be waiting.' He removed the hands-free from his right ear and threw it on his desk.

'I'm sorry about the mess,' Coleman said, shaking both detectives' hands before clearing the boxes off the two seats. 'We're expanding. We were supposed to be moving premises, but a few months ago the company across the hall from us went bust.' He shrugged indifferently. 'Recession, you know? So we decided to take their offices instead. It's easier, but no less stressful.' He pointed to the phone on his desk. 'Delivery companies are slick little bastards. If you let them, they'll walk all over you.'

Hunter and Garcia nodded politely.

'So?' Coleman clapped his hands together. 'What can I do for you?'

'We're looking for a documentary about West Coast

artists that was produced by your network,' Hunter said, taking a seat.

'Do you know the name of this documentary?'

Hunter checked his notebook. 'Yes, it's called *Canvas Beauty, The Upcoming Talents from the West Coast.*'

Coleman cocked his head back. '*Canvas Beauty*?' he said with a surprised chuckle. 'Wow. That was three maybe four years ago.'

'Three,' Hunter confirmed.

'I was in the production team for that. Very low budget stuff.' Coleman took off his glasses and started polishing them with a piece of cloth. 'That documentary was a fluke. A promotional trick. You sure that's the one you want?'

Hunter rested his left elbow on the arm of his chair and his chin on his knuckles. 'What do you mean, a fluke?'

'The only reason it was shot in the first place was because of our regional director at the time,' Coleman explained. 'His daughter was an artist, a painter. She'd been trying to break into the scene for some time without much success. So suddenly a new documentary script found its way to the top of our schedule. You know the drill – include a few truly talented upcoming artists, heavily feature his daughter in the middle of it all and hope for the best.'

'Did it work?'

Coleman nodded hesitantly. 'I guess it did its job. She got noticed and I think she's doing OK with her art. That regional director left us a couple of years ago, so I wouldn't really know.'

'What's her name?' Garcia asked. 'The regional director's daughter?'

'Ummm . . .' Coleman started fidgeting with a ballpoint pen.

'Martina,' he remembered. 'That's it, Martina Greene. May I ask why you're interested in that particular documentary?'

'We just wanna have a look at it and find out which other artists were featured,' Hunter replied. 'Were they filmed individually? I mean, on different locations, on different days?'

Another chuckle from Coleman. 'Nope. As I said, it was *really* low budget. Even our director wouldn't be able to justify spending real money on it. So we crammed the whole thing into one day's shooting. We got all the artists together one afternoon at the . . .' he looked away for a second as if struggling to recall, '. . . Moca Museum in South Grand Avenue.'

'Were they all women?'

Coleman frowned and thought about it for an instant. 'On that particular documentary, yes.'

'And do you know if it was aired again? Maybe recently?'

'I can check, but I wouldn't think so. As I said, it wasn't a very good piece of work.' He pulled himself closer to his computer and typed something into his keyboard.

When the result came back a few seconds later, he repositioned his computer monitor so Hunter and Garcia could have a look. 'Nope, aired once two weeks after it was produced and that was it.'

'Do you have any more recent documentaries or interviews in the same vein as that one?' Garcia asked. 'I mean, featuring Los Angeles female painters?'

A look of interest came over Coleman's face. 'Anyone in particular?'

'If you could just show us whatever you have, we'd be very grateful,' Hunter was quick to answer. He didn't want Coleman's curiosity piqued further.

Too late. Once a reporter, always a reporter.

Coleman twitched in his chair before returning to his computer. 'When you say "more recent", how recent do you mean?'

'A year, maybe two.'

This time the search took a little longer.

'OK, in the past two years we've produced three programs on painters,' Coleman said, 'but they weren't exclusively on Los Angeles or Californian artists.'

Garcia frowned. 'That's it, three programs in two years?'

'Very few people are interested in the art of painting, or in the life of modern painters,' Coleman explained, sitting back in his chair. 'We live in a capitalist world where money rules, Detective, and to us viewing numbers is what translates into money – advertising time. If we air a documentary on hip-hop, rap, or whatever trendy new singer is storming the charts, our viewing numbers hit the roof. We air one on paint-ers or any less popular branch of the arts, that number drops to less than a third, even during prime time. Get the picture?'

'Could we get copies of all three,' Hunter said, 'together with the *Canvas Beauty* one?'

'Of course.'

'We'll also need a copy of the work log for the *Canvas Beauty* documentary. Names of everyone who worked on it – cameraman, make-up artists, production and editing team . . . everyone.'

'No problem. I'll put you in touch with Tom, our archives guy. He'll get you whatever you need.'

As Hunter closed the door behind him, Coleman reached for the phone and dialed the private number of a very good friend of his: Donald Robbins, the lead crime reporter at the *LA Times*.

Sixty-Five

The CCTV files from Mr. Wang's convenience store had finished uncompressing. He wasn't sure what he was hoping to find from the footage, but the Missing Persons investigator's assumption that Kelly Jensen had been abducted from Santa Monica, either while parking her car, or walking from it to her apartment building didn't sit right. Even in the dead of night, San Vicente Boulevard was way too busy. Cars drove by every ten seconds or so. Someone could look out the window at any time. It was just too risky. A risk that her killer could've easily avoided by taking Kelly from her much quieter studio in Culver City. And the small parking lot at the back provided a perfect location for an abduction. It was secluded and badly lit. If Hunter were the one planning to kidnap Kelly, that's where he'd have done it from.

Hunter checked his watch. It was late. Before leaving the office, he quickly read through the email he'd received from Jenkins, a good friend from the Records and Identification Division. It contained all the information he'd requested about Whitney Myers and her time with the force, but Hunter had found it hard to concentrate. The punishing headache that had been pounding his brain for the past two hours was threatening to intensify. He needed food. But the cupboards and the fridge back in his place hadn't seen supplies in days. Besides, the only thing he knew how to cook well was popcorn, and he'd already had his share of it this month. He decided to go for something a little healthier. He printed out the contents of the attachment to Jenkins' email, grabbed the laptop and headed for his car.

Uncle Kelome's, a small Hawaiian restaurant in Baldwin Hills, served the best Aloha-style shrimp in the whole of Los Angeles. Hunter loved the food and the relaxed atmosphere. And right now there was nothing that he needed more than to relax, even if only for a few minutes while having his favorite, Volcano Shrimp Platter. The fact that their bar also kept a respectful stock of single malt Scotch was a welcome bonus.

Hunter placed his order at the counter and took a table at the far end of the dining room, hidden away from the often noisy bar. He sat down and buried his head in his hands. His headache was so intense it felt like his brain was about to burst inside his head.

A waitress brought him his drink and placed it on the table in front of him.

'Thank you,' he said without looking up.

'Not a problem, but if you'd like those files I promised you, I'm gonna need my ID back.'

Hunter lifted his head too quickly, and for a fraction of a second his vision was filled with blurry dots. His eyes quickly refocused on Whitney Myers' face.

She smiled.

Hunter didn't.

'Can I sit down?' she asked, already pulling out the chair opposite him.

Despite himself, Hunter appraised Myers. She looked different tonight. Her hair was loose, falling over her shoulders. She was wearing a dark blue pencil skirt suit. The top button on her blazer was undone, showing a silk white blouse underneath. Her make-up was so light it was almost invisible, but it skillfully accentuated her features. Hunter noticed that the group of guys sitting at the table to his right had all turned to look at her; two of them were almost drooling. Hunter's eyes moved from Myers to the glass in front of him and then back to her.

'Balvenie, 12-year-old single malt,' she announced before touching her glass against his. She was drinking the same. 'It's always a pleasure finding someone else who appreciates a proper drink.'

Hunter placed his hands on the table but didn't say anything.

'Wow, you look shattered,' she continued. 'And I'm sorry about that.' She gestured towards the cut above his eyebrow before placing a palm on the left side of her torso. 'You were right, my ribs aren't broken, but they're bruised to shit.'

Still silence from Hunter, but it didn't seem to bother her.

'I must admit, your file is quite a read. A child prodigy. Really?' She pulled a face. 'Attended the prestigious Mirman School for the Super Brainy on a scholarship, and cruised through their entire curriculum in two years. After that, Stanford, also on a scholarship. Received your PhD in Criminal Behavior Analysis and Biopsychology at the age of twenty-three? That's impressive.'

Not a word from Hunter. Myers carried on.

'Made detective in record time and was immediately asked to join the RHD ... now that really *is* impressive. You must've kissed a lot of ass or impressed the hell out of some important people.'

Still nothing from Hunter.

'Now a detective with the infamous HSS, and you're affectionately called the one-man zombie squad by most of your department.' She smiled. 'Cute nickname. Did you come up with that yourself?'

She continued, unfazed by his lack of response.

'Your specialty is ultra-violent crime, and you hold an impressive arrest record. Your book is still mandatory reading at the FBI National Center for the Analysis of Violent Crimes. Have I left anything out?'

Hunter had never written a book, but one of his university professors was so impressed with his thesis paper on Criminal Conduct that he forwarded it to his friend at the FBI academy in Virginia, who passed it on to the academy director. A few weeks later a young Robert Hunter was invited to Quantico to talk to a class of experienced officers and instructors. The one-day talk became a week-long seminar, and at the end of it the director asked Hunter's permission to use his thesis as required reading material for all field officers. Now no one graduates from Quantico without reading it.

'So you read my life story,' Hunter finally said. 'It must've been a pretty boring few minutes.'

'On the contrary. I thought it was very colorful.' Myers smiled again. 'Though there's a strange gap. For a couple of years it seems you just disappeared off the face of the earth. Not a scrap of information on you anywhere. And my research team is the best there is.'

Hunter said nothing.

'I have to ask you this: why the hell did you become a cop? With a résumé like that you could be with the FBI, NSA, CIA, take your pick.'

'Do you have an obsession with getting me a new job?'

She smiled.

The waitress brought Hunter his shrimp platter. As she walked away, Hunter's eyes moved from his glass to Myers. 'I ordered orange juice.'

'I know,' she replied casually. 'But you would've ordered Scotch anyway. I was just saving you some time.' She paused. 'You must be hungry. Look at the size of that platter.'

'Would you like some?'

She shook her head. 'I'm fine, thanks. Knock yourself out.'

Hunter dipped a jumbo shrimp into the pot of hot sauce and took a bite.

Myers waited a few seconds. 'If you're as good as your file says you are, then you've also checked me out, and by now you will know I lied.'

Hunter nodded. 'There's no ex-boyfriend.'

Myers studied Hunter's face for a moment. 'But you already knew that yesterday, right?'

He nodded again.

'If you knew I was lying, why didn't you take me in?'

'No point. You used to be a cop. You knew there was really nothing we could do to force you to tell us who your client really is. If you didn't want to co-operate, we would've just wasted a lot of time. And time is something I don't have. Call it a little professional courtesy.'

Myers smiled. 'Bullshit. You thought you could find out whom I was working for on your own. But it wasn't quite so easy, was it?'

They regarded each other for a moment.

'The reason I was in Kelly Jensen's apartment last night was because I wanted to follow a hunch,' Myers finally admitted, taking a sip of her drink.

'And that hunch was . . . ?'

'That Kelly's disappearance and the disappearance of the woman I'm looking for were connected.'

Hunter put his fork down.

'I didn't find anything in her apartment to confirm that hunch. She wasn't taken from there. But there are other similarities that are hard to ignore.'

'What other similarities?'

'How many victims?' Myers countered. 'How many victims have you got so far? And I'm seriously not fucking around this time. If you wanna know what I know, you've gotta talk to me.'

Hunter sat back and used a paper napkin to wipe his mouth. 'Kelly Jensen was the second victim.'

Myers nodded and placed a photograph of an attractive brunette on the table. 'Was this the first victim?' She held her breath.

Hunter's eyes moved to the picture. On looks, the woman in it could've been Laura or Kelly's sister. He shook his head. 'No, that's not her . . . Who is this?'

Myers breathed out. 'She's not on any Missing Persons list,' she continued. 'Her father tried to report her as missing but MP ran her through their regular six-point checklist. She met only one condition, so they weren't immediately prepared to allocate time to her.'

'Who is she?' Hunter repeated.

Myers sat back. 'Her name is Katia Kudrov. She's the principal violinist concertmistress with the Los Angeles Philharmonic.'

'A musician?'

'That's right.' Myers paused. 'The first victim, was her name Laura Mitchell?'

Hunter sat back in his chair. It was obvious that Myers had done her homework where missing persons were concerned.

Myers waited.

'Yes, Laura Mitchell was the first victim we found.'

The tips of Myers' fingers moved straight to her upper lip. 'She was also a painter. This killer is after artists.'

'Wait up, it's too soon to get to that conclusion. And *artist* is too vast a field. If we're gonna go down that path then we'd have to include dancers, actresses, sculptors, magicians, jugglers . . . the list goes on and on. So far, he's kidnapped and killed two painters, and that's all we have to go on. The fact that Katia's profession falls into the *vast* category of being an artist is a simple coincidence at this point.' Hunter tapped the picture on the table. 'When did she go missing?'

'Four days ago. Laura went missing about a week after Kelly, right?'

'You're good with names and dates.'

'Yes, I'm *very* good with names and dates. So we have no specific time signature between kidnapping and murder?'

'*We*?'

Myers glared at Hunter. 'Katia Kudrov is still my *private* case. At the moment she's a missing person, not a homicide victim. I spent most of today checking Katia's background against Kelly's.' She placed a folder on the table. 'Other than being the same age and sharing some physical characteristics, they've got absolutely nothing else in common. No substantial link.'

Hunter went silent again.

Myers leaned forward. 'Trust me, Robert, the last thing I wanna do is work with the LAPD. But the only way we'll be able to get a better idea if your psycho has really kidnapped Katia without wasting precious time is if we share what we know.' She tapped the folder she'd just placed on the table. 'And the optimum word here is *share*. So if I tell you what I know, you tell me what you know. And don't even think about giving me the classified information excuse bullshit. I'm not a reporter. I have as much to lose as you do if any of the information about this case leaks. We want the same thing here – to catch this fucker. Your victims are already dead. Katia may still be alive. Do you really wanna waste time?'

After reading the file on Whitney Myers that Jenkins had sent him, Hunter wasn't surprised that she wasn't prepared to give him any information on her investigation for free.

For a long while they simply stared at each other in silence. Myers was trying hard to read Hunter's expression. But she certainly wasn't expecting his next question.

'Did *you* kill them?'

Sixty-Six

The uncomfortable silence stretched between them. Neither Hunter nor Myers moved. Neither of them broke eye contact. But Myers' stare lost all its warmth.

Hunter had read all the information Jenkins had sent him on Myers' last ever case with the LAPD.

Myers had been called to try and resolve a situation that had developed in a tower block in Culver City a few years ago. A 10-year-old boy had managed to gain access to the roof of an apartment block and was sitting on the ledge, eighteen floors off the ground. The boy, who everyone knew by the name of Billy, wasn't responding to anyone, and understandably, no one wanted to approach him. His parents had died in a car crash when he was only five, and since then he'd been living with his aunt and uncle, who'd become his legal guardians. They'd gone out for the afternoon and left Billy alone in the apartment.

Billy had no history of mental illness, but the few neighbors who knew him said that he was always very sad, never smiled, and never played with any of the other kids.

Myers saw no other way other than to break protocol and go up to the roof without waiting for the proper backup team.

The report Hunter had read had said that Myers had

spent only ten minutes trying to talk Billy down when he simply got up and jumped.

Myers was so distraught that she'd had to take time off work, but she'd refused to see the police shrink. Two days after the incident, Billy's uncle and aunt jumped from the same spot Billy did. Their wrists were tied together by a zip-tie handcuff. A suicide pact from two grief-stricken guardians would've been the conclusion, if not for the fact that three neighbors had seen a woman who fitted Myers' description leaving the building minutes after Angela and Peter hit the ground.

'Peter and Angela Fairfax,' Hunter clarified.

'Yes, I know who you're referring to.' Her tone was firm.

'Did you push them off that roof?'

'What the fuck does that have to do with this?'

Hunter finally had a sip of his whiskey. 'You just asked me to share information from an ongoing investigation with someone I only just met. You used to be a cop, so you know that's against protocol. But I don't mind breaking it, if it means I'll get a step closer to catching this guy. The problem is: the file I read on you says there's a big chance that you handcuffed two innocent people together and then threw them off the top of an eighteen-story-high building. If you're a real loose cannon, then this conversation ends here.' He retrieved Myers' private investigator's ID from his pocket and placed it on the table in front of her. She didn't reach for it. Her gaze could've burned a hole in Hunter's face.

'What do you think?'

Hunter's left eyebrow lifted slightly.

'The file I read says that you're a good judge of character. So, I wanna know: do you think I could've pushed two innocent people off a rooftop?'

'I'm not here to judge you. But I wanna hear the truth – from you, not from a file written by an Internal Affairs investigator and some police shrink.'

'And I wanna hear your opinion.' Her voice was defiant. 'Do you think I pushed two innocent people off a building?'

Myers' credentials before the rooftop incident were impeccable. She'd worked very hard to make detective and she took pride in being one. She was good at it, one of the best. Her track record proved it. Even after leaving the force and becoming a private investigator, her success rate was impressive. Hunter knew that people like her didn't just flip, didn't just lose their mind out of the blue. He considered her a moment longer and then leaned forward.

'I think you allowed yourself to get personally involved with that case,' Hunter said in a steady voice. 'But you were an experienced detective, so it must've been something that rocked you pretty badly. My guess is that you suspected something really bad was happening in that family. To Billy in particular. But you didn't have enough evidence to substantiate it. I think that maybe you went back to try and get an explanation from Billy's guardians, but things went badly wrong.'

No reaction from Myers.

'If I'm right . . . then I would've probably done the same thing.'

Myers sipped her drink slowly, her eyes still on Hunter's face. She placed the glass back down on the table. Hunter held her stare without flinching.

'She jumped,' Myers said calmly. 'Angela Fairfax jumped.'

Hunter waited.

'That day I was the first to reply to a potential jumper,' she began. 'I made it there in two minutes flat, and started breaking protocol straight away. I had no choice. I just didn't have the time to wait for backup. My intelligence on the boy was almost none. When I got to the rooftop, I found this kid sitting with his legs dangling from the edge of the building. He was just sitting there with his teddy bear, drawing onto a pad of paper. Billy was tiny. He looked so fragile . . . so scared. And that's why I couldn't wait for backup. A strong gust of wind and he would've taken off like a kite.'

She tucked a strand of loose hair behind her left ear.

'He was crying,' she continued. 'I asked him what he was doing sitting on the edge of that building. He said he was drawing.' She had another sip of her drink, a long one. 'I told him that wasn't a very safe place to sit and draw. Do you know what he said?'

Hunter said nothing.

'He said that it was safer than being in his apartment when his uncle was home. He said that he missed his mom and dad so much. That it was unfair that they had to die in a car crash and not him. That they didn't hurt him like his uncle Peter did.'

Hunter felt something catch in his throat.

'I could see the boy was hurting,' Myers proceeded, 'but my priority was to get him away from that ledge. I kept on talking to him, all the while taking small steps forward, getting closer and closer in case I needed to reach for him. I asked him what he was drawing. He ripped the sheet of paper from the pad and showed it to me.' For the first time her eyes moved away from Hunter's face to a blank spot on the tabletop. 'The drawing was of his bedroom. Very simple, sketched using lines and stickman figures with skewed faces. There was a bed with a little stickboy in it.' Myers paused and swallowed dry. 'A bigger stickman was lying on top of him.'

Hunter listened.

'And here comes the sucker punch from hell: standing right next to the bed was a stickwoman.'

'His aunt knew.' It wasn't a question.

Myers nodded and her eyes became glassy. 'They were his guardians. They were supposed to protect him. Instead, they were raping his soul.' She finished her whiskey in one gulp. 'Right there and then I promised him that if he came with me, if he got off that ledge, his uncle would never hurt him again. He didn't believe me. He asked me to cross my heart and hope to die. So I did.' A heartfelt pause. 'That was all that was needed. He said he believed me then because I was a police officer, and police officers weren't supposed to lie, they were supposed to help people. Billy got up and turned towards me. I offered him my hand and he extended his tiny little arm to take it. That's when he slipped.'

'So he never jumped as the report said?'

Myers shook her head.

Neither of them spoke for a few moments.

The waitress returned to the table and frowned as she saw Hunter's uneaten platter. 'Something wrong with the food?'

'What?' Hunter shook his head. 'Oh no, no. It's fantastic. I haven't finished it yet. Just give me a few more minutes.'

'I'll have one more of these.' Myers pointed to her empty glass. 'Balvenie, 12-year-old.'

The waitress nodded and went on her way.

'I lunged towards him,' Myers continued. 'My fingers brushed his tiny hand. But I just couldn't grip it. He was so fragile that his body almost disintegrated when he hit the ground.'

Hunter ran his hand through his hair.

'It took me two days to build up the courage to go back to Billy's building.' She paused to find her words. 'Actually, I think what built up inside me wasn't courage – it was pure hate. I didn't want a confession. I wanted to teach them a lesson. I wanted them to feel at least a fraction of the fear Billy felt.' Her voice was suddenly coated with anger. 'He was a 10-year-old boy, so hurt and so scared that he'd rather jump off the top of a building than go back to the family that was supposed to love him. You're a psychologist. You know that 10-year-old boys aren't supposed to commit suicide. They shouldn't even understand the concept.'

The waitress returned with Myers' drink and placed it on the table.

'I got to their apartment and confronted them. Angela started crying, but Peter was as cold as ice. He couldn't have cared less. Something took over me right there and then. So I forced them to cuff themselves to each other, and took them to the rooftop. To the same spot Billy had fallen from. And that's when it happened.'

Hunter leaned forward but said nothing, allowing Myers to continue at her own pace.

'Angela started crying uncontrollably, but not because she was scared. The guilt inside her just exploded and she let everything out. She said that she was so ashamed of herself, but she had been terrified of what Peter would do to her and Billy if she told anyone. Peter also used to rape and beat her up too. She said that she thought about taking Billy and running away, but she had nowhere to go. She had no money, no friends and her family didn't care for her. That's when Peter lost it up there. He told her to shut the fuck up and slapped her across the face. I almost shot him for that.'

Myers paused for another sip.

'But Angela beat me to it. The slap didn't faze her. She said she was tired of being afraid. She was tired of being helpless against him, but not any more. She looked at me and her eyes burned with determination. She said, "Thank you for finally giving me the chance to do something. I'm so sorry about Billy." Then, without any warning, she threw herself off the rooftop. Still cuffed to Peter.'

Hunter was studying Myers, searching for signs of dissembling – rapid facial movements, fluttering of the eyes. She displayed only a sorrowful calm.

'Angela was a heavy-built woman. Peter was tall and skinny. He wasn't expecting it. Her weight pulled at him like a crane, but he managed to hold her for a few seconds. Long enough for his frightened eyes to look at me. Long enough for him to ask for my help.' A pause. 'I just turned and walked away.'

They sat in silence for a while as Hunter digested the story.

'So what do you have to say? Do you think I'm lying?' Myers finally asked.

That was why Myers had never recounted those events to anyone investigating her case years ago. Hunter knew no Internal Affairs investigator would have believed her. On the contrary, they'd crucify her for seeking revenge.

'As I said,' Hunter said, 'I would've done the same thing.'

Sixty-Seven

Hunter and Myers talked for over an hour more. They shared information. She told him how the evidence she'd collected suggested that Katia Kudrov had been taken from inside her apartment in West Hollywood. She told him about the sixty messages on Katia's answer machine, and how they were all exactly twelve seconds long. She told him about the sound analyses on the last message, the deciphering of the hoarse whispering voice – 'YOU TAKE MY BREATH AWAY ... WELCOME HOME, KATIA. I'VE BEEN WAITING FOR YOU. I GUESS IT'S FINALLY TIME WE MET.' – and why they believed the kidnapper had made the last call from inside her bedroom, probably while watching her shower.

Myers handed Hunter a copy of all the recordings, including the deciphered last one, together with several files. Her research was as good as she had said it was.

Hunter kept his side of the bargain, but he told Myers only what she really needed to know. He told her about the stitches to the victims' mouths, but not to their lower bodies. He never mentioned that the killer left any devices inside his victims. He also didn't say anything about the bomb, the spray-painted messages. He said the killer had used a knife and simply left it at that.

Hunter finally finished his shrimp platter before leaving Uncle Kelome's. His headache wasn't gone, but it was now bearable. Hunter contacted Operations and asked them to get started straight away on a file on Katia Kudrov.

Back in his apartment, he sat in his living room, nursing a new glass of single malt. He didn't even bother with the lights. Darkness suited him just fine. His brain kept going over everything Myers had told him. There was no concrete evidence that the same person who'd taken Laura Mitchell and Kelly Jensen had also abducted Katia Kudrov, but Hunter's mind had already started finding links in the method of their disappearance.

Katia had been abducted from inside her own apartment. That was consistent with the way in which Laura Mitchell, the first victim, had been kidnapped. Despite his suspicions, Hunter had yet to find out from where Kelly Jensen had been taken.

The phone messages left on Katia Kudrov's answering machine also bothered him. The fact that they were all twelve seconds long was evidence enough that they'd been left by the same person. One message a day, over sixty days. That again implied that they were dealing with someone patient and self-disciplined. A person who didn't mind waiting. It was almost like a game he played with his victims. But why twelve seconds? It wouldn't have been a random choice, he was sure.

Hunter played through the copy of the recordings Myers had given him. He heard the kidnapper's hoarse whisper, first as a mass of static sound, then as the deciphered voice. He rewound it and played it again. Over and over.

Hunter sat back in his beaten-up black leather sofa and rested his head against the backrest. He needed to watch the CCTV footage from Kelly's studio parking lot, but he was exhausted. His eyelids were starting to feel heavy. And when sleep came Hunter's way, he always grabbed it with both hands.

He fell asleep right there in his living room. Five consecutive and dreamless hours, something that very rarely happened. When he woke up, he had a stiff neck, and the taste in his mouth was as if he had eaten from a garbage can, but he felt rested and his headache was mercifully gone. He had a long shower, allowing the warmth and strong jet of water to massage his neck muscles. He shaved with an old razorblade that seemed to rip the hairs from his face instead of cutting them. He cursed. He had to go the grocery store sometime soon.

After making himself a strong cup of black coffee, Hunter returned to his living room and to the laptop he'd brought home with him.

Mr. Wang's hidden parking lot camera was set to record twenty-four hours a day, but Hunter had a feeling he'd only need to watch the night footage. This killer didn't strike him as someone who'd risk hanging around an abduction scene in the middle of the day, in plain view of everyone. If Kelly Jensen had really been taken from her studio location, chances were, it would've been done at night.

Because the parking lot was secluded and mainly used by shop owners, the movement of cars and people was minimal. Anything out of the ordinary would stand out. There was no need for Hunter to watch every minute of the fifty-six hours of night footage he had. After a quick test, he found out that he could speed up playback to six times its original playing speed and still be able to spot anything suspicious. That meant it would take him just over an hour to go through a whole eight hours. Hunter checked his watch – 6:22 a.m. He had enough time to skim through the first recorded night before making his way to Parker Center.

He didn't need to watch it for long.

The timestamp at the bottom right-hand corner of the screen read 8:36 p.m. when an old Ford Fiesta entered the parking lot and stopped directly behind Kelly's Trans-Am. Hunter sat up and slowed the footage down to normal playing speed. A few seconds later someone stepped out of the car – male, tall, well built. He leaned against the driver's door and nervously looked around the lot as if checking if anyone else was around. He looked uncomfortable as he lit up a cigarette. Hunter paused the picture and enhanced it by zooming in, but the quality he got from the laptop's imaging application wasn't great – too pixilated and grainy – so he couldn't properly make the man's face. He was sure the LAPD computer guys would be able to clean it up. Hunter pressed play again. Thirty seconds later, the passenger's door opened and a leggy blonde stepped out. She moved around to where the nervous male was standing, kneeled down in front of him, undid his belt, pulled down his trousers and took him in her mouth.

Hunter smiled and rubbed his chin. Just a couple of thrill seekers. He sped up the footage again. The couple moved from oral to full-blown sex – over the hood and against the driver's door. They were there for thirty-eight minutes.

Hunter moved on. At 9:49 p.m. Mr. Wang jumped into his pickup truck and left, leaving only Kelly's car in the parking lot. At 10:26 p.m. Hunter slowed the footage down once again.

'What the hell?'

He leaned closer to the screen and watched the events that unfolded in the next minute as his jaw dropped.

'Sonofabitch.'

Sixty-Eight

In complete darkness she sat shivering, curled up into a tight ball. She felt lightheaded, nauseous and every muscle in her body ached with feverish intensity. Her throat scratched as if she'd swallowed a ball of barbed wire.

She had no real idea of how long she'd been locked up in that cell. She guessed a few days. There was no way she could be sure. The room had no windows and the weak light bulb inside the metal mesh box on the ceiling only came on for a few minutes at a time. The intervals were uneven. Sometimes four, sometimes five times a day. But the light always came on just before she was given food. It was like training a lab rat.

She was given four meals a day, slid to her on a plastic tray through a special hatch at the bottom of the cell's heavy wooden door. The cell was small, ten paces long by eight wide, with bare brick walls, concrete floors, a metal-framed bed and a bucket on the corner, which was emptied once a day.

She moved her head and felt the room spin around again. The dizziness seemed to never go away. She wasn't even sure if she was awake or asleep. It felt as if she was caught somewhere between the two states. The only thing she was sure of was that she was scared – really scared.

He watched her bring her hands to her face and wipe away the tears that never seemed to stop. He wondered how much more scared she'd be if he made a noise. If he made her realize that she wasn't really alone. If she knew he was right there, hiding in the darkness, just three paces from her. How would she react if he extended his hand and touched her skin, her hair? How terrified would she be if he whispered something in her ear?

He smiled as he watched her shiver one more time. Maybe it was time she found out.

Sixty-Nine

Between pausing and fast-forwarding, Hunter spent another half an hour studying the CCTV camera footage from Kelly Jensen's studio parking lot. There were three main sections that interested him. The first was timestamped between 10:26 and 10:31 p.m. The second from 11:07 to 11:09 p.m. And the last one from 11:11 to 11:14 p.m.

The drive from Hunter's apartment in Huntingdon Park to Parker Center took him twenty-five minutes. He went straight into the IT Division, but at that time in the morning there was no one there except a new eager-to-impress recruit to the team. He was wearing a freshly ironed white shirt and a conservative gray tie. His matching suit jacket was resting on the back of his chair. No one in IT ever wore a shirt and tie, never mind a suit.

The young recruit told Hunter that Brian Doyle would probably come in late. He'd gone out celebrating the night before. The long-standing investigation he'd been personally involved in had finally come to an end. They'd successfully apprehended a serial pedophile after a sting operation that had lasted the whole day.

'The guy they caught . . .' the recruit told Hunter, 'he's married with two kids – one is ten, the other is twelve years old. Those are exactly the ages of the kids he used to groom online.' He shook his head as if the entire world had lost its logic. 'Is there anything I can help you with, Detective?' the recruit asked, jerking his head towards the laptop under Hunter's arm.

'What's your name, kid?'

'Garry, sir.' He offered his hand. 'Garry Cameron.'

Hunter shook it. 'I'm Robert, and if you call me *sir* one more time, I'll arrest you for defamation.'

Cameron smiled and nodded.

'I'm afraid I need to talk to Jack, Garry. I need him to run a few pieces of video footage through one of his super applications.'

Cameron's smile widened. 'Well, that's my field of expertize – video and audio analyses. That's the main reason I was transferred here.'

Hunter let out a surprised chuckle. 'I'll be damned. So I guess you're just the man I need.' He placed the laptop on Cameron's desk and they both waited in silence while it booted up. Hunter brought up the video player application and queued up the pre-selected segments. 'This is the original footage, taken from a private CCTV camera,' he explained before pressing play.

Cameron put on his computer glasses and leaned forward. The footage started off with an empty parking lot, except for a candy white Trans-Am T-top with dark tinted rear windows. The picture quality wasn't good, made worse by the lack of lighting.

'Nice car,' Cameron noted.

They watched for only a few seconds before a mysterious male figure approached the lot on foot from the right. He was tall, somewhere between six two and six four with a strong, football player's physique. He was wearing dark clothing; shoes, trousers, gloves, skullcap and a jacket with its collar pulled up. The problem was: Mr. Wang's camera was on the east side of the lot, facing west, and so was the stranger. So far he could only be seen from the back. He stopped by the driver's door to the Trans-Am, reached inside his jacket and retrieved a long, flat piece of metal that resembled a school ruler. Like a professional car thief, the man slid the stick of metal down through the window slot and into the car door. In one quick movement he yanked it up. He tried the handle and the door opened as if he'd used a key.

'You don't look like a CATS, Detective,' Cameron said, referring to the Commercial Auto Theft Section of the LAPD without diverting his attention from the screen.

'I'm not.'

On the screen, the man bent down, put his hand inside the car and popped the hood.

Cameron frowned.

The man quickly rechecked the lot's entrance – no one was coming. Without ever facing east he moved to the front of the car and lifted the hood before bending over the engine and reaching for something in the main block. There was no way they could see exactly what he was doing, but whatever it was, it only took him three seconds. He closed the hood and returned to the driver's side. One more look around before opening the door and disappearing inside and into the back seat.

'Strange,' Cameron commented. 'What's this about?'

'You'll see.'

The video application jumped straight to the next section Hunter had queued up. Cameron checked the timestamp clock at the bottom right-hand corner of the screen and noticed that the footage had jumped forward thirty-six minutes.

'I take it that our mysterious man is still inside the car?' Cameron asked.

'Never moved.'

They carried on watching. This time a slender brunette appeared, coming in from the same direction the man did earlier – Kelly Jensen. Her hair was tied back in a ponytail. She was wearing blue jeans, flat shoes and a faded brown leather jacket.

'Oh shit,' Cameron murmured, already guessing what was about to happen.

Kelly approached the car and searched her handbag for her car keys. Oblivious to the fact that someone was already inside waiting for her, she opened the door and got into the driver's seat. The darkness, the position of the car, and the angle in which Mr. Wang's camera was set, made it impossible for Hunter and Cameron to see through the windscreen. Zooming in on the picture didn't help either.

Cameron pulled his glasses from his face and rubbed his eyes.

Nothing happened for the next two minutes. When the timestamp at the bottom of the screen read 11:11 p.m. the passenger's door opened and the man stepped out of the car. He paused and looked around slowly, checking he was still alone. Satisfied, he made his way to the other side, opened the driver's door and retrieved the keys from the ignition before opening the trunk. As if lifting nothing heavier than a shopping bag, he picked Kelly up with both arms. She was knocked out cold, but it was easy to tell she was still alive.

The man carefully placed her in the trunk and stood still for a long while, looking down at her as if admiring her. He finally returned to the front of the car, opened the hood and tweaked something in the engine block again. Moments later he got into the driver's seat and took off.

'Shit,' Cameron said, looking at Hunter, his complexion paler than minutes ago. 'What do you need me to do?'

'I've looked at this footage several times,' Hunter said. 'That guy doesn't face the camera once, but he looks around a few times, checking his ground.'

Cameron nodded. 'Yeah, I noticed that.'

'OK, so I was wondering – if we slowed this thing down completely, and then moved it frame by frame, we might be lucky enough to get at least a partial face shot in there somewhere.'

'It's possible,' Cameron said, checking his watch. 'I can start working on it right away. I'll have to transfer the footage to my computer and then analyze it again using professional software, but it shouldn't take me more than an hour, two at the most.'

Hunter placed a card on the desk. 'Call me the moment you get anything.'

As he turned to leave, Cameron stopped him.

'Detective, is there a chance she's still alive?'

Hunter didn't say anything. He didn't have to.

Seventy

'Sonofabitch!'

Garcia exclaimed as he watched a copy of the footage Hunter had left with Cameron in ITD. The timestamp on the screen showed that Kelly Jensen had been taken on the 24th February. Their suspicion was that Laura Mitchell, the first victim, had been abducted between the 2nd and the 5th of March.

'So he abducts Kelly first, but murders her second,' Garcia said.

Hunter nodded.

'Why?'

'If we're right about the killer projecting the image of the person he wanted them to be onto his victims, then it's just a matter of time before they do or say something that'd break that spell. Something that'd make him see them for who they really are.'

'Laura broke the spell first.'

'It looks that way, yes.'

Garcia returned his attention to the footage Hunter had retrieved from Mr. Wang's shop. 'Do we have a facial shot?'

'No yet, but ITD are working on it.'

Garcia's eyes returned to his computer screen and the footage. 'You were right when you said that we were dealing with someone who is patient.'

'Not only patient,' Hunter replied. 'He's calm, collected and confident. He staked out Kelly's studio location for several nights no doubt, before making his move. And when he did, he was precise. No time wasted, no struggle, no chance for her to react. This guy is different, Carlos. He takes his victims from places where they are supposed to feel safe; their homes . . . their work studios . . . their cars . . .'

Garcia nodded. 'Judging from that footage, what would you say he is . . . ? Six two, six three . . . ? Weighs around two hundred pounds . . . ?'

'That sounds about right. And that is consistent with the perpetrator's height theory from the skullcap fibers retrieved from the brick wall in Laura's studio. I've called Forensics and told them to pick Kelly's Trans-Am up from Santa Monica and go through every inch of that cockpit and boot.'

Garcia watched the footage one more time in silence.

Hunter had also gotten in touch with the bureaus' Traffic Divisions. The killer had driven Kelly's car out of her studio parking lot and onto Los Angeles' streets, and there were thousands of traffic and CCTV cameras spread across town. Kelly's Trans-Am was an easy car to spot, so the killer would've wanted to swap vehicles as soon as possible. He probably had a van waiting and ready to go someplace close, but he was clever, he didn't just dump her car and leave. A classic Trans-Am abandoned on a side street some-where would've raised too many eyebrows. It would've alerted the police to start looking for Kelly almost immedi-ately. The killer also knew not to return her car to the studio's parking lot. From his surveillance, he would've known that Kelly never left it there overnight. He wouldn't want to risk one of the shop owners noticing it and calling the cops. Instead, he'd driven it back to Santa Monica and parked it in the same spot she always did – right in front of her apartment block. Rule one of being a criminal: raise as little suspicion as possible. This guy seemed to have written that rule.

Hunter was hoping that a traffic camera somewhere had picked up some of that journey. It was a long shot, but right now, any shot was worth taking.

'Anything from Operations on any stitched victims? Anything anywhere in the country?' Garcia asked.

Hunter had asked the Office of Operations to start a nationwide search – any deaths where a brunette female victim had been found with stitches to her mouth, sexual organ, or both. If the killer was really transferring his feelings and projecting the image of the person he once loved onto his victims, there was a good chance that that person had died in a similar way.

'Nothing so far.'

'How far back are we searching?'

'Twenty-five years.'

'Really? That long ago?'

Hunter leaned against his desk. 'We might as well cover all angles.'

'What do you mean?'

'What if we're right about the love theory, but the person the victims remind our killer of isn't an ex-wife, or girl-friend, or even someone he's been infatuated with all his life. What if it's someone else? Someone he also loved. Someone he'd never hurt no matter what?'

Garcia thought about it for a brief moment. 'His mother?'

Hunter nodded. 'It's a possibility. Either his mother or a guardian – like an aunt, an older sister or cousin or something.' Hunter paused and reached for a folder on his desk. 'Have you ever heard of Katia Kudrov?'

Garcia frowned and shook his head at the same time. 'Who's she?'

Hunter pulled a portrait out of an envelope.

Garcia's heart skipped a beat. 'Holy shit. She's almost the spitting image of Laura and Kelly. Who the hell *is* she?'

Hunter took his time telling Garcia everything that had happened since he met Whitney Myers.

'This is a copy of Whitney's investigation file. She's covered every angle. She even has her own forensic specialist.'

'And . . . ?' Garcia started flipping through the pages.

'Nothing substantial. The fingerprints found belonged to Katia herself, her father or the person she was seeing at the time.'

Garcia's eyebrows arched.

'He's not a suspect. He wasn't even in the country at the time of the abduction. It's all there, have a look through later.'

'So her father never filed a Missing Persons report?'

Hunter shook his head. 'Not officially. That's why she wasn't in any of the lists MP sent us. Last night was the first I ever heard of her.'

'Do you think our killer has her?'

'I'm not sure. Sometimes I think my mind is chasing ghosts.'

'What kinda ghosts?'

Hunter shrugged and started picking at the scab that had formed on the cut above his eyebrow.

'I think there are several similarities in the way Katia, Laura and Kelly were abducted. But then again, there are only so many ways a person *can* be abducted. That's why I'm worried about wasting time and chasing a connection that might not even be there. As Whitney said, officially Katia Kudrov isn't even a Missing Persons case, she was never reported.' He picked at the scab too hard and a tiny blob of blood started to form. Hunter wiped it away with the heel of his hand. 'Our research team is already looking into the background of Laura and Kelly, searching for any more connections other than looks and profession. I've asked them to include Katia in that search.'

Hunter's cell phone rang and he fumbled for it in his jacket pocket. 'Detective Hunter.'

'Detective, it's Garry Cameron from ITD.'

'Garry . . . tell me you got something.' His eyes darted towards Garcia expectantly.

'Sorry, Detective, no facial image whatsoever,' Garry sounded defeated. 'I went through every single frame of the footage you gave me, enhancing them every way I could. The guy never gets himself into a revealing angle.' A quick pause. 'In a couple of frames there's a flash of skin but that's all. All I can tell you other that what you've already seen is that he's Caucasian. I'm really sorry, Detective.'

Hunter disconnected and closed his eyes. He needed some sort of break in this investigation. Four people were dead. James Smith was still missing after that bizarre phone call, and if Katia Kudrov had been taken by the same person who took Laura and Kelly, she was running out of time fast.

Seventy-One

Like a contagious disease, Hunter's bad luck seemed to spread throughout every aspect of the investigation. The documentaries he and Garcia got from the A & E TV network revealed nothing. Bryan Coleman was right about the *Canvas Beauty* production: it looked low budget right from the starting credits. Laura Mitchell and Kelly Jensen did appear in it, but for no longer than a few minutes each. They mainly spoke about how living in the West Coast had influenced the way in which they painted.

As Coleman had said, the majority of the piece concentrated on Martina Greene, the daughter of the old A & E TV regional director. The whole thing played more like an advertisement than anything else. Besides Martina, Laura and Kelly, only two other female painters appeared in the documentary – one of them, just like Martina, was naturally blonde. The other one was much older – in her fifties. Hunter checked with both of them, neither had seen nor spoken to Laura or Kelly since. Neither of them recognized James Smith from the picture Hunter showed them either.

Hunter's team was checking the background of every single person whose name was on the *Canvas Beauty* documentary credits list. So far, everyone had checked out, but the list was long.

The other three documentaries Hunter and Garcia had obtained from the A & E TV network featured several painters from all over the country – none of them brunette females in their thirties.

Doctor Hove's lab had confirmed that the dust retrieved from under Kelly Jensen's nails had come from a mixture of mortar and red clay, consistent with common wall bricks. That meant that she could've been kept absolutely anywhere, from a self-built underground bunker to an inside room or an outside garage.

Hunter's traffic camera gamble didn't pay off either. The closest road camera to Kelly Jensen's art studio was a mile away. Her Trans-Am was never spotted on the night she was taken. The South Bureau Traffic Operations' captain had explained that most of the inner-city cameras were only infraction activated – like going through a red light or breaking the speed limit. They didn't film twenty-four hours a day. The ones that did were strategically positioned on main roads, avenues and interstates. Their principal function was to alert Traffic Divisions about congestion hotspots and accidents.

Early the morning after Kelly's disappearance, a camera in Santa Monica picked up her car as it traveled down San Vicente Boulevard going west, in the direction of her apartment building. But the cameras don't monitor the whole of the boulevard. The vehicle was lost as it approached the final stretch that led to the beachfront.

As Hunter had requested, Forensics had picked up the car from Santa Monica and gone over every inch of its interior and boot. The hairs found matched to Kelly Jensen. The few dark fibers retrieved from the driver's seat matched the ones found on the wall behind the large canvas in Laura

Mitchell's apartment. They came from the same skullcap. There were no fingerprints.

It was close to midnight, and for the first time since the beginning of spring the sky had clouded over. Menacing rain clouds and strong winds were closing in from the north, bringing with them the unmistakable smell of wet grass and turf. Hunter was sitting in his living room, reading through reports from his research team into Laura, Kelly and Katia's professional and personal lives. Their backgrounds were totally different from each other. Other than physically having the same overall look and being an artist by profession, the team hadn't found any other links between the three women.

Laura had come from a success-story family. Her father, Roy Mitchell, started his life slum-poor. Having run away from violent and abusive parents when young, most of the food Roy ate in his early years came from trash cans in the back alleys of hotels and restaurants. He was only fourteen when he started selling discarded secondhand books he bought from hotel staff. By the age of eighteen he'd opened his first bookstore, and from there business prospered. His autobiography – *Back Alley Books* – topped the US non-fiction book chart for twelve weeks, and spent a further thirty-three in the top twenty-five. He married the young lawyer who helped him set up his book business, Denise, at the age of twenty. Laura was the younger of their two children.

Kelly, on the other hand, had had a pretty unadventurous life. Born into a small, church-going family in Montana, she was destined to become just another Treasure State housewife, tending to her husband, kids and garden. Her arts schoolteacher recognized her talent when it came to painting, and for years kept on telling her that she shouldn't walk away from her gift.

Katia came from the richest of all three families, but she never took anything for granted. She became a violinist of her own accord, and no matter how much money her family had, talent and dedication can't be bought. Everything she'd achieved, she did it through her own hard work.

Hunter put the report down and stretched his arms high above his head. From his small bar, he poured another double dose of single malt. He needed something comforting and rich on the palate this time. His eyes rested on the bottle of Balblair 1997 and his mind was made. He dropped a single cube of ice in his glass and heard it crack as the dense, honey-colored liquid hit it. He brought the glass to his nose and breathed in the sweet, vanilla oak vapors for a moment. He took a small sip, allowing the alcohol to reach every corner of his mouth before swallowing it. If heaven had a taste, this would be pretty close to it.

Hunter stared out his window at a city that he had never really understood, and that was getting crazier and crazier by the day. How could anyone understand the madness that went around in this town?

A thin sheet of rain had started falling. Hunter's gaze dropped to the files and photographs scattered on his coffee table. Laura and Kelly stared back at him with terrified pleading eyes, their ragdoll smiles grotesquely outlined by rough stitches and black thread.

Knock, knock.

Hunter frowned as his eyes first shot towards his front

room door and then quickly to his watch. Way too late for visitors. Besides, he couldn't even remember the last time someone knocked on his door.

Knock, knock, knock. A lot more urgent this time.

Seventy-Two

Hunter put down his glass, grabbed his gun from his holster, which was hanging from the back of a chair, and approached his front door. There was no peephole. Hunter hated them: they provided any assailant with a very easy kill shot. Just wait until the lens darkens and put a bullet through it. Training and instinct told him to stay to the right of the doorframe, out of reach of the door swing. That would avoid him being slammed in the face if anyone kicked the door in as he unlocked it. It would also put Hunter out of the direct blast path of a powerful weapon, should anyone be waiting to blow a hole through the door.

He undid the main lock and pulled the door back, letting it rest, fractionally open, on the security chain. From the outside, only part of his face was visible through the gap.

'Expecting the bad guys?' Whitney Myers asked with an amused grin.

She was wearing a cropped, black leather biker's jacket with an AC/DC T-shirt underneath. Her blue jeans were faded and torn at her left knee, a look that was perfectly complemented by her silver-tip cowboy boots. Hunter looked her up and down. He was not amused.

'Are you gonna invite me in or shoot me with that gun you're holding behind your back?'

Hunter closed the door, undid the security chain and pulled it back open again. He was also wearing faded jeans – though his weren't torn – but not much else.

It was Myers' turn to look him up and down. 'Well, somebody is a gym bunny.' Her eyes paused at the tight muscles of his abdomen before slowly moving up to his chest, making sure she grabbed a good look of his biceps, and then finally back to his face.

'Did you get lost on your way to a rock gig or something?' He stood on the doorway, his gun still in his right hand. 'What in the world are you doing here . . . and at this time of night?'

As her gaze moved past Hunter and into his apartment, Myers' expression changed. 'I'm sorry . . . are you . . . with someone?'

Hunter allowed the embarrassing moment to stretch for a couple of seconds before shaking his head.

'No.'

He stepped back and fully opened the door, giving her a silent invitation.

Hunter's front room was oddly shaped, with furniture that looked to have belonged to the Salvation Army. There were four mismatched chairs around a square, wooden table that he used as his computer desk. A laptop, together with a printer and a small table lamp were crammed onto it. A few feet away from the far wall was a beaten-up black sofa. The coffee table in front it was overflowing with pictures and police reports. Across the room Myers saw a glass bar with an impressive collection of single malt Scotch.

'I can see you're not a man who cares for extravagant decoration.'

Hunter gathered the pictures and papers from the coffee

table into a pile and moved them out of the way. He reached for a white T-shirt that was on the back of one of the chairs and put it on.

Myers looked away, hiding her disappointment. She approached the dark wood sideboard to the right of the glass bar where a few lonely picture frames were arranged. Two of the photographs were black and white and looked to be old. Both were of the same smiling couple. Hunter looked like his father, but he had his mother's understanding eyes, Myers noted. Most of the other photographs showed Hunter and another man, heavier and about two inches taller. From Myers' research she knew he was Hunter's old RHD partner, Scott Wilson, who'd died in a boat accident a few years ago. Two other photographs showed Hunter receiving commendations from the Mayor of Los Angeles and the Governor of California. The last picture, the one hiding right at the back was of a younger-looking Hunter dressed in a graduation gown and holding a university diploma. He looked like he'd just conquered the world. His father was proudly standing by his side. His smile could've brightened a dark day.

With his arms folded, Hunter stood by the window, waiting.

Myers' eyes moved from the pictures to the glass bar and the neatly arranged bottles. 'Do you mind if I have a drink?'

'If you promise to tell me why you're here, sure, go right ahead.'

She poured herself a double dose of Balblair 1997 and dropped a single cube of ice in it.

Hunter's face remained impartial but he was impressed. 'Good choice.'

Myers had a sip of her drink. 'Do you have a CD player?'

Hunter's eyes narrowed. 'Why? Are you suddenly in the mood for some *Back in Black*?'

She smiled and her gaze moved momentarily down to her shirt. 'That *is* my favorite AC/DC album, but we can listen to it later if you like. Right now, you've gotta listen to this.' Myers pulled a CD case from her handbag. ''Cause you won't believe me if I'd told you.'

Seventy-Three

The rain was coming down a little harder now, drumming against the window just behind Hunter. The wind had also picked up.

'Give me a sec,' he said before disappearing down a small corridor. Moments later he returned with a portable stereo system.

'I found this on the Internet, almost by chance,' Myers said as Hunter cleared the table, placed the stereo on it and plugged it in.

'What is it?'

'An interview.'

Hunter paused and looked up. 'With Katia?'

Myers nodded and handed him the CD. 'It was first aired by KUSC Radio. It's a dedicated classical music FM station.'

Hunter nodded. 'Yeah, I know it. It's run by the University of Southern California.'

Myers pulled a face. 'I didn't know you were into classical music.'

'I'm not, but I read a lot.'

Myers moved on.

'The entire interview is about an hour long with a few classical pieces thrown in so the whole thing isn't just talk. In the first half, Katia is talking to the radio DJ, answering questions he puts to her. In the second half, she's answering questions that were phoned or emailed in by listeners.' She tilted her head to one side. 'I'm not that cruel, so I'm not gonna make you listen to the whole thing. I've copied only the important bits.'

Hunter slotted the CD in, pressed play, and adjusted the volume.

'Welcome back. This is KUSC Radio, the best in classical music in Los Angeles and California.' The DJ's voice sounded exactly like what most people would expect the voice of a classical music station DJ to sound like – velvety and soothing. 'We're back with our special guest this afternoon, someone most of you will need no introduction to. The Los Angeles Philharmonic concertmistress, Katia Kudrov.'

A small section of a violin solo faded in for several seconds and then out again.

'OK, just before the break we talked about your early beginnings and how much you struggled to dominate your instrument, but now we're moving onto something a little more personal – love and romance. Is that OK?'

There was a small pause, as if Katia was considering something.

'Yeah, sure, as long as you don't make me blush.' Her voice was delicate but not fragile. There was confidence in her tone.

'I promise I won't. OK, you describe yourself as a hopeless romantic. Why?'

A timid chuckle. ''Cause I am, really. And here comes the first blush. My favorite movie is *Pretty Woman*.' Giggles.

'Yeah, I'd say that's reason enough to blush,' the DJ laughed.

'I'm like a little girl when it comes to love. I know this

might sound naïve, but I'd love for that kind of fairy tale to exist.'

'The "true love" fairy tale?'

'Yes. The magical make-you-float-on-air kind of love. Sparks flying the first time you set eyes on someone and you just know you were made for each other.'

'Have you ever been that much in love?'

Another chuckle. 'No, not yet. But there's no rush, and I have my music. That really does make me float on air.'

'I'd say your music makes us all float on air.'

'Thank you.' A short pause. 'And now I'm really blushing.'

'So, judging by your comment about sparks flying the first time you set eyes on someone means you believe in love at first sight?'

'Absolutely.'

'And what would someone have to say or do to grab your attention?'

'Nothing.'

'Nothing?'

'Nothing. I believe that love is a lot more than words, or looks. It's something that hits you and then just takes over, without any warning. I believe that when you meet the person you're supposed to spend the rest of your life with—'

'The proverbial "soul mate"?' the DJ interrupted.

'Yes, your soul mate. I think that when we meet that person, we just know. Even from a silent moment. Even if he doesn't say a word at first.'

'OK, I guess I can see what you mean, but he can't be silent forever. He'll have to say something eventually. So what would that have to be? How would he grab your attention?'

'He wouldn't have to do or say anything in particular, but let me tell you my favorite romantic story.'

'OK.'

'As a teenager, my grandmother's first ever job was as a flower girl in a street market in Perm in the old Soviet Union. My grandfather worked in a tailor shop, just a few streets from the market. Her first day at work was the very first time he saw her, and just like that, he fell madly in love. My grandfather was an attractive man, but he was also very, very shy. It took him sixty days to gather up the courage to finally say something to her.'

'Sixty?' the DJ commented.

'Every morning on his way to work he walked past her stall. Every morning he'd promise himself that'd be the day he'd speak to her. And every morning when he saw her, he'd become too nervous. Instead of speaking to her, he'd just walk on in silence.'

'OK, so what happened?'

'What my grandfather didn't know was that my grandmother had also fallen in love with him from the first day she saw him. Every day she watched him walk past the flower stall, and every day she hoped that he'd stop and ask her out. So one morning, he gathered all the courage he could muster, walked up to my grandmother, looked her in the eye and managed to whisper five little words: "You take my breath away."'

Myers reached over and pressed the pause button.

Hunter's memory flashed back to the deciphered answering machine recording Myers had given him a few days ago. The very first words Katia's kidnapper had said had been exactly those – YOU TAKE MY BREATH AWAY . . .

By the way Myers looked at Hunter, he knew that there was more to come.

Seventy-Four

'Fifty-nine days walking past the flower stall in silence,' Myers said, her stare fixed on Hunter. 'Fifty-nine silent messages left on Katia's answering machine. And I'm sure you remember the first five words on the sixtieth message.'

Hunter nodded but said nothing.

'Now this next part of the interview comes after a couple of commercial breaks. The DJ is asking Katia questions that were phoned or emailed in by listeners.' She pressed the pause button again and the interview resumed. It started with animated laughter.

'OK,' the DJ said, 'I've got another question here from one of our callers. This is going back to you being a hopeless romantic, and about you finding your knight in shining armor.'

'OK . . .' Katia sounded hesitant.

'The question is: you said that you believe that love is a lot more than words, or looks. You also said that you believe that when you meet the right person, your "soul mate", you'll just know. Even from a silent moment, like your grandparents. What I'd like to know is how long is that moment? How much silence do you need before you know?'

'Umm.'

Laughter from the DJ. 'That's not a bad question. So how

long is that moment? How quickly do you think you'll be able to know if you've met the right person?'

There was a pause as Katia thought about it. 'Twelve seconds,' she finally replied.

Hunter's stare met Myers but neither said a word.

'Twelve seconds?' the DJ asked. 'That's a strange number. Why twelve?'

'Well, I'd probably know in ten seconds flat, but I'd give it another two seconds just to be absolutely sure.' Katia and the DJ both laughed.

'That's a very good answer,' the DJ agreed.

Myers reached over and pressed the stop button. 'Before you ask,' she said, 'I checked, the station has no record of who called in with that question.'

'Remind me when that was aired again?'

'Eight months ago, but this recording was passed on to other radio stations.' She retrieved a notebook from her bag. 'KCSN in Northridge, KQSC and KDB in Santa Barbara, KDSC in Thousand Oaks and even KTMV, which is a smooth jazz station. It's been aired all over the court. I got this from KUSC's website. Anyone can listen to it online, or download it. Even if the kidnapper wasn't the one who called in with the question, he could've heard the interview and got his idea from there.' She had another sip of her Scotch. 'You and I know that those twelve seconds of silence in every message weren't just coincidence.'

Hunter said nothing.

'You know what this means, don't you?' There was excitement in Myers' voice. 'Katia's abduction is about *love*, not hate. Whoever took her is desperately *in love* with her. So that pretty much discards the possibility of your sadistic killer being the one who kidnapped her.'

Hunter remained silent. His expression gave nothing away.

'Katia had been seeing the new conductor for the Los Angeles Philharmonic, Phillip Stein, for the past four months. He was, and still is, completely obsessed with her. But she broke it all off just a few days before the tour ended. He didn't take the break well at all.'

'But he couldn't have done it. He flew straight to Munich after their last concert in Chicago. I read your report.'

'And you double-checked that just to be sure, didn't you?'

Hunter nodded. 'Any other lovers, ex-boyfriends . . . ?'

'Her previous boyfriend lives in France, where she was before coming back to the US. If she had any other lovers, she kept them well hidden. But I don't think her kidnapper was a lover.' She paused for a moment. 'I think we're dealing with an obsessed fan. Somebody who is so in love with her his whole reality is distorted. That's why he took what she said in that interview so tremendously out of context. His wants to give her her fairy-tale love story.'

Myers almost jumped out of her skin when Hunter's phone vibrated against the tabletop, announcing a new incoming call. The caller ID read *Restricted call*.

He didn't even have to answer it to know that his night was about to get a whole lot darker.

Seventy-Five

Rain was still falling by the time Hunter got to Cypress Park, Northeast Los Angeles. He hadn't said anything after he disconnected from the call. He hadn't said a word during it either. He'd just listened. But Myers knew from the defeated way he closed his eyes for just a second – they had another victim.

Cypress Park was one of the first suburbs of Los Angeles. Developed just outside the downtown area at the beginning of the twentieth century, it had been created as a working-class neighborhood, whose main attraction was its proximity to the railroad yards. That's where the victim's body had been found, inside one of the abandoned buildings along the tracks.

The old railroad yards still occupied a vast area, but great parts of it were now just wastelands. One of these wastelands was located directly behind Rio de Los Angeles State Park. Half a mile north from there, still inside this desolated area and sandwiched between the train tracks and the LA River was an old maintenance depot. On a rainy, moonless night, the flashing police lights could be seen from quite a distance.

Forensics were already there.

Hunter parked next to Garcia's car. A young policeman, wearing a standard issue LAPD raincoat and holding what could only be described as a kid's size umbrella, came up to his door. Hunter pulled his collar up and tighter around his neck, refused the umbrella, and started walking up to the brick building. His hands were tucked deep inside his pockets. His eyes were low, searching the ground, doing his best to avoid stepping into any puddles.

'Detective Hunter?' a man called from the perimeter.

Hunter recognized Donald Robbins' voice – the pain-in-the-ass *LA Times* reporter. He'd covered every case Hunter had been involved in. They were old friends without ever being friends.

'Is this victim related to the case you're already investigating? Perhaps a painter as well?'

Hunter didn't lose stride or look up, but he wondered how the hell Robbins had found out about the victims being painters.

'C'mon, Robert. It's me. You're after another serial killer, aren't you? Is he an artist stalker?'

Still not even an acknowledgement from Hunter.

The outside of the brick building was a mess of graffiti and colors. Garcia, together with two police officers, was standing under an improvised canvas shelter by the entrance to the old depot. The metal door directly behind them had been graffitied with the silhouette of a long-haired pole dancer bending forward. Her spread legs created a perfect upside-down V shape.

Garcia had just zipped up his forensic Tyvek coveralls when he saw Hunter coming around the corner.

'You *have* noticed that it's raining, right?' Garcia said as Hunter reached the shelter.

'I like rain,' Hunter replied, using both hands to brush the water off his hair.

'Yeah, I can see that.' Garcia handed him a sealed plastic bag containing a white hooded coverall.

'Who called it in?' Hunter asked, ripping the bag open.

'Old homeless guy,' the officer closest to the door confirmed. He was short and stout with a bulldog-like face. 'He said that he sometimes sleeps here. Tonight, he wanted to get out of the rain.'

'Where's he now?'

The officer pointed to a police car twenty-five yards from where they were.

'Who talked to him?' Hunter looked at Garcia, who shook his head.

'I just got here.'

'Sergeant Travis,' the officer replied. 'He's with him now.'

Hunter nodded. 'Have any of you been inside?'

'Nope, we got here after Forensics. Our orders are to stay out here soaking our asses in this shitty rain and act like nightclub doormen to all of you big Homicide boys.'

Garcia frowned and looked at Hunter.

'I guess you were right at the end of your shift when you got this call, right?' Hunter said.

'Yeah, whatever.' The officer ran two fingers over his peach-fuzz moustache.

Hunter zipped up his coveralls. 'OK, Officer . . . ?'

'Donikowski.'

'OK, Officer Donikowski, I guess you can do your night-club doorman job now.' He nodded at the door.

Garcia smirked.

The first room was about fifteen feet wide by twenty deep. The walls were also covered in graffiti. Rain spat onto the floor through a windowless frame to the left of the door. Discarded food cans and wrappers were piled up in one corner, together with an old straw mattress. The floor was littered with all different sorts of debris. Hunter could see no blood anywhere.

The familiar, strong crime-scene forensic light was coming from the next room along, where hushed voices could be heard.

As they approached the door, Hunter picked up on a mixture of smells – mostly stale urine, mold and accumulated garbage. All of them the kind of odors you'd expect to find inside an old, derelict building, sometimes used by drifters. But there was a fourth, fainter smell. Not the kind of putrid stench you get when a body starts to rot, but something else. Something Hunter knew he'd smelled before. He paused and sniffed the air a couple of times. From the corner of his eye he noticed Garcia doing the same thing. He was the one who recognized it first. The last time Garcia smelled that same smell he'd thrown up within seconds. This time was no different.

Seventy-Six

The second room was smaller than the one Hunter and Garcia were in, but identical in shape and state of deterioration – graffitied walls, windowless frames, piles of garbage on the corners and all sorts of debris scattered around the floor. Doctor Hove and Mike Brindle were standing by a door on the far wall that led into a third chamber. The same portable tactical X-ray unit they'd used in the basement of the preschool in Glassell Park had been set up on the floor next to them. Three paces to the left of the unit, lying on her back, was the naked body of a Caucasian brunette female. Hunter could see the thick black thread used to stitch her mouth and lower body from across the room. There was very little blood surrounding the body.

'Where's Carlos?' Doctor Hove asked. 'I thought he was waiting for you outside.'

Hunter didn't reply, didn't move, didn't breathe. He just stood perfectly still, his eyes fixed on the brunette's face. Her skin had turned a light shade of purple, indicating blood pooling. Like the two previous victims, the lower part of her face had swollen, due to the stitches to her mouth. But even so, there was something familiar about her. Hunter felt his skin burn as adrenalin ran through him.

'Robert,' the doctor called again.

Hunter's eyes finally refocused on her.

'Are you OK?'

'I'm fine.'

'Where's Carlos? I thought he'd be with you.'

'I'm here,' Garcia said as he walked through the door behind Hunter. He looked a little paler than a moment ago. The strange, faint smell they'd picked up outside was more prominent in the room. Garcia brought his hand to his mouth and cringed as he fought to keep his stomach from erupting again.

Hunter approached the body in silence and crouched down next to it. Her face was starting to puff up. He didn't need to touch her to know that her body was now in full rigor mortis. She'd been dead for at least twelve hours. Her eyes were closed, but everything about her features looked familiar. The nose, the cheekbone structure, the shape of the chin. Hunter moved closer still and had a look at her hands and fingers. Most of her fingernails were broken or chipped. Despite the purpling of the skin, at first glance Hunter could see no severe hematomas. There were no cuts or abrasions either. The swelling to her body wasn't due to physical abuse.

Hunter moved around to the other side. She had a single-color tribal tattoo on her right shoulder.

Garcia was studying the body in silence from a standing position, his hand still covering his nose and mouth.

'Do you know who she is?' the doctor asked, noticing the way Hunter kept looking back at her face. 'Is she another painter from your list of missing persons?'

Garcia shook his head. 'I can't place her. I know the face is a little swollen, but I don't think she was on the lists.'

'She's not a painter,' Hunter said, standing back up again. 'She's a musician.'

Seventy-Seven

Garcia's eyes returned to her face and he frowned. He'd had a very good look at Katia Kudrov's photographs since Hunter told him about her. The woman on the floor didn't look like Katia.

'It's not Katia Kudrov,' Hunter said, reading what his partner was thinking.

Garcia frowned harder.

'You know her?' he asked.

'She looks familiar. I've seen her before, I'm just not sure where.'

'So how do you know she's a musician?' Brindle this time.

'She's got calluses on all the fingertips of her left hand, except her thumb, where the callus is on the first joint.'

Brindle looked hesitant.

'String instrument musicians get those,' Hunter explained. 'The fingertip ones from pressing down on the strings, and the thumb joint one from sliding their hands up and down the instrument's arm, like a violin, cello, guitar, bass, whatever.'

Doctor Hove nodded. 'One of my Forensics technicians is learning to play the guitar. He's always complaining his finger-tips hurt like hell and keeps on picking off the loose skin.'

Hunter turned around and looked in the direction of the room he came in from. 'She was found in this room?'

Brindle nodded. 'At the exact location she is right now. Unlike the victim from Glassell Park, we didn't need to turn her over to use the X-ray machine. She was found on her back. There's no indication that anyone has touched the body either.'

Hunter looked around at the ceiling and walls for an instant. 'What's in that room?' He nodded towards the next chamber.

'Same as in here and the previous room,' Doctor Hove replied. 'More graffiti and garbage.'

Hunter moved closer and pulled the creaking door open. The forensic light was strong enough to illuminate most of the next chamber.

'There's no bed, or table, or counter, or anything? She was just left in here on the floor?'

'No,' Brindle clarified. His head tilted back a fraction and his eyes moved towards the ceiling. 'Upstairs.'

Hunter peeked inside the third room again. The staircase was to the left of the door, hugging the wall.

'I've got two agents up there working the scene,' Brindle continued. 'It looks like she was left on a wooden table.' He knew what Hunter would ask next and nodded before the question came. 'The table was lifted about a foot off the ground by wooden blocks, just like in Glassell Park.'

'The words . . . ?'

Brindle nodded again. '*It's inside you*. Painted onto the ceiling this time.'

Garcia had a quick look inside the next room. 'So she managed to get off the table, come all the way down those stairs, and out here before finally dying?'

'Before collapsing,' Doctor Hove said, grabbing both detectives' attention again. 'Death took a while to come, but not before tremendous suffering.'

'And she probably crawled her way down here,' Brindle took over. 'She must've been a very strong woman, physically and mentally. Her will to stay alive was nothing short of exceptional. The kind of pain she went through, most people wouldn't have been able to move at all, never mind make it all the way down here.'

Hunter's stare moved to the X-ray unit on the floor and the laptop screen. It seemed to be turned off.

Brindle and Doctor Hove followed his gaze. 'Given what we know and the fact that the MO and signatures are the same,' the doctor said, 'I'm sure the killer used the same trigger mechanism he used before, but this time it didn't trigger a fan-out knife or a bomb. Let me show you.'

Garcia cleared his throat uncomfortably while the doctor brought the laptop back to life.

'We'd just finished capturing this when you arrived,' Brindle explained.

As the image of the object left inside her body materialized on the screen, both detectives moved closer.

No one said a word.

Hunter and Garcia squinted at the same time, trying to make sense of what they were looking at.

'No way,' Hunter said. 'Is that what I think it is?'

Brindle and Doctor Hove nodded in unison. 'We think so.'

A couple more seconds and Garcia finally saw it, his eyes widening in disbelief.

Seventy-Eight

The digital clock on Hunter's microwave read 3:42 a.m. when he stepped back into his apartment and closed the door behind him. He wasted no time walking into every room and turning on all the lights. For now he just didn't want any more darkness. He was tired, but for the first time he welcomed insomnia. He wasn't sure he'd have the strength to deal with the nightmares he knew would come as soon as he closed his eyes.

After the body had been removed and taken to the morgue, Hunter and Garcia had spent a long time looking around the old depot, especially the room upstairs. It was a large chamber, which had probably been used as one of the main storage areas. Two of the walls were lined from floor to ceiling with long wooden shelves. A large carpenter's workbench occupied the center of the floor. As Brindle had said, it had been raised about a foot off the ground by wooden blocks. There was so much garbage and debris around the place, Forensics could take weeks analyzing it, and maybe months to process it all. The exact same words as before – IT'S INSIDE YOU – had been spray-painted onto the ceiling, just like in the butcher's shop. If there'd been any tire tracks on the soft ground outside, the rain did a good job of washing them away.

The homeless man who'd found the body was in his late sixties, frail and undernourished. He'd walked a long way, hoping to have a roof over his head for the night and escape the rain that he had smelled in the air an hour before it started. He never saw anyone around the old depot. Just the girl lying on the floor, naked, with her mouth stitched up like a ragdoll. He never touched her. He never even got close to her. And by the time Hunter talked to him, he still hadn't stopped shaking.

It had been exactly seven days since they had found the body of Laura Mitchell. Kelly Jensen's body was discovered three days after that, and now they had a new unidentified female victim. Counting Doctor Winston and the young Forensics assistant who died in the explosion in the autopsy room, they had five victims in one week. Hunter knew that while their investigation was moving at a snail's pace, the killer was sailing with the wind.

In the kitchen, Hunter poured himself a glass of water and drank it down in large gulps, as if trying to put out a fire somewhere inside him. He was sweating as if he'd just run five miles. He reached for his cell phone and dialed Whitney Myers' number before walking over to his living room window. The rain had only stopped ten minutes before. The sky was dark and dull. Not a single star.

'Hello . . .' Myers answered after a single ring.

'It's not her . . .' His voice was heavy. 'It's not Katia.'

'Are you sure?'

'Positive.'

An uneasy pause.

'Do you know who she is?' Myers pushed. 'Is she on the MP list?'

'No, she's not on the list. But she looks familiar.'

'Familiar? In what way?'

'I think I've seen her before. I just can't think where.'

'Police environment . . . ?'

'I don't think so.'

'Court of law . . . ? Witness . . . ? Victim . . . ?'

'No, somewhere else.'

'A bar . . . ?'

'I don't know.' Hunter ran his hand through his hair and let his fingertips rest at the back of his neck. Unconsciously they traced the contour of his ugly scar. 'I don't think I've ever met her or seen her on the streets or in a bar or anywhere like that. I think I've seen a picture of her. Maybe in a magazine or an advertisement . . .'

'She's that famous?'

'I don't know. I might be wrong. I'm wracking my brain here trying to remember, but I've got nothing, and I'm dead tired.'

Myers said nothing.

Hunter moved away from the window and started pacing his living room.

'If you get me a photo of her, maybe I can help,' Myers offered.

'No one will recognize her from the crime-scene photos. She's been dead for over twelve hours. The killer could've dumped her there yesterday, or even the day before. We were lucky that a homeless drifter wanted to use the place for shelter tonight, or else she could've been decomposing by the time we got to her.' Hunter paused by his bookcase, absentmindedly browsing through the titles. His eyes stopped as he reached the fifth book on the top shelf. 'Shit!'

'What? What happened?'

Hunter ran his hand over the spine of the book.

'I know where I've seen her before.'

Seventy-Nine

Hunter had to wait until 7:30 a.m. to find out for certain who the latest victim was. The central branch of the Los Angeles Public Library on West 5th Street could easily be called Hunter's home away from home, he spent so much time in there. Its opening time was 10:00 a.m., but he knew most of the staff, and he knew that one of them in particular, Maria Torres from Archives, was always there very early.

Hunter was right. He'd seen the victim's face before. He'd passed her picture many times as he walked through the Arts, Music and Recreation department on the library's second floor. One of her CDs, *Fingerwalking*, was featured on the middle shelf of the 'we recommend' display in the jazz guitar section. The display faced the main walkway. Its cover was a black-and-white close-up of her face.

From the library, Hunter made it to the LA morgue twenty minutes after Doctor Hove had called him saying she was done with the autopsy. Garcia was already there.

The doctor looked more than exhausted. No amount of make-up could disguise the black circles under her eyes, and they looked as if they'd sunken deeper into her skull. Her skin looked tired, with the pallor of someone who hadn't seen the sun in months. Her shoulders were hunched forward, as if she was having trouble carrying the invisible weight on them.

'I guess none of us had much sleep,' Garcia said, noticing Hunter's heavy-looking eyelids as he joined them by the entrance to the autopsy room. 'I tried you at home . . .'

Hunter nodded. 'I was in the library.'

Garcia pulled a face and checked his watch. 'Ran out of books at home?'

'I knew I'd seen the victim before,' Hunter said. 'Her name is Jessica Black.' He pulled a CD case from his pocket.

Garcia and Doctor Hove took turns looking at the cover.

'There's another picture inside,' Hunter said.

The doctor pulled the cover booklet out and flipped it open. Inside there was a full body picture of Jessica. She was standing with her back against a brick wall. Her guitar resting against it by her side. She had on a sleeveless black shirt, blue jeans and black cowboy boots. The tattoo on her right shoulder was clearly visible. Doctor Hove didn't need to check it again. She knew it was exactly the same tattoo the victim on her autopsy table had on her shoulder. She'd looked at it for long enough.

'I just found out about her fifteen minutes ago,' Hunter explained. 'I called Operations from the car and asked them to get me an address and whatever else they can on her. We'll check it after we leave here.' He nodded at Garcia who nodded back. 'Missing Persons don't have her,' he continued; 'she was never reported missing.'

Silence took over as they entered the autopsy room and paused by the examination table. All eyes settled on Jessica's face. The stitches had been removed from her lips, but the scars where they'd dug so deep into her skin remained.

There were scratch marks all around her mouth. Hunter could tell that Jessica herself had made them in blind panic, as she desperately clawed at the stitches with whatever was left of her nails. How much she'd suffered, no one could even begin to imagine.

'We were right,' the doctor broke the silence. Her voice was throaty. 'The killer burned her from the inside.'

Garcia shook off a shiver. 'How?'

'Using exactly what we thought he'd used. He inserted a signal flare inside her.'

Garcia closed his eyes and took a step back. Last night, it had been the faint smell of burned human flesh inside the old depot that had made him sick to his stomach. It was one of those smells you never forget. And Garcia had never forgotten it.

'Well, not exactly a signal flare,' the doctor corrected herself, 'but a variation of one.' She indicated the long counter behind her where a metal tube had been placed inside a metal tray. The tube was five inches long by half an inch in diameter. 'This is the aluminum tube that was placed inside her.'

Hunter moved closer to take a better look. The tube was sealed at one of its ends. No one said anything, so Doctor Hove moved on.

'Signal – or warning – flares are the most common type of flares out there. They're also quite easy to obtain. You'll find them in any boat at the marina or even in road safety kits, which can be easily purchased from pretty much anywhere. But they aren't the only type of flares you can get . . .' she paused and allowed her eyes to return to the aluminum tube inside the tray, '. . . or create yourself.'

'Heat flares,' Hunter said.

The doctor nodded. 'Precisely. Unlike signal flares, their main purpose isn't to burn bright and produce a warning signal. Their purpose is just to burn *hot*.' She picked up the tube. 'Essentially, a flare is just a container, a tube packed with chemicals that can produce a brilliant light or intense heat without an explosion. And that's exactly what the killer created and inserted into his victim.'

'How long did that burn for?' Hunter asked.

The doctor shrugged. 'Depends on what chemicals were used and how much of each. This is going up to the lab straight after here. But the killer wouldn't have needed much at all. Heat flares burn at ridiculously intense heat. Just a few seconds of direct contact would be enough to completely carbonize human flesh.' She paused and slowly rubbed her face. 'The damage that that fan-out knife caused to the second victim . . .' she shook her head, 'that's cotton candy compared to what we have here.'

Garcia drew a deep breath and shifted his weight from foot to foot.

Doctor Hove turned the tube over and showed them a small click button at its sealed-off base. 'Same sensitive impact-activated trigger mechanism. When her feet touched the ground, this thing clicked and produced a tiny spark. Enough to ignite the chemicals inside the tube. Similar to an oven lighter, really.'

'How can a fire ignite and keep on burning inside a human body?' Garcia asked. 'Doesn't it need oxygen?'

'The same way a flare ignites and burns underwater,' Hunter said. 'It uses an oxidizing agent, which directly feeds the fire with oxygen atoms. Underwater flares carry a higher oxidizer mixture, so even in an environment with no oxygen, the fire never dies.'

Garcia looked at Hunter as if he were from outer space.

Doctor Hove nodded again. 'The higher the oxidizer mixture, the stronger the initial deflagration.'

Hunter hadn't thought of that.

'And in English that is . . . ?' Garcia asked.

'When the initializing spark hits the chemicals, it produces an . . . impact, so to speak. That impact causes the whole thing to ignite at once, but not to explode. That uniform ignition is a deflagration – a combustion a few steps short of an explosion. Deflagration creates a bubble of super-heated gas. In this case, that bubble would've shot out the top of the flare canister like a bullet a millisecond before the fire. That bubble had to expand until it lost strength.' Doctor Hove closed the fingers of her right hand into a fist and then reopened them slowly, creating a bubble-growing illusion. 'It wouldn't have propagated much, probably only millimeters, but while it was expanding, whatever it touched, it completely vaporized it.'

Garcia felt his stomach start to churn again.

'The pain she must've suffered is . . . indescribable,' the doctor confirmed. 'Most fire victims die from smoke inhalation, not from the injuries sustained. Basically, their lungs collapse because they can't process the smoke and they suffocate – sometimes even before they feel any pain at all from their scorched flesh. But that's not the case here. There was no smoke. She felt every last pinprick of pain that came to her.' She placed the metal tube down and let go of a deep breath. 'As you know, the second victim was severely mutilated from inside. She suffered a lot, but that mutilation caused intense loss of blood. We all know that when a human being loses a certain amount of blood, the body simply shuts down, like going into hibernation or being anesthetized. The person starts to feel cold and tired, the pain disappears and they fall asleep before dying.' She ran her hand over her mouth. 'But not if you're burned. The blood loss is minimal. There's no hibernation or anesthetized effect. There's only grotesque pain.'

Eighty

Doctor Hove pointed to a clear plastic bag on the metal counter behind her. Its contents seemed to be a small gooey mass of soft tar.

'That's all that was left of her entire reproductive system. It's been scorched beyond any recognition by heat and fire. Even *I* couldn't tell what was what.'

Not a word from Hunter or Garcia. The doctor carried on.

'Her uterus, ovaries, and bladder exploded inside her abdominal cavity. Death came from a series of major organ failures, but that would've taken some time. During that time, she felt every ounce of pain her body could've taken. Until it could take no more.'

Garcia's eyes kept going back to the plastic bag with the blackened contents.

'Was she drugged?' Hunter asked.

'Without a doubt, but toxicology results will take a couple of days. My guess is that the killer used Estazolam again.'

'Any signs of malnutrition or dehydration?'

Doctor Hove shook her head. 'None. And just like the previous victim, I won't be able to tell if she was sexually assaulted or not.'

By the time Hunter and Garcia made it back to Parker

Center, their research team had compiled a three-page report on Jessica Black.

Born in South Los Angeles, she had turned thirty less than a month ago. The report went on to explain about her poor childhood, how she lost her mother when she was only nine, and about her fascination with acoustic guitars because of an old blues guitar man she saw in the park when she was a child. It also explained about her rise to fame once her videos were posted onto YouTube. Her concerts were sold out weeks in advance. She and her boyfriend, Mark Stratton, who was also a guitarist, but with a metal band called Dust, shared an apartment in Melrose.

Hunter tried the apartment phone number – no answer. He tried Mark's cell phone – straight to his voicemail. He didn't leave a message.

Hunter and Garcia made it to Melrose in forty-five minutes. Jessica and Mark's apartment was on the top floor of a private condo surrounded by a forest of California Bay trees in North Kings Road. The building's concierge, Scott, was a tall and reedy man in his late-twenties with a shaved head and a trendy goatee. He said that he hadn't seen Jessica for a few days. Five to be exact.

'How about Miss Black's partner?' Garcia asked.

'Mark? He's been away for ... four days now,' Scott replied. 'His band, Dust, is just about to release their new album, so they hit the road for a bunch of pre-tour gigs before the real tour begins.'

'Do you know when he's supposed to be back?'

Scott shook his head. 'Not exactly, but it'll be a few weeks.'

Hunter's eyes roamed the building's entry lobby and settled on the security camera in the far-left corner.

'How many CCTV cameras are there in the building?' he asked.

'Four,' Scott said. 'One just outside the main entrance, that one here in the lobby.' He pointed to the camera Hunter had spotted. 'One on the entrance to the underground garage, and one inside the elevator.'

'And how long do you keep your CCTV footage?'

'For a month. Everything is stored into a hard drive.'

'We're gonna need copies of everything, going back to the day you last saw Miss Black.'

'Sure, that's not a prob . . .' Scott hesitated for an instant. 'Something wrong?'

'Well, four days ago we had a fuse box overload and all the cameras went down for a few hours in the middle of the night. And if I remember correctly, it happened on the day Mark left on tour.'

Hunter remembered what Myers had told him about the CCTV cameras in Katia Kudrov's apartment building in West Hollywood. They had all conveniently gone down the night she disappeared. A fuse box overload.

'We'll need copies of whatever you have.'

'Sure.'

'How about any visitors?' Garcia asked. 'Do you remember anyone calling in on or around the day you last saw Miss Black? Maybe delivering something, a workman checking something . . . Any reason to go up to their apartment?'

'Mark and Jessica didn't really have people over. They preferred to go out, which they did a lot. Anyway, every visitor, service or delivery has to go through the front desk and details are always taken down.' He checked the computer log. There was nothing.

'Did you notice anyone suspicious hanging around the

building on the days prior to Mark leaving on tour?' Garcia asked.

Scott laughed. 'Other than Mark and Jessica we have two up-and-coming Hollywood actresses, one rock singer, one rapper, one TV presenter and two radio DJs living here. There are always strange and eager people around just waiting to get a glimpse of their idols, or an autograph or photo.'

Hunter took down the name of the concierge on duty the night the cameras went down – Francisco Gonzales. He'd be on duty again later that evening.

As they got back to the car, Hunter tried Mark's cell phone again. Still voicemail. He needed to get in touch with Mark as soon as possible. He needed access to their apartment. He called Operations and asked them to get back to him with Dust's manager's name, office and cell phone number. While they were at it, he asked them to get Jessica's manager's details as well.

Hunter disconnected and ten seconds later his cell phone rang.

'Talk about fast response,' Garcia joked.

'Detective Hunter,' he said, bringing the phone to his ear. He listened for a moment. 'You're kidding me. When? . . . Where is he? . . . OK, we're on our way.'

'What's going on?' Garcia asked as soon as Hunter closed his phone.

'James Smith has been arrested.'

Eighty-One

James Smith was sitting alone inside interrogation room number two on the second floor of Parker Center. His hands were cuffed together, and he had them resting on the metal table in front of him. His fingers were picking at each other, anxiously. His eyes were fixed on the far wall, as if watching some invisible movie being played on a screen only he could see.

Hunter, Garcia and Captain Blake were regarding Smith from the other side of the two-way mirror in the adjacent observation room. Hunter paid particular attention to his eyes and facial movements.

'He's not our guy,' Hunter said in a steady voice. He kept his arms folded over his chest.

'What?' Captain Blake blurted out with annoyance. 'This is the first concrete lead we've managed to follow through since we found the first victim. Since Jonathan died in that autopsy room seven days ago for no reason. You haven't even spoken to him yet.'

'I don't have to. He's not our killer.'

'And you know that how?' Her hands moved to her hips. 'Or you gonna tell me that together with your lip-reading ability you're also psychic?'

'Do you know where he was arrested, Captain?'

She glanced at Garcia, who gave a tiny shrug.

'I haven't looked at the arrest report yet. Why?'

'Lakewood,' Hunter said. 'He was arrested in Lakewood.'

'OK, and . . . ?'

'Around the corner from Laura Mitchell's apartment.'

'Your point is . . . ?'

'He was arrested because I told Operations to send two teams of plain clothes officers to stake out her place.'

The captain frowned. 'When did you do that?'

'After I talked to him on the phone.'

'You knew he'd go back to her place?'

'I suspected he'd observe it.'

'Observe it? Why?'

'Because his mind refuses to believe something has happened to Laura Mitchell. He needed to check it out for himself.'

The captain's stare returned to Garcia for a moment before moving back to Hunter. 'You better start making sense, Robert. And right now is a good time.'

Hunter finally turned and faced Captain Blake. 'When we spoke on the phone, he thought I was a detective with the fraud squad.'

'Fraud squad? Why?'

'Because *that's* his crime, Captain – impersonating. We all know James Smith isn't his real name. Nevertheless, he's managed to obtain a driver's license, an ID card, a library card, maybe even a passport, all under a false identity. That can get him one to five years inside. But as he said on the phone to me, that's not enough to trigger a major investigation. That's why he couldn't understand why his photo had hit the papers. Why we were after him. When he found out I was with the Homicide Division, he hesitated for a moment, then there was a distinct change in his voice.'

'Like what?'

'Trepidation ... fear, but not for himself, or of being caught.'

The captain looked lost.

'The reason why he hesitated was because at first he couldn't figure out why Homicide would be after him. But as we all know, he's far from stupid. He quickly realized that it must've been something linked to his obsession.'

'Laura Mitchell,' Garcia said, comprehending.

Hunter nodded. 'We know that they exchanged phone numbers at the exhibition. We checked Laura's cell phone records. Just a couple of days before the presumed time-frame of her disappearance, she received a call from a payphone in Bellflower.'

'That's the next neighborhood along from Norwalk,' the captain said. 'Smith's apartment is in Norwalk, right?'

Hunter and Garcia nodded.

'Only one call?'

'That's right. My guess is that they talked that day, maybe arranged to talk on the phone again later that week or even meet up somewhere. She didn't turn up or he got no reply on his next call. He kept on trying, still no answer. He got worried, maybe a little annoyed. When I mentioned Homicide on the phone to Smith, it took him just a few seconds to make the connection.'

'So he started staking out Laura Mitchell's place to try to spot her, get some sort of confirmation,' Garcia said.

'That's what I figured he'd do,' Hunter agreed.

'Well, for someone who isn't stupid, that's a pretty dumb thing to do, don't you think?' the captain shot out. 'You're gonna tell me that he didn't at least suspect her place would've been watched?'

'You saw the pictures of his collage room, right? He's been obsessed with Laura Mitchell for years. The kind of obsession that overrides rational thought, Captain – pure, undying love. Of course he knew it was dangerous. Of course he knew he could be caught. But he couldn't help it. He needed to find out. He needed to make sure she was OK.'

'Like an addiction?'

'Stronger than an addiction, Captain. It's a compulsion.' Hunter turned towards the officer in the room. 'Has he requested a lawyer yet?'

'Not yet. He said he wanted to talk to you.'

All eyes moved to Hunter.

His gaze returned to James Smith for a moment longer. 'OK, let's do it.'

Eighty-Two

James Smith's eyes darted towards Hunter as soon as he entered the interrogation room.

'I'm Detective Robert Hunter of the Homicide Special Section. We talked on the phone a couple of days ago.' Hunter placed a tray with a coffee pot and two mugs on the metal table. 'Coffee?'

'She was kidnapped and murdered?' Smith's voice was edgy and concerned. His eyes looked haunted.

'It's fresh.' Hunter poured two cups and slid one over towards Smith. 'And you really look like you could use some.'

Smith's eyes didn't leave Hunter's face. 'Laura was kidnapped and murdered?' He pleaded rather than asked this time.

Hunter pulled the chair across the table from Smith and sat down before sipping his coffee.

'They told me I was being arrested on suspicion of the kidnap and murder of Laura Mitchell.'

'Yes, she was kidnapped . . . and murdered,' Hunter said and paused for a second. 'Everyone in the station has their money on you. They think you did it.'

Smith closed his eyes for a fraction of a second and breathed out a heartfelt breath. 'When?'

Hunter regarded him.

'When was she murdered?' There was pain in his voice.

'A few days before we knocked on your door.' In contrast, Hunter's voice was calm and collected.

Smith kept his eyes on Hunter but his stare was distant. The kind of stare you get when your mind is somewhere far away.

'We know that you talked to Laura on the last night of her exhibition at the Daniel Rossdale Art Gallery. And we've seen the room inside your apartment.'

His focus returned to Smith's stare.

'I have the right to have an attorney present, don't I?'

'Of course you do, but I'm not here to interrogate you.'

Smith chuckled. 'Really? So what's this, a friendly chat? You're here to be my buddy, is that it?'

'Right now, you need all the friends you can get.'

'Friends won't help. You already said that everyone's money is on me. Your mind is already made up. You'll believe what you wanna believe no matter what.'

'Try me.' Hunter leaned forward.

Smith's focus moved to the two-way mirror and the tension intensified. 'Do you really think I'd be able to hurt Laura . . . in any way?' His gaze returned to Hunter. 'I love her in a way you'll never understand.'

Hunter allowed the moment to settle.

'The kind of love that strangles your heart and keeps you awake at night?' he countered. 'The kind of love that makes it hard for you to breathe when she's near, even if she never notices you? The kind of love that if you have to wait forever for just a simple touch, or a kiss, you will?'

Smith went silent.

'Yes, I know the kind of love you're talking about.'

Smith interlaced his fingers together so tight his knuckles started to lose their color.

'Is that how you loved her?' Something in Hunter's voice made Smith believe that maybe he understood.

'I knew Laura from the bank. Way before she became a famous painter.' Smith's tone was full of melancholy. He gave Hunter a sad headshake. 'But she didn't know me. She never noticed me. I don't think she even knew I existed. I spoke to her a couple of times back then, in the coffee room. She was always nice, don't get me wrong, but every time I talked to her, I had to reintroduce myself. I was never important or attractive enough for her to remember who I was.' His eyes filled with sadness. 'I wasn't even invited to her leaving party.'

Inside the observation room, Captain Blake turned to Garcia. 'We need a list of names and photographs of all bank employees from Laura Mitchell's section during her last six months there.'

Garcia was already on the phone. 'I'm on it.'

On the other side of the glass Smith relaxed the tight grip on his hands and blood returned to his knuckles. 'I stayed with the bank for another two years after she left. But I followed her career from the beginning. I read every article, attended every exhibition. I even started liking and appreciating art.' A sliver of confidence crept into his eyes. 'Then one day I looked in the mirror and decided that I wouldn't be weak any more. I decided that I *was* important and attractive enough for her to notice me, I just needed to polish off some rough edges.'

'So you created your new identity,' Hunter pressed.

'More than an identity. I created a whole new *person*. New diet, strict exercise program, new haircut, new hair color, colored contact lenses, new wardrobe, new attitude, new way of talking, new everything. I became someone she would notice. Someone she would talk to and flirt with. Someone she'd like to spend time with. I became James Smith.'

Hunter had to admire his determination.

'I went to every one of her exhibitions. But I still couldn't sum up the nerve to say hello to her again. I was scared she'd recognize me. That she'd see straight through me . . . that she'd laugh at me.'

Hunter knew exactly why. Changing a person's appearance is easy – it can be done in one afternoon or, in the case of changing a person's body shape, with the right diet and exercise program – a few months. Changing a person's personality is much harder, though – it requires work, determination, willpower and it can take years. Smith used to be a shy, low self-esteem, low-confidence, scared-of-rejection person, and though he looked completely different on the outside, he was yet to overcome all his personality glitches.

'She approached you that night, didn't she?' Hunter concluded.

Smith nodded. 'I was so surprised, I stuttered.' A glimpse of a smile graced his lips as he remembered.

'Did she give you her number?'

'Yes.'

'Did you call her?'

'Yes.'

'Do you remember when?' Hunter leaned forward and placed his elbows on the table.

'I remember the day, the time, and everything that was said.'

Hunter waited.

'It was the 4th March, at 4:30 p.m. I used a payphone and called her on her cell. She was on her way to her studio. We talked for a while and she asked me to call her back just before the weekend. She said that maybe we could go out for a drink or even dinner. She practically asked me out.' Smith's eyes moved from Hunter's face to the far wall for a long moment. When they moved back to Hunter, a liquid sheen had formed over them. 'You're a detective. Do you really think that after all I've done, after so many years trying to get her attention, trying to get her to notice me, to talk to me . . . when she finally does, I'd hurt her in any way?'

'Why did you run when we knocked on your door?'

'I panicked,' Smith replied with no hesitation. 'I knew that I had broken the law by living under a false identity. I know that I could be locked away for several years for it. Suddenly the police were at my door. I did what most people in my shoes would do, I didn't think, I just ran. Before I had time to consider, my picture was in every paper in town. I knew then that something was definitely not right. That's when I called you.'

Hunter remained silent. His stare locked on Smith's face. He'd said all that without flinching, without vacillating and without breaking eye contact with Hunter. If he was lying, Hunter decided, he was a master at it.

'*She* approached me that night,' Smith said again. '*She* smiled at me. *She* flirted with me. *She* gave me her number and asked me to call her. *She* wanted to have dinner with me . . . to go out on a date with me.' Smith faced the two-way mirror. 'I'd been dreaming about the day she'd finally noticed me for years. My dream had just come true. Why in the name of God would I hurt her?'

Eighty-Three

Hunter splashed some cold water over his face and stared at his tired reflection in the mirror. James Smith had requested an attorney. No matter what happened, without actual proof of any involvement between Smith and Laura Mitchell, the LAPD could only hold him without charge for a maximum of forty-eight hours. Captain Blake was already talking to the DA's office about charging Smith with fraud and impersonation. That way, they could keep him off the streets for longer, at least until they had more information on him, his story and his whereabouts on the nights of all three murders.

After leaving the interrogation room, Hunter had finally managed to get in touch with Mark Stratton, Jessica Black's boyfriend. Experience counted for nothing in these situations. There was no easy way to tell someone that their life had just been wrecked. That the person they loved the most had been taken away from them by a brutal killer. People dealt with loss and pain in their own way, but it was never easy.

Hunter didn't disclose every detail over the phone. He kept the information down to the bare minimum. Not surprisingly, Stratton thought the call was a prank at first, a very bad joke from one of his buddies. Many of them were notorious for their dark and distasteful sense of humor. Hunter knew denial is the most common initial shock reaction to sad news. When realization finally set in, Stratton broke down the way most people did. The same way Hunter had broken down years ago when a RHD detective knocked on his door to tell him his father had been shot in the chest by a bank robber.

Hunter splashed some more water on his face and wet his hair. The darkness inside him was lurking around again, murky and deep.

Stratton told Hunter that he'd be making his way back to LA as soon as possible – sometime today, and that he'd call Hunter as soon as he got back. Jessica Black's body still had to be positively identified.

Garcia was reading something on his computer screen when Hunter got back to his desk. 'Are you OK?' he asked. He understood exactly how difficult making those calls was.

Hunter nodded. 'I'm fine. Just needed to cool down, that's all.'

'Are you sure? You don't look fine.'

Hunter approached the pictures board and studied the photographs of all three victims again.

'Robert,' Garcia called, his voice just a few decibels louder.

Hunter turned and faced him. 'His interval between kidnapping and murdering his victims is shortening.'

'Yeah, I noticed that,' Garcia agreed. 'Kelly Jensen was the first to be kidnapped. She was killed almost three weeks later. Laura Mitchell was taken about a week after Kelly, but she was the first to die. We still don't know for sure, but it looks like Jessica Black went missing no longer than five days ago, and she turned up dead yesterday. It went from weeks to days. So either Jessica Black lost no time in break-ing his spell, or he's simply losing patience.'

Hunter said nothing.

Garcia sat back in his chair and pinched his chin. 'I was just checking the results from your national search on brunette victims with any sort of stitching to their mouths, sexual organs or both.'

'And . . . ?'

'Not a goddamn thing. It seems like most of the files only date back fourteen to fifteen years. Beyond that, we've got almost nothing.'

Hunter thought about it for a moment. 'Damn.'

'What . . . ?'

'Police records only started to be properly digitized . . . what? Maybe ten, twelve years ago at a stretch?'

'Something like that.'

'The problem is that the amount of everyday cases is so huge, most police departments around the country don't have the budget or the personnel to deal with the backlog. Most cases older than maybe fifteen years are probably just sitting inside boxes, getting dusty, down in basement stor-age rooms. Database searches will *never* get to them.'

'Great. So even if we're right, but it happened over fifteen years ago, we'll never know?'

Hunter was already typing away on his computer. 'Police files and databases might not be properly backlogged yet, but . . .'

Garcia waited but nothing else was forthcoming. 'But what?'

'But newspaper ones certainly are. I was stupid, I should've thought of that at first and searched the national news archives as well as the police ones.'

Hunter and Garcia searched the net and specific newspaper databases for hours, scanning through any piece that flagged up according to their search criteria. Three and a half hours later Garcia started reading a 20-year-old local newspaper article and felt a shiver run down his spine.

'Robert,' he called, placing both elbows on his desk, clasping his hands together and squinting at his screen. 'I think I might have something here.'

Eighty-Four

Los Angeles was a trendy nightclub Mecca full of see-and-be-seen clubs, which made the existence of a local bar like the Alibi Room a blessing. It dated back to the days of smoke-filled interiors and drunken games of pool. The place was really just one room with some vintage carpet, a line of locals bellied up to the bar, a single pool table with iffy geometrics and dead rails, a decent jukebox packed with rock albums and the best dive bar attraction of all time: cheap booze.

Whitney Myers spotted Xavier Nunez as soon as she walked through the door. He was sitting at one of the few low oak tables next to a window to the left of the bar. Two bottles of beer and a basket of corn tortillas were on the table in front of him.

Nunez was an odd-looking man. In his mid-thirties, he had a shaved head, long pointy face, large dark eyes, bowl ears, small crooked nose, pitted skin and lips so thin they looked like they'd been drawn using a marker pen. The slogan on his shirt read – *Tell your tits to stop staring at me*.

Nunez was another of Myers' contacts, whom she paid very handsomely when she needed information. He worked for the Los Angeles County Department of Coroner.

'Nice shirt,' Myers said as she came to his table. 'Get loads of girls when you wear it, do you?'

Nunez took a swig of his beer and looked up at her. Nunez was about to comment on her remark, but Myers smiled at him, and all he could do was melt in his seat.

'So, what have you got for me?'

Nunez reached for the plastic folder on the seat next to him.

'These were really hard to get.' He spoke with a heavy Puerto Rican accent.

Myers had a seat across the table from him.

'That's why I pay you so well, Xavier.' She reached for the folder but he pulled it away from her.

'Yeah, but special circumstances cases are *really, really* hard to get, d'you know what I mean? Maybe I deserve a little extra for it.'

Myers paused and smiled again, but this time there was no warmth in it. 'Don't go there, honey. I can be very nice when you play the way the game should be played. You know that I pay you more than enough. But if you wanna play hardball, trust me . . .' she placed her hand on his and gave it a subtle but firm squeeze, '. . . I can become a real bitch. The kinda bitch you and your homies don't wanna fuck with. So are you sure you wanna roll like this?'

Something in her voice and her touch made Nunez' mouth go dry.

'Hey, I was just joking. I know you pay me enough. I was talking more like you know . . . you and me . . . dinner . . . sometime . . . maybe . . .'

The warmth came back to her smile. 'As attractive as you are, Xavier, I'm already taken,' she lied.

He tilted his head from side to side. 'I'd settle for mean-ingless sex.'

Myers finally took the folder from Xavier. 'How about you settle for what we agreed?' Her voice was menacing.

'OK, that will do too.'

Myers flipped open the folder. The first photograph was of Kelly Jensen's face. The stitches to her mouth hadn't been removed yet. She stared at it for several seconds. Though she'd been told about it by Hunter, seeing the photographs brought a new dimension to the evil of the crime.

Myers moved to the next picture and froze. They were of the second set of stitches to Kelly Jensen's body. Hunter had never told her about those. She had to take a deep breath before moving on. The next photo was a wide shot of Kelly Jensen's entire body. Myers studied it carefully.

'Where are the cuts?' she whispered to herself, but it didn't escape Xavier's ears.

'Cuts?' he said. 'There are none.'

'I was told the killer used a knife to kill her.'

'Apparently he did. But he didn't cut her on the outside.'

Myers looked questioningly.

'He inserted it into her.'

Myers' whole body turned into gooseflesh.

'And the knife is no knife I've ever seen. There's a picture of it in there.'

Myers quickly leafed through all the photos until she found it.

'Jesus Christ . . . What in the name of God . . . ?'

They were dealing with a monster here. She had to find Katia. And fast.

Eighty-Five

Hunter looked up from his computer screen. Garcia had his stare fixed on his PC monitor, his brow creased in a peculiar way.

'What have you got?'

A couple more seconds before Garcia finally looked up. 'A 20-year-old article.'

'About what?'

'A family murder/suicide. Husband found out that his wife was sleeping with someone else, lost his head, killed the someone else, his 10-year-old kid, his wife and then blew his head off with a shotgun.'

Hunter frowned. 'Yes, and . . . ?'

'Here's where it gets interesting. It says that the husband stitched parts of his wife's body shut before killing her.'

Hunter's eyes widened.

'But that's all. It gives no further details as to which body parts.'

'Did he shoot his wife?'

'Again, it doesn't say, and that's what's strange about it. It's a potentially big story, but the article is quite brief.'

'Where did this happen?' Hunter got up and approached Garcia's desk.

'Northern California, Healdsburg in Sonoma County.'

Hunter took control of Garcia's computer mouse and scrolled through the article. It was about five hundred words long. Garcia was right, it was too brief, mentioning what happened almost by passage. No specific details were given other than the ones involved. The victims had been Emily and Andrew Harper – mother and son, and Emily's lover, Nathan Gardner. Emily's husband, Ray Harper, had carried out all three executions before shooting himself in the couple's bedroom. There were two pictures. The larger of the two showed a two-story white-fronted house with an impeccable lawn, completely surrounded by yellow crime-scene tape. Three police vehicles were parked on the street. The second picture showed a couple of county sheriff deputies bringing a dark polyethylene body bag out of the front door. The expression on their faces told its own story.

'Is this the only article?' he asked. 'No follow-up?'

Garcia shook his head. 'Nope, I've already checked. Nothing on the Harper case prior or after that date. Which again, I find hard to believe.'

Hunter scrolled up and checked the name of the newspaper – the *Healdsburg Tribune*. He checked the name of the reporter who covered the story – Stephen Anderson. After a quick search, he had the address and phone number for the newspaper headquarters.

The phone rang for thirty seconds before someone answered it on the other side. The person sounded young. He told Hunter that he'd never heard of a reporter called Stephen Anderson, but then again, he'd only been with the paper for six months. He was with the newspaper's Sonoma University trainee program. After asking around, the kid returned to the phone and told Hunter that according to one of the most senior reporters, Mr. Anderson had retired nine years ago. He still lived in Healdsburg.

Hunter disconnected and got the operator for Sonoma County. Stephen Anderson's name wasn't listed. He clicked off again and called the Office of Operations. Less than five minutes later he had an address and phone number.

Eighty-Six

It was just past eight in the evening when Stephen Anderson answered his phone inside his home office on the outskirts of Healdsburg. Hunter quickly introduced himself.

'Los Angeles Police Department?' Anderson said, sounding worried. His voice was husky. Hunter could tell it came from years of smoking rather than natural charm. 'Are you sure you've got the right person, Detective?'

'I'm certain,' Hunter replied, motioning Garcia to listen in.

'And what will this be about?'

'An article you wrote twenty years ago flagged up on one of our searches. Unfortunately the article is quite brief. I was wondering if you wouldn't mind giving us a few more details on it.'

Even down the phone line, the silence that followed felt uncomfortable.

'Mr. Anderson, are you still with me?'

'Call me Stephen, and yes, I'm still here,' he said. 'Twenty years ago ... That must be the Harper family murder tragedy.'

'That's right.'

A new brief silence. 'You said my article flagged up in an LAPD investigation search. I'm guessing, a homicide investigation?'

'That's correct.'

Hunter heard the sound of a lighter being flicked a couple of times.

'You have a victim over there that's been stitched up?'

This time the silence came from Hunter. Anderson was quick on the uptake. Hunter chose his next words carefully.

'It sounds like there could be similarities between the Harper case and one of our ongoing investigations, yes, but as I said, your article doesn't describe what happened in great detail.'

'And those similarities would be the stitching of the victim's body?'

'I didn't say that.'

'Oh, c'mon, Detective, I spent thirty-five years as a reporter. I know that the similarities you're referring to couldn't just be a jealousy-fueled family murder/suicide, or someone blowing his head off with a shotgun. You're an LA cop – the city where the freaks come out to play. You probably have crimes like those happening on your doorstep every week. From my article, the only unusual aspect about the Harpers incident is the mentioning of stitches.'

There was no doubt about it, Anderson was quick on the uptake. Hunter conceded.

'Yes, we have a case here where stitches have been applied to the victim's body.'

The silence returned to the line for a moment.

'Do you remember any more details?' Hunter pushed. 'Or is the reason why your article was so brief with no follow-ups was because that was all the information you ever had on the case?'

'Do you know anything about Sonoma County, Detective?'

'The biggest wine production county in California,' Hunter replied.

'That's correct.' Anderson coughed a couple of times to clear his throat. 'You see, Detective, Sonoma lives off its wine production county status in every possible aspect – not only by producing great wine. There are special events every month of the year all around the county which pull in the crowds. Agricultural festivals, holiday celebrations, street fairs, music carnivals and more. There's always something happening somewhere.'

Hunter could already see where Anderson was going with this.

'We can't compare to Los Angeles or Vegas, but we have our share of tourists. Publicizing something as horrific as what happened that day would've benefited no one. The *Tribune* wouldn't have sold any more copies than it did on a day-to-day basis either.' Anderson coughed again, a lot heavier this time. 'I didn't get to see the scene, but yes, I did find out the details. On that same day I was approached by Chief Cooper and Mayor Taylor. We talked for a long time, and it was decided that it would be in the town's best interests if the paper didn't sensationalize the story, and by that I mean I agreed to play it down. So between the police, the mayor and the paper, a very heavy lid was placed over the whole incident.'

'We really need to know those details, Stephen.'

The pause that followed felt laden.

'You're not gonna be breaking your promise to the police chief or the mayor,' Hunter insisted. 'None of what you tell me will go any further, but I do need to know those details. It could save lives.'

'It's been twenty years, I guess,' Anderson said after taking a long drag of his cigarette. 'Where would you like me to start?'

Eighty-Seven

'I knew the Harpers quite well,' Anderson began. 'You have to understand that Healdsburg isn't a big town, even today. Back then we didn't have more than maybe nine thousand people living here. Ray Harper was a shoemaker and his wife, Emily, was a teacher in the primary school. They'd been married for over fifteen years, and I guess, like in so many longstanding marriages, things weren't a bed of roses any more.'

Hunter was busy taking notes.

'Emily started sleeping with another schoolteacher, Nathan Gardner, which in a city this small, isn't a very smart idea, unless you think you're invisible.'

Hunter heard Anderson take another drag of his cigarette.

'Somehow Ray found out during that year's winter school break. Now Ray had always been a very calm person. I'd never known him to lose his head. Actually, I'd never known him to even raise his voice. He was just your regular, every-day, church-going, quiet kinda guy. And that's what was so out of character about what he did.'

Garcia looked like he was about to ask something but Hunter lifted his hand, stopping him. He didn't want to rush Anderson.

'Well, that day Ray completely lost control, as if he was possessed. He went over to Nathan's apartment and killed him first, before going back to his house and killing his kid, his wife, and then splattering his brains all over the walls with a double-barreled shotgun.'

Anderson coughed and Hunter waited as he heard the cigarette lighter being flicked on again.

'How did he kill them?'

'That was the reason why Chief Cooper and Mayor Taylor asked to talk to me that day. Because of the way Ray went about his killing business. Ted Bundy is a boy scout compared to what he did.' Anderson paused. 'In Nathan's apartment, Ray tied him down and used a meat cleaver to cut his . . . penis off.' A longer pause this time. 'That was it. Nothing else. Ray simply left him there to bleed to death. Now, you might ask – how come Nathan didn't scream his head off and alert the whole neighborhood. Well, the reason would be because Ray used a shoe needle and thread to stitch Nathan's mouth shut.'

Garcia's eyes flickered towards Hunter.

'Ray went from Nathan's apartment back to his house . . .' Anderson continued, '. . . killed his kid inside his truck, and then did the same thing he did to Nathan to his wife, Emily. He stitched her mouth shut too.'

Hunter had stopped writing.

'But it didn't end there.'

Hunter and Garcia waited.

'Ray took what he'd cut off Nathan with him, shoved it inside his wife, and stitched her shut as well.'

Garcia flinched but Hunter's face remained neutral. His blue eyes locked onto a blank page in his notebook.

'I still can't believe that Ray did what he did. Not the Ray Harper we knew. It just couldn't have been the same person. As I said, it was like he was possessed.'

A short pause, a new cigarette drag.

'After stitching his wife shut, Ray sat on the floor in front of her and blew his brains all over the room with his shotgun.'

'And you're sure those facts are correct?' Hunter asked. 'You said you never saw the crime scene for yourself.'

A nervous chuckle.

'Yes, I'm sure. I didn't see the crime scene, but I saw the pictures with my own eyes. Those images will be imprinted in my brain forever. Sometimes I still have nightmares about them. And the words . . .'

'Words?' Hunter cocked his head forward.

There was no response.

'Stephen?' Hunter called. 'Are you still there? What words?'

'Ray left his wife tied to their bed all stitched up. But before blowing his head off, he used blood to write something on the wall.'

'And what did he write?' Garcia asked.

'He wrote the words – *He's inside you.*'

Eighty-Eight

Hunter came off the phone with the Healdsburg Police Department after speaking to Anderson and went straight down to Captain Blake's office. He caught her as she was getting ready to go home for the day.

'I need to go up to Healdsburg first thing tomorrow morning,' he said, letting the door close behind him. 'I'll be away for one, maybe two days.'

'What?' She looked up from her computer screen. 'Healdsburg? Why the hell?'

Hunter ran her through everything he'd found out. Captain Blake listened to the whole story in absolute silence, her face immutable. When he was finished, she breathed out as if she'd been holding her breath for minutes.

'When did all that happen, again?'

'Twenty years ago.'

Her eyebrows lifted. 'Let me guess, because that case is older than fifteen years, the files aren't in the Unified California Police Database, nothing's been digitized, right?'

Hunter nodded. 'I've searched by date, town and victim names. There's nothing. The records will be in paper form in the Healdsburg PD storage archives.'

'Great. So other than the newspaper article and the reporter's story, what do we have?'

'I just got off the phone with Chief Suarez in Healdsburg. He wasn't the chief back then. He was transferred and relocated from Fair Oaks nine years ago, a year after the entire Healdsburg Police Department was moved to its new location. He hadn't even heard of the Harper case.'

Captain Blake paused and looked at Hunter sideways. 'Wait a second. Why are you going to Healdsburg? Homicide case files would've been filed with the Sonoma District Attorney's office, and that's in . . .'

'Santa Rosa,' Hunter confirmed. 'I've called them as well.' He pointed to his watch. 'After office hours. There was nobody there who I could talk to. But if the case files aren't in the California Police DB, it means that either the Sonoma DA's office don't have them, or they're piled up in some dusty room still waiting to be digitized. I'd like to have a look at the crime-scene pictures and the autopsy reports if I can get them, but the police and the DA case files won't help us much. They'll just describe what happened back then in a little more detail than Stephen did. It was a family murder/suicide, Captain. Open and shut case. No witness accounts, no investigation records, if there even was one. They had nothing to investigate. Wife sleeps with another man, husband gets jealous, loses control . . . the lover and the whole family pays the ultimate price. Case closed. We have replica cases up and down the country.'

Captain Blake sat back on her chair and rested her chin on her knuckles. 'And you wanna talk to someone who was involved in the case?'

Hunter nodded. 'The old chief of police retired seven years ago, but he still lives in Healdsburg. Somewhere near Lake Sonoma. I don't really wanna talk to him over the phone.'

The captain saw something shine in Hunter's eyes. 'OK, talk to me, Robert. What are you really after? Do you think our killer came from Healdsburg?'

Hunter finally had a seat on one of the wingback chairs in front of the captain's desk. 'I think our killer was there, Captain. I think he saw that crime scene.'

Captain Blake studied Hunter for a beat. 'A trauma?'

'Yes.'

'You mean . . . a shock trauma, induced by what he saw?'

'Yes.' Hunter ran a hand over his left arm and felt the bullet scar on his triceps. 'The similarities between what happened in Healdsburg twenty years ago and what we have happening here today are too strong to be coincidental.'

Captain Blake said nothing.

'The way Ray Harper killed his family . . . the way he killed his wife's lover . . . even big city, seasoned Homicide detectives would find such a crime scene hard to deal with, never mind a small town's police department whose idea of a tough crime is probably jaywalking.'

The captain started fidgeting with one of her earrings. 'But hold on. If the Healdsburg Police Department did their job properly, then not many people would've had access to that crime scene. Presumably officers and the sheriff's coroner, that's all.'

Hunter nodded. 'That's why I need to talk to the old chief of police, and hopefully find the crime-scene logbook. We need to establish the whereabouts of everyone who had access to it that day.'

The captain's eyes stayed on Hunter while her brain searched for answers. 'Could a similar kind of trauma occur just by looking at the crime-scene pictures?'

Hunter considered. 'It would depend on how mentally

vulnerable the person was at the time. But yes, deeply disturbing photographs can easily initiate something inside a person's mind.'

Captain Blake paused while she thought about it. 'But the kills aren't exactly the same as the one in Healdsburg. Our victims aren't tied down. The words he uses aren't exactly the same either.'

'That's not uncommon, Captain. A trauma can be like a large picture that's flashed in front of your eyes. Not everyone will remember every single detail perfectly. Adaptation is also a major consequence of crimes derived from early traumas. That's what he's doing.'

Captain Blake closed her eyes and shook her head slowly.

'There's one more thing, Captain,' Hunter said, standing up. 'Emily Harper, the woman that was stitched shut and killed in Healdsburg twenty years ago was a schoolteacher.'

'Yeah, I know, you told me that. And . . . ?'

Hunter paused by the door. 'She taught arts and music.'

Eighty-Nine

Hunter thought about driving to Healdsburg, but even with zero traffic it would've taken him at least seven hours to cover the four hundred and fifty miles. Spending over fifteen hours on the road was simply out of the question.

So Hunter caught the 6:30 a.m. nonstop flight from LA's LAX to Healdsburg municipal airport. The flight was on time, and by 8:10 a.m. Hunter was driving his rental Chrysler Sebring out of the relatively empty Hertz forecourt.

Even without a map or an in-car navigation system, it took Hunter no longer than fifteen minutes to get from the airport to the Healdsburg Police Department in Center Street.

Chief Suarez was in his late fifties, stocky, intimidating, with a presence that projected itself without him having to speak. He looked like a man who had spent way too much time in the same job. As he'd told Hunter over the phone, he'd never heard of the Harper case. It had happened eleven years before he was transferred to Healdsburg. But Chief Suarez was also a very thorough and inquisitive man, and overnight he researched what he could.

'One of the first people I met when I moved here was a guy named Ted Jenkins,' the chief told Hunter after showing him into his office. 'Coffee?' he gestured towards an aluminum thermal flask on his desk.

Hunter shook his head. 'I'm OK, Chief, thanks. I grabbed one as I was leaving the airport.'

Chief Suarez laughed. 'Yeah, and I bet it tasted like cat piss.'

Hunter conceded. 'Probably just a step above it.'

'No, no. You've gotta try this.' He grabbed a mug from a tray on top of the metal filing cabinet by the window and poured Hunter a cup. 'No one makes coffee like my Louise. She's got a gift. Like a family secret. How do you take it?'

Hunter had to admit that even from that distance, the coffee smelled incredible. 'Black is great.'

'I like you already. That's how coffee is *meant* to be drunk.' The chief handed Hunter the cup.

'You were telling me about Ted Jenkins,' he said before having a sip. 'Wow.' His eyes widened.

Chief Suarez smiled. 'Good, isn't it? I'll ask Louise to make you a flask before you leave.'

Hunter nodded his thanks.

'OK. Ted Jenkins. He's the editor for the *Healdsburg Tribune*. Back then he was just a reporter. I had a drink with him last night after I got off the phone with you. He certainly remembers what happened. A terrible case where a cheated husband lost his head and killed his wife, his kid, the wife's lover and then blew his own head off with a shotgun. Huge for a place like Healdsburg, but for an LA cop . . . ?' Chief Suarez leaned forward, placed both hands on his desk and interlaced his fingers. 'One of the reasons I made chief of police is because I'm a very curious man, Detective. And your phone call yesterday got my curiosity steaming.' He paused and took a sip of his coffee. 'I looked you up. Had a quick chat with your captain this morning too.'

Hunter said nothing.

The chief reached for his reading glasses and his eyes moved to a notepad on his desk. 'Los Angeles Police Department – Homicide Special Section. Your specialty – ultra-violent crimes. Now that's something us folks over here only see in movies.' His eyes returned to Hunter over his spectacles. 'Your captain told me you're the best there is. And that got my old brain thinking. Everyone knows Los Angeles is a crazy town, Detective. Gangs, drugs, drive-by shoot-outs, serial killers, mass murderers, killing sprees, and worse. Why would a murder case that happened twenty years ago in a small town like Healdsburg interest the Homicide Special Section in LA?'

Hunter sipped his coffee.

'So late last night I went down to our archives room to look for the case files. Turns out that anything older than ten years was stuck under piles and piles of junk inside unmarked cardboard boxes at the back of a smelly and cobweb-filled room. It took me and an officer nearly five hours to find them.' He tapped a very old-looking paper folder next to his desktop PC.

Hunter moved to the edge of his seat.

'Imagine my surprise when I saw the pictures and read the reports of what had *really* happened.' He handed the file to Hunter.

Hunter flipped it open and the first photograph he saw made his heart skip a beat.

Ninety

The woman was in her late twenties, early thirties. It was hard to tell from the photo because her face was swollen and battered, but even so, Hunter could see she'd been pretty, very pretty.

A large bruise covered the left side of her forehead, eye and cheekbone. Her shoulder-length black hair was wet and sticking to her face. Her large hazel eyes, that Hunter was sure had once dazzled many men, were wide open. Her terrifying fear was frozen in them like a snapshot. Just like Laura, Kelly and Jessica, her lips had been stitched tightly shut with thick black thread, but the stitches were neat and tidy, unlike those on the victims in Los Angeles. Blood had seeped through the needle punctures and run down to her chin and neck. She was alive when he stitched her up. A brownish substance had also accumulated between her lips and at the corners of her mouth – vomit. She had been sick and the discharge had had nowhere to go.

The second picture was a close-up of the words that had been written the wall – HE'S INSIDE YOU. Ray Harper had used blood to write them. The third picture showed the next set of stitches on her body. Her groin and inner thighs were also smeared with blood that had seeped through the puncture wounds. She'd been tied to the bed by her wrists and ankles in a spread-eagled position. But the bed had been tipped on its end and pushed up against a wall, placing the victim in a standing position and facing the inside of the room.

Hunter moved to the next picture – a male body lying on the floor directly in front of the bed and the female victim. His entire head and most of his neck were missing. A double-barreled shotgun was lying partly over his torso and partly in an enormous pool of blood. Both of his hands were resting on the gun's stock. From the destruction to his head, Hunter knew he'd discharged both rounds simultaneously, and that the barrel ends had been placed under his chin.

Hunter skipped the rest of the photos and skimmed over the report and the autopsy files. He finally found what he was looking for as he got to the last page inside the folder – the crime-scene log sheet. Eight different people had had direct access to the Harper crime scene that day – the county coroner, a county forensic investigator, the county sheriff together with two of his deputies, Chief Cooper and two other Healdsburg police officers.

'Are Officer Perez or Officer Kimble still with the police department?' he asked Chief Suarez.

The chief scratched a thin scar under his chin. 'Officer Perez retired four years ago. He lives just down the road from me. His son is with the fire department. Officer Kimble passed away a few years back. Pancreatic cancer won that battle.'

'I'm sorry to hear that.' Hunter's attention returned to the log sheet. 'Do you know any of these deputies from the County Sheriff's Office, Peter Edmunds or Joseph Hale?'

The chief nodded. 'Sure, but they aren't deputies any more. Peter Edmunds is Captain of Field Services and Operations and Joseph Hale is Assistant Sheriff of the Law

Enforcement Division. They both live in Santa Rosa. They're great guys.'

Hunter rubbed his eyes for an instant. The county coroner, the county forensic investigator, the county sheriff, and Healdsburg old chief of police, Chief Cooper, would all be over sixty-five years of age today. It wasn't impossible but there was very little chance any of them would've become a serial killer in their old age. That meant that everyone who had attended the crime scene was accounted for, unless someone hadn't been logged in. But if that was the case, Hunter had no way of finding out who else had seen the scene. Instinctively he flipped through the files and the pictures again and suddenly frowned. Something caught his eye. He returned to the photographs, this time studying every picture attentively. When he reached the last one, he flicked back to the files and scanned them again, all the way to the last page.

'Are these all the case files or is there another folder somewhere in your archives room?' he asked.

'That's it. Nothing else.'

'Are you sure?'

Chief Suarez arched his eyebrows. 'Yes I'm sure. I told you, it took us five hours to find those files. We've been through every single one of the old boxes, and believe me, there were quite a few of them. Why?'

Hunter closed the folder on his lap.

'Because there's something missing.'

Ninety-One

The drive to Chief Cooper's house took Hunter less than fifteen minutes.

He stepped out of the car, and as he closed the door behind him, a woman came out onto the house's porch. She was in her mid-sixties, slender but not skinny. She wore a simple blue dress and a pocketed apron. She had a long angular face framed by straight gray hair falling to her shoulders.

'Morning,' she said with a smile. Her voice was a little hoarse, as if she'd been fighting off a cold. 'You must be the detective from Los Angeles Tom mentioned.' Her blue eyes fixed on Hunter's face. They were as tender as her voice.

'Yes, ma'am,' Hunter said, approaching her. He produced his credentials and she scrutinized them like a seasoned pro.

'My name is Mary,' she offered, extending her hand. 'Tom's wife.'

'It's a pleasure to meet you, ma'am.'

They shook hands and Hunter was surprised by how much strength she packed in her tiny hand.

'Tom is down by the lake, fishing.' She shook her head in a mock-disapproving way. 'He's always fishing. Well . . .' she laughed, 'at least it gives him something to do. Or else he'd be hammering things in the house all day long.'

Hunter smiled back politely.

'Just follow that path over there all the way down the small hill,' she said, pointing to a narrow trail that seemed to lead deep into the woods to the right of the house. 'You can't miss him.' She paused and quickly assessed the sky. 'Do you have a raincoat in that car of yours?'

'I'm afraid I don't.'

Mary gave him a sweet smile. 'Wait just a minute, then.' She walked back into the house. A few seconds later she reappeared carrying a police-issue raincoat. 'Rain ain't far away, you better take this or you might catch a cold.' She handed him the coat. 'Tom's got enough coffee and cakes with him to feed the two of you for a day and a half.'

Hunter thanked her again and disappeared down the trail. It twisted left and right several times, getting steeper the deeper Hunter moved into the forest. It led down to a secluded spot by Lake Sonoma. He paused as he reached a rock and dirt landing at the bottom of the path. There was no one there. The lake was placid, still even. Hunter took a step back and listened for a moment. Something didn't seem right.

Suddenly he swung around, drawing his gun.

'Woah, easy.' The man standing about five feet from him with his hands up in the air was in his late-sixties, tall and lean. He had two tiny tuffs of white hair over his ears, black rimmed glasses pushed up all the way to the bridge of his nose, and a cotton white moustache that seemed way too thick for his thin face and lips. Despite his age, he still looked like he could handle himself in any sort of fight.

'You heard me coming up behind you?' His voice was commanding.

'Something like that,' Hunter replied, his gun still targeting the old man.

'Damn, I'm either losing my touch or you've got fantastic

hearing. And that was a fast draw if I've ever seen one.' He waited a few seconds. 'I'm Tom Cooper. You must be Detective Robert Hunter from the Los Angeles Robbery Homicide Division. Do you mind if I lower my hands?'

'Yeah, sorry about that.' Hunter flicked the safety into place and holstered his gun.

'You're not very light on your feet, though. I could hear you coming from halfway down the hill.'

Hunter looked down at his now dirt-covered boots. 'I wasn't expecting a stealth exercise.'

Chief Cooper smiled. 'Sorry, old habits die hard.' He offered his hand.

Hunter shook it firmly.

'I'm all set up over here.' He pointed to another trail that went around some trees and to the left. Hunter followed him into a second clearance where a fisherman's chair and a small weave basket packed with food were arranged by the water. 'Help yourself to some coffee and cake if you like. Do you fish?'

'I tried it once when I was a kid.' Hunter shook his head as he poured coffee from one of the two large thermal flasks into a cup. 'I wasn't any good at it.'

Chief Cooper laughed. 'No one is good at it if you only do it once. I've been doing it for years and I still have a lot to learn.' He reached for a thin fishing rod, grabbed a couple of live black lugworms from a container, and pushed their slimy bodies through the hook. 'I prefer live bait, it's . . .'

'Nicer for the fish,' Hunter finished. 'And since you don't keep them, might as well give them a nice treat in exchange for having their mouths hooked.' He had a sip of his coffee and nodded. It was just as good as the one he had back at the police station.

The chief studied Hunter curiously before looking at his setup. 'No fish net or containers to take my catch back up to the house.' He nodded. 'You're observant, but I guess you wouldn't be a detective if you weren't.' He swung his hook into the lake. 'OK, I know you didn't come all this way to learn about fishing or to shoot the breeze. You said on the phone that you needed to talk to me about the Harper case.'

Hunter nodded. 'Do you remember it well?'

Chief Cooper stared back at Hunter and his playful tone had vanished. 'You don't forget a crime scene like that, Detective. I don't care how experienced you are. I know you've been through the station first 'cause Chief Suarez just called me. You saw the pictures, right? Could anyone forget those images?'

Hunter said nothing.

'You didn't tell me much over the phone, but I guess you didn't have to. The way I see it, the only reason the LAPD RHD would be interested in a 20-year-old case from a small town is because you guys must have something down there that's pretty close to what happened here.'

Hunter stared at his reflection in the water for a moment. 'If I'm right, Chief, it's a lot closer than you think.'

Ninety-Two

Chief Cooper slotted his fishing rod into the appropriate hook next to his chair and turned to face Hunter.

'When I left LA this morning, my main concern was finding the log sheet for the Harper crime scene. There are only eight names on it.' He retrieved his notebook from his jacket pocket. 'Yours and two of your officers, Kimble and Perez. The Sonoma County sheriff at the time, Sheriff Hudson and two of his deputies, Edmunds and Hale. The county coroner at the time, Doctor Bennett and a forensic investigator, Gustavo Ortiz. Is that right?'

Chief Cooper didn't have to think about it. He nodded immediately.

'Can you remember if anyone else saw that scene, anyone at all? Someone who somehow wasn't logged onto the sheet?'

The chief shook his head firmly. 'No one else saw the scene. Not once we got there.' He poured himself some more coffee. 'The Harper house was only about a block away from the old police station. Tito, their neighbor at the time, called the station saying he heard a gunshot. Tito was, and still is, a pretty accomplished hunter. So when he said he heard a shotgun being fired, I knew it couldn't have been a mistake. I was at the station when he called. It took me less than a minute to get there. I was first at the scene.' He paused and looked away. 'I'd never seen anything like it. Not even in case studies. And to tell you the truth, I hope I never see anything like it again.'

The sky was getting menacingly dark and the wind had picked up a notch.

'A minute after I got to the house, Officers Kimble and Perez arrived. I knew straight away I had to get the County Sheriff's Office involved. Despite our restricted experience with homicides, we all knew the protocol. We immediately isolated the house. No one other than the three of us had access to the scene.'

'Until the sheriff and the coroner arrived,' Hunter added.

'That's right. As you said, Doctor Bennett, who is now retired, had an investigator with him, Gustavo Ortiz. He's now the chief coroner investigator for Santa Clara County. Sheriff Hudson had two deputies with him, Edmunds and Hale.'

Hunter nodded. 'Chief Suarez told me. Edmunds is a captain now and Hale is assistant sheriff. They both live in Santa Rosa.'

Chief Cooper confirmed this. 'No one else entered the house or saw the scene. I am sure because I was there until all the photographs were taken and the bodies removed.'

Thin rain started falling, but neither man moved.

'The Harpers had a son, right? Andrew,' Hunter said.

Chief Cooper nodded slowly.

'I've been through all the files down at the station. There's no photograph of the body, no autopsy report and no mention of what happened to him. It's like all the files on the kid are missing.'

The way Chief Cooper looked at Hunter made the hairs on the back of his neck stand on end.

'His files aren't missing. They aren't there because his body was never found.'

Ninety-Three

'What?' Hunter cleared the rain from his eyebrows and stared back at Chief Cooper. 'Never found? So how did you know he was murdered?'

The chief let out a deep sigh. His glasses were so heavy with rain Hunter could barely see his eyes. 'The truth is that we didn't know. But that was what the evidence told us.'

'What evidence?'

Chief Cooper finally pulled the nylon hood of his rain-coat over his head and retreated a few steps back to the shelter of a large tree. Hunter followed him.

'The Harpers tragedy happened on a Sunday,' the chief explained. 'Every Sunday, without fail, for the six years previous to that day, Ray took his son fishing. Sometimes to Lake Sonoma, sometimes to Rio Nido, and sometimes to Russian River. They're all within driving distance. I went with them several times. Ray was a great fisherman, and his boy was starting to get pretty good at it too.

'Tito, the neighbor who called in "shots fired", saw Ray and his kid packing the truck a couple of hours before he heard the shot. The owner of the gas station a few blocks away from their house also confirmed seeing the kid in the passenger's seat of Ray's truck while Ray went into the store to buy some ice cream. Andrew never came back to the house with his father. When Forensics checked the truck, they found the kid's shirt and shoes. There was blood on the shirt, on the shoes, on the car's dashboard, and on the inside of the passenger's door. The kid's blood. The lab confirmed it.'

'Wasn't there an investigation into the boy's disappearance?'

'Yes, there was. But we found nothing other than what I just told you. We don't know where he took his son, Detective – Sonoma Lake, Rio Nido or Russian River. There are also acres and acres of forest surrounding Healdsburg and the rivers. He could've killed his son and buried or left him to the wolves somewhere in the forest. He could've weighted the kid's body down and dumped him in the lake or the river. Finding the body without knowing where he went that day was a pretty impossible task. Though we did try, we never found it.'

The chief took off his glasses and rubbed the bridge of his nose where the pads had left two sunken red marks.

'Ray was a good man, but he suffered from depression,' he continued. 'I think he found out about Emily's affair a few days earlier because there was thought put into what he did. It wasn't your typical loss of control murder, though it might've looked that way from all the mess and blood. We figured Ray found out that Emily saw her lover when she thought it was safe to do so. So he got his kid out of the house and killed him first, disposing of the body somewhere. He then went over to Nathan Gardner's apartment, disfigured him and left him there, bleeding to death, but not before stitching his mouth shut. After that, Ray returned to his house to confront his wife, and to complete his crazy killing plan.'

Chief Cooper paused and looked straight into Hunter's eyes.

'And I have no doubt that in Ray's plan, no one was coming out alive. *No one*.'

Ninety-Four

Garcia stood across the room from the unmade bed, staring at the mess of clothes and objects on the floor.

Mark Stratton, Jessica Black's boyfriend, had cut short his band's pre-tour and come back to LA in the early hours of the morning. Garcia accompanied him to the morgue so he could positively identify her body.

No matter how physically or mentally strong anyone is, seeing a loved one lying naked on a cold metal morgue's body-tray will cut through their defenses. Despite all the stitches having been removed, Jessica's face seemed to have frozen with an expression of terror and pain. Mark didn't have to ask if she'd suffered.

His legs gave away within seconds of him being in the room, but Garcia managed to grab him before he hit the floor.

Hunter had told Mark over the phone that there was a possibility that Jessica had been abducted from inside their own apartment. He explained that it was very important that the police and a forensic team had a look at it as soon as possible. It was also very important that he didn't disturb anything. It didn't quite work that way.

Since Mark had come off the phone to Hunter late yesterday, he hadn't stopped shaking. He had incessantly called his home number and Jessica's cell phone, leaving message after message. He just couldn't think straight. Emotions took over and he had lost it, destroying his hotel room in anger and frustration.

Without knowing what had happened, the rest of his band had to kick his door in and hold him down. It took the tour manager a couple of hours to get things organized, including a flight back to LA. By then Mark was tramp-drunk, and at the airport he wasn't allowed to board the plane.

'Aviation rules,' explained the young woman at the airline counter. 'He's way too inebriated to fly. I'm sorry.'

That had been the last daily flight back to Los Angeles. In the end, they had to hire a private plane to take him back.

After a cab dropped him by his private condo, Mark, still half-drunk, stumbled rather than walked through his front door. At that moment all hope of things not being disturbed inside his apartment was lost. He didn't stop calling Jessica's name for hours, walking from room to room, turning lights on and off as if she would suddenly magically appear. He opened her wardrobe and rummaged through her clothes. He emptied drawers and cupboards. He lay down on their bed, hugged her pillow and cried until he had no more tears left.

Mark was now sitting quietly in his kitchen, his eyes bloodshot and sore.

Garcia picked up a photo frame from the bedroom floor – Jessica and Mark holidaying somewhere sunny. They looked happy and in love.

He returned the frame to the dresser, turned to face the unmade bed once again and considered what to do. They couldn't cordon off Mark and Jessica's apartment because it wasn't an official crime scene. The chances of him getting a Forensics team dispatched to the apartment before confirming Jessica had been abducted from there were less than slim. The chances of that Forensics team finding any sort of clue in a scene that had been compromised and completely messed with were virtually none.

Garcia walked out of the room, down the long corridor and into the living room. On the stylish glass table that sat between the sofa and the wall-mounted TV set, he found several music magazines. The top one had Jessica on its cover. Out of pure curiosity he flipped it open and looked for the article. It was a two-page interview through which she talked about being a successful musician and her life in general, but one subheader caught his attention – *On Love*. Garcia allowed his eyes to skim through the section, but just a few lines in he paused. A chill ran down his spine as if he'd been suddenly hit by an arctic wind. He read the lines again just to be sure.

'No fucking way.' He grabbed the magazine and rushed back to his office.

Ninety-Five

Hunter left Chief Cooper's house by Lake Sonoma just before lunchtime, but he wasn't ready to fly back to LA just yet. His mind was batting thoughts back and forth and he needed to organize them before moving on. He remembered driving past the city library on the way to the chief's house. He decided to start there.

The building was a single-story structure that couldn't even be compared to some of LA's high-school libraries. Hunter parked in the adjacent lot, pulled the collar of his jacket tight against his neck and dashed to the entrance. The rain that had started earlier was still coming down.

The woman at the information desk lifted her eyes from her computer screen and smiled sympathetically as Hunter came through the door.

'I guess you forgot your umbrella, huh?'

Hunter brushed the water off his hair and sleeves before smiling back. 'I wasn't expecting the heavens to open.'

'Spring downpour. We're famous for those over here. It'll pass soon enough,' she offered with a renewed smile and a couple of paper tissues.

'Thanks.' He took them and dried his forehead and hands.

'I'm Rhonda, by the way.'

They shook hands.

'I'm Robert.'

Rhonda was in her mid-twenties with short, spiky, black-dyed hair. Her face was ghostly pale and her make-up was one step short from being full goth.

'So . . .' she said, fixing Hunter with her dark eyes. 'What brings you to Healdsburg's library? Actually, what brings you to Healdsburg at all?'

'Research.'

'Research? About Healdsburg's wineries?'

'No.' Hunter thought for a second. 'I guess I'm looking for an old school yearbook.'

'A yearbook? An old friend, huh? From which school?'

Hunter paused. 'How many schools are there in Healdsburg?'

Rhonda laughed. 'It doesn't look like you know much about this research of yours.'

Hunter agreed with a smile. 'The truth is: I'm just trying to find a picture of a kid who lived here many years ago.'

'A kid?' Her expression changed to concern and she took a step back from the counter.

'No, look, I'm a cop from Los Angeles,' Hunter said, producing his badge. 'Something that happened here twenty years ago has suddenly become of interest to us. I'm just trying to gather some information, that's all. A picture would help.'

Rhonda studied the badge and then Hunter's face. 'Twenty years ago?'

'That's right.'

She hesitated for a beat. 'So you must be talking about what happened to the Harpers. And if you're looking for a picture of a kid, you must be talking about Andrew Harper.'

'You knew him?'

She looked uncertain. 'Sort of. I was only five when it happened. But he used to come to our house sometimes.'

'Really? How come?'

'We lived in the same street. He was friends with my brother.'

'Does your brother still live here?'

'Yep. He's an accountant and runs his own practice in town. You probably drove past his office on your way here.'

'Do you think I could have a chat with him?'

Another hesitant moment.

'Whatever information he can give me might help a lot,' Hunter pushed.

Rhonda regarded Hunter for a second longer.

'I don't see why not.' She checked her watch. 'I'll tell you what. It's coming up to my lunch break. Why don't I take you there and introduce you to him?'

Ninety-Six

Rhonda said hello to Mrs. Collins at the reception desk in the anteroom of her brother's small accountancy practice and pointed to his office door.

'He's not with anyone, is he?'

Mrs. Collins smiled kindly as she shook her head.

'I think he was just getting ready to go out for lunch, dear. You can go right in, Rhonda.'

Rhonda knocked twice and pushed the door open before a reply.

Ricky was pretty much the opposite of his sister. Tall with neatly trimmed hair and a sportsman's physique, he was dressed conservatively in a light gray suit, baby blue shirt and a blue on red tie. The introductions were quick and to the point, and Ricky's smile dissipated once Rhonda told him why she'd brought Hunter to see him.

'I'm sorry, but I don't see how I can help,' he said to Hunter, looking a little rattled. 'I was ten when it happened and we weren't even here, remember?' He directed the question to Rhonda, who nodded. 'It happened during Christmas vacation and we had gone over to Grandma's house in Napa. We only heard about it when we got back.'

'I understand, and I don't want you to tell me about the incident. I know you know nothing about that. But if you could tell me a little about Andrew himself, that could help. Rhonda told me that you were friends?'

Ricky looked at his sister in a reprimanding way. 'I guess.' He shrugged. 'He . . . didn't have many friends.'

'Why was that?'

Another shrug. 'He was very quiet and shy. He much preferred spending time with his comic books than with people.'

'But you guys did spend some time together, right? Played games, that kinda stuff?'

'Yeah, sometimes, but not always. He was . . . different.'

Hunter's eyes narrowed a fraction. 'In what way?'

Ricky paused and checked his watch before crossing to the door to his office and sticking his head outside. 'Mrs. Collins, if anyone calls, I'm out for lunch.' He closed the door behind him. 'Why don't you have a seat?'

Hunter took one of the two chairs in front of Ricky's desk. Rhonda preferred to lean against the window frame.

'Andrew was . . . sad most of the time,' Ricky said, returning to his desk.

'Did he ever tell you why?'

'His parents argued a lot, and that really upset him. He was very close to his mother.'

'Not so close to his father?' Hunter asked.

'Yes, he was as well, but he talked about his mother more.'

Hunter's cell phone vibrated in his pocket and he subtly checked the display window – Whitney Myers. Hunter returned the phone to his pocket without answering it. He'd call her later.

'Kids always talk about their mothers,' Rhonda offered.

'No.' Ricky shook his head firmly. 'Not the way he did.

He talked about her as if she was a goddess. Like she couldn't do anything wrong.'

'Idolizing her?' Hunter asked.

'Yes. He put her on the pedestal. And when she was sad, he was *really* sad.' Ricky started fidgeting with a paper clip. 'I know that sometimes he used to watch his mom cry and that just ate away at him.' A nervous chuckle escaped Ricky's lips. 'He used to watch her a lot . . . in a weird way.'

Rhonda cocked her head. 'What does that mean?'

Ricky's eyes moved from her to Hunter, who kept his face steady.

'Andrew told me about this secret hiding place he had. And I know he used to spend a lot of time there.'

Hunter knew that a secret or special place wasn't uncommon amongst kids. Especially ones like Andrew – sad, quiet, with few friends – the bullied ones. It's usually just an isolated location where they can get away from everything and everyone that upsets them. A place where they feel safe. But if a child starts reverting to it more and more, it's usually because they feel the need to increase their isolation – from everyone and everything. And the consequences can be severe.

'That's not so bad,' Rhonda said. 'Me and my friends used to have a secret place when we were kids.'

'Not like Andrew's,' Ricky countered. 'At least I hope not. He took me there one day.' A muscle flexed on his jaw. 'He made me promise to never tell anyone.'

'And . . . ?' Rhonda asked.

Hunter waited.

Ricky's eyes moved away from both of them. 'I'd pretty much forgotten about that place.' His stare returned to Hunter. 'His secret place was this secluded bit in the attic in his house. Their attic was packed with boxes and boxes of junk and old furniture. There was so much stuff piled up that it created a wall, a partition of sorts, dividing the attic into two separate spaces. If you went up there via the stairs in the house, you could only see one of them. The other one was completely hidden behind this barricade of stuff. You couldn't even get to it, unless you started moving things. And you'd have to move a lot of things.'

'And this hidden space in the attic was Andrew's secret place?' Rhonda asked.

'That's right.'

'But you just said no one could get to it,' she challenged.

'Not through the house,' Ricky clarified. 'Andrew used to climb up the trellis on the outside wall and get in through this tiny round window on the roof.'

'The roof?'

'Yes. He was good at it too. He could climb that wall like a real-life Spiderman.'

'So what was so strange about his secret attic place?' Rhonda asked.

'It was directly above his parents' bedroom. He said that when they were in the room, he could hear everything.'

'Oh my God.' Rhonda pulled a face. 'You think he used to listen to them while they were doing it?'

'More than that. You remember his house, right?'

She nodded.

He turned towards Hunter. 'It was an old-style wooden house, with high ceilings. Andrew had scraped away at the gaps between some of the wooden planks in the attic's floor, at different locations. I know because he showed them to me. Through them he could see the entire bedroom. He used to spy on his parents.'

'No way,' Rhonda said with wide eyes. 'That's just nasty. What a pervert.' She cringed.

'But what freaked me out about the place,' Ricky continued, 'was that in this little corner I saw a few cotton balls and rags stained with blood.'

'Blood?' Hunter asked.

'Blood?' Rhonda repeated.

Ricky nodded. 'I asked him about it. He told me it was from a nosebleed.'

Hunter frowned.

'When Andrew was younger he'd got really ill with flu, and that somehow messed up the inside of his nose. I know that's true because it happened in school a few times. If he started sneezing or if he just blew his nose a little too hard, blood would go everywhere.'

Hunter sensed Ricky's uneasiness. 'But you didn't believe the bloody cotton balls and rags came from his nosebleed, did you?'

Ricky looked at his sister and then at the paper clip he'd been fidgeting with. It was all bent and out of shape. He lifted it up and showed it to Hunter. 'I saw some of these on the floor next to the cotton balls. They also had blood on them. Maybe he was picking at his nose with paper clips, who knows? As I said, he was stranger than most. I didn't know what was going on, but the whole place felt creepy. I told Andrew that I had to go home and got out of there as quick as I could.'

Hunter knew why the bloody cotton balls, rags and paper clips – Andrew was self-harming. He was substituting pain for pain, trying to take hold of his suffering. He couldn't control the emotional pain he went through every time his parents argued, so, to disconnect from that hurt, he created his own, by inflicting his own wounds. That way he could calmly watch himself bleed, detached from his own suffering and his underlying rage. It was a pain he could completely control, down to how deep the cut was, and how much he'd bleed.

Ricky paused and rubbed his face with both hands.

'Look, I know Andrew was a little weird, but most 10-year-old kids are in one way or another.' His eyes moved to Rhonda. 'Some of us still are.'

She flipped him her middle finger.

'But he was a nice kid,' Ricky continued. 'And if you ask me, I think that what his father did was a very cowardly act. Andrew never had a chance. He didn't deserve to die.'

Everyone went silent.

To Hunter, all the pieces were starting to fall into place.

Ninety-Seven

The room he was in was illuminated only by candles – twelve in total. Their flames flickered in an unsynchronized dance, bouncing shadows against the walls. He raised his eyes towards his naked body reflected in the large wall mirror. Bare feet on a cold cement floor, strong legs, broad shoulders, athletic body and icy cold eyes. He stared at his face for a long while, analyzing it carefully before twisting his body left, then right, checking his back.

He walked over to the table on the corner and picked up one of the many pre-paid cell phones on it, dialing a number he knew by heart.

It rang twice before it was answered by a calm but firm voice.

'Do you have the information I asked you for?' he asked, his eyes moving to the workstation in front of him.

'Yes, it wasn't a problem.'

He listened carefully.

The information was more surprising than upsetting, but his face displayed no signs of anxiety. He disconnected and ran his right hand over the large blood-coated needle and thread he'd left on the workstation.

He'd have to change his course of action, adapt, and he didn't like change. Deviating from well-laid plans meant increasing his risk, but right now, he wasn't sure it mattered any more.

He checked his watch. He knew exactly where she'd be in a few hours' time. The information had been so easy to come by it made him laugh.

He faced the mirror once again and stared deep into his own eyes.

It was time to do it again.

Ninety-Eight

'Shit!'

She checked her car's clock and cursed under her breath as she turned into her street in Toluca Lake, southeastern San Fernando Valley. She had no doubt she'd be late, and she hated being late.

The gala charity fundraising event was scheduled to start in seventy-five minutes' time. The drive from her house alone would take her at least half an hour. That gave her around forty-five minutes to have a shower, do her hair and make-up and get dressed. For a woman who took as much pride in her appearance as she did, that was almost impossible.

Her secretary had reminded her in plenty of time, as she'd asked her to, but an accident on Hollywood Freeway cost her an extra thirty-five minutes, and in an event where the Mayor of Los Angeles, the Governor of California and quite a few A-list celebrities were supposed to be attending, being late wasn't the best plan of action.

To save time, she decided that she'd have her hair up and tied back. She also had a pretty good idea of which dress and shoes she'd be wearing.

Her home was a large, two-story, cul-de-sac house by Toluca Lake itself. She knew the house was way too big for her alone, but she had fallen in love with it when she was first property searching.

She parked her Dodge Challenger on her paved driveway and her eyes involuntarily checked the dashboard clock again.

'Shit, shit.'

She'd been so concerned with the time and being late that she didn't even notice the white van parked on the street, almost directly in front of her house.

She stepped out of her car and fumbled inside her handbag for the key while walking to her front door. As she got to the porch, she heard a ruffling noise coming from the trimmed shrubs of her small front yard. She paused and frowned. A few seconds later the noise returned. It sounded like some sort of scratching.

'Oh, please don't tell me I've got rats,' she whispered to herself.

Suddenly she heard a sniffing cry and a tiny white puppy stuck its head through the bushes. It looked frightened and hungry.

'Oh my God.' She crouched down, put her handbag on the floor and extended a hand. 'Come here, little one. Don't be scared.' The puppy stepped further out of the bushes, sniffing at her hand.

'Oh, you poor thing. I bet you're hungry.' She patted its head, running a hand up and down its white fur. It was shivering. 'Would you like some milk?'

She did not hear him walk up behind her. In her crouched position it was easy for him to dominate her. His strong hands pushed her forward into the bushes where the white puppy had come from, while at the same time pressing a wet cloth over her mouth. She tried to react, dropping the puppy and desperately trying to reach behind her to grab hold of her assailant. But it was too late; he knew it, and so did she.

Within seconds, her world faded to black.

Ninety-Nine

Garcia went straight back to his desk in Parker Center and fired up his computer. He needed to search the Internet for online editions of art magazines and journals.

Two hours later he was starting to get a headache from squinting at the screen, and he still hadn't found what he was looking for. His gaze returned to the copy of the music magazine he'd taken from Jessica Black's apartment and a thought crept into his mind. He considered it for only a few seconds before grabbing his jacket and flying out the door once again.

Garcia wasn't as familiar with the central branch of the Los Angeles Public Library as Hunter was, but he knew they kept a microfilm and database archive on all their magazines and journals. He just hoped their Arts department was as accomplished as Hunter said it was.

Garcia found a free workstation, sat himself down and started searching through articles. He searched for any piece about either Laura Mitchell or Kelly Jensen, especially one-to-one interviews.

It took him just under two and a half hours to find the first one – an interview with Kelly Jensen for *Art Today* magazine. As he read the lines he'd been looking for, he felt a rush of blood inundate his veins.

'This is fucking crazy,' he said, pressing the print button. He collected his printout and returned to his seat. Laura Mitchell was now his next target.

An hour later he got to the end of the list of all the Laura Mitchell interviews he'd found in the system – nothing.

'Fuck!' he cursed under his breath. His eyes were getting tired and watery. He needed a break, a cup of coffee and an Advil.

Suddenly a crazy thought came into his head and he paused for a moment, considering the alternatives.

'Oh, what the hell,' he whispered as he decided that it was worth a shot.

Garcia wouldn't find a better collection of art magazines and articles on Laura Mitchell than the ones they'd uncovered inside the dark room in James Smith's apartment. Smith seemed to have collected everything that was ever published on her. He was still under custody, and his apartment was still seized by police as part of an ongoing investigation.

Garcia stood by the door to the dimly lit collage room, staring at the magazines and newspapers piled just about everywhere.

'Damn!' he whispered to himself. 'This is gonna take me forever.'

In fact, it took him two hours and three piles of magazines and journals. Laura Mitchell's last interview had been with *Contemporary Painters* magazine, eleven months ago. It was a small article – less than fifteen hundred words.

He almost choked when he read the lines.

'Sonofabitch.'

Every hair on his body stood on end. He knew that this kind of coincidence just didn't exist.

As he rushed out of the building, his cell phone rang in his pocket. He checked the display window before answering it.

'Robert, I was just about to call you. You're not gonna believe what I just found out—'

'Carlos, listen,' Hunter interrupted urgently, 'I think I know who we're after.'

'What? Really? Who?'

'I have no doubt he doesn't go by his real name any more, but his original name was Andrew Harper. I need you to get in touch with Operations and the research team immediately. We need everything and anything we can get on him.'

Garcia stopped walking and frowned at nothing. His memory searching for the name. 'Wait a second,' he remembered, 'isn't that the name of the kid Stephen told us about on the phone? The one who was murdered by his father?'

'Yep, that's him, and I don't know how he got away, but I don't think he was murdered that day.'

'Come again?'

'I think that somehow he survived. And I think he was in the house when it happened, Carlos.'

'What?'

'I'll tell you everything when I get back to LA. I'm at the airport now. I'll land at LAX in about two hours. But I think the kid was hiding in the house.'

'No way.'

'He watched his father violate his mother's body, stitch her shut, write a blood message on the wall and then kill her before blowing his own head off . . .'

Garcia stayed silent.

'I think the kid saw everything. And now he's repeating history.'

One Hundred

Clouds were gathering when Andrew Harper turned his van into State Highway 170, going north. From the back seat of the brown station wagon in front of him, a kid of about nine smiled and waved at him, an ice-cream cone in his hand. It wasn't as if Andrew ever needed reminders for his mind to take him back to that day, they were everywhere he looked, but at the sight of the kid and his ice cream, Andrew twitched like a cow shaking off flies as vivid images flooded his memory. In an instant, he was transported back to his father's truck that Sunday morning. His father had driven just a couple of blocks before stopping at that gas station.

'I have a surprise for you,' Ray Harper said, turning to face little Andrew who was sitting in the passenger's seat. His lips smiled but his eyes betrayed him. 'But first, let me go get you some ice cream.'

Andrew's eyes widened. 'Ice cream? Mom doesn't like me to have ice cream. She said that since my cold, ice cream isn't good for me, Dad.'

'I know she doesn't, but you like ice cream, don't you?'

Andrew nodded eagerly.

'One single scoop can't hurt. This is a special day, and if you like ice cream, you can have ice cream. What flavor?'

Andrew thought about it for a beat. 'Chocolate brownie,' he said, his happiness almost oozing through his pores.

A few minutes later Ray came back to the car with two cones. Andrew bit into his as if the whole thing would vanish in thin air if he didn't eat it immediately. Less than a minute later he had finished his cone and started licking his fingers.

Ray had just finished his ice cone when a single, powerful sneeze exploded out of Andrew, and with it came blood. Andrew didn't manage to cover his nose in time and blood splattered everywhere: dashboard, windshield, door, but mainly all over his shirt. The nosebleed that followed was short but intense, enough to drip onto his trousers and shoes. Ray instantly reached for Andrew, tipped his head back slightly and used the edge of Andrew's shirt to clear the smudges around his nose and mouth. The bleeding stopped within two minutes.

'OK,' Ray said with an apologetic frown. 'Maybe it wasn't such a good idea after all.'

Andrew smiled before looking down at his bloody shirt and cringing.

'It's OK, kiddo,' Ray said, putting a hand on the kid's head. 'I said I had a surprise for you, remember?' He reached behind his seat, and from under his coat he retrieved a gift-wrapped box. 'This is for you.'

Andrew's eyes lit up. 'But it's not my birthday and it's not Christmas yet, Dad.'

'This is a pre-Christmas present. You deserve it, son.' Sadness masked Ray's face for an instant. 'Go ahead, open it. I know you'll like it.'

Andrew ripped the paper from around the box as fast as

he could. He loved presents, though he never got many of them. His whole face morphed into one huge smile. The top item was a brand new T-shirt. On its front was a large Wolverine print, Andrew's favorite character from the X-Men Marvel comics.

'WOW!' was all he could say.

'Go ahead, check the next one,' Ray urged him.

Andrew could tell what it would be even before opening the box – a new pair of trainers, also covered in Wolverine and X-Men prints. Andrew looked at his father, half-shocked.

'But, Dad, these are really expensive.' He knew his family had been struggling with money lately.

Ray's eyes became glassy. 'You deserve a lot more, son.' He paused for an instant. 'I'm sorry I could never give you all that you deserve.' He kissed Andrew's forehead again. 'Why don't you try everything on? That way you can get rid of that dirty shirt.'

Andrew hesitated.

Ray knew how shy his son was. 'I'll go and get us a couple of sodas and you can get changed, OK?'

Andrew waited until his father had reentered the gas station's shop and quickly stripped off his bloody shirt and threw it in the back seat. The scar on his chest from last night stuck out from the other ones across his torso because it was so red and itchy. He rubbed it gently with the tips of his fingers. He'd learned never to use his fingernails in case the wounds started bleeding again. By the time Ray returned to the truck with a paper bag and two bottles of Mountain Dew, Andrew's favorite soda, he was dressed in his new shirt and trainers.

'They look great on you, kiddo,' Ray said, handing him a bottle.

Andrew smiled. 'I'll have to take the shoes off, Dad. They'll get dirty when we get to the lake.'

Something in Ray's eyes changed. His whole being was filled with grief and sorrow. 'I have to tell you something, son. We're not gonna go fishing today.'

The sadness was mirrored on Andrew's face. 'But Dad, Mom said that if I caught a big fish today, you wouldn't fight any more. She promised.'

Tears returned to Ray's eyes but he held them there. 'Oh, honey, we won't fight any more. Never again.' He placed a hand on the boy's nape. 'Not after today.'

Andrew's eyes glistened with happiness. 'Really? You promise, Dad?'

'I promise, kiddo, but I need you to do something for me.'

'OK.'

'I have something very important to do today, that's why we can't go fishing.'

'But it's Sunday, Dad. You don't work on Sundays.'

'What I have to do today isn't work. But it's something very, very important.' He paused for an instant. 'You told me once that you have a secret place, isn't that right?'

Andrew looked concerned.

'Do you still have it?'

The boy nodded shyly. 'Yes, but I can't tell you where it is, Dad. It's secret.'

'That's OK. I don't want you to tell me where it is.' He reached under his seat for something. 'What I need you to do is go to your secret place and stay there all day long. You can play with these.' Ray showed him three six-inch figurines – Wolverine, Professor X and Cyclops.

'Wow.' Andrew couldn't believe his eyes. It got better and better.

'What do you say? Do you like your presents?'

'Yes, Dad. Thank you very much.' He reached for the toys.

'It's all right, son, but can you do that for me? Can you go to your secret place and just stay there until tonight, playing with your new toys?'

Andrew slowly peeled his eyes from the figurines and refocused them on his father's anxious face. 'You won't fight with Mom again?'

Ray gave him a coy headshake. 'Never again,' he whispered.

'Promise?'

'I promise, son.'

Another animated smile. 'OK then.'

'Don't come out until tonight, you hear?'

'I won't, Dad. I promise.'

'Here.' Ray gave him the paper bag. 'There are chocolate bars – Butterfingers; I know they're your favorite – some Pringles, a cheese and ham sandwich and two more bottles of soda, so you don't get hungry or thirsty.'

Andrew took the bag and looked inside.

'Don't eat everything at once or else you'll be ill.'

'I won't.'

'OK then. Is your secret place close by? Can you walk there?'

'Yes, I can walk there, Dad. It's not far.'

Ray hugged his son again, this time for a very long time. 'I love you, Andrew. I'll always love you, son, no matter what. Please remember that, OK?'

'I love you too, Dad.' While his father battled with tears,

Andrew opened his door and skipped on down the road with his new shirt, trainers and toys. His father had promised never to fight with his mother again. It was the happiest day of his life.

One Hundred and One

Andrew turned on the radio, hoping that music would help push the memories away, but it was already too late. His mind was on a rollercoaster trip, and the memories and images just kept on coming.

He remembered that it had taken him only a few minutes to get back to his house after leaving his father at the gas station. He stuck the figurines in his coat pocket, jumped the fence and waited in the bushes that led to the backyard. He just wanted to make sure his mother wasn't out there. It was too cold for her to sit out back anyway. Dashing to the wall, he started climbing up the trellis as he did every day, this time being even more careful than usual not to dirty his new trainers. He squeezed through the small round window at the top and entered his secret place.

The first thing he did, as always, was to take off his shoes and slip into a thick pair of woolen socks. The attic floorboards were steady, and he'd identified the squeaky spots long ago, but he still had to be careful when moving around up there. Andrew had already developed a way of tiptoeing and sliding his feet across the floor that allowed him to move around in almost total silence.

Andrew placed the three figurines on top of a wooden crate in the corner and stared at them with smiling eyes. His gaze flicked over to a bag of cotton balls and a box of paper clips on the floor by the crate. He felt something warm start growing inside him. Something he hadn't felt in a long while. Suddenly he stuck his tongue out at the cotton balls and paper clips, mocking them. He wouldn't be needing them any more. His father had promised him that he'd never fight with his mother again. And his father always kept his promises. They would go back to being a happy family like they used to be. And that meant that he wouldn't have to initiate his own pain any more.

Andrew slotted himself in his favorite corner and grabbed a handful of comic books. He'd read them all, but he didn't mind.

He must've been sitting there, flipping through his magazines for almost two hours when he heard a noise inside his parents' room. Andrew put the comics down and looked through one of the many gaps he'd created in the floor. His mother had just walked into the room. She was wrapped in a fluffy yellow towel. Her hair was still wet and combed back. Andrew took his eye off the gap before his mother let go of her towel. He'd seen her naked before, but it had been by mistake. She'd been standing on a blind spot from any of Andrew's floor gaps. When she finally reappeared, she had nothing on. Andrew knew it was wrong to look at his mother or father naked. He'd seen them hiding under the covers, making strange noises. He knew that's what all the kids in school called *a fuck*, but from where he was standing, neither of them looked like they were enjoying it very much.

He went back to his comics, knowing that he had to be extra quiet now, but then he heard the door to his parents' room being slammed shut with tremendous violence. His eye returned to the gap and his breath froze for several seconds. His father was standing by the shut door, but his face was almost unrecognizable, covered in so much rage it frightened Andrew down to his soul. His father's hands, arms and shirt were soaked in blood. His mother was standing naked and paralyzed across the room from her husband.

'Oh my God. What happened? Where's Andrew?' she asked, panic stalking her voice.

'You don't have to concern yourself with Andrew, you lying whore,' Ray blasted in such an angry voice the room almost shook. 'You should concern yourself more with your fucking lover.'

Emily hesitated.

'I don't think you'll be fucking him any more.' From his pocket he took something out. To Andrew it looked like a very bloody piece of meat.

Emily let out a strangled cry. 'Oh my God, Ray. What have you done? What on God's earth have you done?' Her hands shot towards her open mouth in absolute terror.

'I made sure that Nathan, that pathetic excuse for a man, will never wreck another home again.' He smiled a satanic smile. 'I also made sure that he won't be able to say a word when he meets his maker. You could say that his lips are sealed.' He took two steps in Emily's direction.

She took one pace back and tried to cover her body with her hands.

'Why did you have to do it, Emily? Why did you have to destroy our family? Why did you have to betray my love this way? Why did you have to make me do these things?' Spit flew from Ray's mouth. He returned the bloody piece of meat to his pocket. 'Do you remember what we used to say to each other?' He didn't wait for a reply. 'We used to say – *You are the one, honey. You are the one I've been looking for all my life. You are my soul mate. We'll never be apart because you are the person I want to spend the rest of my life with.* Do you remember that?'

Silence.

'ANSWER ME.'

Ray's yell was so loud and full of rage, Andrew immediately wet himself up in the attic.

'Ye— yes.' Emily had started crying and shivering so violently she was almost hyperventilating.

'But I wasn't the one, was I? You lied to me, you deceitful bitch. You made me believe that what we had was sacred . . . special . . . everlasting. But it wasn't, was it? I wasn't enough for you.'

Emily's lips wouldn't move.

'Was he the one?' Ray asked. 'Was Nathan the one for you?' He moved a step closer. Emily's back was against the wall. She had nowhere else she could go. 'Did you love him?'

No reply.

'Did. You. Love. Him . . . ?' Something changed in Ray's entire demeanor, like someone else was taking over. Someone beyond evil.

Emily's voice was completely gone. Her vocal cords frozen by sheer fear. In a reflexive and thoughtless action, she nodded ever so slightly.

That was all Ray's rage needed to erupt.

'If that's what true love means to you, then you should have it. You should have it inside you forever. You and him, together as one – forever.' He moved towards her with such speed and purpose that not even an army of soldiers could have stopped him. His closed fist hit the side of her head with so much power she collapsed to the ground, unconscious.

Above them, Andrew was petrified, too scared to respond,

his voice had disappeared and his eyes had almost lost the ability to blink. His mind too young and naïve to cope with all the images. But he never moved. He never took his eye off the gap.

For the next hour Andrew watched the monster inside his father surface.

Ray dragged Emily's body to the bed and tied her down. He then grabbed a long piece of thick black thread and a needle, and proceeded to meticulously stitch her mouth shut. He retrieved whatever strange piece of bloody meat he had with him, spread Emily's legs apart and forced it into her before stitching her shut. Ray then used her blood to write something on the wall. The letters were big enough for Andrew to be able to read them – HE'S INSIDE YOU.

Ray tipped the bed on one end so his wife was in a standing position and pushed it against the far wall.

Tears streamed out of Andrew's eyes.

From the box on top of the wardrobe, Ray took his double-barreled shotgun, sat on the floor directly in front of Emily, crossed his legs, rested the shotgun on his knees and waited.

He didn't have to wait long. A few minutes later Emily opened her eyes. She tried to scream but the stitches on her lips kept most of the sound trapped inside her body. Her disbelieving eyes rested on her husband's face.

He smiled at her.

'Was this what you wanted, Emily?' His tone had changed – serene, understanding, as if he'd suddenly found eternal peace within himself. 'This is all your fault. And I hope you rot in hell for it.' Ray tilted his head back and placed the barrels of the shotgun under his chin. His finger tightened its grip on the trigger.

Emily convulsed in anticipation of what was about to happen, and in realization of what Ray had done. He'd lost his mind completely. She was certain he'd killed their son, her lover. The contents of her stomach catapulted into her mouth and were blocked by Ray's stitching. She panicked and started to choke. Oxygen couldn't find its way into her lungs.

With his head tilted back, Ray took a deep breath and pulled the trigger. And on that last fraction of a second just before the shotgun hammers were released, he saw them. Hidden between the wooden ceiling boards. He saw them because the light reflected on them and they blinked.

He saw his son's terrified eyes staring straight down at him.

One Hundred and Two

She woke up but didn't open her eyes. She knew she hadn't been unconscious for too long – five, ten minutes maximum. As the damp cloth was pressed against her nose and mouth back at her front door, she recognized the characteristic smell straight away – ether. She also realized that in her crouched position, ambushed by a surprised attack coming from behind her, and against an opponent that was certainly stronger than she was, fighting would have been pointless.

Instinct immediately kicked into action. As soon as she realized that her attacker was using an anesthetic to subdue her, she knew exactly what kind of reaction he'd be expecting from her. She played along, holding her breath for as long as she could and faking a struggle. Her initial mouthful of ether would no doubt knock her out, but not for too long. If she could act convincingly enough that she was fighting her attacker and gasping for air, he would believe that she'd taken in enough breaths to render her unconscious for a long while.

It worked.

Her assailant didn't hold the cloth to her nose for longer than twenty-five seconds, believing she was under.

Now, Captain Blake remained totally still and silent. She could hear the rattling of a car engine. She felt the hard floor under her vibrate and bump every so often. She opened her eyes very slightly to get a better idea of her environment. There was no doubt: she was lying down in the dark back cabin of a van, speeding somewhere. Her hands were tied behind her back, but her feet weren't restrained. That could give her a chance. Her cell phone and handbag were gone – no surprise there.

For now she knew there was nothing she could do but wait.

She had always been very in tune with her mind's clock. She figured they had driven for about an hour before they came to a complete stop. The van seemed to be moving at a reasonable speed for most of the journey, which meant that somehow they'd managed to avoid most of the stop-start traffic Los Angeles was so famous for. Wherever he'd taken her, she was pretty sure it was somewhere out of town.

She heard the driver's door open and then slam shut. He was coming for her. It was show time.

She quickly slid down towards the back door, getting as close to it as she could. She would only have one chance at this. She brought her knees close to her chest and waited. This time the element of surprise was on her side. She heard the doors being unlocked and prepared herself.

As the doors opened, she kicked out as hard as she could. Her feet thundered against her captor's chest. For the first time in her life she wished she had worn stiletto heels to work.

As she'd predicted, it caught her captor totally by surprise. It knocked the breath out of him and sent him tumbling backwards, straight to the ground.

She threw her body forward and pushed herself to the edge of the van's back cabin. Her legs were shaking so hard from fear and adrenalin she was unsure if she'd be able to stand up. As she fought to steady them and jumped out of the van, her eyes quickly scanned her surroundings. The van was parked in front of a large old building, but there was nothing else around except wasteland, unkempt vegetation and the narrow road they'd obviously taken to get there.

Her gaze dropped to the floor and fear rose in her throat like a tsunami. Her captor was gone.

'Fuck!'

Panic took over and she started running in the direction of the road, but she didn't have the proper shoes for it and her hands were still tied behind her back. All she managed was an awkward, wobbly dance for a few strides before her legs were hooked from under her with amazing force and precision. She hadn't even heard him come up behind her again.

She hit the ground hard with a thud, shoulder first, then head. Her vision blurred and all she could see was a figure towering over her.

'So, clever bitch wants to play rough, huh?' His voice was calm but very menacing. 'Well, check this out.'

His fingers closed into a fist.

'It's pain time, whore.'

One Hundred and Three

Whitney Myers checked her watch before answering her cell phone after the third ring.

'Whitney, I've got some information for you,' Leighton Morris said in his usual overexcited voice. Morris was another of Myers' LAPD contacts, who she called upon every now and then when she needed inside information.

'I'm listening.'

'That detective you asked me to keep an eye out for, Robert Hunter . . . ?'

'Yeah, what about him?'

'He boarded a plane early this morning.'

'A plane? Where to?'

'Healdsburg in Sonoma County.'

'Sonoma County? What the hell? Why?'

'That I don't know. But it's certainly something to do with the case he's investigating at the moment, which by the way, is very hush-hush.'

'He left this morning, you said?'

'That's right, and he just booked a return ticket for this afternoon.' There was a brief pause. 'Actually, he should be boarding pretty soon.'

Myers checked her watch again. 'Into LAX?'

'You got it.'

'Do you have the flight details?'
'Right here.'
'OK, text them to me.'
She disconnected and waited.

One Hundred and Four

There were no delays, and Hunter landed at LAX right on schedule. With no luggage to collect, he walked through the gates just minutes after touching down. Garcia was already there, waiting for him with a folder under his arm.

'Are you parked on a meter?' Hunter asked.

Garcia pulled a face. 'Are you crazy? This is official business. We've got perks.'

Hunter smiled. 'OK, let's grab a coffee and I'll run you through everything I got. Anything from Operations or the research team yet?'

'Not a scrap so far. I just checked with them.'

They found an isolated table towards the back of the Starbucks in Terminal One. Hunter proceeded to tell Garcia all he found out about the Harpers. He told him about Andrew's secret place in the attic and the peepholes. He told him about the self-harming and that he was sure that Andrew had somehow survived and witnessed everything that happened that day, twenty years ago. After that, Andrew had vanished.

'If his father was that brutal, how did Andrew survive?'

'I don't know exactly what happened that day. No one does except Andrew. But he's alive. And the pressure cooker in his head finally blew.'

'You mean something triggered it?'

Hunter nodded.

'And there were no pictures of him whatsoever?'

'I couldn't find any. It's a small town, small school. Back then the school's yearbook only featured high-school students. Andrew was in fifth grade when it happened.' He rubbed the scar on his nape. 'I think we were right about the killer using projection and transference together with a deep love for the person the victims remind him of.'

'His mother. The person he loved the most at that age. The person he'd never hurt, no matter what.'

'No matter what.'

'Oedipus complex?'

'I don't think he was in love with his mother in a romantic way, but he was a very shy kid with few friends. His parents were everything to him. In his mind, they could do no wrong.'

'Could his feelings have mutated into a combination of maternal and romantic love all rolled up into one?'

Hunter considered the theory. 'It's possible, why?'

'OK, it's my turn. Let me show you what I found out.' Garcia flipped open the folder he'd brought with him and took out the music magazine he'd found in Jessica Black's apartment. He quickly ran Hunter through what had happened with Mark Stratton, how he'd failed to control himself, and how he'd completely trashed a possible abduction scene. 'By chance I came across this magazine when I was in their apartment. There's an interview with Jessica Black in it. In a particular section, the interviewer asked her about love.'

'What about it?'

'He asked her what true love meant to her.' Garcia pushed

the magazine over to Hunter and pointed to some high-lighted lines. 'That was her answer.'

Hunter's eyes went over the lines and he paused. His heart skipped several beats. He read them again.

'To me true love is something uncontrollable. Like a fire that burns really bright inside you and consumes everything around it.'

'A fire that burns bright inside you?' Garcia said, shaking his head. 'It didn't sound like a coincidence to me. So I went back to the office and searched the net . . . found nothing. I then remembered you told me how good the magazine archives were at the public library, so I took a trip downtown.'

'And . . . ?'

'I found this.' From the folder he retrieved a copy of the printout he had got from the library and pushed it over towards Hunter. 'An interview with Kelly Jensen for *Art Today* magazine. Another question about true love and how she viewed the subject.' He pointed to the highlighted lines. 'Check her answer out.'

Love hurts, and true love hurts even more. I must admit that I haven't been very lucky in that department. My last experience was very painful to me. It made me realize that love can be like a crazy knife that sits inside you, and at any moment it can simply flick open. And when it does it cuts you. It slices through everything inside you. It makes you bleed. And there's very little you can do about it.

'Shit,' Hunter whispered, running a hand through his hair.

'In the library I couldn't find any similar articles on Laura Mitchell. Then I had this crazy idea of going back to James Smith's apartment.'

'Best collection of magazines and articles you'll ever find on Laura.'

'Exactly,' Garcia agreed. 'It took me a few hours, but I found this.' He handed Hunter the copy of *Contemporary Painters*.

Another question about love. Hunter read the highlighted lines – *True love is the most incredible thing. Something you can't control. Something that explodes inside you like a bomb when you're least expecting it and you're totally consumed by it.*

'He's giving them love,' Garcia said. 'Not his love, but what they consider to be true love, according to what he'd read. According to their own words.'

Hunter agreed mutely. 'His mind is in a real mess. He's got no understanding of what love is. And I'm not surprised. To Andrew real love was what his parents had between them, but what he witnessed that night shattered that understanding into a million little pieces, and he's been trying to put them back together ever since.'

'OK, but why now?' Garcia asked. 'If the trauma occurred twenty years ago, why is he only acting now?'

'Traumas aren't straightforward, Carlos,' Hunter explained, 'no psychological wound is. Many traumas suffered by people at one stage or another in their lives will never manifest themselves into actions. A lot of the time not even the traumatized person knows what catalyzes it. It just suddenly explodes inside their heads and they have no control over themselves. In Andrew's case, just seeing Laura, Kelly or Jessica's picture on a magazine or newspaper could've done it.'

'Because they didn't just resemble his mother physically, but they were the same age she was when she died, and they were all artists.'

'Exactly.' Hunter's cell phone started ringing – the screen said *Restricted Call*.

'Detective Hunter,' he said, bringing the phone to his ear.

'Hello, Detective. How did you like my birth city?'

Hunter's surprised stare shot in Garcia's direction. 'Andrew . . . ?'

One Hundred and Five

Garcia's eyes widened in surprise. He thought he'd heard wrong, but the expression on Hunter's face left little doubt.

'Andrew Harper . . . ?' Hunter repeated, keeping his voice steady.

A chuckle came down the phone. 'No one has called me Andrew in twenty years.' The sentence was delivered in a calm tone. His voice like a muffled whisper. Hunter remembered the whispering voice he'd heard on the recording Myers had retrieved from Katia Kudrov's answering machine.

'Do you miss being called by your real name?' Hunter's tone matched Andrew's.

Silence.

'I know you were there, Andrew. I know you saw what happened that day in your house. But why did you run? Where did you go? Why didn't you allow people to help you?'

'Help me?' He laughed.

'No one could've coped with what you went through alone. You needed help then. You need help now.'

'Cope? How could anyone cope with watching his father transform into a monster right in front of his eyes? A father who only hours earlier had given me the best presents I'd ever got. A father who'd promised me that everything would be fine. That there'd be no more fights. A father who said that he loved my mother and me more than anything. What kind of love is that?'

Hunter didn't have an answer.

'I've researched you. You used to be a psychologist, didn't you? Do you think you could've helped me cope?'

'I would've done my best.'

'That's bullshit.'

'No, it isn't. Life isn't meant for us to go through it on our own. We all need help from time to time. No matter how strong or tough we think we are. A person alone just can't deal with certain life situations. Especially not when you're only ten years old.'

Silence.

'Andrew?'

'Stop calling me Andrew. You don't have the right to do that. No one does. Andrew died that night, twenty years ago.'

'OK. What name would you like me to call you?'

'You don't need to call me anything. But since you were so kind to fuck everything up. To go digging into something you had no right to, I have a surprise for you too. I take it that your phone has video-streaming capabilities, right?'

Hunter frowned.

'I'm sending you a short video I made earlier. I hope you enjoy it.'

The line went dead.

'What happened?' Garcia asked.

Hunter shook his head. 'He's sending me some sort of video.'

'A video? Of what?'

Hunter's phone beeped – *Incoming video request.*

'I guess we're just about to find out.'

One Hundred and Six

Hunter immediately pressed the yes button accepting the request. Garcia moved closer and craned his neck. Their eyes were glued to the small progress bar on Hunter's cell phone screen as it filled itself up very slowly. Time seemed to drag.

The phone finally beeped again – *Download complete. Watch it now?*

Hunter pressed yes again.

The picture was grainy, the quality substandard. It had obviously been recorded using a cheap cell phone camera, but there was no doubt who they were looking at.

'What the fuck?' Garcia moved even closer.

Tied to a metal chair in the center of an empty room was a woman. Her head was slumped forward, her dark hair falling over her face covering her features. But neither Hunter nor Garcia needed to see her face to know who she was.

'Am I going crazy?' Garcia asked, wide-eyed, the color draining from his face.

No words left Hunter's lips.

'How the fuck did he get Captain Blake?' Garcia's eyes were still cemented to the screen.

Still silence from Hunter.

The video played on.

Captain Blake slowly lifted her head and Hunter felt something close tight around his heart. She was bleeding from the nose and mouth and her left eye had almost swollen shut. She didn't look drugged, just in severe pain. The picture focused on her face for just a few more seconds before fading to black.

'This is crazy,' Garcia said, fidgeting like a kid.

Hunter's phone rang again. He answered it immediately.

'If you're wondering,' the whispering voice said, 'she's still alive. So I'd be very careful of your next move. 'Cause how long she stays that way depends on it. Back off.'

The line disconnected.

'What did he say?'

Hunter told him.

'Shit. This is so messed up. Why take the captain? And why send us a video? That's completely contrary to his MO. He hasn't done that with any of the previous victims.'

'Because Captain Blake isn't like any of the previous victims, Carlos. She doesn't remind him of his mother. He didn't take her for that reason. She's security . . . a bargaining tool.'

'What?'

'On the phone he said, "Be very careful of your next move. 'Cause how long she stays alive depends on it. Back off." He's using her as a guarantee.'

'Why?'

''Cause we're getting close, and he wasn't expecting it. We know who he is . . . or used to be. He knows it's just a matter of hours before we catch up with him.'

Garcia bit his bottom lip. 'He's panicking.'

'Yes. That's why the video. And when they panic and deviate from their original plan, they make mistakes.'

'We don't have time to wait for him to make a mistake, Robert. He's got the captain.'

'He's already made the mistake.'

'What? What mistake?'

Hunter pointed to his phone. 'He sent us a video. We need Internet access.'

'Internet?' Garcia frowned. 'Can we trace it?'

'I don't think so. He's not that stupid.'

'So why do we need the Internet?'

Hunter looked around and saw a thirty-something man sitting at a table in the corner. He was typing into his laptop.

'Excuse me, are you online?'

The man looked up, his gaze quickly jumping from Hunter to Garcia, who was right behind his partner. The man nodded skeptically. 'Yeah.'

'We need to borrow your computer very quickly,' Hunter said, having a seat and pulling the laptop towards him.

The man was about to say something when Garcia placed a hand on his shoulder, showing him his badge.

'Los Angeles Homicide Division, this is important.'

The man lifted both hands in the air in surrender and stood up.

'I'll be right over there.' He pointed to the corner. 'Take your time.'

'Why do you need the Internet all of a sudden?' Garcia asked, taking a seat next to Hunter.

'Give me a sec.' He was busy Googling something. A web page loaded and he scanned it as fast as he could.

'Fuck.'

Hunter grabbed his phone and watched the video again, frowning at it.

'Damn.'

He Googled something else. A new page loaded and he scanned it again. 'Oh shit,' he whispered, checking his watch. 'Let's go,' he said, standing up.

'Go where?'

'Santa Clarita.'

'What? Why?'

'Because I know where the captain is being held.'

One Hundred and Seven

Aided by Garcia's car's lights and siren, they were eating ground fast. They hooked onto Interstate 405 and Garcia hit the fast lane doing eighty-five miles an hour.

'OK, how do you know where the captain is being held?' Garcia asked.

Hunter played the video again and showed his partner. 'Because she told me.'

'Huh?'

'Pay attention to her lips.'

Garcia's attention diverted from the road for just a second, enough for him to notice the captain's lips moving ever so slightly.

'I'll be damned.'

'The captain knew there was only one reason Andrew was shooting this video. She knew we would watch it.'

'More to the point,' Garcia added, 'she knew *you* would watch it. So what did she say?'

'St Michael's Hospice.'

'What?'

'That's why I needed the Internet. I thought she'd said St Michael's *Hospital*. But there isn't one, there never was. So I watched the video again and realized she'd said *hospice*, not hospital. St Michael's Hospice in Santa Clarita closed down nine years ago, after a fire destroyed most of the building.' Hunter typed the address into Garcia's GPS navigational system. 'There it is.'

'Shit,' Garcia said. 'Out towards the hills. Completely isolated.'

Hunter nodded.

'So if we suspect that's where the captain is being held, why are we going there without a SWAT team?'

'Because Andrew said that how long the captain lived depended on our actions. He's somehow monitoring what we do.'

'How?'

'I don't know, Carlos. But he called me just minutes after I landed. I'd been away less than a day. How the hell did he know I'd gone to Healdsburg this morning?'

Garcia had no answer.

'SWAT teams are great, but they aren't exactly subtle. If Andrew gets a sniff that we might know where he is, he'll get to Captain Blake a lot faster than we or any SWAT team can get to him. And then it's game over.'

'So what are we gonna do?'

'Everything we can. We might be able to surprise him. He doesn't know that we know. The surprise factor is on our side. If we do this right, we can end this – now.'

Garcia stepped on the gas.

One Hundred and Eight

In Santa Clarita they drove up Sand Canyon Way in the direction of the hills and turned right into a small narrow road that ran another five hundred yards towards the entrance to the old St Michael's Hospice.

'We better come off-road somewhere around here and walk the rest of the way,' Hunter said as they got within two hundred yards of the entrance. 'I don't wanna alert him that we're coming.'

Garcia nodded and found a hidden place behind some tall trees to leave the car.

They quickly walked the rest of the way through the high vegetation and found a covered position about seventy-five yards from the derelict St Michael's Hospice building.

It was a two-story rectangular structure covering around one thousand square feet. Most of the outside shell had crumbled, the majority of the roof had caved into the top floor, and there were clues everywhere that a large fire had taken place some time ago. At certain spots they could see right through the building. Debris was scattered all around the grounds.

'Are you sure about this?' Garcia asked. 'There seems to be nothing here.'

Hunter pointed to the ground around what used to be the building's main entrance – a series of fresh tire tracks.

'Someone has been here recently.'

The tracks led away from the front of the building and disappeared around and towards the back – the only place where the walls seemed intact. Hunter and Garcia spent a few minutes observing from a distance, looking for surveillance cameras or any other signs of security or life. Nothing.

'Let's get closer,' Hunter said.

The tire tracks stopped by a large staircase and wheelchair ramp that led down into the building's underground floor. There were several footprints on the steps, going in both directions. They all seemed to belong to the same person.

'Whatever's happening here, it's down there.' Garcia nodded at the stairs.

Hunter pulled out his gun.

'Only one way to find out. Are you ready for this?'

Garcia grabbed his weapon. 'No, but let's do it anyway.'

One Hundred and Nine

Surprisingly, the double swing doors at the bottom of the staircase weren't locked. Hunter and Garcia pushed them open and stepped inside.

The first room was an old-style reception lobby. A battered semicircular counter was fixed to the wall on the left. Broken furniture was scattered around everywhere, covered in dust and old rags. Beyond the reception counter there was another set of swing doors.

'I don't like this one bit,' Garcia whispered. 'There's something just not right about this place.'

Hunter looked around slowly. He still could see no surveillance cameras or any other type of security against intruders. He nodded at Garcia and they both carefully approached the new set of doors.

Hunter tried the handles – unlocked. They moved through.

The doors led them into a wide corridor, stretching for about thirty-five feet. One single dim light bulb kept it from plunging into total darkness. From where they were standing they could see only one door, halfway down the corridor.

'OK, I'm not one to believe in vibes, or auras, or crap like that,' Garcia said, 'but there's definitely something fucked-up about this place. I can feel it in my soul.'

They kept moving stealthily forward until they reached the lonely door on their left. Again – unlocked. They moved inside.

The room was about twenty-five feet by twenty, and was kitted out like a carpenter's workshop. A large wooden drawing desk, a heavy-duty workstation counter, two old metal filing cabinets, wall-mounted shelves, and a paraphernalia of instruments and tools hanging from the walls and scattered around the room.

Hunter and Garcia stood still for a moment, taking everything in. When they finally approached the drawing desk, they froze.

'Holy shit,' Garcia whispered. His eyes settled on the building plans and the photographs on the desk. They showed one item only. An object they'd seen before. The fan-out knife that was retrieved from inside Kelly Jensen's body.

Across the room, Hunter recognized the items inside a small box on top of the workstation – the self-activating clicking mechanism. There were three of them, ready to be used. Next to them he found another box with two aluminum tubes. Hunter and Garcia didn't need to look at them closely to know exactly what they were – practice runs for the flare that was inserted into Jessica Black's body. This was his creative chamber of horrors, Hunter thought. His death factory.

'Look at this,' Garcia said, checking some of the other drawings on the desk. 'Plans for the bomb used on Laura Mitchell.'

An uneasy silence followed.

Garcia allowed his eyes to roam the room one more time. 'He can build almost any sort of torture and death instrument in here.'

Hunter's eyes were also rechecking the room – ceiling, corners, strategic places ... Still he could see no surveillance of any kind.

'Here we are!' Garcia said, reaching for a sheet of paper he found stuck to the wall.

'What have you got?'

'Looks like the underground floor plan for this place.'

Hunter moved closer and studied the drawing. The corridor they were in led into a new, transversal hallway. That hallway went around in a large squared path. Four corridors, and according to the plans they were looking at, each corridor held two rooms. There was no other exit on the other side. The only way out was to come back to where they were and go up the stairs they'd come down from.

Garcia felt his blood run cold. 'Eight rooms. He can keep up to eight victims here at once?'

Hunter nodded. 'It seems that way.'

'Fuck. This guy is sick.'

Hunter paused and turned around. He had noticed something hanging from the wall before, but he didn't pick up on it. A large metal key ring with several skeleton keys.

'I bet these open the rooms.'

Garcia nodded. 'Let's go give them a try.'

They stepped out of the drawing room and, as quickly and quietly as they could, moved onto the transversal hallway at the end of the corridor they were in. They came out exactly at the center of the hallway. In total, this corridor stretched for sixty or seventy feet. Just like the previous one, a single dim light bulb behind a metal mesh on the wall kept it from total darkness.

'So, what would you like to do?' Garcia asked. 'Split up or go together?'

'Let's give ourselves a better chance and move together. That way we can cover each other.'

Garcia nodded. 'Good call. Which way?'

Hunter pointed right.

Once again they moved in almost complete silence. They quickly got to the first room towards the end of the corridor. A very sturdy and thick timber door. At the bottom of it there was a food hatch. Hunter fumbled through the keys in the large key ring, trying each one. He found the correct key on his third attempt.

Hunter gave Garcia a quick nod, who responded in the same way. They were as ready as they'd ever be.

Both detectives held their breath as Hunter stood with his back against the wall to the right of the door and pushed it open in one fast movement. Immediately, Garcia stepped inside, both of his arms stretched out, his weapon held by a double-hand grip. He was followed a fraction of a second later by Hunter.

The room was in complete darkness, but the tiny amount of light that seeped through from the corridor outside allowed them to understand its setup. It was small, maybe only ten feet in depth by seven wide. There was a metal bed pushed up against one of the walls and a bucket on the floor to the right of the bed; nothing else. The walls were made of red bricks and the floor was concrete. It looked like a medieval dungeon, and if fear had a smell, that room was drenched in it. There was no one in there.

Garcia breathed out and cringed. 'Damn, look at this place, man. Stephen King couldn't have imagined this hellhole.'

Hunter closed the door silently and he and Garcia moved on. The corridor swung left. Hunter went through the same process, trying each key as he reached the first door in this new hallway. The room was identical to the first one and again in total darkness. There was no one in there either.

Garcia started fidgeting.

They reached the next door and the process started again. As Hunter pushed the door open and they stepped inside with their weapons at the ready, they heard a faint and frightened cry.

One Hundred and Ten

Hunter and Garcia paused by the door. Both of their guns aiming at whoever or whatever had made that noise, but neither of them fired. Due to the darkness, it took Hunter a couple of seconds to spot her. She was pressed against one of the corners of the room, curled up into a tiny ball. Her knees were tight against her chest. Her arms hugging her legs so hard the blood seemed to have drained from them. Her eyes were wide open, staring at the door and the two new arrivals. One word could describe her whole being – fear.

Hunter recognized her straight away – Katia Kudrov.

He holstered his gun and quickly lifted his hands up in a surrender gesture.

'We're Los Angeles police officers,' he announced in the calmest voice he could muster. 'We've been looking for you for a while, Katia.'

Katia burst into tears, her body convulsing with emotion. Hunter stepped into the room and approached her very slowly.

'You're gonna be OK, we're here now.'

Her eyes were still wide, staring at Hunter as if he was an illusion. Her breathing was coming to her in bursts. Hunter feared she was too shocked to speak.

'Can you talk?' he asked. 'Are you hurt?'

Katia sucked in a deep breath through her nose and nodded.

'Ye— yes, I can talk. No— no, I'm not hurt.'

Hunter kneeled down before her and took her in his arms. She hugged him tight and broke down in a barrage of desperate tears and high-pitched yelps. Hunter felt as though he was absorbing her fear through his skin.

Garcia stood by the door, both hands wrapped firmly around his gun, his gaze incessantly moving up and down the corridor outside.

Katia's eyes met Hunter's. 'Than— thank you.'

'Are there others here?'

She nodded. 'I think so. I never saw anyone. I'm never let out of this room. The lights are always off. But I'm sure I heard something one day. I mean, I heard some*one*. Another woman.'

Hunter nodded. 'You are the first one we found, we've gotta look for others.'

Katia's arms tightened further around Hunter. 'No . . . don't leave me.'

'We're not leaving you. You're coming with us. Can you walk?'

Katia breathed out and nodded.

Hunter helped her stand up. She looked much skinnier than the pictures he'd seen of her.

'When was the last time you ate?'

She gave him a tiny shrug. 'I don't know. The food and the water are drugged.'

'Do you feel dizzy?'

A succession of quick nods. 'A little, but I can walk.'

Hunter's questioning gaze moved to Garcia.

'We're good here, let's move.'

Hunter moved Katia in between him and Garcia and drew his weapon again. They stepped towards the door cautiously, ready to brave the corridors again.

All of a sudden all the lights went off.

They were left in absolute darkness.

For an instant all three of them were frozen to the spot. Katia let out another cry, but the fear in her voice this time almost chilled the air.

'Oh my God, he's here.'

Hunter reached for her again. 'It's all right, Katia. It's gonna be OK. We're still here with you.' As his hand touched her arm, he felt her shivering.

'No yo— you don't understand. It won't be OK.'

'What do you mean?' Garcia whispered.

'He's like a ghost. He moves like a ghost. You can't hear him when he comes for you.' She started crying and her voice faltered. 'And . . . he . . . he can see you but you can't see him.' Her breathing accelerated. 'He can see in the dark.'

One Hundred and Eleven

Hunter pulled Katia into his arms again.

'Katia, it'll be OK. We'll get out of here.'

'No . . .' Desperation took over her voice. 'You're not listening. We can't hide from him. There's nowhere we can go where he won't find us. We won't get out of here alive. He could be standing behind you right now and you wouldn't know. Unless he wanted you to.'

That statement sent a shiver up Garcia's spine and he mechanically extended his left arm like a blind man, feeling the space around him – nothing but air.

'I could never see him,' Katia continued, 'but I sensed him many times, right here, in the room with me. He wouldn't say a word. He wouldn't make a sound, but I knew he was there, watching me, just observing. I never heard him come in or go out. He moves like a ghost.'

'OK,' Hunter said. 'The three of us moving blind isn't a great idea. We won't be able to cover each other.'

'What do you wanna do?' Garcia whispered.

'Katia, stay in here. Stay in the room.'

'What?'

'I've been checking every inch of this place. He's got no surveillance. There are no cameras, no microphones, nothing. He might know that we're here, but there's no way he can be sure that we've gotten to you or to anyone else. If you stay in the room just like you've been doing since the day you were captured, he's got no reason to be angry with you.'

'No . . . no. I'd rather die than stay here alone for another second. You don't know what I've been through. I can't stay here. Please don't leave me here to face him again. You can't leave me here alone.'

'Katia, listen, if the three of us move out of this room together right now, and if this guy can see in the dark and move as silently as you said he can, we've got no chance.'

'No . . . I can't stay here alone. Please don't make me stay here alone. I'd rather die.'

'I'll stay with you.' Garcia said. 'Robert is right. We won't be able to cover each other if we move out of here together. He could easily pick us out one by one and we wouldn't even know. I'll stay here with you. As Robert said, he doesn't know which room we're in. For all he knows you're here, alone, just like you were minutes ago. I'll stay. There's no way he can know I'm with you. If this door opens without the person identifying himself, I'll smoke the bastard.' He cocked his gun and Katia jumped.

'It's a good idea,' Hunter agreed.

'Why don't you stay too,' Katia pleaded. 'Why can't we all just wait for him in here and fight him together? We've got a better chance that way.'

'Because he might not come directly here,' Hunter explained. 'We know for sure that he's got at least one more victim held hostage. Our captain. He might go straight for her just to punish us. I have to try and find her before he gets to her. I can't just sit here and wait. Her life depends on it.'

'He's right, Katia,' Garcia said.

'We can't waste any more time,' Hunter took over again. 'Trust me, Katia. I'll be back for you.'

Garcia put his arm around Katia and slowly brought her back into the room.

'Good luck,' he said as Hunter closed the door behind him and took a deep breath.

This already looks like a bad idea, he thought. *Walking around in pitch-dark corridors, fighting a killer blind. What the hell am I thinking?*

Hunter knew that there were about twenty feet between him and the end of the corridor. No more doors on this stretch. He moved cautiously, but he moved fast. The hallway swung left again. He stood still, listening as hard as he could.

Nothing except absolute silence.

Hunter had always been good at identifying sounds. Sneaking up on him would be a tough task. Though Katia had told him that Andrew could see in the dark and move like a ghost, he couldn't believe anyone could be that quiet.

He was wrong.

One Hundred and Twelve

Andrew stood just a few meters from Hunter, observing, his breathing so quiet and smooth that even a person standing inches from him wouldn't have noticed him. He'd heard the entire conversation just moments earlier. He knew Garcia had stayed in the room with Katia. But he'd deal with them later. A satisfied smile parted his lips. He could see the anxiety on Hunter's face. He could sense the tension in his movements. Hunter had guts, Andrew had to give him that. He'd knowingly walked into a fight he couldn't win.

Hunter started moving forward again. His left hand in constant contact with the corridor's internal wall as he searched for the next door.

Five steps were all he managed.

The first blow came to his gun hand, so powerful and precise it almost snapped his wrist in two. Hunter never heard a thing. He never sensed another presence. Katia was right. Andrew could see in the dark. There was no other way he could have delivered such an accurate strike.

Hunter's gun left his hand like a rocket propelled into the air. He heard it hit the ground somewhere in front of him and to his right. Instinctively, he pulled back and assumed a fighting position, but how do you fight when you can't see or hear your opponent?

Somehow Andrew had moved around Hunter, because the next blow came from behind him, straight to the lower back. Hunter was catapulted forward and he felt an agonizing pain creep up his spine.

'I guess you decided not to take my advice,' Andrew said, his voice firm and confident – familiar to Hunter. 'Bad move, Detective.'

Hunter turned in the direction of the voice and blindly delivered a punch around chest height. He hit nothing but air.

'Wrong again.' This time the voice came from Hunter's left, just inches away.

How could he move so fast and so quietly?

Hunter twisted his body and swung his elbow around as fast and as hard as he could, but Andrew had moved again. And again, Hunter hit nothing.

The next punch hit Hunter in the stomach. It was so well placed and powerful he doubled over and tasted acrid bile in his mouth. No time to react. A quick follow-up punch hit him on the left side of his face. Hunter felt his lip split and the bitter taste in his mouth was quickly substituted by a metallic and sharp one – blood.

Hunter swung his arm around again. A desperate attempt from someone who knew this war was lost. He couldn't even defend himself. The only thing he could do was wait for the next blow. And it came in the form of a low kick to the knee. A jolt of pain ran up Hunter's leg and gravity sent him plunging to the floor. His back and head slammed against the wall behind him hard. Andrew wasn't only invisible and soundless; he knew how to fight too.

'The question is,' Andrew said, 'should I keep on beating you up until you're dead . . . or should I use your gun and end this with a bullet to your head?'

'Andrew, you don't have to do this.' Hunter's voice was heavy, defeated, and gurgling in blood.

'I told you not to call me Andrew.'

'OK,' Hunter accepted it. 'Do you want me to call you Bryan? Bryan Coleman?' Hunter had finally recognized his voice.

Silence, and for the first time Hunter sensed Andrew's hesitation.

'That's the new identity you chose for yourself, right? Bryan Coleman? Director of Production at the A & E TV network. We sat face to face just a couple of days ago.'

'Wow,' Andrew said, clapping his hands. 'Your reputation is well deserved. You figured out something no one else could.'

'Your identity isn't a secret any more,' Hunter carried on. 'Whatever happens here tonight, the LAPD know who you are now. You can't stay in the dark forever.' Hunter paused, took a deep breath and felt his lungs burn with pain. 'You need help, Bryan. Somehow, alone, for twenty years, you managed to cope with something that no one could handle on their own.'

'You don't know anything, Detective. You have no idea what I've been through.'

Andrew had moved again. His voice was now coming from Hunter's right.

'I spent three days in that attic, hiding, scared, trying to decide what to do.' He paused. 'I decided I didn't wanna stay in Healdsburg. I didn't wanna be taken away to some orphanage somewhere. I didn't wanna be the kid everyone had pity on. So I waited into night-time and then I ran. It was quite easy to hide in the back of a truck at the interstate gas station.'

Hunter remembered that the Harpers' old family house was less than half a mile from Interstate 101.

'You'd be surprised how easy it is for a kid to survive on the streets of a big city like LA. But being away from Healdsburg didn't help. For twenty years I've had the same images playing in my head every time I close my eyes.'

Hunter coughed a red mist of blood. 'What happened in your house twenty years ago wasn't your fault, Bryan. You can't blame yourself for what your father did.'

'My father loved my mother. He gave his life for her.'

'He didn't give his life *for* her. He took his life as well as hers in a moment of rage.'

'BECAUSE SHE BETRAYED HIM.' The shout came from directly in front of Hunter, but too far away for him to react. 'He loved her with every beat of his heart. It took me years to understand what had really happened. But now I know that he took her life and his for love . . . pure love.'

Hunter had been right, Andrew's vision of what true love meant was completely distorted, but arguing it right now was pointless. Hunter needed to try and calm him down, not irritate him further.

'It's still not your fault,' he said.

'SHUT UP. You don't know what happened. You don't know what caused my father to lose his mind. But I'll tell you . . . I did. I told him. It was *all my fault.*'

One Hundred and Thirteen

Hunter sensed the anguish and pain in Andrew's voice. Pain that came from deep inside. Something he had been carrying with him for all these years.

'How do you think my father found out about Mr. Gardner and my mother?' Andrew asked.

Hunter hadn't thought of that, but he didn't need to reflect for long to know the answer.

'I saw them together one day. I saw them in my parents' room, in my parents' bed. I knew what they were doing was wrong ... really wrong.' A desperate quiver had found its way into Andrew's voice, the memory still way too vivid in his mind. 'I didn't know what to do. Somehow I knew that what my mom was doing would destroy her marriage to my father. I didn't want that to happen. I wanted them to be happy again ... together.' He hesitated for an instant.

'So you told your father,' Hunter whispered.

'A week before it all happened. I told him that I saw Nathan Gardner coming into our house one day. That was all I told him, nothing else.' The hurt in his voice grew stronger. 'I didn't know that my father would be capable of ...' He trailed off.

'Still not your fault,' Hunter said again. 'As you've said,

you didn't know your father would react the way he did. Your intention was to save your parents' marriage, to keep them together. His reaction wasn't your fault.'

Silence took over for a moment.

'Do you know what I remember the most about my mother?' Andrew had moved yet again. 'She told me that when I was her age I'd find someone just like her – beautiful . . . talented . . . Someone I could fall in love with.' He paused for a second. 'I've waited for that birthday for twenty years. For the day that I could finally start choosing my perfect partner.'

Suddenly everything started to make sense to Hunter. They'd been right. The women Andrew Harper kidnapped symbolized a combination of maternal and romantic love. He wanted to fall in love with them, but he also wanted – needed – them to look like his mother. She had told him that when he was thirty, her exact age when she died, he'd find his perfect match, someone just like her. Hunter had checked Andrew's birth certificate. His birthday was on February 22 – two days before Kelly Jensen, his first kidnap victim, had been taken. Andrew had been searching for his victims for a while, but his subconscious prohibited him from taking any action until his thirtieth birthday. In his fragile mind, his mother's words were a rule that couldn't be broken. He had been waiting for that birthday for a very long time. And he'd lost no time when that day arrived. Andrew's mind had distorted what his mother had said in a way only a severely traumatized mind could.

'So you found them,' Hunter said. 'Women who looked just like your mother. Who were as talented as she was—'

'No one could ever be as talented as my mother.' Anger returned to Andrew's voice.

'I'm sorry,' Hunter corrected himself. 'You found candidates for your love . . . and took them from their homes . . . studios . . . cars . . . But you couldn't fall in love with them, could you?'

Silence.

'You took them and you held them captive. You watched them in silence every day, just like you did with your mother. But the longer you watched them, the more they reminded you of her, didn't they? That's why you couldn't touch them in a sexual way, or in any other way. You couldn't hurt them either. But unfortunately the memory of your mother brought back something else.'

Hunter wiped his mouth of the blood.

'It reminded you of her betrayal to your father's love,' he continued. 'Her betrayal to *your* love. Her betrayal to your family. And in the end, instead of falling in love, you hated them. You hated them for that betrayal. You hated them for the exact same reason you took them in the first place. For reminding you of your mother.'

Andrew didn't reply.

'So just like your father, you allowed rage to take over, and when it did, it took you right back to that day and what you saw him do to your mother.'

Again, no reply, but Hunter sensed anxiety in the air.

'We found the interviews, Andrew. We found the questions you put to them about true love.'

'I gave them what they always wanted.'

'No, you didn't. You distorted their words. Just like you distorted your mother's words. Your mother *did* want you to find love, but not this way. You need help, Andrew.'

'STOP CALLING ME ANDREW.' The yell reverberated all around the underground floor. 'You think you know me?

You think you know about my life, my pain? You don't know SHIT. But if you like pain, I'll give you pain.'

The fresh blow hit Hunter on the right side of his face, filling his mouth with blood again, and sending him back to the floor. It took him several seconds to regain composure.

'And now, I have a surprise for you, Detective . . .'

There was an uneasy silence, followed by the sound of something heavy, like a sack of potatoes, being dragged across the floor.

'Wake up, bitch.'

Hunter heard faint slapping sounds, as if Andrew was tapping someone's cheeks, trying to revive them.

'Wake up,' he said again.

'Umm,' a female voice whispered and Hunter held his breath.

'C'mon now,' Andrew said. 'Wakey, wakey.'

'Umm,' she said again.

From the sound she made Hunter could tell that she was gagged, and in a lot of pain.

'Captain . . . ?' he called, jerking his body forward.

Andrew laughed. 'Where do you think you're going?' He rammed the heel of his boot onto Hunter's chest, sending him crashing against the wall behind him again.

'Umm . . . umm . . .' She sounded frantic, but the gag around her mouth had been tied too tight.

'Captain . . . ?' Hunter called again in a desperate breath.

'I guess it's time we all said goodbye to each other,' Andrew said. 'I'm sick of this shit.'

'Ummmmmm!' This time her tone was full of fear.

'Andrew, don't do this.' Hunter tried moving forward one more time, but again he was kicked back to the wall. He coughed a few times before regaining his breath.

'She's got nothing to do with this. *I* broke your rules, Andrew, not her. If you gotta punish anyone, punish me.'

'Ohhh, how noble, Detective,' Andrew said with disdain. 'You cops are all the same. You all want to be the hero. You never know when to quit, when to give up. Even when it's so obvious you just can't win. And that makes you predictable. So guess what, Detective?'

The pause that followed filled the air with dread.

'This time you don't get to save the day.'

'PLEASE, ANDREW, NO.' Hunter sensed the determination and rage in Andrew's voice and knew he'd run out of time. He lunged himself forward with all the strength he had left, but they had moved again. Hunter reached nothing. 'Captain . . . ?' But all he heard was her dying gurgling cry; a split second later he felt a gush of warm blood hit him across the face and chest.

'NO . . . NO . . . CAPTAIN . . . ?'

Silence.

'Captain . . . ?'

'Sorry, Detective,' Andrew said, sucking in a deep, fulfilling breath. 'I don't think she's listening any more.'

The smell of blood intoxicated the air.

'Why, Andrew? Why did you have to do this?' Hunter shivered with anger.

'Don't be sad, Detective. There's no reason to miss her so much . . . because you're about to join her.' Andrew laughed again. 'Isn't it some sort of dishonor for a cop to be killed with his own gun?'

Hunter heard the sound of a semi-automatic gun being chambered.

In the dark, Andrew lifted Hunter's gun and aimed it directly at his head. Hunter knew it was over. There was nothing more he could do. There was nothing more he could say.

Hunter took a deep breath, and despite the darkness, he kept his eyes open, defiantly staring straight ahead.

The deafening blast that came a fraction of a second later filled the corridor with a sick burning smell.

One Hundred and Fourteen

Bright, burning light exploded in the corridor like a flash grenade. Suddenly, everything was illuminated. Andrew let out such a painful roar it was like he'd been stabbed through the heart, but the pain came from his eyes, as he was almost blinded by the intensity of the brilliance, amplified thousands of times by his night-vision goggles.

Andrew instinctively reached for the device and lifted it from his eyes, but the damage was already done. His eyes were struggling to cope with the light blast they'd received directly to the retina, and he felt dizzy and confused.

It took Hunter just a split second to realize what had happened. From the corner of his eye he could see Garcia standing at one of the turns of the corridor. On the floor in front of him was a flare, burning intensely – one of the trial flares he'd seen just minutes earlier in Andrew's 'factory'.

Garcia had soon realized that the only way anyone could see in the dark was by using a light-enhancing device, like night-vision goggles. And he knew exactly how they worked. From Katia's cell, he had heard Hunter and Andrew fighting. He couldn't just sit there and wait. He knew Hunter was great in hand-to-hand combat, but he wouldn't stand a chance against an opponent he couldn't see. Garcia remembered the 'factory' and the flares. Even in the darkness, he knew he wouldn't get lost in corridors structured to go around in a squared pattern. All he needed was a second of bright light, but to Andrew it would feel like a bomb had gone off inside his eyes.

That was exactly the chance Hunter needed. Without thinking, and in a fraction of a second, he threw his body forward towards Andrew. Garcia did exactly the same. Both of them collided with Andrew at the same time, sending him thundering against the wall. He slammed head first into it with incredible force. The roles had completely reversed. Andrew was totally blinded by the explosion of light, and entirely disoriented by the heavy knock to his head. Just like Hunter moments earlier, Andrew swung his arm around in a desperate attempt to defend himself. But how do you defend yourself from opponents you can't see?

Garcia immediately delivered a well-placed and powerful punch to Andrew's solar plexus. Hunter followed it up with one to his jaw. Andrew's head jolted backwards and hit the wall again with a dull crack.

He passed out immediately.

The last thing Hunter and Garcia saw just before the flare extinguished was Whitney Myers' lifeless body lying on a pool of her own blood on the floor. Her throat slit the entire length of her neck.

One Hundred and Fifteen

Thirty-six hours later – USC University Hospital – Los Angeles.

Hunter knocked twice and pushed the door open. Captain Blake was sitting up in her adjustable bed. Its backrest inclined about forty-five degrees. Her face had been cleaned of all the dried blood, but it still looked black and blue and very battered. Her left eye, lips and nose were still swollen. She looked exhausted, but she certainly didn't sound that way. Her good eye moved towards the door and widened in surprise at the sight of what Hunter and Garcia had brought with them.

'Flowers and chocolate?' she asked skeptically. 'Are you guys getting soft on me? 'Cause two soft detectives is the last thing I need in my department.'

Hunter stepped into the room, and placed the flowers on the small table next to her bed. Garcia did the same with the chocolates.

'You're welcome, Captain,' Hunter said. His bottom lip was also cut and swollen. His eyes carried only half of the sparkle they usually did.

'I'm sorry about Whitney Myers,' the captain said after an uneasy silence.

Hunter said nothing, but the sadness in his eyes intensified.

He knew that Myers' dedication and determination had led her to the killer's clutches, and he could do little to save her. He felt guilty for not answering her call when he was in Healdsburg, and for not calling her back.

'How did Andrew Harper get to her?'

'She was at the airport the day I came back from Healdsburg,' Hunter said. 'And so was Andrew. He spotted her after making the call to me, followed her, and took her as she climbed into her car.'

'How did he know who she was?'

'He probably started following me after Carlos and I talked to him in his office. That same night Whitney and I met in a restaurant in Baldwin Hills. It wouldn't have taken him long to connect the dots.'

'And why was she at the airport?'

'Because she knew I wasn't telling her everything. She had contacts everywhere, even inside Parker Center.'

Captain Blake didn't look surprised.

'Through them she found out I was onto something. She guessed I knew about the kidnapper. And if I wasn't prepared to share information, then she'd find out for herself. She was a very good detective.' He looked away. 'And a very kind person.'

'So she decided to tail you?'

'According to her partner, that was the initial idea, yes.'

The silence returned to the room for a moment longer.

'The other woman?' the captain eventually asked. 'The kidnap victim.'

Hunter nodded. 'Katia Kudrov. She's the violinist concert-mistress for the LA Philharmonic. She was the woman who Whitney was hired to find.'

The captain nodded. 'How is she?'

'Terrified, a little dehydrated and malnourished, but Andrew Harper never touched her. Physically she hasn't been hurt.' He paused for an instant. 'Psychologically . . . she'll need help.'

'Is he talking?'

Hunter tilted his head to one side. 'The psychiatrists are making progress little by little. But this will be a long process. Understandably, Andrew's mind is in a complete mess. We were right. He was kidnapping women who reminded him of his mother, but we were wrong in the assumption that sooner or later they did something to break his projection spell – and made him realize that they weren't who he wanted them to be.'

'On the contrary,' Garcia took over. 'They reminded him of her too much. That remembrance awoke a 20-year-old suppressed feeling that he probably didn't even know it was there . . . and it wasn't *love*.'

'Hate,' Captain Blake guessed.

'Anger,' Hunter corrected her. 'Violent anger. Subconsciously he blamed her for betraying his father . . . destroying his family. He used the knowledge he gained through his interviews and the questions about *true love* to mimic what happened that day in his house. To punish his mother time and time again.'

'How come he wasn't killed by his father?' the captain asked.

Hunter explained that Andrew's father never intended to kill him in the first place. 'Andrew saw everything that happened that day from the attic, and then hid there for three days. When he escaped the house, he hid in the back of a truck at the interstate gas station. By chance, the truck was destined for Los Angeles.'

'He's been here all this time?'

Garcia nodded and took over. 'He slept in the ghettos in South Central and shined shoes in West Hollywood for money. At the age of fourteen he managed to get a job in a clockmaker's and locksmith shop in South Gate. The shop was a family-owned business, run by a childless couple in their sixties – Ted and Louise Coleman. That was where he learned about time triggers, precision mechanisms, building complicated devices, and to pick locks. In fact, he became an expert. It was also where he adopted his new name and identity.'

'Sonofabitch,' the captain said, reaching for the glass of water on the side table.

'He joined *Contemporary Painters* magazine as a runaround boy at the age of nineteen.' Garcia carried on. 'The magazine belongs to the DTP Corporation. They also own *Art Today* magazine and several others, together with the A & E TV network. He was very intelligent, and moved up the ranks fast.'

'A great place to keep an eye out for any female painter or musician who reminded him of his mother,' Hunter added.

'And here's the surprise fact,' Garcia again. 'The St Michael's Hospice building . . . he owns it.'

'*Owns* it?' The captain's stare jumped from detective to detective.

Garcia nodded. 'Bought it a year ago, eight years after a fire destroyed it.' He shrugged. 'What was left of the building was just rotting away. Nobody wanted it, least of all the old owners. He got the whole thing for two thousand bucks. The building was way too far out of town to be crawling with teenagers, drug addicts and drifters. A perfect isolated location. Nobody ever went up there. Few people even knew it existed.'

'What I don't get,' the captain said, 'is why he didn't kill his victims at the hospice? Why take them somewhere else?'

'Because no matter what, they still reminded him of his mother,' Hunter said. 'Despite his anger for what he considered her betrayal, his love for her was undeniable.'

'And that's why he created those trigger mechanisms,' Garcia added. 'So he didn't have to be there when they died. A sort of detachment.'

'Exactly,' Hunter agreed.

'He still could've done that at the hospice,' Captain Blake pushed. 'He could've locked them in a room and left them to their fate.'

'If he did, he'd still have to deal with their dead bodies,' Hunter explained. 'Re-enter the room, dispose of them . . . His brain couldn't cope with the emotion of seeing someone who reminded him so much of his mother dead.'

'The easiest way to avoid all that,' Garcia concluded, 'leave them to their fate somewhere else.'

Captain Blake gently brought her fingers to her swollen lips. 'So the psychiatrists will have a field day with him.'

'More like a summer camp,' Garcia came back. 'The kind of traumatized mind he's got is the stuff of dreams for criminal behavior psychologists.'

The captain's eyes searched for Hunter's. He nodded.

'So after killing six people, this monster will probably end up in a psychiatric institution instead of getting the death penalty,' Captain Blake said, shaking her head. 'As always, we bust our asses to catch the crazy psychos out there, and the goddamn lawyers and the state let them loose.'

'He ain't going loose, Captain,' Hunter said.

'You know what I mean, Robert.' The captain paused and looked at the flowers Hunter had brought her. Her lips almost broke into a smile, but she held it back.

'How did you know?' Hunter asked. 'How did you know where you were?'

Captain Blake explained about how she was abducted, how she pretended to have breathed in large amounts of ether, and her attempt to break away when they got to the hospice.

'When I started running towards the road, I saw the hospice's old sign. I guess I was lucky he decided to make that video. I was afraid I hadn't moved my lips enough for you to be able to read them. I thought he'd see me doing it, so I pretended to be disoriented and moved my lips incoherently, throwing the words in as I did it.'

'Great thinking,' Hunter admitted.

'It saved my life.'

Garcia smiled.

'What are you smiling at?' Captain Blake said, glaring at him.

'I just realized that this is the first time that at the end of a big case I'm not the one with my face all smashed in.'

'Well, that can be easily arranged,' she replied, giving him the evil eye.

'Nope, I like my face like this,' Garcia said. The smile didn't go away.

Everyone went quiet for a moment.

'Thank you,' the captain finally said, looking at Hunter.

Hunter tilted his head in his partner's direction. 'Carlos saved us all when he came up with the flare idea.'

'Well, somebody had to think of something,' Garcia said.

There was a knock at the door and a nurse popped her head through the door.

'OK now, that's enough for today. You must all leave Miss Blake to rest,' she said, her gaze settling on Hunter.

'Rest?' Captain Blake shot back almost laughing. 'Honey, if you think that I'm gonna spend another night in here, you're the one who needs a doctor.'

'The doctor said you should spend at least another twenty-four hours in here under observation,' the nurse replied.

'Do I look like a woman who needs to be observed?'

Hunter lifted both hands in the air and looked at Garcia. 'We've gotta go anyway. We'll leave you two to sort this out.'

'There's nothing to sort out,' the captain blurted. 'I ain't spending another night in here. And that's final.' She could have killed the nurse with her look.

Hunter paused by the door and whispered in the nurse's ear. 'I suggest you sedate her.'

'Oh don't worry, sugar-lips, I was already warned about her.' She tapped her right breast pocket and winked at Hunter. 'I have a needle with her name on it.' She studied Hunter's face for a moment. 'Would you like me to have a look at those cuts and bruises, sweet pie? It looks like you might need a stitching job.'

Hunter and Garcia exchanged a quick look.

'I'll be fine.' Hunter shook his head.

'Are you sure? I'm very good with needle and thread.'

'Positive,' they both said in unison.

One

'Oh my God, I'm late,' Melinda Wallis said, springing out of bed as her tired eyes glanced at the digital clock on her bedside table. Last night she'd stayed up until 3:30 a.m., studying for her Clinical Pharmacology exam in three days' time.

Still a little groggy from sleep, she clumsily moved around the room while her brain worked out what to do first. She hurried into the bathroom and caught a glimpse of her reflection in the mirror.

'Shit, shit, shit.'

She reached for her makeup bag and started powdering her face.

Melinda was twenty-three years old and according to an article she'd read in a glossy magazine a few days ago, a little overweight for her height – she was only five foot four. Her long brown hair was always tied back into a ponytail, even when she went to bed, and she would never go outside without at least plastering her face with foundation to hide her acne-riddled cheeks. Instead of brushing her teeth, she quickly squirted a blob of toothpaste into her mouth just to get rid of the night taste.

Back in the room, she found her clothes neatly folded on a chair by her study desk – a white blouse, stockings, a knee-length white skirt and white flat-soled shoes. She got dressed in record time and sprinted out of the small guesthouse in the direction of the main building.

Melinda was attending the third year of her Bachelor of Science in Nursing and Caretaking degree at UCLA, and every weekend, to fulfill her job-experience curriculum, she worked as an in-house private nurse. For the past fourteen weekends she'd been working for Mr. Derek Nicholson in Cheviot Hills, West Los Angeles.

Just two weeks before she was hired, Mr. Nicholson was diagnosed with advanced lung cancer. The tumor was already the size of a plum stone and it was eating away at him fast. Walking was too painful, sometimes he needed the help of breathing apparatus, and he spoke only in a barely audible voice. Despite his daughters' pleas, he declined to start chemotherapy treatment. He refused to spend days locked inside a hospital room and chose to spend the time he had left in his own house.

Melinda unlocked the front door and stepped into the spacious entry lobby before rushing through the large but sparsely decorated living room. Mr. Nicholson's bedroom was located on the first floor. As always, the house was eerily quiet in the morning.

Derek Nicholson lived alone. His wife had passed away two years ago, and though his daughters came to visit him every day, they had their own lives to attend to.

'I'm sorry I'm late,' Melinda called from downstairs. She checked her watch again. She was exactly forty-three minutes late. 'Shit!' she murmured under her breath. 'Derek, are you awake?' she called, crossing to the staircase and taking the steps two by two.

Derek Nicholson had asked her on her first weekend at the house to call him by his first name. He didn't like the formality of 'Mr. Nicholson'.

As Melinda approached his bedroom door, she caught a noseful of a strong, sickening smell coming from inside.

Oh, damn, she thought. It was obviously too late for his first bathroom break.

'OK, let's get you cleaned up first . . .' she said, opening the door, '. . . and then I'll get you your breakf—'

Her whole body went rigid, her eyes widened in horror and the air was sucked out of her lungs as if she had been suddenly propelled into outer space. She felt the contents of her stomach shoot up into her mouth and she vomited right there by the door.

'God in heaven!' Those were the words Melinda had intended to say as she moved her trembling lips, but no sound came from them. Her legs began to give way under her, the world began to spin, and she held on to the door-frame with both hands to steady herself. That was when her horrified green eyes caught a glimpse of the far wall. It took her brain a moment to understand what she was seeing, but as it did, primal fear and panic rose inside her heart like a thunderstorm.

Two

Summer had barely started in the City of Angels and the temperature was already hitting 87°F. Detective Robert Hunter of the Los Angeles Robbery Homicide Division (RHD) stopped the timer on his wristwatch as he reached his apartment block in Huntingdon Park, southeast of downtown. Seven miles in thirty-eight minutes. Not bad, he thought, but he was sweating like a turkey on Thanksgiving Day and his legs and knees hurt like hell. Maybe he should've stretched. In fact, he knew he should stretch before and after exercising, especially after a long run, but he could never really be bothered to do it.

Hunter took the stairs up to the third floor. He didn't like elevators, and the one in his building was nicknamed 'the sardine trap' for a reason.

He opened the door to his one-bedroom apartment and stepped inside. The apartment was small but clean and comfortable, though people would be forgiven for thinking that the furniture had been donated by Goodwill – a black leatherette sofa, mismatched chairs, a scratched breakfast table that doubled as a computer desk, and an old bookcase that looked like it would give under the weight of its overcrowded shelves at any minute.

Hunter took off his shirt and used it to wipe the sweat off his forehead, neck and muscular torso. His breathing was already back to normal. In the kitchen, he grabbed a pitcher of iced tea from the fridge and poured himself a large glass. Hunter was looking forward to spending an uneventful day away from the Police Administration Building, and the RHD headquarters. He didn't get many days off. Maybe he'd drive down to Venice Beach and play some volleyball. He hadn't played volleyball in years. Or maybe he could try to catch a Lakers game. He was sure they were playing that night. But first he needed a shower and a quick trip down to the launderette.

Hunter finished his iced tea, walked into the bathroom and checked his reflection in the mirror. He also needed a shave. As he reached for the shaving gel and razor, his cell phone rang in the bedroom.

Hunter picked it up from his bedside table and checked the display – Carlos Garcia, his partner. Only then he noticed the small red arrow at the top of the screen indicating that he had missed calls – ten of them.

'Great!' he whispered, accepting the call. He knew exactly what ten missed calls and his partner on the phone that early on their day off meant.

'Carlos,' Hunter said, bringing the phone to his ear. 'What's up?'

'Jesus! Where were you? I've been trying you for half an hour.'

A call every three minutes, Hunter thought. This was going to be bad.

'I was out, running,' he said, calmly. 'Didn't check my phone when I walked in. I only saw the missed calls now. So what have we got?'

'A hell of a mess. You better get here quick, Robert. I've never seen anything like this.' There was a quick, hesitant pause from Garcia. 'I don't think anyone has ever seen anything quite like this.'

Three

Even on a Sunday morning, it took Hunter almost an hour to cover the fifteen miles between Huntingdon Park and Cheviot Hills.

Garcia hadn't given Hunter many details over the phone, but his evident shock and the slight trepidation in his voice were certainly out of character.

Hunter and Garcia were part of a small, specialized unit within the RHD – the Homicide Special Section, or HSS. The unit was created to deal solely with serial, high-profile and homicide cases requiring extensive investigative time and expertise. Hunter's background in criminal-behavior psychology placed him in an even more specialized group. All homicides where overwhelming brutality or sadism had been used by the perpetrator were tagged by the department as 'UV' (ultra-violent). Robert Hunter and Carlos Garcia were the UV unit, and as such, they weren't easily rattled. They had seen more than their share of things that no one else on this earth had seen.

Hunter pulled up next to one of several black-and-white units parked in front of the two-story house in West LA. The press was already there, crowding up the small street, but that was no surprise. They usually got to crime scenes before the detectives did.

Hunter stepped out of his old Buick LeSabre and was hit by a wave of warm air. Unbuttoning his jacket and clipping his badge onto his belt, he looked around slowly. Though the house was located in a private street, tucked away in a quiet neighborhood, the crowd of curious onlookers that had gathered outside the police perimeter was already substantial, and it was growing fast.

Hunter turned and faced the house. It was a nice-looking two-story red-brick building with dark-blue-framed windows and a hipped roof. The front yard was large and well cared for. There was a two-car garage to the right of the house, but no cars on the driveway, except for more police vehicles. A forensic-unit van was parked just a few yards away. Hunter quickly spotted Garcia as he exited the house through the front door. He was wearing a classic white hooded Tyvek coverall. At six foot two, he was two inches taller than Hunter.

Garcia stopped by the few stone steps that led down from the porch and pulled his hood down. His longish dark hair was tied back into a slick ponytail. He also promptly spotted his partner.

Ignoring the animated herd of reporters, Hunter flashed his badge at the officer standing at the perimeter's edge and stooped under the yellow crime-scene tape.

In a city like Los Angeles, when it came to crime stories and reporters, the more gruesome and violent the offence, the more excited they got. Most of them knew Hunter, and what sort of cases he was assigned to. Their shouted questions came in a barrage.

'Bad news travels fast,' Garcia said, tilting his head in the direction of the crowd as Hunter got to him. 'And a potentially good story travels faster.' He handed his partner a brand new Tyvek coverall inside a sealed plastic bag.

'What do you mean?' Hunter took the bag, ripped it open and started suiting up.

'The victim was a lawyer,' Garcia explained. 'A Mr. Derek Nicholson, prosecutor with the District Attorney's office for the State of California.'

'Oh that's great.'

'He wasn't practicing anymore, though.'

Hunter zipped up his coverall.

'He was diagnosed with advanced lung cancer,' Garcia continued.

Hunter looked at him curiously.

'He was pretty much on his way out. Oxygen masks, legs weren't really responding the way they should . . . The doctors gave him no more than six months. That was four months ago.'

'How old was he?'

'Fifty. It was no secret he was dying. Why finish him off this way?'

Hunter paused. 'And there's no doubt he was murdered?'

'Oh, there's absolutely no doubt.'

Garcia guided Hunter into the house and through the entry lobby. Next to the door there was a security-alarm keypad. Hunter looked at Garcia.

'Alarm wasn't engaged,' he clarified. 'Apparently, arming it wasn't something they did often.'

Hunter pulled a face.

'I know,' Garcia said, 'what's the point of having one, right?'

They moved on.

In the living room, two forensic agents were busy dusting the staircase by the back wall.

'Who found the body?' Hunter asked.

'The victim's private nurse,' Garcia replied and directed Hunter's attention to the open door in the east wall. It led into a large study. Inside, sitting on a vintage leather Chesterfield sofa, was a young woman dressed all in white. Her hair was tied back. Her eyes were raspberry red and puffed up from crying. Resting on her knees was a cup of coffee that she was holding with both hands. Her stare seemed lost and distant. Hunter noticed that she was rocking her upper body back and forth ever so slightly. She was clearly in shock. A uniformed officer was in the room with her.

'Anybody tried talking to her yet?'

'I did,' Garcia nodded. 'Managed to get some basic information out of her, but she's psychologically shutting down, and I'm not surprised. Maybe you could try later. You're better at these things than I am.'

'She was here on a Sunday?' Hunter asked.

'She's only here on weekends,' Garcia clarified. 'Her name is Melinda Wallis. She goes to UCLA. She's just finishing a degree in Nursing and Caretaking. This is part of her work experience. She got the job a week after Mr. Nicholson was diagnosed with his illness.'

'How about the rest of the week?'

'Mr. Nicholson had another nurse.' Garcia unzipped his coverall and reached inside his breast pocket for his notebook. 'Amy Dawson,' he read the name. 'Unlike Melinda, Amy isn't a student. She's a professional nurse. She took care of Mr. Nicholson during the week. Also, his two daughters came to visit him every day.'

Hunter's eyebrow arched.

'They haven't been contacted yet.'

'So the victim lived here alone?'

'That's right. His wife of twenty-six years died in a car accident two years ago.' Garcia returned the notebook to his pocket. 'The body is upstairs.' He motioned to the staircase.

As he took the steps up, Hunter was careful not to interfere with the forensic agents as they worked. The first-floor landing resembled a waiting room – two chairs, two leather armchairs, a small bookshelf, a magazine holder, and a sideboard covered with stylish picture frames. A dimly lit corridor led them deeper into the house, and to the four bedrooms and two bathrooms. Garcia took Hunter all the way to the last door on the right and paused outside.

'I know you've seen a lot of sick stuff before, Robert. God knows I have.' He rested his latex-gloved hand on the door-knob. 'But this . . . not even in nightmares.' He pushed the door open.

Four

Hunter stood by the open door to the large bedroom. His eyes registered the scene in front of him, but his logical mind was having trouble comprehending it.

Centered against the north wall was an adjustable double bed. To its right he could see a small oxygen tank and mask on a wooden bedside table. A wheelchair occupied the space by the end of the bed. There was also an antique-looking chest of drawers, a mahogany writing desk, and a large shelf unit on the wall opposite the bed. Its centerpiece was a flat-screen TV set.

Hunter breathed out but didn't move, didn't blink, didn't say a word.

'Where do we start?' Garcia whispered by his side.

Blood was everywhere – on the bed, floor, rug, walls, ceiling, curtains, and on most of the furniture. Mr. Nicholson's body was on the bed. Or at least what was left of it. He'd been dismembered. Both legs and both arms had been ripped from his body. One of his arms had been hacked at the joints into smaller pieces. Both of his feet had also been separated from his legs.

But what baffled everyone who entered that room was the sculpture.

On a small coffee table by the window, the victim's severed and hacked body parts had been bundled up and arranged together into a bloody, twisted, incomprehensible shape.

'You've gotta be kidding me,' Hunter whispered to himself.

'I'm not even going to ask. 'Cos I know you've never seen anything like this before, Robert,' Doctor Carolyn Hove said from the far corner of the room. 'None of us have.'

Doctor Hove was the Chief Medical Examiner for the Los Angeles County Department of Coroner. She was tall and slim with deep penetrating green eyes. Her long, chestnut hair was tucked away under the hood of her white coverall, her full lips and petite nose hidden under her surgical mask.

Hunter's attention moved to her for a couple of seconds and then to the large blood pools on the floor. He hesitated for a moment. There was no way he could walk into that room without treading on them.

'It's OK,' Doctor Hove said, motioning him and Garcia inside. 'The entire floor has been photographed.'

Still, Hunter did his best to circumvent the blood. He approached the bed and what was left of Mr. Nicholson's body. His face was caked in blood. His eyes and mouth were wide open, as if his last terrified scream had been frozen before it came out. The bed sheets, the pillows and the mattress were ripped and torn in several places.

'He was killed on that bed,' Doctor Hove said, coming up to Hunter.

He kept his attention on the body.

'Judging by the splatters and the amount of blood we have here,' she continued, 'the killer inflicted as much pain as the victim could handle before allowing him to die.'

'The killer cut him up first?'

The doctor nodded. 'And the killer started with the small, non-life-threatening pieces.'

Hunter frowned.

'All his toes were cut off, together with his tongue.' Her

stare moved back to the revolting body-part sculpture. 'I'd say that was done first, before he was dismembered.'

'He was alone in the house?'

'Yes,' Garcia answered. 'Melinda, the student nurse you saw downstairs, spends the weekends here, but she sleeps in the guesthouse above the garage you saw up front. According to her, Mr. Nicholson's daughters came by every day and spent a couple of hours with him, sometimes more. They left last night at around 9:00 p.m. After putting him to sleep and finishing up in the house, Melinda left Mr. Nicholson at around 11:00 p.m. She went back to the guesthouse and stayed up until three-thirty in the morning, studying for an exam.'

It wasn't hard for Hunter to understand why the nurse never heard anything. The garage was all the way up front and about twenty yards away from the main building. The room they were in was right at the back of the house, the last one down the corridor. Its windows faced the backyard. They could've had a party in here and she wouldn't have heard it.

'No panic button?' Hunter asked.

Garcia pointed to one of the evidence bags in the corner of the room. Inside it was a piece of electric wire with a click button at the end of it. 'The wire was snipped.'

Hunter's attention focused on the blood splatters all over the bed, furniture and wall next to it. 'Was the weapon found?'

'No, not yet,' Garcia replied.

'The spit-like blood pattern and the jagged edge of the wounds inflicted indicate that the killer used some sort of electrical sawing device,' Doctor Hove said.

'Like a chainsaw?' Garcia asked.

'Possibly.'

Hunter shook his head. 'A chainsaw would be too noisy. Too risky. The last thing the killer would've wanted would be to alert anyone before he was done. A chainsaw is also a harder tool to control, especially if your aim is precision.' He examined the body and the bed for a while longer before moving away from it and approaching the coffee table and the morbid sculpture.

Both of Mr. Nicholson's arms were awkwardly twisted and bent at the wrist joints, forming two distinct, but meaningless shapes. His feet had been cut off and bundled together in a peculiar way with the arms and hands. All of it was held in place by thin but solid pieces of metal wire. Wire had also been used to attach a few of his severed toes to the edges of the two pieces. His legs had been laid flat side-by-side, and formed the base to the sculpture. Everything was covered in blood.

Hunter circled it slowly, trying to take every detail in.

'Whatever this is,' Doctor Hove said, 'it's not something anyone can put together in a couple of minutes. This takes time.'

'And if the killer took the time to put it together,' Garcia added, moving closer, 'it's gotta mean something.'

Hunter took a few steps back and stared at the macabre piece from a distance. It meant nothing to him.

'Do you think your lab could create a life-size replica of this?' he asked Doctor Hove.

Under her surgical mask, she twisted her mouth from side to side. 'I don't see why not. It's already been photographed, but I'll call the photographer back in and ask him to get a snapshot from all angles. I'm sure the lab can get it done.'

'Let's do it,' Hunter said. 'We're not gonna figure this out here and now.' He turned towards the far wall and froze. It was so covered in blood that he almost didn't notice it. 'What in the world is that?'

Garcia's stare moved to Hunter and then back to the wall. He breathed out a heavy sigh.

'That . . . is everybody's worst nightmare.'